Wayward Son

In An Instant Series – Book 1

Lisa Bingham

Wayward Son; In An Instant Series, Book 1

ISBN: 978-1-7327270-1-4
ISBN eBook: 978-1-7327270-0-7

Library of Congress Control #2018910488

Edited by Nancy Peterson.
Cover design by JJS Marketing & Design LLC
Author photo by Julie Hess.
Interior book design by Bob Houston eBook Formatting

For more information, you may contact the author at: www.lisabinghamauthor.com;
www.Facebook.com/lisabinghamauthor.

Other Works by Lisa Bingham

The Taggart Brothers Series
Desperado
Renegade
Maverick

Women at War Series
Into the Storm
After the Fall

The Bachelors of Aspen Valley Series
Accidental Courtship
Accidental Family
Accidental Sweetheart

Discover Lisa Bingham

On her website
www.lisabinghamauthor.com

On Facebook
www.Facebook.com/lisabinghamauthor

For news on upcoming releases and previous
publications, you can sign up for Lisa's newsletter
through her website www.lisabinghamauthor.com.

Dedicated to Irish Winters.

Thanks for persuading me to test my wings.

ONE

October
Larkspur, Wyoming

Sleet splatted on the hood of Whit Patterson's truck, the noise a perfect accompaniment to the cacophony of thought marching through his head. He'd parked well away from the familiar Queen Anne farmhouse. Far enough that he had a vantage point of the bright squares of light spilling into the darkness, but not so close that someone might see his vehicle obscured beneath the willows.

The wipers whined as they swept away the moisture, leaving streaks in the glass that added to the surreal scene in front of him. Whit had spent so much time in that house as a kid, he could have described every board, every shingle from memory. He'd bounded up those steps a million times and slammed the front door at least that many.

There had been a part of him that had expected to pull up to the curb and step into the past. He'd been shaken to discover that the structure had a few more cracks and dings, missing shingles and peeling patches of paint. Whit supposed the changes were inevitable, but he still found them...unsettling.

He shifted in his seat, wincing at the twinge of bruised ribs. One hand rested on the wheel, the other on the gearshift—as if his body hadn't quite made up its mind whether to go or stay. He knew it would be a mistake not to pay his respects. But that didn't prevent the little voice inside him that whispered: *run!*

The wipers pushed aside the soggy accumulation of ice, giving him a clear picture again. Across the lane, the weather had caused the Victorian's windows to fog at the edges. That, combined with the bands of moisture left in the wake of his wipers, made the figures inside the structure seem fuzzy and out of focus. Their silhouettes congregated and dispersed like schools of fish on the other side of the glass. In a strange, otherworldly way, Whit felt as if he were gazing upon a scene that was both past and future. Pleasure...

And pain.

Although he knew that he should pass through the gate, knock on the door, and add his sympathies to the mourners, he couldn't bring himself to do it. Not when, now and again, he caught a glimpse of Finley Fitzpatrick circling through the rooms.

The familiar silhouette caused his chest to ache with regret.

Finley seemed to flit from group to group, never staying long or offering more than a few words. To others, it might have looked as if she were working the crowd. But Whit knew it was avoidance that inspired her restlessness. Finley hated crowds. She was a self-proclaimed introvert, preferring an evening at home reading a book or an afternoon hiking. She'd never been fond of parties or clubbing, let alone a somber gathering like this one.

Whit followed her progress from the dining room to the entry, then to the formal sitting room. Rather than approaching the knot of people, she crossed to the window, and for several moments, he could see her so clearly that his heart lurched.

She looked good.

No.

"Good" didn't come close to describing her. She was absolutely beautiful.

But then, she'd always been pretty to Whit. Even when she'd been a knobby-kneed teenager with braces and freckles, her hair permed and frizzled from one of her mother's failed attempts to help Finley fit in with the "popular girls", she'd been the most beautiful person in the world to him. Her smile could brighten his day more than the summer sun. She only had to look at him to make his adolescent hormones race and his hands begin to sweat.

He swiped his palms across his jeans, a self-deprecating grimace twisting his lips. Apparently, she still had the power to do that.

She backed away from the window and disappeared. Whit sighed, trying to psyche himself into braving the congregation of townspeople who'd gathered for Norm Campanella's wake. But he couldn't do it. He'd endured his share of dangerous situations, but the thought of entering a room where everyone knew his history—good, bad, and decidedly ugly—seemed monumentally unappealing.

Thankfully, the door opened, and Pastor Willis and his wife appeared. They paused to speak to a figure that Whit couldn't see. Then, the minister opened a black umbrella, holding it high as he linked arms with his wife. Moments later, the door closed and they hurried toward a station wagon parked near the end of the lane.

The couple's departure seemed to signal to the other mourners that a suitable length of time had been spent in expressing one's grief because a gradual exodus ensued. Whit leaned deeper into the shadows watching his childhood pass by: JoAnn Throop, his second-grade teacher; Wally Coombs, the owner of the bowling alley; Neal Pottersheim, the editor of the weekly paper. He watched them shrug into coats, don gloves, and pull hats down low before stepping into the night. One by one, their cars pulled away from the mounds of autumn leaves and disappeared into the storm. Until finally...

Whit's truck and a small hatchback were the only vehicles left.

His pulse knocked at the side of his throat. It was time to approach the house. If he didn't do it now, Finley would leave before he had a chance to let her know that he'd tried to get here in time for the funeral.

Tried and failed.

The door to the vintage Bronco squeaked as he opened it. Automatically, his hand touched the pistol holstered in the small of his back. Without really knowing how he'd managed to get his feet to move, he crossed the lane, pushed the iron gate out of the way and strode up the buckling sidewalk. Once he'd reached the top of the stairs, he hesitated only a moment before knocking.

Then he waited, knowing that the next person he saw would be Finley.

The only woman he'd ever loved.

Finley Fitzpatrick gathered the flotsam left by the mourners, stuffing napkins and plastic utensils into a garbage bag. She knew she didn't have to clean up—the Compassionate Service Committee from the church would be here soon enough. But she needed a few minutes to push away the incessant noise which still echoed in her head—the murmured regrets, the choruses of "let us know if we can do anything", or "I'm here if you need me."

Her hand darted out for a half-eaten cookie on a plate, more cups. And more. And more. As if a person's grief could be washed away with hot tea and coffee and a few hours of chatter.

It hadn't been her choice to hold the wake in the Campanella home. If she'd had her way, Finley would have arranged for everyone to return to the church. Neutral territory. A place where folk might think twice before rechewing the same old rumors behind her back. It was painful being at the Campanellas'. There were too many memories. Too many things she wanted to forget. As she'd moved from person to person, accepting the sympathies of those who'd come to pay their respects, the rooms seemed hollow without the people who should have been here.

Norm and Martha.
And the Sinful Six.

A knock came from the door, making her jump. Finley glanced at the clock and frowned. Apparently, the Compassionate Service ladies had arrived sooner than expected.

Sighing, she left the bag on the dining room table. She'd hoped for a few more minutes to absorb the emptiness of the house. She wasn't sure what would happen to the beautiful Queen Anne. It would probably be sold so the funds could be added to the trust that paid for Clint Campanella's care. Soon, the walls would be stripped of pictures and the furniture emptied away. Then, one of the happiest chapters of Finley's life would truly be gone.

The rapping came again and she called out, "Coming!"

As soon as the women entered, Finley would offer her farewells and leave. Not for home. She couldn't bear that added stress at the moment.

She threw the door open wide, adopted what she hoped looked like a sincere smile, then froze.

Whit.

Whit Patterson had returned to Larkspur.

"Hello, Finley."

She couldn't have said how many times she'd hoped for this moment—*dreamed* of this moment. Yet, everything she'd imagined the reunion might be skittered away beneath a wave of anger, shame, abandonment and...

Joy.

She wanted to pound at his chest with her hands, then throw her arms around his neck and never let go. But she couldn't do either. Her limbs seemed locked in place while her eyes scoured his form, taking in every detail: the battered cowboy hat beaded with moisture; the light spilling over the sharp planes of his face; the faint cleft in his chin; and that oh-so-familiar half-smile.

He was taller than she remembered, broader in the shoulder, even narrower in the hips—was that even possible? Or had he simply lost the last of his teenage awkwardness to a thoroughly masculine body, one that was still quite accustomed to hard work? Or maybe, the strength she saw was an illusion caused by the bulky Carhartt coat he wore.

"Mind if I come in?"

The words finally managed to break her from the tangling effects of the past and she quickly took a step backwards.

"O-Of course."

"Of course," he could come in?

Or *"of course,"* she minded?

He moved past her—big and broad and infinitely male— his arm inadvertently brushing hers, causing a frisson of gooseflesh to race from that point of contact through her chest. Finley resolutely ignored the sensation.

It's the cold, nothing more.

Despite her inner protestations, her heart seemed to flutter in her chest like a wounded bird as she shut the door behind him.

"I-I'm afraid you've come too late for the services." The moment the words left her mouth, she could have kicked herself. The last thing she needed was for Whit to take her remarks as criticism.

But he stood with his fingertips tucked into the pockets of his jeans, his body relaxed, his expression inscrutable while her own body raged with so many emotions that she couldn't seem to catalog them.

Curiosity, resentment, excitement.

And a longing that nearly stole the breath from her body.

"Yeah, I know. I tried to get here in time, but I got delayed at work, then an accident closed I-80 for a couple of hours. How was it? The funeral?"

He swept his hat from his head, raking his fingers through the longish waves. The light from the overhead bulb seemed to gild the gold-brown strands. She was relieved to see that he hadn't completely lost his boy-next-door looks, even though a wealth of experience radiated from his eyes.

Old eyes.

Old beyond their years.

She realized that he was waiting for an answer to his question so she offered a soft laugh. "Short. Just like he ordered. The music was beautiful. Amber Guinn even managed to make a postlude of *Take Me Out to the Ball Game*. I don't think anyone but his closest friends noticed."

Whit was worrying the brim of his hat in his hands—a tell-tale sign of his discomfort. He'd always been so careful with his hats...

"Did anyone else show up?"

She knew without having been told that he wasn't speaking about the residents of Larkspur. He was inquiring about the rest of the Sinful Six.

"No."

She'd meant her response to be simple. Matter-of-fact. But she feared that he would hear a measure of her disappointment. She'd been so sure that someone from their group would come and help her shoulder the burden of Norm's passing.

But she'd been alone.

Just as she'd been for years.

She must have telegraphed a portion of her thoughts, because Whit's eyes narrowed thoughtfully.

"Not even Javi?"

Javier Bartolomé served as a S.W.A.T. and K-9 officer in Jackson Hole. Under normal circumstances, he would have been the first to arrive.

"He had a training session in Seattle and couldn't get away. He'll be gone for another ten days. P.J. has been stationed in the Middle East. He's still got nearly a year left of his tour."

Peter James Gallagher—who had always squeamish at the sight of blood or needles—had made the improbable career decision of becoming an Air Force Pararescueman. A PJ.

"And Liam?"

She folded her arms, sighing. Liam Hanny had seemed the most "traditional" of their group. He'd graduated with a full-ride scholarship to Stanford, completed a bachelor's degree, a masters, a PhD. Then, he'd gone on to teach at Berkley.

She clutched her elbows a little tighter to her chest. "He's...uh...dropped off the grid."

"What do you mean?"

"He was teaching that day when an armed gunman made his way through campus. Liam's classroom was one of the ones that was targeted. From what I've been able to gather, Liam was severely injured and a few of his students were killed. He finished out the semester, then resigned. No one around here has been able to find him. His parents are absolutely sick about it."

"Oh, shit." Whit grimaced then offered, "Sorry. I shouldn't curse. I—"

She laughed softly, a warmth inexplicably settling into her breast at his consternation. Classic Whit Patterson. He'd always been so overtly chivalrous around her—a direct contrast to Clint Campanella who'd been determined to treat her like "one of the boys."

At least until she'd begun to grow breasts.

"I think Liam's situation definitely deserves an 'oh, shit' reaction."

Whit offered a sheepish grin, but the smile disappeared as a somber light entered his eyes. "And Clint. How's he doing?"

The last of their infamous childhood gang, Clint Campanella was probably the least changed of them all.

"Still the same."

A severe line appeared between Whit's brow. "Is he...is he still at the hospital then?"

She'd forgotten that Whit had left after the first few weeks. About the time they'd all realized that Clint may never recover from his injuries.

"No. He's in a convalescent home on the outskirts of town. Norm thought of bringing Clint here to the house, but that's about the same time they diagnosed Norm's cancer, so he figured he'd wait until he was sure he could beat the leukemia."

The man had fought it too. For nearly six years.

Whit seemed to digest that information. Then he looked up again, his gaze scanning the familiar entry hall, the archway that led to the formal parlor on the left, the dining room on the right, the steep, narrow staircase leading to the upper rooms.

"Look, are you staying here? With the Campanellas?"

"No!" She couldn't account for the need to be very clear on that point. "I stopped by a lot, just to check on Norm—especially in the last few weeks. But I've never lived here."

A flicker of something that looked like relief flashed across his features, then was gone as quickly as it came.

"Am I interrupting?"

"No." She hesitated only a moment before saying, "Actually, I was about ready to leave. The Compassionate Service Committee will be here any minute to clean up."

A look akin to horror crossed his features and he cast a quick glance toward the window as if he could see the army of minivans heading in their direction.

"Yeah, I'll get going too. I wouldn't want…"

To be seen?

To be cornered?

To be confronted?

He began worrying his hat again.

"Finley, I know you've been at it all day—and you probably want to go home and put up your feet or get out of your heels or…whatever, but…" He seemed to wrestle with his words before asking, "I wondered if you could tell me how to find Norm's grave, then maybe give me directions to the convalescent home?"

Finley supposed that she could draw him a map—or have him follow her car. But even though her body throbbed with weariness, she reached for her coat instead. "If you don't mind bringing me back here later, I'll go with you and show you the way."

For a moment, his eyes grew dark. Warm. And oh, so green. Then they became shuttered. Expressionless.

"I'd like that."

TWO

*W*hit opened the door to the Bronco for Finley, but squelched the urge to help her slide onto the high bench seat as he might have done years ago. Too much time apart lay between them. And he didn't think that he could touch her without coming completely unglued.

Finley.

She hadn't changed a bit—at least not in any way that counted. Her hair hung long and wavy, a dark autumn gold. A faint scar was still visible over her right eye, a product of an ill-planned hike in the Tetons. Even better, she still watched him beneath her lashes when she thought he wasn't looking and that made him feel…

Good.

Better, in fact, than he had in a damned long time.

Despite the twelve hour drive it had taken to get here, Whit felt a jolt of energy as he circled the front of the truck to climb behind the wheel.

"I can't believe you still have the old Bronco," Finley said with a grin as she fastened her seatbelt.

That smile hit him like a hot punch to the gut, but he resolutely thrust the sensation away, focusing on her comment instead.

"Why wouldn't I? It's a classic."

He'd rescued the '79 Bronco from a scrap yard before he'd even had a license to drive. Then he'd picked up every odd job he could wrangle to finance the spare parts needed to get it back into shape. He would never sell it. The truck had too much sentimental value for him to ever let it go.

But when he twisted the key, it took longer than usual for the engine to kick over.

"Yeah. It's a classic," Finley muttered.

The sass lacing her comment filled his veins like a tonic. Once again, unbidden, his lips slid into the semblance of a grin.

When was the last time someone had been able to make him smile?

"Nothing's wrong that can't be fixed with a tune-up."

He adjusted the windshield wipers, then flipped the defroster to HIGH, waiting for the air to clear the mist from his windows.

"I'm sorry you missed the funeral," Finley said— probably more to fill the awkward silence than for any other reason.

"Yeah, me too. I got here a few minutes before people started leaving the wake."

"You should have come in."

"I…uh…I was gearing myself up to approach the house when the pastor and his wife left."

Again, her lips twitched. "Yeah. Once the refreshments gave out, people were ready to go."

The glow of the dashboard assured him that she really didn't think that was the reason.

"You must be exhausted," he murmured, knowing even as he said the words that Norm's passing wasn't the only reason for the shadows in her eyes. He recognized the emotions that hung there, dark and unexpressed, like a bruise on her soul. Didn't he encounter the same thing staring back at him from his mirror every morning?

Damn, it had been so long since he'd seen her.

"A little." A wealth of sentiment lay behind the confession. "I came over early this morning to let the church ladies in so they could start setting out dishes and food." She glanced at the dashboard. "Is it really that late?"

The clock glowed 7:15. But the darkness brought by the autumn storm made it seem even later. Whit suddenly realized that he was adding more duties to the long day she'd already had.

"Maybe this is a bad idea. The cemetery doesn't have any lighting, so I probably wouldn't be able to see much. After everything you've been through today, I hate to drag you out there."

"I don't mind. Honest. Norm's grave is located near one of the lanes. The lights from your truck will be enough for you to see."

Whit nodded, not sure if he trusted himself to speak. The fact that Finley was willing to do this for him—after dark, in the middle of a sleet storm—conveyed the fact that she understood. He might have been kept from the funeral due to events outside his control, but he didn't want to delay much longer before paying his respects.

He put the Bronco into gear, pointing it toward the end of the lane.

"Which way?"

"East. He's in the old pioneer cemetery."

Whit pulled the Bronco onto the main road, then shot another glance in Finley's directions.

She was so freakin' beautiful. It had taken every ounce of control he'd ever possessed to stay away from her all these years. Her image haunted his dreams and popped into his head when he'd least expected it. He'd resigned himself to the fact that he would never see her again—and it was all for the best.

But when he'd heard of Norm's passing…

He couldn't stay away from her a moment longer.

Realizing the dangerous path his thoughts were taking, Whit cleared his throat, searching for something—anything—innocuous to say.

"I thought they weren't burying folks in the old graveyard anymore," he said as he eased the Bronco's speed up to the limit.

"Norm and Martha owned plots bought by his grandparents back in the twenties, so the new rules don't apply. Besides, I don't think Norm would be very happy if he weren't buried next to Martha."

Memories of Martha Campanella flooded into his mind. Clint's mother had died nearly a dozen years ago of pneumonia. When Whit thought of her, he recalled big hair and an equally big heart. She hadn't seemed daunted by the noise Clint and his friends made when they'd burst through the door. In fact, she'd seemed to encourage the din. Over the years, her kitchen had become the meeting point for the Sinful Six. She'd greeted them with plates of after-school sandwiches, cookies and glasses of milk. Then she'd subtly pointed them in the direction of an adventure—collecting frogs at the pond, bottle-feeding newborn heifers, gathering cattails from the ditch banks. She'd been the one to teach Whit that there was no shame in crying or saying you were sorry, even if you were a boy.

Whit and Finley rode in silence for several minutes. Perhaps it was the safety of the shadows that pressed in upon them, or the soft splat of sleet hitting the windshield, but there was no awkwardness to the quiet. A part of Whit could almost deny the years that had separated them. His headlights picked out the old, familiar landmarks—the fork in the road that led to town on the right and the highway on the left, the farm implement dealership near the crossroads, the Dairy Delight hamburger joint with its parking lot filled with teenagers and their souped-up cars.

But then, interwoven between all that seemed familiar were stark differences—the housing development planted in what had once been the Sato family's pasture, the strip mall and gas stations built along the road, a stoplight erected at the edge of town.

He slowed for a red light, waiting for several minutes even though there was no traffic coming in the opposite direction.

"I never thought I'd see the day when Larkspur sported a stoplight."

Finley's expression grew rueful. "We have three now. The new freeway tends to bring more traffic into town during the day." She shrugged. "But at night, the streets are as sleepy as ever."

She pointed to an intersection ahead of them. "You'll want to take the old highway."

He nudged his signal, then turned. The streets became dark again as they headed away from the glow of town.

Once again, the Bronco grew quiet, the slush from the road hissing beneath his tires.

"It's about a half mile up ahead."

Whit appreciated the reminder. As a kid, he hadn't paid all that much attention to the old cemetery. Sure, he knew where it was. There'd been Halloweens when the Sinful Six had driven down its narrow lanes in the hopes of seeing the famed Gray Lady ghost, who, according to urban legend, roamed the grounds in search of her missing baby. But there'd been a glibness to their visits, an unspoken belief in their own immortality. Whit doubted that any of them had ever really absorbed the fact that the weather-eroded headstones marked the resting spots of so many people.

He touched his brakes when he saw the wrought iron fence that heralded the boundaries of the property. A pair of stone pillars with an elaborate arch allowed him access inside.

"Head all the way to the end of the lane. It's right there against the outer ditch."

He drove slowly, the beams of his headlights picking out the monuments on either side—tall sandstone obelisks that honored entire pioneer families; smaller, simpler stones that memorialized individuals; and the heartbreaking lambs and angels that marked the passing of a child.

At the end of the gravel road, he flicked on the high beams. Just as Finley had said, he could see the spot where a freshly upturned grave had been heaped with flowers.

The sight suddenly made everything more real. Until now, a part of him had shied away from the truth—that the man he'd regarded as a substitute father had died. It had all seemed so otherworldly to him—receiving the news, traveling for hours…

Seeing Finley.

Unable to avoid the power of her name, he looked at her then. But he couldn't hold her gaze for long.

She knew.

Finley had always been the only person on earth who'd understood him. She'd been fully aware of the shit at home which had driven him to spend more and more time at the Campanellas' as a kid. And she understood the reasons why he'd stayed away for the last ten years.

"I should have come back before now."

He didn't realize that he'd spoken the words aloud until they rasped through his throat.

"Norm understood why you stayed away."

Whit gripped the steering wheel.

"I should have tried harder to get here for the funeral."

Finley reached for his hand, and for a moment, a jolt of white-hot sensation rushed through his veins. Images raced through his head like flashbulbs.

The first time they'd met.

The first time they'd danced.

The first time they'd kissed.

Without thinking, he jerked away—then regretted his reaction when the connection between them was severed as quickly as it was formed.

"Sorry, I—"

"Go pay your respects. I'll wait in the car to give you a little privacy."

He heard the stiffness to her tone. Damn it, he didn't want her to think he was the same prick he'd been all those years ago. He wanted to call back the moment, but her posture warned him against saying anything.

Besides, what could he say to make any of this easier?

I'm sorry I'm being an asshole?

I'm sorry I've been away so long?

I'm sorry I kissed you all those years ago?

No. He could never be sorry for that kiss. It had been his one chance to touch her, hold her.

Taste her.

"I'll be back in a minute."

Finley waited until the door had closed behind Whit before allowing herself to exhale.

What had she been thinking? Grabbing onto him like that?

She felt her cheeks grow hot at the memory of the lightning bolt of need which had shot through her at that innocent touch. Dear sweet heaven above, she'd thought she was over all that. She hadn't seen Whit in years. Years and years. And it would be an understatement to say they hadn't separated on the best of terms. There shouldn't be anything at all between them. Certainly not any…*feelings.*

Feelings?

Was that really the proper term for it?

She pressed a hand to her chest as if she could ease the pounding of her heart. She had to keep a level head. Whit would be leaving soon—maybe even tomorrow. No doubt, he would be in and out of town within a few days.

With no idea of the emotional devastation he left in his wake.

Finley laced her fingers together, then clenched them so tightly in her lap that the joints gleamed white. Concentrating on the image, she willed herself to ignore the physical ache as much as her emotional turmoil. It was for the best, really. The moment the community gossips discovered Whit was in town, they would be at it again. Finley certainly couldn't afford to get wrapped up in any of it. If she wanted to get out of this place herself, she needed to stay away from controversy. She was at least five hundred dollars away from her goal. That meant extra shifts at the diner and squirreling away her tips. She couldn't afford any distractions, let alone anything as monumental as Whit Patterson.

She leaned forward to wipe the steam away from the windshield. But even after telling herself she mustn't get involved, she couldn't help noting the slump to his broad shoulders. He stood with his hands shoved into the pockets of his bulky jacket, his head bowed. Then, to her infinite surprise, he dragged his hat from his head and placed it over the piles of flowers mounding the grave.

She took a gulp of air—half gasp, half sob. Whit had always been so fanatic about his hats. He'd often proclaimed that a cowboy's hat was like a good marriage. It took time and patience and effort to find the right one, make it your own, and maintain the relationship.

Leaving it at Norm's grave was a love offering to the single adult who had helped Whit negotiate the pitfalls of adolescence and become the man that he was.

Even if that man felt he was inordinately flawed.

She sobbed again, then caught the tell-tale sound in her throat. Blinking furiously, she tried to think of something— *anything*—which would help her drive the tears away.

Puppies.

Sunflowers.

Roast beef sandwiches.

But in that moment—with his body illuminated in the Bronco's high beams—she came to a sudden, rushing revelation.

Nothing had changed between Whit and her. At least not on her part.

Heaven help them both.

Finley seemed oddly quiet as they left the cemetery—not that Whit had expected to be greeted with a burst of conversation. No, there was more to it than that. She sat with her hands clenched in her lap, her face turned to the window. And she was…sniffing?

Damn.

She was crying.

Too late, he realized that he probably shouldn't have brought her to the cemetery. She'd already had a rough day, and the last thing she needed was another reminder of her grief.

"I'm sorry."

She whipped to look at him, giving him a glimpse of tears. Then she returned her attention to the window again, surreptitiously wiping her cheeks.

"About what?"

"I should have let you go home. You've had a tough day, I'm sure. The last thing you needed was to come with me."

Again, she seemed to wipe her eyes, then she turned to meet him with a smile that was too wide, too bright, too…non-Finley.

"Nonsense! It would have been difficult giving directions, and I…"

The words petered away, clearly requiring too much effort. Finally, she sighed and the woman he knew returned—one who was vulnerable and thoughtful and sad.

"Don't mind me. I-I'm hungry and…a bit emotional."

"Didn't you eat at the wake?"

She grimaced. "No, I…I couldn't really settle into one place long enough."

Knowing Finley, she'd probably been nervous that the event would be a fitting tribute, that her guests would be comforted, that there would be enough food. Introvert that she was, the noise and chatter and the large group of people had probably sapped her of what little energy she'd had left.

"Look…would you like to stop and get dinner?"

She opened her mouth, closed it. Then seemed to give in to her moral dilemma.

"Yeah, actually. But not in public. I-I don't want to…"

"Feel like you're onstage again?"

Even in the dimness of the cab, he saw the flicker of relief in her blue eyes.

"Yeah." She bit her lip, then pointed to a road leading back to town. "Turn right there. I've got an idea."

Within a few miles, he realized that she was directing him toward the diner on the outskirts of town.

"Park in the rear, over there, next to the employee entrance." As soon as he'd pulled to a stop, she jumped from the Bronco. "I'll be right back."

True to her word, she soon appeared carrying a large sack and a drink holder with two cups.

Whit leaned across the seat, opening the door.

"I hope you don't mind soda."

"No. That's great." Truth was, he'd drink molten lava if it meant that he could spend a few more minutes in her company.

As soon as she'd handed him the carrier, she climbed up beside him.

"The Compassionate Service Committee should be finished by now. We have to go back to the Campanellas' to get my car, so why don't we eat there?"

"Sounds good."

Whit didn't need directions to return to the Campanellas'. He eased back onto the two-lane highway and headed to the one place where he'd ever felt like he belonged.

Sure enough, by the time they pulled into the lane, the only car they saw belonged to Finley. A single light glowed from the living room as if it had been left to welcome them back.

Finley led the way inside, crossing through the entryway to the kitchen in the rear. She switched on the light, flooding the room with a golden glow.

"Have a seat." She motioned to the large farmhouse table surrounded by chairs. Whit knew from experience that the table could expand to hold the Sinful Six and their dates for the prom, or homecoming, or a birthday.

Finley began unloading to-go containers from the sack. Opening his own, Whit found thick slices of homemade wheat bread stacked with shredded lettuce, tomatoes, pepper jack cheese and thinly shaved roast beef.

"That used to be your favorite," she took her own seat.

"Oh, yeah." His mouth watered at the mere sight of the meal, but he managed hold off his hunger long enough to shrug out of his jacket.

When he started to sit, he caught her looking at him. Hard.

But then she glanced down at her food, making him wonder if he was placing too much weight on her reaction.

He waited until she reached for the hand-cut fries piled into the container before grabbing his sandwich. With one bite, he was transported into the past. No one made a sandwich like the Busy B. The bread was thick and soft, the meat savory, the cheeses sourced from one of the local dairies. The whole thing was topped off with the Busy B's famous herb aioli and a wedge of near-dill pickle pulled straight from one of Herb Boyington's crocks.

Whit couldn't help the moan that eased from his throat.

Finley grinned. "Good?"

"Heaven."

A comfortable silence filled the corners of the room as they ate. It was only when he'd managed to take the edge off his hunger that Whit said, "So what do I need to know to get caught up on your life?"

The question seemed to startle her. Finley had always appeared surprised when he asked her personal questions. Obviously, she hadn't caught on to the fact that he wanted to know everything about her.

"I, uh…" She took a sip from her soda. "There's not much to tell. I've been here, in Larkspur."

Whit frowned. "You didn't finish college?"

She'd had a partial scholarship. What had happened?

"No. After the accident…I was forced to drop out." She shrugged. "Mom divorced. Again. Then, she injured her back and needed surgery. And Norm seemed so…lost. Especially when we didn't know what would happen with Clint. So, I stayed."

She did her best to make light of the situation, but Whit could see the shadows gathering in her eyes again. The Finley he remembered had wanted to become a surgical nurse. It must have been heartbreaking to have that choice ripped away from her.

"Right now, I'm a waitress at the Busy B. It's good work, decent money."

But not what she'd wanted to do.

"I'm actually planning to go back to school. With luck, I'll start winter semester. If not, I'll take some courses in the summer."

"That's great."

"What about you, Whit?"

For a moment, the kitchen throbbed with uncertainty. Too late, Finley must have realized that she'd strayed into sensitive territory. But Whit was used to answering such questions. He'd long ago learned that there were things about his past that most folk really didn't want to know. He skipped those parts automatically.

"I've been around. Done a little traveling. For a few years, I'd find a job as a ranch hand, stay for six months to a year, then move on. It took a while before I found my footing. Then I went back to school myself and landed a position that was more...permanent. I work outside of Reno, now."

Had he said too much? Given too much away?

Did it seem pitiful or needy that he'd spent most of his time away from Larkspur bouncing from job to job? Or had he managed to sound as if that way of life appealed to him? He couldn't tell from her expression, so he bent over his food again. He could fill her in on the rest, how he'd fought to get through college and into a career he enjoyed. But after all the crap he'd mentioned, he feared it would ring of overcompensation, so he changed the subject instead.

"Where did you say Clint was staying?" Whit asked the question as casually as he could. But once again, he knew he'd failed miserably.

"It's a convalescent facility they built about a year ago near the old hospital. It's really nice. Sunny. The nurses there are fantastic."

He could tell that Finley was trying to keep her tone matter-of-fact. But the shadows had returned to her eyes and the slight lift to her brows conveyed a different message.

Are you sure you want to go there, Whit? Are you sure you're up to it?

"Do you…uh…think they'd mind if I visited?"

Finley shook her head. "The nurses would love it, I'm sure." She set the rest of her sandwich down and pushed her food away. "Not many people visit him anymore."

Shit.

Whit's guilt wrapped around his throat even tighter, and he abandoned his own food, reaching for the cold cup of Pepsi. Not surprisingly, Finley had remembered that it was his drink of choice. She couldn't know that he hadn't drunk it in years. He couldn't take a sip without remembering hot summers and cold colas with his friends.

"I take it you see Clint regularly."

Of course, she would. She and Clint had been an item for a long time before the accident. They'd been *engaged*.

Until Whit had ruined everything.

Everything.

"I try to drop by several times a week," she murmured.

Whit had to look away. He couldn't take the sympathy that darkened her eyes to a stormy blue.

"Do they…uh…have specific hours?"

"No. Not really." She offered a rueful half-laugh. "I don't suppose they'd be too thrilled to see a stranger show up in the middle of the night, but they welcome family involvement, so they don't have too many rules."

Whit absently rubbed his thumb over the condensation gathered on his cup. "I'm not really family."

At that, Finley's eyes softened. "Aren't you? You were always the closest thing Clint had to a brother."

"A brother who betrayed him."

THREE

*T*he words blurted from Whit's lips before he could contain them, spilling into the silence and setting ripples of emotion into play. He watched as a montage of reactions flashed across her features: shock, grief, guilt.

Then shame.

Unable to help himself, Whit sprang to his feet, nearly knocking over his chair in the process. "Thanks for the dinner, Finley. What do I owe you?"

"N-nothing."

"I'd like to pay my half, at least."

"No! Phil gave me the meals on the house. He's always spoiling me, bullying me into eating more."

Whit was glad that someone was doing it.

He opened his mouth to offer his own list of advice: drive safely, use your seatbelt, lock

your doors.

But he didn't have a right to tell her anything. He'd lost any possibility of that a long time ago.

"I'll let myself out."

"Okay."

He'd hoped to make a clean exit, but as he snagged his jacket and strode to the door, she followed him.

"Drive safely," she offered quietly.

Damn.

"Make sure you use your seatbelt."

He knew he shouldn't, but he paused once his hand closed over the doorknob. The need to turn and look at her again was overwhelming. When he met her gaze, it was like a sucker punch to the gut.

This might be the last time he ever saw her.

The. Very.

Last.

Time.

"'Bye, Finley."

He was halfway out the door when he heard, "Will I see you tomorrow?"

Shit, shit, shit.

His boots seemed to stick to the porch and he glanced over his shoulder to find her silhouetted in the light, her hair spilling around her shoulders.

Whit knew that most men probably wouldn't have given Finley a second glance. She was what a person might call "handsome". Her features were too angular, her skin freckled—and her body lacked the curves that most men found appealing.

To Whit, she couldn't have been more beautiful. More vulnerable.

He wanted to say "no". He wanted to jump into his Bronco and drive as far and as fast away from this place as he could.

But he couldn't bring himself to say the word.

"I've got a couple of things to do in town, but I won't leave without talking to you again."

Why in hell had he said that? He would only be prolonging the inevitable.

"Thanks. I'll be at the Busy B in the morning. After that, you can find me either at Norm's or my mom's place."

He nodded. "'Bye Finley."

Whit was halfway through town before he realized where he was and where his current course would take him. A glance at the clock reassured him that it was only a little past eight. Not the best time for a visit. But maybe it wasn't the worst time either.

Sighing, he turned down one of the side streets, then turned again. Ahead of him, he could see a glowing sign.

GREENSPRINGS CONVALESCENT HOME.

As soon as he pulled into a parking place, he nearly backed out again. What on earth did he think he could accomplish? It wasn't as if Clint would welcome a visit.

But he couldn't really refuse, either.

Whit's heart felt as if it would jump right through his skin, but he forced himself to step out, lock the Bronco, then cross the parking lot to the automatic doors.

Just as Finley had stated, an effort had been made to make the facility seem more like a home. The walls were made of split pine, and the pieces of furniture were Stickley knock-offs. Artificial pine trees sparkled with fairy lights, and stuffed bears and moose adorned the side tables and book shelves.

He crossed to a reception desk and waited for a woman wearing dark green scrubs to finish with her charts. A nametag identified her as Sharla.

Her smile was warm. "May I help you?"

"I wondered if I could visit Clint Campanella? I know it's late, and I'd be happy to come back another time if—"

"No, no. I'll show you the way."

Whit realized that he'd unconsciously hoped that the staff would refuse to let him enter and send him back into the storm. Now, he had no choice but to follow things through.

"He's in the Teton wing," the woman said as they passed through a set of fire doors. From there, a series of halls radiated out like the spokes of a wheel. She chose the passage on the far right. "He has a lovely room at the end where he gets lots of sunshine during the day. Are you family?"

Whit mentally stumbled for a reply. "I-in a way. I...We were close friends back in the day."

"I'm sure he'll be pleased that you dropped by to see him." As promised, the woman stopped at the last door. "He's on a ventilator at the moment due to a recent bout of pneumonia, but it's only temporary, so don't let it startle you. Stay as long as you like. I'll be at the reception desk if you need anything."

"Thank you."

He waited until she'd left before knocking softly, then opening the door.

Whit wasn't sure what he'd expected—certainly not a tackling hug or a hearty slap on the back. But even though he'd kept his expectations low, nothing could have prepared him for what he found.

Finley had said that Clint hadn't changed much. But she was wrong. So wrong. The figure in the bed looked nothing like the friend that Whit had known since childhood. The old Clint was tall and broad and athletic with an Adonis-like face that caused a stir with the girls wherever they went. Whit, who preferred to remain in the background, had always been grateful for Clint's good looks and charisma. With Clint around, there was never a shortage of fun or excitement, but Whit didn't have to be the one to maintain it. If he got tired of all the limelight, he could simply step away.

But this...this was a ghost of the man Clint had once been. His body was incredibly thin. He lay in a half-reclining position, his arms propped on pillows, hands curled into loose fists around foam grips. Beneath the blanket, his legs seemed oddly twisted. A tube in his throat helped him breathe, causing his chest to rise and fall, rise and fall, in measured amounts. But it was his face that drew Whit's attention the most.

The cuts and lacerations from the accident had healed, but they would never be erased. Thick ropy scars spread out like a macabre spider's web from a spot over his left eye—mirroring the crazed glass which had shredded his skin as he'd been thrown from the car. And his eyes...they were still dark, but they'd lost the intensity that invariably convinced Whit to join whatever crazy new scheme his friend had devised. Only partially open, those eyes stared into the shadowed corners of the room. The blue depths were devoid of the fire and emotion that had once seemed to blaze from his core.

"Hey, Clint. It's me. Whit."

He didn't expect an answer. But that didn't mean that Whit didn't look for the tiniest flicker that might tell him that Clint was still in there.

The door bounced shut behind him and the room filled with the soft *hiss...hiss...*of the ventilator.

Whit wasn't sure what to do now that he'd announced himself. More than anything, he wished he still had his hat so he had a way to keep his hands busy. As it was, they hung uselessly at his sides until he plunged them into the pockets of his coat.

An effort had been taken to give the room a homey touch. Whit supposed that either Norm or Finley was responsible. Or both. A brightly colored quilt had been folded at the foot of the bed. The walls were adorned with old football jerseys and rodeo posters. Clint's bull-riding trophies lined the shelves on the opposite side of the room. A stuffed bull regarded Whit with button eyes from a recliner in the corner, and the vinyl hospital-style couch had been softened with pillows adorned with horses—Finley's touch, Whit suspected.

Suddenly, Whit didn't know what to do. He probably shouldn't be here at all. If Clint hadn't been in a vegetative state, he would have launched himself at Whit, called him a bastard, and begun pummeling him with his fists. Instead, he lay still. So still.

"I don't know if...uh...you can hear me or not..." Whit paused, knowing that once the words were said—even if Clint couldn't understand them—it would be a confession.

"I'm sorry. So, *so* sorry. I don't know what I can ever say or do to make things right between us. I handled things...badly."

That was the understatement of the world.

The figure on the bed seemed to pull at him, drawing Whit closer, until finally, he sat on the edge. One of his hands closed around Clint's and gently squeezed.

He'd thought that his friend's skin would be cool to the touch. But Clint's fingers were warm. And if Whit moved his thumb a bit...he could feel the slow, steady beat of the man's pulse.

"I can't offer you an explanation for what I...what we...no, what *I* did." His throat felt so tight that he could barely speak. "I...I loved her, Clint."

The words shimmered in the air like tinkling glass. Shattered glass. And Whit tried to block out the images of that night. The chaotic activity of the first responders, the harsh lights of the hospital.

The pain.

A head injury had resulted in Whit having no memory of the wreck or the hours preceding it, but the aftermath had been seared into his brain.

Damnit all to hell. He shouldn't be here. He didn't have the right to waltz back into town, have dinner with Finley, then show up here as if...

As if what?

As if nothing had happened?

The past few years were evidence enough that none of them had escaped the repercussions of that night. They'd all been injured, to varying degrees, but it was the emotional scars that still lingered. Due to one single, careless moment of weakness, the bonds of the Sinful Six had been tested, and their friendships hadn't been able to survive the strain. As soon as it became clear that Clint wouldn't recover, they'd all scattered.

Everyone but Finley.

Whit jumped to his feet and strode to the door. But he couldn't help looking back one last time.

"I'm so sorry." The words seemed to tear themselves from his throat. Then he strode down the hall and into the miserable night.

It was dark when Finley let herself into the house.

Her *mother's* house.

If that wasn't a statement on her failure as a grown-up, Finley didn't know what was. She and Alice Fitzpatrick had never really been close. Alice had spent her life frantically trying to push her daughters into the town's "socially elite." She'd envisioned them hanging with the popular kids at school, becoming cheerleaders and trend-setters. But Finley had been more concerned with getting good grades, while Billie…well, Billie had been…*Billie*.

Finley closed the door as noiselessly as she could, wincing when the latch hit home. But her mother, who lay slumped in the easy chair in front of the flickering television set, didn't lift her head. On the side table, Finley could see an empty wine bottle tipped on its side next to a highball glass.

"You don't need to be tiptoeing around." The announcement came from Billie who appeared in the doorway leading into the hall. "She's been out cold for an hour."

As if to emphasize her point, Billie took a book from the shelf nearby and dropped it onto the hardwood floor. Finley jumped, but her mother didn't even flinch.

"See?"

Finley sighed and shrugged out of her jacket, hanging it on the coat tree next to the door.

"When did you get home?"

"An hour ago. By that time, she'd ploughed through her secret stash of whiskey, what was left of the wine, and I'm pretty sure a bottle of cooking sherry."

"She's out of control again."

"She's always out of control," Billie offered. "Some days she just hides it better."

Finley supposed that Billie had a point, but she was too tired to argue with her about the best way to handle Alice, so she moved down the hall toward her bedroom. Billie, unfortunately, trailed along behind her.

"You'd better be prepared. I hear that Whit Patterson is back in town."

In typical Billie fashion, her sister skipped the small talk altogether and shot straight into dangerous waters. Idly, Finley noted that the town grapevine must have gone into overdrive to spread the news so quickly. The only place Whit could have even been seen was the Busy B parking lot. In any event, there was no sense in denying the truth.

"Yeah."

Billie's mouth dropped and her eyes widened. "You've seen him."

The comment emerged more as an accusation than a statement, but Finley refused to react.

"He dropped by after the wake."

Billie leaned against the doorway, folding her arms, her head shaking from side to side. "Figures. He was afraid to show his face, so he slunk into town after everything was over."

"Actually, an accident closed I-80 for several hours, or he would have been here on time."

"Uh huh."

Finley bristled at her sister's automatic assumptions about Whit, but she was too tired to object. Since the accident, Billie had pinned all the blame for the accident on Whit—much like the rest of the town. But there'd been more to her attitude than that. She'd mulishly held a private grudge against Whit and the rest of Finley's friends—and Finley had never really understood why. She doubted a sense of sibling overprotectiveness had anything to do with it.

"Look, Billie, I'm exhausted and I need to go to work early tomorrow morning. So, unless there's a point to this discussion…"

"No point," Billie said straightening. "Just a warning. That man ruined your life—and Clint's and Javi's and PJ's and Liam's. If you decide to get mixed up with him again, you're an even bigger fool than I took you for."

With that, Billie turned and padded to her own room further down the hall. And even though Finley wanted to march after her sister and defend what little time she might spend with Whit…

She had a feeling that, in this instance, Billie might be right.

The air was cold and crisp the next morning, the sun glinting off a fine layer of ice on the cars in the parking lot as Whit gathered the rest of his belongings from the cheap "no-tell motel" where he'd stayed the night. After stuffing his toiletries into a duffel bag, he cast one last glance around the room to make sure he hadn't left anything behind. Then, he slid his pistol into the holster at the back of his waist and tugged his shirt tails down to cover it.

Time to get out of Dodge.

But as he closed the door behind him and threw his bag into the back of the Bronco, he didn't experience the relief he'd anticipated. Instead, his thoughts were crowded with images of Finley and her crystal blue eyes.

Hell.

Sliding behind the wheel, he debated what to do next. He'd promised that he wouldn't go before saying goodbye, but if he were smart, he'd head for the freeway before either of them could get into this reunion shit too deeply.

His phone chirped in his pocket, and he sighed.

"Patterson here."

"Hey, Whit. How's the vacation going?"

Whit immediately recognized the voice. Thayne Ruff was one of his fellow officers in Nevada's "cow cop" Agricultural Enforcement Unit.

"I wish it were a vacation, Thayne."

"Yeah, I heard you had a funeral."

Not wanting to go down that road, Whit nudged the conversation into a different direction. "What's up?"

"Listen, how far are you from Redmond?"

"Not far. About fifteen miles or so."

"You got a way to take down some information?"

"Sure."

Whit reached for the pen and the small notebook he kept tucked in the glove compartment.

"I've been tracking a lead on the missing cattle from the Rocking B Bar Ranch, and I've had some reports of a semi heading your way carrying a full load of livestock with what might be altered brands. There's a big auction in Redmond coming up, so maybe our rustlers are thinking they could offload their take. I've got the Wyoming Livestock Board Investigators in the loop, but I wouldn't mind another set of eyes."

"I'd be glad to help."

"Let me give you the particulars I've scrounged up so far."

Thayne rattled off tag numbers and descriptions of the vehicles in question, then asked, "How much longer are you thinking of staying?"

Whit opened his mouth to inform Thayne that he'd been planning on leaving within an hour, give or take. But as he stared down at his own scrawled handwriting, he found himself hesitating. It didn't make much sense to volunteer to keep an eye peeled for a suspicious load of cattle, then leave the same day, did it? He looked up and grimaced. Then again, he didn't look forward to another night spent in the hotel from hell, either.

"I don't know yet. My plans are up in the air right now."

"You should take some time off. That's beautiful country. Hell, I can't even remember the last time you took a personal day, let alone a vacation."

Whit worked because it gave him less time to think and brood. But...

For the first time, his gaze lifted up, up, focusing on a point beyond the hotel where the nearby mountains were etched against the morning sky. Even in the dim light, the yellows, golds, and scarlets of the autumn foliage were startlingly beautiful.

"I'll keep you posted, Thayne."

"Thanks, bud."

As he placed his phone back into his pocket, Whit sighed. Only minutes ago, he'd been sure about his decision to leave Larkspur. But now…

Well, he couldn't leave before at least taking a look for Thayne. Could he?

"Can I get you anything else, Mr. Clumsky?"

"No. Thanks, Finley."

Finley left Aldo Clumsky the bill for his food, then stepped to the next set of customers.

"More coffee?"

"Thank you."

She knew better than to engage Manuel Sarta in conversation. The owner of the local bank came into the diner every morning like clockwork. He ordered two eggs, scrambled; two pieces of bacon, crisp; two pieces of wheat toast, dry; then drank two cups of coffee, black. Through it all, he read the morning papers with the concentration of a copyeditor, and he tolerated no interruptions.

After filling his second cup, Finley backed away, then returned to the kitchen to check on her orders.

With the weekend approaching, traffic at the diner had been crazy. RV's on their way to Jackson or Yellowstone filled the parking lot. The booths and tables were crowded with tourists and locals alike looking for a quick, hearty breakfast with the flavors of a home-cooked meal.

"Ray, how's that steak and eggs order coming?"

"Give me two more minutes."

She gathered up several plates and delivered them to table twelve. "Banana-strawberry waffles, lumberjack special, and moose pancakes for the little one."

Finley took special care placing the last plate in front of the toddler in a booster seat. His mouth formed a perfect O when he saw the moose-shaped pancake complete with a maraschino cherry nose, chocolate chip eyes, and whipped cream adorned antlers.

"Can I get you anything else?"

"Hot sauce?"

The query was made by the "father" of the group, a kid really, with the straggly beginnings of a beard.

"There's Tabasco in the carrier with the mustard and catsup. Or I could bring you fresh salsa."

"Salsa sounds great."

"Be right back."

She was hustling toward the kitchen again when the jingling of the bell drew her eyes to the front door.

Whit.

His frame seemed to fill the doorframe before he stepped inside and stood for a moment in indecision.

Had he come for breakfast?

Or to say goodbye?

A part of her heard the beginnings of the whispers, then saw the heads begin to turn. Ignoring the reaction, she snagged a menu from a nearby rack and made a beeline for Whit—even though hostessing wasn't her job.

As soon as she was close enough, she snagged his wrist, pulling him toward the last empty table she had left in her section. Thankfully, Whit seemed willing to follow her lead, trailing behind her to the rear booth.

Only then did she turn and stammer, "D-did you come here for breakfast…or…"

He seemed to feel a measure of her discomfort. Without the blanket of darkness and the white noise of the storm, their second meeting seemed…exposed.

"I, uh…wondered if we could talk. But if you're busy, I could order something to eat."

"Perfect."

She waited until he'd been seated, placed the menu in front of him, then said, "I need to take care of a couple of tables, then I've got a break coming up. If you can wait a little longer…"

"Sure."

"Great. Great!" She wasn't sure why she was so pleased with his response. Finley was under no illusions that he would be staying long in Larkspur. Even now, he had the looks of a man who was wondering how to offer bad news.

"Take a look at the menu and…I'll be back."

She dodged away from him, wondering why it was so hard to talk to Whit. Sure, he'd been gone a long time. But in the past…

The past.

Therein lay the crux, she supposed.

They had a past together, and they hadn't separated under the best of terms.

She ladled salsa into a ramekin, then gathered up the plates which had been left in the window. Within ten minutes, she'd managed to handle all of her customers. Then she found Megan, who was about to come on shift.

"Hey, listen. Could you cover my tables while I take my break?"

"Yeah, sure. No problem."

"I might run a little late, but I'll be sitting in the back booth if you need me."

"Don't worry about it."

"Thanks."

FOUR

*F*inley filled two glasses with ice water, then returned to Whit. As she set the drinks on the table, she asked, "Have you decided what you want?"

He opened his mouth, seemed to change his mind, then said, "Do you have time to ...sit?"

"Sure. I got Megan—Megan Phipps—to cover my tables."

She slid into the seat opposite Whit—then had the irrational thought that she should have put him at a table. She'd forgotten how *big* he was. At 6'5", he'd always towered over her. But all these years later, he'd filled out from being a gangly teenager. His shoulders were broad, his arms muscular. A part of her wanted to push the Carhartt away so she could discover where the layers of clothing ended and the powerful shape of his body began.

Stop it!

Finley took a quick sip of water, spilling part of it over her hand. Choking, she tried to get her breath again.

"You okay?" Whit asked.

"Fine. Fine." She finally managed to catch her breath, then used a napkin to wipe up the water.

She'd always been like this around Whit—nervous, clumsy, tongue-tied. She'd often wondered if that's why she'd ended up dating Clint. Clint was easy to be around. She could say anything to him. Even if she messed up, he would merely laugh and throw his arm around her shoulders. But Whit…

Whit was a whole new brand of intense. When she was near him, her brain short-circuited and her tongue stuck to the roof of her mouth. It was always incredibly *important* that he think well of her, even though she'd never had any reason to believe otherwise.

She looked up to find Whit watching her closely.

"Is something wrong?"

Finley shook her head, then let the pent-up air leave her lungs in a long, slow whoosh.

"I don't know why I get all worked up like this. Last night I was fine, but this morning…I-I…"

His smile was rueful. "It's easier in the dark, isn't it?"

"Yeah." The word emerged half-uttered, half-sighed when she realized that he shared a portion of her nervousness.

"We never had any trouble in the dark, did we?" he murmured.

The words throbbed into the space between them, seeping into the nooks and crannies of her body, filling her with a warmth that she hadn't felt in a very long time.

True. They'd never had any trouble in the dark. A shadowy dimness brought with it an illusion of privacy, intimacy, the sense that anything said would remain in confidence and that transgressions would never be discovered by anyone else.

They'd been so wrong.

Whit reached across the table to take her hand, and the action was so unexpected that she jumped. He held onto her, refusing to let her evade the contact.

"I never wanted to hurt you, Finley."

She'd forgotten about his eyes. They were green with flecks of brown and gold. Summer eyes.

"I know that."

"I should have stuck around longer. I shouldn't have left you to deal with the fallout on your own."

Finley didn't know what to say, so she shook her head, then tightened her fingers around his.

"You did the right thing, Whit."

"Did I?" His free hand rubbed idly through the condensation circles left on the table. "I'm not so sure."

"It's not like you had a choice."

No, no, no! That was the *wrong* thing to say.

Whit didn't seem angry. A corner of his mouth tipped in a rueful smile, but to her surprise, he didn't try to back away.

The old Whit would have stood up and left.

"I saw him last night." He met her gaze again. "Clint."

Even though she knew what Whit would have found when he entered Clint Campanella's room at the convalescent center, her heart began to thud against her ribs in a slow, measured beat.

"You warned me, but...I don't know. I expected...a reaction."

Her thumb seemed to stray of its own volition, exploring the bumps and valleys of his knuckles, then moving back again. In the light, she could see the scars. They'd healed, for the most part, becoming thin almost imperceptible streaks. She wondered how many scars there were under his clothes. He'd been ejected from the car like Clint, but his face hadn't been cut. Instead, Whit had sustained a concussion, a broken leg, broken ribs, a cracked collar bone. But even those injuries were nothing compared to what had happened to him inside. In those first few days after the accident, he'd refused to talk or meet with a counselor. He'd held his emotions bottled tightly inside him.

"I know what you mean," she said softly. "Every time I visit Clint, I feel like there should be something—a glance, a twitch of the fingers, a shift of his head—that will show me that he knows I'm there. I swear, there are times when I *feel* him and I know that a part of his spirit is still there. I can imagine exactly what he'd say to me or how he'd grouse about still being in bed. But there's nothing tangible to give me evidence that anything I offer is getting through."

He nodded. "I thought the same thing. I expected him to jump from the bed and come at me with fists swinging, swearing at me for what a...fucking mess I've made of everything."

Finley's chest grew tight. "You can't still blame yourself."

When he looked up, his eyes were fierce. "Why not? I'm the one that started everything. I should have kept a lid on my feelings, not...tempted you...kissed you..."

The memories swept over her like a rolling tide, burying her in sights and sounds and sensations that she'd tried so hard to bury. The surge of adrenaline, the roar of the crowd, the grunts and snorts of the livestock in the pens.

And Whit, riding that bull, his body whipping like a rag doll as he struggled to remain seated for two seconds, four, eight. When he'd kicked free and fallen to the ground, the bull had whirled, nearly kicking him in the ribs. Then the bullfighters had intervened and Whit had bounded to his feet.

As he'd made his way from the arena, there had been no thought, no warnings of what would ensue. He'd strode toward Finley, his jaw set, his eyes aglow. But not for the win.

For her.

For her.

Finley wrenched her thoughts back to the present, refusing to go down that road of memories. Nothing good could come from it.

"The past is over, Whit," she said firmly. More to convince herself than Whit.

The words seemed to echo around them in the narrow booth. Finley watched as Whit carefully chose his words, then opened his mouth to offer a comment, but before he could, a shadow loomed above them and Finley looked up to find Nelson Grove standing next to their table.

"Finley, Whit. I've been trying to find the two of you. Little did I know that you'd end up at the Busy B together."

There was no censure behind the comment, but Finley felt her cheeks flaming nonetheless.

Thankfully, Whit drew the man's attention away from her.

"Mr. Grove."

Whit gently withdrew his hand from Finley's and held it out to the local lawyer, shaking it firmly. Finley couldn't help feeling a slight chill at the loss of the contact.

"I wonder if the pair of you could drop by my office tomorrow. Say, around three?"

Finley scrambled to think. "I...I get off at three, so I might be late."

"Let's make it half-past, then. That will give me time to contact my other clients and set up a conference call, if necessary."

"Conference call?" Whit stiffened.

"Nothing to worry about. I've been tying up one or two loose ends with Norm's will. If we could meet, I'll be able to wrap everything up with a neat little bow and hand it off to his executor to finalize. Good day to you both."

Finley waited until the man had moved out of earshot. "What was that all about?"

"I have no idea."

"Finley?" A woman with a long braid poked her head around the corner. "Things are picking up again. Are you about done?"

Finley waved to her co-worker. "I'll be right there." Then she turned to Whit. "Sorry. I've got to get back to my shift. What would you like to eat?"

Whit shook his head. "Nothing, thanks. I've got a few things I need to do. I'll swing by your house to pick you up tomorrow afternoon if you want."

Once again, that pool of warmth seemed to spread through her body. Like a silly high school wallflower, she found herself thinking: *He wants to spend time with me.*

With me.

Immediately, she slammed on the emotional brakes.

Stop it! You're not a girl anymore, and this isn't high school. The stakes were so much higher now that she knew the consequences.

"Do you remember where I live?"

"Mm-hmm."

She wasn't sure why it pleased her so much that he did. "Give me your cellphone."

Whit reached into his pocket, then handed his phone to her.

She turned it on, her thumbs working quickly over the screen before offering it back to him. "That's my number. If you need to get in touch, give me a call. I'll have to take a quick shower and change after my shift tomorrow, but I'll try to be ready by twenty after three."

Unable to help herself, she paused to meet his eyes one last time. "Thanks, Whit."

Then she beat a hasty retreat.

Whit's Bronco rumbled to a stop at the end of the dirt lane leading to his childhood home. Twisting the key, he sat looking at the old clapboard house, listening to the engine *tic-tic-tic* as it cooled beneath the autumn breeze.

It felt surreal, staring at the ramshackle building which had brought him so much grief as a kid. He'd always been embarrassed by this place. He'd done everything he could to keep his friends from seeing the rusted vehicles in the yard, the old washing machine riddled with bullet holes, the heaps of scrap iron and the waist-high weeds. Even the house itself was a disgrace, with a porch awning that had collapsed on one side and the tar paper showing through the shingles. The windows were bare and filthy, some of them broken and filled in with plywood, and the stoop had spots where the boards had given way due to rot.

What a dump.

Whit had almost convinced himself that he'd remembered the place being worse than it really was. But this…

This was proof positive that he'd done the right thing by leaving Larkspur. Getting away from Elvis Patterson had been the best thing he'd ever done.

Not for the first time, Whit wondered if things would have been different if his mother had been around when he was a kid. He'd never known her. According to Elvis, she'd been out of the picture as soon as Whit was born. Whit had only been five when Elvis had told him that his mom had either died of an overdose or drunk herself to death. Then again, Whit had learned early on not to believe a single word that came out of his father's mouth. The man had his own share of substance abuse problems, and as far as Whit was concerned, Elvis Patterson couldn't be trusted drunk, and he couldn't be trusted sober.

That's why Whit had avoided this place and spent most of the time after school at the Campanellas'. They must have known what was going on. Looking back on it now, Whit realized there was no way they hadn't guessed something was wrong. He'd been a dirty, grubby kid with too-small clothes and holes in his shoes. But the Campanellas had never made him feel anything but loved. Martha Campanella would insist that he and the other kids wash up after school. Then she'd *tut-tut* over the grass stains on his knees or the rips in his T-shirt, and the next thing he knew, there'd be a clean pair of pants or a folded shirt waiting for him on the edge of the tub. For the longest time, Whit had thought the clothes belonged to Clint. It wasn't until later, when Whit grew noticeably taller than his friend, that he realized she must have bought him spare pairs so that she could rotate him into a selection of clean clothes any time he visited.

The Bronco's door squeaked as Whit stepped to the ground. Although he tried to close it again as quietly as possible, he still managed to set the dozens of dogs barking away in the kennels set up under the trees.

A familiar anger twisted his gut. More than once, he'd emptied those kennels while his father was on one of his binges. But, invariably, Elvis always managed to fill them up again. Soon, there'd be a new collection of mangy mutts behind the bars, their legs shivering in fear, their ribs pressing against their fur.

The cruelty was repugnant to Whit, but not a surprise. After all, his father hadn't taken care of his own son any better than he had the animals.

He stepped toward one of the kennels, squatting so that he could push his fingers through the bars.

"Hey, there. Hey."

He'd tried to keep his voice quiet, gentle. But the animal shrank toward the far side of his enclosure and cowered in the corner.

Damnation. No creature should ever have to live like that.

"Get away from my dogs!"

The shout came from the house, and even though his back was turned, the hairs on Whit's neck stood on end. As he slowly stood, hands held out to show he was unarmed, Whit couldn't still the instinctive response to run.

Run to the Campanellas, to the Sinful Six. Anywhere but here.

He turned to face his father, fighting the shock he felt when he saw Elvis for the first time in years. Although the house and the yard remained the same, Elvis seemed to have aged twenty years. His hair—what was left of it—was gray and stringy, his features hollow. His shoulders stooped over a body which seemed frail and crooked. As Whit watched, the man staggered slightly before reaching to brace his hand against the porch support.

"Well, well, well. If it isn't the prodigal son," he rasped.

Judging by the slight slur to his words, Elvis wasn't completely drunk. Not yet. But he was well on his way.

"Elvis."

Whit had stopped calling his father by any other title about the time he'd turned eight—and he didn't see a reason to change now. In his mind, calling Elvis "Dad" would be a farce. The only person who had ever earned that title had been Norm Campanella.

Whit's footsteps soughed through the too-long grass as he crossed to the front porch.

"I never thought you'd have the guts to come back here," his father said with a sneer that revealed a mouth of missing and rotting teeth.

"Not surprising. You never had a very high opinion of me, even when I was younger."

"That's because I knew what you were. What you would become," his father growled. "And I was right, wasn't I?"

Whit didn't bother to respond. Anything he said would merely provide fuel to the fire, and his father loved to argue.

"I've come to get some of my stuff. That is, if you haven't hawked it all."

Elvis' eyes narrowed. "Anything you left behind is mine now, boy. I bought and paid for everything in that rathole room of yours."

Let it go. Don't say anything.

"Did you hear me, boy?"

How could he not?

Whit had lived with that voice dogging him every day of his life. Even after putting hundreds of miles between them, Whit had lived with the echoes swimming in his brain.

"Don't ignore me, you little bastard!"

Elvis grabbed Whit by the elbow. But Whit wasn't that scrawny kid who feared a beating anymore. When Elvis tried to shove him off the porch, Whit suddenly turned and grabbed a fistful of his father's shirt. Before the man could respond, Whit had pinned him to the porch support with such force that the man's breath exploded from his lungs in a single fetid exhalation.

"Don't touch me. Ever. Again. Maybe you haven't noticed, but I'm not a little boy you can bully and hit and scream into submission. I'm a grown man and I'm wise to your piss-poor attempts to mold me into your little toady. I'm going into that house, and I'm going to see what few personal possessions I might have left from my childhood. Then I'll leave you to your miserable existence and you'll never hear from me again. Agreed?"

Elvis' eyes had grown wide. Whit held him easily with one fist, taking most of Elvis' weight so the older man teetered on tiptoes. Too late, Elvis must have realized that Whit towered over him by at least a foot and outweighed him in muscle-mass two to one. Wisely, he offered a weak nod.

But Whit wasn't quite finished. "Furthermore, if I hear that you've hit someone again, especially a kid, I'll be back and I'll pound you into the ground. And give those dogs food and water. Right now."

Whit let go and Elvis sagged, catching himself with the porch railing. But Whit didn't bother to see what happened next. The quicker he checked his old bedroom, the faster he could be out of this dump, once and for all.

"See you tomorrow, Finley."

"'Bye, Megan. Thanks for your help today."

Finley pushed through the outer door and strode toward her car. Her mother had already called, requesting she drop by the pharmacy. And Billie needed her to pick up a couple of newspapers for her never-ending "dream job searches." After a full shift, Finley wanted a hot shower, a power nap, and something to eat.

Her phone chirped and she resisted the urge to swear. Her mother and sister seemed to know the instant she walked out the door—and they both were under the misconception that, since Finley had "nothing better to do", she should become their personal gopher.

She was tempted to ignore the ringing, but finally sighed and snatched her cell from the outer pocket of her bag. But when she unlocked the screen, she found that there was a text waiting.

From Whit.

Since a cool breeze was gusting from the nearby canyon, she waited until she'd climbed into the car, started the engine, then adjusted the heat. Then she dropped her bag onto her seat so that both hands would be free.

She touched the icon which would take her to the texting app, then sat back, smiling.

HOW WAS WORK?

It took only a couple of seconds to respond.

GOOD.

BET UR TIRED. U MUST HAVE GONE TO WORK AT…6? 5.

There was a long silence, and Finley had begun to believe that he'd finished, but then a series of chirps revealed a longer text.

WENT BY MY OLD HOUSE TODAY. SAW ELVIS. HE DIDN'T SEEM 2 HAPPY 2 SEE ME. I GOT A CHANCE 2 LOOK AROUND ROOM. MOST OF MY STUFF GONE. NO SURPRISE. BUT I'D HIDDEN MY CHAMPION BUCKLES. RESCUED THEM. AND A COUPLE DZ. DOGS.

WHICH BUCKLES?

CHEYENNE, SLC, PHOENIX.

There was a slight pause, then,

JACKSON.

Jackson Hole, Wyoming.

The last rodeo.

Their infamous kiss.

Even now, the memory of that kiss was enough to cause a warmth to flood her body, and with the heat of remembered awareness came a gnawing sensual hunger that she'd never been able to push aside.

She wanted Whit Patterson.

Even now.

There was no way that she was going to tell him that. Not even in a text. But she couldn't leave their exchange at that. Especially not when he'd spent the afternoon with his father.

R U OK?

The pause was longer this time, and she wondered if she'd presumed upon their old friendship too much. Elvis and Whit had never really got along, but Finley had probably known more than anyone how badly Whit had been neglected and even abused.

Just when she feared that she might have embarrassed Whit, another text appeared.

I'M GOOD. MADE ME REALIZE HOW MUCH NORM AND MARTHA HELPED ME OUT. GLAD I HID THE BUCKLES. THEY MEANT A LOT 2 ME.

The buckles themselves, or the memories they inspired?

Finley hesitated, wondering if she had the guts to prod him into recalling those memories.

GLAD YOU FOUND THEM. I'D LOVE 2 SEE THEM. I HAVE FOND MEMORIES OF YOUR WINS AS WELL. ESPECIALLY THE LAST ONE.

Would that be the end of it? Would he decide to break off?

U SURE?

O YEAH.

There was a moment's pause.

MAYBE WE CAN MAKE NEW MEMORIES.

Hunger slid through her veins like hot molasses. He must have felt it too. This overwhelming awareness whenever they were near. She'd tried her hardest to ignore it, but even sitting across from him at the booth that morning had seemed to bring every inch of her skin alive so that she could all but feel the heat radiating from his own body.

I'D LIKE THAT.

TOMORROW?

Her thumbs trembled as she typed,

I'D LIKE THAT EVEN MORE.

C U THEN.

She paused, unsure how honest she should be. But with only a short time remaining of his stay, she realized that she had to make her own feelings clear.

CAN'T WAIT.

There was a moment before he responded with,

ME EITHER.

By the time she tucked her phone away, she found herself thrumming with energy. And more. Her body all but vibrated with anticipation. Running her mother's and sister's errands were the last thing she wanted to do, so she turned on the radio, blasted her favorite Adele tune, and enjoyed the sunlight that played peek-a-boo through the storm clouds gathering up above. It wouldn't be long before the cold would arrive for good and the snow would start falling. But today, there was enough of a golden glow to lift her spirits and make her feel…

Alive.

FIVE

*F*inley considered a half-dozen activities—
everything from grocery shopping to playing
hooky and going to a matinee. But somehow,
she found herself driving toward Greensprings to visit Clint.

There had been a time, when they'd still had hopes of
Clint's recovery, that Finley visited him every day—even
though it meant a half-hour drive to Redmond. But as the
years had passed, it had become more difficult to see him so
often. By the time Greensprings had been built and Clint had
been transferred closer to home, she'd come more for Norm's
sake—so that the older man would know that his son wasn't
forgotten and to make sure that her surrogate father was
taking care of himself. Now, she was ashamed to admit that
she hadn't been to Greensprings since Norm had died nearly
a week ago.

As she entered the facility, she could see that Sharla was
already manning the reception desk.

"Finley! It's good to see you."

"Hi, Sharla. How's Clint doing?"

For a moment, a frown flitted around the woman's brows. "He can't seem to shake the after-effects of his latest bout with pneumonia, which has him feeling a little sorry for himself. We've got him on a ventilator, but with luck, he'll be off it by the end of the week. Go on back, I'm sure he'll be glad to see you."

Over time, Finley had become accustomed to the way the staff spoke of Clint as if he displayed his emotions and was aware of everything that went on around him. But it could still be disconcerting. Early on, the staff had explained to Finley that knowing exactly what Clint might be experiencing was difficult to determine. He might be able to process light or color, sounds or smells. The staff had begun new forms of therapy, encouraging Finley and Norm to stimulate as many of his senses as possible—and there were times when Finley could have sworn he'd reacted to those efforts. But his condition had remained relatively the same.

Finley was surprised that she hadn't worn a path through the carpet to the concrete beneath considering the number of times she'd traversed the hall. She paused at the open door, taking in the fact that Clint had been moved from the bed to the recliner. Apparently, the breathing difficulties he'd had lately hadn't weakened him too much. Opposite the chair, a television bolted to the wall had been turned to a children's television program with bright flashing colors and cheerful music.

"Hi, Clint."

Finley kept her tone bright as she approached him and bent to kiss him on the top of his head. The movement dislodged the chain she wore around her neck, and for a moment, the engagement ring that Clint had given her fell free and sparkled in the light shining through his windows. She could have sworn that his eyes tracked the glittering flecks of light that danced on the opposite wall, but then he blinked and the sensation passed.

"How are you?"

She turned her back to the ugly folding sofa, trying not to remember the countless mornings she'd come to visit and discovered that Norm had spent the night there. He'd been such a constant presence in Clint's life that she wondered if Clint knew that his father had died or had sensed his absence. Finley had been the one to tell him the news herself.

"I'm sorry I haven't seen you in a while," she said as she sat on the side of the bed. "Things have been a little crazy with all the preparations for your father's funeral. It turned out to be a beautiful service—shorter than an hour, like he'd requested." She reached to squeeze his hand. "Nearly the whole town came to the church or the wake. They asked about you, so you might have one or two extra visitors in the next few days."

At first, it had been easy to talk to Clint. Finley had prattled on about her life, her sister's string of jobs, the latest events in town. But after so many years of one-sided conversations, she sometimes felt as if she'd run out of things to say. Clint wouldn't know many of her co-workers. They'd moved to the valley after the accident. And the town itself had changed with a sudden surge of sub-divisions and new businesses. So, invariably, she found herself falling back on the weather or other inconsequential topics.

Poor, Clint. If he was aware of her chatter, he'd probably grown incredibly bored.

"It was really cold yesterday. We had a sleet storm, so things were icy. But today, the sun is shining and it feels more like autumn."

For a moment, the only noise in the room was the muted cartoon sound effects and the soft *hiss...hiss* of his ventilator.

"I saw Whit yesterday."

The moment the words left her mouth, she wished that she could bring them back. Her gaze automatically flew to his face—and for a moment, she saw a shift in his expression, then a twitch to his fingers. Had it been a reaction? Or merely a natural muscle spasm?

"He looked good," she continued, watching him more closely. "He said he came by to see you, so maybe you remember?"

Again, his fingers seemed to twitch.

"After the wake, he made a special point to get directions so that he could come see you as soon as possible. It was important to him."

Nothing.

Oh, well. Perhaps she'd tired him out.

"You look good today. Much better than when I saw you last. Maybe you're finally getting over this bug you've had."

Another slight twitch.

"We finished our book last time, didn't we?" Finley dug through her bag for her phone. "Is there a different story you'd like to read?"

They'd been through several dozen classics, from *Huckleberry Finn* to *The Count of Monte Cristo* to *The Great Gatsby.* Then, they'd moved on to Agatha Christie, Tom Clancy and Tolkien. Their latest forays into great literature had been Dahl's *Willy Wonka and the Chocolate Factory,* and *Going Solo.*

But after connecting to her reading app, Finley—who had a fondness for romantic fiction—realized that her favorite historical author had released a new book. It had been nearly a year since the last one and…

Why not?

"We're going to try something new today, Clint, so, get comfortable."

She clicked DOWNLOAD, waited for the text to appear, then settled more comfortably on the bed and began reading aloud.

"'Chapter One. Lady Clarissa Darlington was late— which put her in a very unfortunate situation, especially where the Duke of Claremore was concerned….'"

It was only a little after six-thirty in the morning when Whit gave up on getting any sleep at all at the Red Rock Motor Inn. He was too damn tall for the cheap hotel mattress that had been advertised as a queen-size but was actually a double. Added to that was the rhythmic pounding coming from the other side of the wall and a woman's voice shouting, "Stan, Stan! Oh, sweet potato, sweet potato, sweet potato *pie*!"

Whit rolled to sit on the side of the bed, resting his elbows on his knees. He *did not* want to know *what* had been going on in that room—or what pie had to do with it—but he was sure as hell happy that the mystery couple had finally called it quits about five in the ever-lovin' A.M…

He had to get out of here.

As he staggered into the bathroom to brush his teeth, Whit realized that he no longer felt the need to leave town, simply this particular cheap hotel.

Grove had thrown him a curve ball by arranging a meeting with Finley and him this afternoon. But even that wasn't what tethered him here. It was a few simple texts—unexpectedly frank texts—from Finley.

MAYBE WE CAN MAKE NEW MEMORIES.

I'D LIKE THAT.

She'd actually texted those words.

I'd like that.

Could it be possible, after all these years, that she was feeling a fraction of the same attraction toward him as he did toward her? Would she actually...*welcome* his attention?

Or was he interpreting more into this than she'd ever intended. Maybe she simply wanted to be friends.

Friends.

If that was all she could ever give him, he'd take it. But if she was willing to consider more...

He'd be the happiest bastard in Wyoming.

Suddenly, the hours between now and when he'd arranged to pick her up seemed incredibly far away. He supposed he could track down the leads he had for Thayne, visit the auction barns, maybe visit Clint one more time.

But he found himself suddenly needing to know what she'd meant by her reply.

When he'd planned this trip to Larkspur, he'd thought he could meet up with her, one last time, and put all the old feelings he'd had for her to rest. He should have known things wouldn't be that simple. Rather than easing, the attraction he'd always felt for her had only lain dormant, glowing like hot coals, waiting for one of her smiles so that his emotions could fan into a flame again.

Could he dare to believe she might feel the same way?

Although he wanted to race headlong toward that thought, he forced himself to pump the brakes. He had to remember that he had a life outside of Larkspur now, and he had responsibilities waiting for him at home. He could stay longer, maybe even a couple of weeks if he called in some favors and took his vacation time. But, eventually, he would have to leave. And judging by what little Finley had told him, she had her own plans, and they didn't include following him to Nevada.

Whoa.

A few flirty texts didn't immediately lead to a commitment. He had to remember that Finley might want nothing more than his friendship, and if that was all she could offer, he wouldn't regret it.

Yeah, right.

Less than twenty minutes later, Whit had managed to take a hot shower, dress, and gather up his things. He wasn't sure what the appointment at Grove's office would bring, but one thing was for damn sure, there was no way he was staying here another night. He'd sleep in his truck before he'd endure another *"Sweet potato, sweet potato, sweet potato pie!"*

As he settled his hat over his brow, slung his duffel bag over his shoulder and firmly closed the motel room door behind him, Whit did his best to keep his eyes straight ahead. Even so, he couldn't miss the pile of pastry boxes and empty pie plates.

Good hell. What had they been doing next door?

The air had a distinct nip to it as he threw his duffel into the back seat, then climbed behind the wheel. Grabbing his phone, he scrolled through his messages, seeing that Thayne had sent him some attachments with photos of the registered brands which had originally been on the stolen cattle. There were also more semi and trailer possibilities.

Taking his notebook out of the glove compartment, Whit added the details to the list he'd made yesterday. He was sure that the Wyoming officials had received the same information, but it couldn't hurt to have another trained eye. After he'd found himself a restaurant offering free Wi-Fi, he would order a gallon of black coffee and take a look at the local classifieds and auction notices. He might even call his boss and make arrangements to stay at least a week. Just to help Thayne out.

Help Thayne *out? Is that what you're telling yourself now?*

He slid his phone back into his pocket and turned the key in the ignition, then jumped when someone banged hard on his window. As he twisted in his seat, his hand automatically reached for his pistol. As he was about to slip it from its holster, he recognized the figure on the other side of the glass.

"Geez, Elvis!"

"You get out of there! You get out of there right now!"

Whit sighed, the rush of adrenaline easing when he recognized the wild look in his father's eyes, the gray tinge to his skin, and the almost feverish spots of red to his cheeks and nose.

Realizing that his father would continue to make a scene—or simply ambush him somewhere else if he didn't find out what was on his mind—Whit turned off the engine and reluctantly eased from the Bronco.

In the past, this was the point when his father would throw himself at Whit, his arm pulled back in preparation for a blow. Whit had learned to duck and cover, thereby protecting his face so that Finley wouldn't see the bruises later on. But he'd grown older and wiser, and his training had shown him ways to protect himself without resorting to fisticuffs. The moment Elvis charged, he grabbed him by the wrist, whirling the man in the other direction while he brought his father's hand up sharply between his scrawny shoulder blades.

"Ow, ow, *ow*!"

"I told you what I'd do if you tried to take another swing at me, old man," Whit said, without heat. As he held his father there, letting him wriggle and squirm until Elvis realized that he wasn't getting away anytime soon, Whit felt years of anger drain from his body.

As a child, he'd cowered, too frightened to fight back. As an adolescent, he'd seethed and longed-for revenge. Now...

He felt nothing but hollowness for the man who'd given him life but had never had a kind word to say to him.

"You bastard," his father spat. "You no-good, thieving *bastard!*"

Whit didn't have a clue what had Elvis in such an uproar. A quick search of his childhood bedroom had assured him that Elvis had stolen, destroyed, or pawned anything Whit had ever owned of value. The only items Whit had taken away with him that day were the championship belt buckles that he'd hidden in a bag stuffed into the heat register.

Elvis suddenly sagged against him, his shoulders hunching in abject misery. "You stole my dogs, damn you. You stole my dogs."

His *dogs*.

Elvis must have realized that as soon as Whit had left the property, he'd called the authorities and informed them about the suffering, shivering menagerie Elvis held captive under the trees.

Elvis sobbed, huge tears rolling down his cheeks. "I know you done it. I know you're the one who took 'em."

Whit pushed his father away from him in disgust. Elvis was mourning the loss of a dozen mutts that he'd penned up and forgotten, but when Whit had lived under his roof, Elvis hadn't spared him a second thought. He'd never considered that he might need to feed or clothe his own son. If it weren't for the Campanellas, Whit probably would have starved to death—or worse, become a man like his father.

"I didn't take them, I notified the authorities, who handed them off to a no-kill shelter that will find them decent homes. But if I'd known the animals would have to spend another hour in those cages, I would have loaded them up myself."

"Damnit, you didn't have the right to take 'em!"

"Any decent human being who'd seen the state they were in—the abject fear—would inherit the *right*, and the *responsibility* to intervene. I merely did what needed to be done."

"But they were *my* dogs," Elvis whined, dropping to his knees.

Whit shook his head. "Go home and sleep off whatever you've been drinking, snorting, or shooting, Elvis."

Then, leaving the old man cowering in the dirt, Whit climbed back into the Bronco, feeling the overwhelming need to get as far away from his father as he could. He'd only been with the man for a few minutes but his misery and despair seemed to cling to Whit like a palpable stink.

Not for the first time, Whit thanked God that the Campanellas had come into his life. He didn't want to imagine what kind of man he would have become without their example. It had been the hours in their home that had taught him the true meaning of love and marriage and friendship. Norm and Martha hadn't just protected his body, they'd nurtured his soul, and they'd provided time with friends who had enriched his life.

And Finley, who could enrich his future.

Whit glanced down at the numbers scrawled on the notepad, then pushed them to the side. It was time to be honest with himself. Sure, he'd originally come for Norm's funeral. And he'd agreed to help Thayne any way he could. But the real reason for staying longer had nothing to do with the past or his job.

It was the fact that this might be his last chance with Finley Fitzpatrick.

Finley slid a plate of eggs and bacon in front of Clive Olsen, then topped off his coffee.

"How does that look?"

"Fine, Finley."

"I'll leave you to finish eating, but I'll check back."

Finley tucked the coffee carafe onto the warmer. Then, since she only had the one table to tend for the moment, she checked the supply of rolled up utensils, straws, and the kids' placemats and crayons.

The bell over the door jingled, causing her to look up. On slow days, customers were allowed to seat themselves, but occasionally, they needed a little encouragement. When she recognized the tall, familiar figure, she straightened, automatically wiping her hands down her apron.

"Hello, Whit."

She loved the smile that spread over his features. This time, the touch of caution was gone, causing his green eyes to glow from within.

"Hey."

Finley felt a slight hitch next to her heart. A smile like that had to be a good sign, didn't it? He wouldn't look at her like that if he'd changed his mind about going with her to Mr. Grove's offices and had come to tell her goodbye.

"I wondered if I could get some coffee. Lots of coffee."

"Black?"

"As black as you've got it."

"Coming right up."

"And I'll take another look at that menu, if that's all right."

"Of course."

She hid her own smile as she gathered the items he'd requested, then followed him to the same back booth where they'd briefly talked the day before.

When she set the coffee mug on the table, he reached for it immediately. "Thanks."

"Rough night?"

The moment the words left her lips, she could have kicked herself for the myriad ribald interpretations.

But Whit merely muttered, "You have no idea." He took a healthy swallow, then asked, "Is there Wi-Fi here?"

"Sure. The password is 'yummy', all lowercase."

His lips twitched at that, and once again, she found herself warming beneath those unconscious reactions. She sensed that, in the last few years, his smiles had become rare.

Finley handed him the menu and he briefly studied it before saying, "I'll have the two-egg breakfast, over-easy, bacon, and toast instead of pancakes."

"What kind of bread?"

"Wheat."

"I'll get that going for you."

She relayed Whit's order to the kitchen, then checked on Clive, slipping his bill onto his table when he said he was ready to go.

There were a few other diners, but none of them in Finley's section. The farmers had come and gone, and it was still early for the normal breakfast rush. Finley grabbed the coffee carafe and headed back in Whit's direction.

"Were you able to get onto the Wi-Fi okay?"

"Yeah, thanks. Hey, do you know where the Double Diamond Auction Barns are located?"

"They're on the other side of town as you head to Redmond. If you follow the old highway, you'll see the signs about a hundred yards before the onramp to the Interstate."

"Thanks."

He was making notations in a small notebook, and just as it had been years before, his handwriting was an illegible scrawl.

"Are you planning on buying cattle?"

He shook his head. "No. I'm making inquiries for work." He leaned to the side to check the dining room behind her. "Are you busy? Can you sit and talk for a minute?"

"Sure."

"I don't want to get you into any trouble."

"It's fine. I don't have any other customers yet."

She sat across from him, resting the carafe on her order pad so the heat from the glass wouldn't mar the table.

"What's up?"

"We're still on for this afternoon, aren't we?" he asked, taking another sip of his coffee.

Finley couldn't help the way that her gaze ran over him. He'd angled himself onto the bench seat, one leg resting on the cushion, so that he could slouch comfortably in the corner. The pose should have given him an indolent air. Instead, it merely emphasized the breadth of his shoulders and the long, lean length of his body. Yet even though he appeared relaxed, there was a barely leashed control to him— as if he were ready to defend himself, if necessary.

Whit had always been that way. Finley had suspected that he'd developed a hair trigger defense mechanism because of his father's temper. But now, so many years later, she realized that it was more than that. He might look laid-back on the surface, but he was always aware of his surroundings, the people, the emotional climate.

He must have noted her scrutiny, but to his credit, he didn't comment. He simply let her look her fill.

As if such a thing were possible.

He was still the same Whit, at least in theory. The years had definitely agreed with him, making the angles of his face sharper, his jaw line more defined. Time in the sun had formed a lighter strip that bisected the tan on his temples, probably from a pair of sunglasses, and faint lines fanned from the corners of his eyes. He had a tiny mole to the side of his nose, and his hair was longer than she'd seen him wear it before, brushed back from the sides and curling slightly at his nape. She could see the faint indentation where his hat usually rested, and the mussed quality only added to his appeal.

Finley knew he would object to the description, but, in her opinion, he was a beautiful man. Perhaps, not traditionally handsome. But it was the little imperfections that made him so intriguing.

Again, his lips twitched—as if he couldn't understand why she continued to stare. He looked away for a moment, took another healthy swallow of coffee. Then he set his mug on the table, twisting it slightly as if adjusting the angle of the handle.

"I wanted to ask you a couple of questions. About Clint."

"Sure."

"How…fragile is he?"

Finley shrugged. "For a person with his health issues, he's been fairly lucky. He's had his rough patches—infections, reactions to his feeding tub. You've probably seen that he's hooked up to a ventilator lately. He seems more susceptible to lung issues—bronchitis, pneumonia—than some of the other long-term patients. There have been a few times when things have been touch-and-go, but he always seems to rally and pull through."

"What's his…" Whit cleared his throat. "What's his life expectancy?"

Again, she shrugged. "No one really knows. The ventilator keeps him restricted to his bed or the recliner, but when he's doing better, he can be placed in a wheelchair."

"Does he ever…go outside?"

"Oh, yeah. He was in a nursing home in Redmond at first, so his outings were kept to the balcony terrace. Honestly, the facility wasn't the best arrangement—not because of his care, but because Norm wasn't able to visit him as much as he'd like. As soon as Greensprings was finished, Clint was one of the first patients to be moved to the facility. At Greensprings, they've got a huge grassy area with a walking path as well as a visitor's porch. Clint spends a lot of time out there when the weather's good. And the staff are fantastic. They've upped his physical therapy to prevent any more muscle loss, and they've tried lots of new neurological therapies to stimulate his senses. When we visit, they encourage us to assume that Clint can hear everything we say. We've been told to talk to him, ask questions, play music, watch television. If we see any kind of reaction, we're supposed to let the nurses know."

"And does he ever…react?"

"Yeah. I think so. Sometimes, it seems as if his eyes are tracking you, or he leans toward a sound." She sighed. "It's hard not to get your hopes up since the reactions could be muscle spasms or unconscious movements. But…there are days when I think he's caught the gist of something I've said, or a certain kind of music can change, I don't know…his energy. And, in my opinion, he loves the sun. He seems so…content…when he's outside with the heat of the sun on his face."

Whit became thoughtful. "Should I…see him again? Or stay away?"

Unspoken between them was the fact that if Clint were fully aware of Whit's presence, he would probably swing first, then ask questions later. But, Finley was tired of holding onto the past. It was high time that everyone else did as well.

"You should go. When Javi visits Clint, he usually buys a pizza, plunks it right down under Clint's nose, and spends the evening watching nonstop soccer—and you know how much Clint hated soccer."

"Yeah, but Javi isn't responsible for putting him in that place."

The words hovered between them like distant thunder, roiling with the storm of emotions which had never blown over.

"You didn't—"

"I was responsible for the accident," Whit said lowly, the words rubbing together like gravel.

"No one knows that for sure."

"Oh, come on, Finley. I was driving—"

She stopped whatever Whit had been about to say with a hand on his. "And Clint was in a raging temper. But you weren't the only one to make him angry that night, Whit. I was part of it too."

For a moment, that kiss, that hot, passionate, arms-straining, legs-tangling kiss hung between them as if it had happened yesterday.

"If he's upset that I've been visiting him all this time, he hasn't said anything about it to me," she offered wryly.

For a split second, Whit looked at her with such raw emotion in his eyes that she was forced to blink. It was as if he were a drowning man and she'd thrown him a rope. But then, it was gone and his green eyes became dark and enigmatic.

"Finley, you've got a table!"

Finley glanced over her shoulder and waved in Megan's direction. "I'll go check on your food. Do you want me to top off your coffee in the meantime?"

"No. I'm good. I'll wait until my meal's ready."

"All right then. I'll be back."

SIX

*a*s Finley hurried back to work, Whit couldn't help the way that his gaze clung to her, taking in the feminine slope of her shoulders, the hollow of her back, and that cute little derriere set off in jeans with a swirl of embroidery on the pockets.

She was so beautiful.

But it wasn't only her outer shell which made her that way. She was kind. Loving.

Empathetic.

Other than the police and his lawyer, he'd never talked to anyone about the accident, not even in passing. Yet, even though they'd merely skimmed over the subject, she'd managed to make him feel...better. Lighter.

Idly, he wondered if Clint was aware enough of his surroundings to know what a lucky bastard his was. For nearly ten years, Finley had stayed by his side and cared for him with the devotion of a...

Wife.

No. They'd never married.

Fiancé?

Whit remembered the ring Finley had worn. It had first appeared on her finger a couple of weeks before the accident, and Whit thought he remembered seeing her wear it in the days afterward. But Whit hadn't seen any evidence of it during this latest visit.

Did she still consider herself engaged to Clint? Or had time and Clint's health given her enough of a reason to set those promises aside?

Whit moved his mug from side to side, wondering why he even bothered to torture himself with such thoughts. If he were smart, he'd pull up stakes and head back to Reno as soon as he'd kept the appointment with Grove. He was certifiable if he considered pursuing anything but friendship with Finley in the amount of time he had left in Larkspur.

But telling himself that and believing it were two different things. The moment Finley stepped into view, his eyes immediately locked onto her again, taking in the thick braid that rested between her shoulder blades, the delicate hands and wrists that carried trays of food or gestured as she spoke to her customers. Each minute detail, each lift of her brows, each smile, each laugh, simply seemed to embed themselves more deeply into his heart, reminding him that this might be his last chance to explore the possibility of a relationship with Finley Fitzpatrick.

Yeah, right. Relationship.

He didn't have that kind of time.

And she might not have the inclination to indulge him in his fantasies.

But he had to try, didn't he?

Before he could answer his own question, she was walking toward him with a tray.

"Here's your bacon and eggs," she said as she set the platter of steaming food in front of him. "And your toast." The smaller plate followed, then a bowl with pats of butter.

"Do you need salsa? There's catsup and hot sauce in the carrier there."

"No. This is great."

"Okay. I'll check back."

She was backing away when he suddenly found himself calling her back. "Finley! We're still on for this afternoon, aren't we?"

"Yeah. If things get crazy around here and I don't get a chance to talk to you again, I'll see you at my Mom's."

Then she flashed him a hundred-watt smile and backed away.

And in that instant, Whit didn't care if he'd only had two hours sleep or he'd had another run-in with his father. Nothing could dim the warmth that settled into his gut by being the recipient of one those smiles.

As soon as she returned home from work, Finley broke the land-speed record showering, blow-drying her hair, and putting on her makeup. But the moment she stood in front of her closet, she froze in indecision.

A dress?

She would look like she was trying too hard.

A sweater?

She would look like she was trying to hide.

"What *are* you doing?"

Finley froze when she recognized her sister's drawl. A quick glance over her shoulder confirmed that Billie was leaning against the door frame.

"Nothing. I have…an appointment in town."

But Finley had never been much good at lying.

"Uh huh. You look a little angsty for an appointment."

Finley's brain knew a response was needed, but she couldn't seem to settle on coherent thought.

"Mr. Grove asked me to drop by for a few minutes."

Billie rolled her eyes. She'd worked the graveyard shift at the call-in center, so Billie must have slept through most of the afternoon because she still wore a T-shirt and a pair of pajama bottoms and her hair looked appealingly tousled. Her sister always managed to look "appealingly tousled" when she rolled out of bed. Finley, on the other hand, needed at least an hour and several cups of caffeine to become coherent.

It wasn't until she heard the distinctive rumble of Whit's Bronco turning at the corner that Finley realized she'd run out of time.

Billie's eyes narrowed. "I take it you found a ride."

Before Finley could stop her, Billie dodged toward the window. Two steps behind her, Finley's cheeks flamed when her sister whirled to confront her.

"Whit Patterson? Are you insane?"

Finley supposed that there were dozens of things she could say to diffuse the situation, but she couldn't think of one. Besides, her sister wouldn't be easily mollified, and Finley didn't have time to come up with a distraction. Whirling, she hurried back to the closet and grabbed the first hanger she touched.

As she hopped into a pair of jeans, Finley felt rather than saw her sister turn to scrutinize her with the intensity of a scientist studying a moth on a pin.

"Have you two been in touch all these years?"

Finley dragged an embroidered blouse over her head to avoid answering. But Billie was more than capable of coming up with her own conclusions, so Finley offered, "We haven't been in touch at all. I've only seen him a couple of times in passing since the funeral."

"And you what? Shook hands, exchanged a half-dozen words, then went your separate ways? You don't expect me to believe that crap, do you?"

Finley felt a slow heat seeping up her neck. "Actually, I…uh, took him to the grave and then…we had something to eat. And I've seen him at the diner a couple of times."

"So, he's been back a few days and the two of you are already dating?"

Finley shot Billie a withering glare, then purposely sat on the edge of the bed with her back to her sister as she dragged on socks and then her boots. "We aren't dating. Good grief, Billie. We ate a sandwich and talked for a little while after the wake. This afternoon, he's merely taking me to Mr. Grove's offices. Then, as far as I know, he's leaving town."

"What does Grove want?"

But Finley had already had more than enough of her sister's interrogation. Jumping to her feet, she spritzed her favorite perfume at her neck, and checked the mirror one last time.

Why had she been cursed with such stick-straight hair?

But there was no time to fuss with it. Grabbing her purse, she raced into the living room, hoping to intercept Whit before he made it to the front door.

"Finley? Finley!"

Billie trotted along behind her, but Finley ignored her sister. Unfortunately, the noise of the engine must have alerted her mother as well, because Alice Fitzpatrick stood at the front window, her lips pressed into a pinched line.

"What's *he* doing here?"

"Whit is taking me…"

What could she say? There would be hell to pay if her mother knew that Finley was on her way to Grove's law offices. Finley wouldn't have a moment of peace until Alice had ferreted out every shred of information so that she could disseminate it and see how it could work to her own advantage.

"He's giving Finley a lift into town," Billie announced.

Both women bracketed Finley with equal looks of incredulity and disapproval.

"Girl," her mother drawled. Originally from Tennessee, her mother tended to lapse into the bourbon-rich vowels of her childhood whenever she was upset. "I didn't take you for being that stupid."

Finley stiffened at her mother's obvious censure. "Mom—"

Alice wasn't finished. "Obviously, you don't remember what happened the last time you got mixed up with that boy. He's nothing but trash, you hear me?"

"Stop it!"

Her mother's views on Whit had never been a secret. Alice had resented him from the very beginning, stating that Whit wasn't the "right" sort of person for Finley or any other Fitzpatrick. Finley had been in her teens before she realized her mother hadn't been referring to his manners, but to the fact that Whit was poor.

"You're not to say a thing. Not a thing!" she whispered vehemently, stabbing her finger in her mother's direction. "If you do, I swear I...I won't give you any of my tips for your car payment this month."

Why her mother had decided she needed a new car was beyond Finley's comprehension. Alice tended to drift in and out of jobs, never realizing that they needed every penny to cover the mortgage and basic bills. They couldn't afford extravagances like a new car—especially since Alice's former vehicle had only been three years old.

Her mother's expression settled into that of a petulant child, but thankfully, she kept her mouth shut as Finley opened the door.

Whit was already on the porch, his fist poised to knock. Her cheeks flamed and she prayed he hadn't overheard anything from inside.

"Ready?" Whit asked.

"Yeah. Oh! Wait a minute." Finley dodged to the far side of the room where she'd left a gift bag on one of the side tables. Then she hurried back, turning to face her mother just as Alice had apparently worked herself up enough to offer a comment. Before Alice could speak, Finley lifted a finger and whispered, "Not a word."

Once outside, Finley didn't feel a whole lot safer from embarrassment than she had indoors. She didn't have to look over her shoulder to know that her mother had returned to the window and watched every move they made. And Billie...

Billie was probably setting up a telescope.

Whit must have caught on to the vibes because he murmured, "Your mother hasn't changed much."

"No. She hasn't."

His lips lifted into a wry grin. "She still doesn't like me all that well, either."

Finley opened her mouth to assure him that her mother thought he was a lovely, lovely person—even if she had to lie through her teeth. But when she met his gaze and saw the sparkle in their depths, she realized that Whit didn't really care what Alice thought. And the idea that Alice Fitzpatrick's longstanding grudge was unimportant to him was…liberating.

Suddenly, the tension fled from her muscles, leaving her relaxed and relieved and…

Happy.

Nevertheless, she still couldn't help murmuring, "Sorry about that," as he opened the door and waited for Finley to climb into the Bronco.

"Don't be. It's got nothing to do with you."

She waited until he'd crossed to the driver's side and started the engine before touching his arm.

"Before we go, I have something for you."

She held out the sack, hoping that he would interpret the offering as the gift she'd intended it to be.

"What's this?"

"Open it and see."

He removed the tissue paper she'd placed on top, then laughed softly. The sound skittered down her spine, then seemed to radiate through her body, causing her cheeks to warm and her body to thrum with anticipation.

"You've been hanging onto this for all these years?" He withdrew a coffee-colored cowboy hat from the bag. "Is this one from the…"

"That last rodeo. Yeah."

Silence spooled between them, thick and rich and sticky with awareness. Whit had placed the hat over her head as a trophy, mere seconds before he'd kissed her.

First kiss.

Last kiss.

"I know how particular you are about your hats. I saw what you did at Norm's grave. I figured this would tide you over until you found a new one."

Whit settled it slowly over his head, and for a moment, she saw him as the twenty-year-old bull-riding champion that he'd been years ago. Then the memory seemed to melt away, leaving her staring at a man she hardly knew.

He'd changed so much. His features were sharper, blunter, his hair longer. Carefully trimmed stubble outlined the stubborn line of his jaw. She could see the spot where too much worrying had etched creases between his brows and deepened the furrows on either side of his mouth. This was the face of a man who'd been to hell and back and lived to tell about it.

He reached up a hand, cupping her cheek in one broad, calloused palm. She had to steel herself not to twist her head, ever so slightly, and plant a kiss against his skin.

Dear sweet heaven above, help me resist him.

"Thanks, Finley." The words were so soft she barely heard them. Then he dropped his hand and backed the Bronco out of the driveway.

Grove's office wasn't at all what Whit had expected. The man didn't have a typical high-powered setup with an oversized desk and lots of shiny surfaces. Instead, he had a small turn-of-the-century bungalow on the edge of town. He admitted Whit and Finley into a room filled with a comfortable couch, two leather wing-back chairs and a low coffee table. Through a half-opened door opposite, Whit was able to see a tidy kitchenette. To the right, glass paned doors led into what must have been Grove's working area where he had an antique roll-top desk and dozens of oak filing cabinets of various sizes and parentage.

"Please, have a seat," Grove stated, gesturing to the couch. "Can I get either of you anything to drink? Water? Coffee?"

Finley shook her head, sinking into one of the wing-back chairs, so Whit took the couch on her right. He couldn't imagine why the local family practice lawyer would want to see him. In his experience, the need for a lawyer was an omen of bad things to come.

He never should have agreed to this meeting.

But even as the words flashed through his head, he looked up at Finley and his gut tightened.

God, she was beautiful.

He would do anything for her—even sitting through this meeting.

If asked, Whit couldn't have pinpointed why he'd always been fascinated by her. As a child, he'd wanted to be as brave and fearless as she'd seemed to be. As a teenager, he'd merely wanted to soak up the glow of happiness that surrounded her. And as he'd moved into adulthood…

He'd wanted her. More than he'd ever wanted any other woman.

"Whit?"

He jerked to attention, realizing that Mr. Grove must have asked him a question.

"Coffee?"

"No. I'm good, thanks."

Just get this over with.

Whit felt a twitchy restlessness rush through his system, and the need to head for the door became nearly overwhelming. He kept flashing back to the last time he'd had any contact with a lawyer—right before they'd slapped the cuffs on his wrists and led him from the Teton County courthouse to a van that would take him to the Teton County jail.

Grove took the other chair and reached for a sheaf of papers. "I had hoped to get the rest of the members involved to join this briefing with a conference call, but alas…" He peered over his reading glasses, his smile benign and fatherly "…technology and I are not always friends, and my secretary, who usually handles these things, is on maternity leave."

Once again, the urge to flee was nearly overwhelming, but Whit tamped it down. If he'd been in trouble with the law again, he wouldn't have been brought to a lawyer first, right?

He tried resting his elbows on his knees and clasping his hands in front of him.

Breathe in and out, in and out.

Grove leaned back, crossing his legs, seeming to refer to the legal documents in his hands. Then he offered a small sigh. "First of all, I want to offer my condolences on the death of Norm Campanella. I know that he held a special place in your lives."

The mere mention of Norm's passing still had the ability to tighten around Whit's throat like a fist.

Breathe, damnit.

A hand touched his arm, and Whit glanced up to find Finley watching him in concern.

She knew. She knew what had him freaking out.

But what should have been an emasculating experience...wasn't. Her eyes flooded with a wealth of understanding and she tugged at his wrist, pulling his fingers apart before lacing one of her hands with his.

So soft, so gentle, so caring.

Why hadn't he been honest with her when they were kids? Why hadn't he let her know from the very beginning how much he'd cared for her. Hell, he'd never wanted a "brotherly" relationship with her. In his mind, Finley had always been his girl. *His.* But he'd never had enough confidence to pursue her. He'd never thought that someone like her—someone so sweet and funny and pretty—would ever have anything to do with a punk from the wrong side of the tracks. She deserved better, not an idiot who routinely let Elvis beat the shit out of him—even though Whit had submitted to Elvis's punishments without retaliating for her sake. Because Finley had once stated that she abhorred violence of any kind.

He would have done anything to earn her approval.

Even let his best friend claim her as his own girlfriend.

The tightness at his throat threatened to strangle Whit. But then, he felt the soft pressure of Finley's grip and her thumb ran in idle circles over his skin.

Soothing the savage beast.

He glanced up again, but Finley's attention wasn't on Grove. It centered on him. When she looked at him that way, the nerves and tension eased, allowing him to drag oxygen into his lungs—even as his soul filled with its own brand of regret.

If only...

Grove dropped the papers he'd been holding onto the coffee table. Too late, Whit realized that the man might get the wrong impression from the way Finley had linked her hand with his. But the lawyer didn't seem to notice. Instead, he was carefully folding his glasses and stowing them in his pocket.

"I could recite all the legal jargon and read directly from the will, but I've found that, when people are grieving, such technicalities are often a little...hard to digest. So, I'll cut to the chase and give you a summary of Norm's wishes. In a few weeks, after things have had time to sink in—and I've hopefully had a chance to contact the other beneficiaries—I'll call you back to my office and we'll have a more detailed chat."

After things have had time to sink in?

A more detailed chat?

Whit couldn't even imagine his previous lawyer employing such a tactic. But then, the man had been a public defender, not a family attorney.

"Norm Campanella had quite a fondness for the two of you, as well as the... What did he call them? The Sinful Six?"

Finley laughed. "Yes. We were a rowdy bunch back in the day."

Grove's beamed at them. "I remember. You always seemed to be together."

Whit felt his hand being squeezed again, and he returned the pressure in kind. Even so, it took every ounce of strength he possessed not to lift her fingers to his lips, graze her knuckles with a kiss, inhale deeply of the perfume she must have dabbed at her wrists.

"It pained Norm that none of you seemed to have much contact anymore." Grove leveled his gaze on Whit. "I can assure you, that he held no ill will against any of you."

Again, Whit felt that a prickling restlessness needling his skin, but he forced himself to listen.

"Since Norm had no other family to speak of, his will was fairly simple. Finley, you've been asked to be the executor, with my assistance, of course."

Her eyes widened. "Are you sure?"

"Quite sure. The house has already been transferred to Clint's name, but the property itself is to be managed by you. Norm intended for it to be rented or leased so that the proceeds could be added to the trust set up for his son's medical care." Grove's eyes twinkled. "He wanted me to impress upon you that the arrangement didn't need to take place immediately. Norm worried that you would feel an obligation to get the house in order as soon as possible. He stipulated that the property was not to be rented for the first three months after his passing."

"Oh."

Finley's response was a bare puff of sound, making it clear that, in her head at least, she'd already begun making lists.

"He has also prepaid the services of the company Two Guys and a Truck to pack things into boxes and deliver them to whatever auction houses, thrift donation centers, or disposal drop-offs you should choose."

A sheen gathered in her eyes and Whit couldn't help himself. He lifted her hand to his mouth and brushed a fleeting kiss against her skin. A haunting floral scent filled his senses.

"He also wanted me to suggest that you not limit the property to housing, but consider how the Queen Anne could be converted into a facility appropriate for business use as well. The three-month grace period will allow you to thoroughly investigate your options."

Whit could feel the tension drain from Finley's limbs. Hopefully, his own reasons for being summoned were equally benign. For the life of him, Whit couldn't think of a single reason why he was here. He hadn't seen Norm or Clint in years. And they had every reason to regard him as the villain in their own family saga.

"That leads me to the next part of his will." Grove steepled his fingers, drumming them together for a moment before saying, "Norm Campanella was wise with his money, and he tended to invest his income in land. In addition, he survived a sister and a great-aunt."

Aunt Geraldine and Great Aunt Maude.

The memories came hard and fast of vacations spent with Clint's Aunt Geraldine. Somehow, the Campanellas had managed to bring them all—the Sinful Six—for at least a week out of every summer vacation. The women lived several miles up the canyon on a sprawling piece of property that had once been an old motel and camping facility. With a gleaming lake, hot springs, pastures, and hiking areas, it had been a kids' Mecca.

"Other than a couple of holdings here in town, which are part of Clint's trust, Norm left the bulk of his property to the six of you: Clint, Finley, Liam, P.J., Javier…and you, Whit."

SEVEN

The words skipped over Whit's consciousness and skittered away before he could capture their meaning.

"What?"

Norm smiled like a secretive Santa Claus.

"Congratulations. You're all the recipients of the Come Back Dude Ranch."

"The...the..." Whit couldn't seem to wrap his mind around the concept. "The what?"

"That's the name of the original motel." Grove sighed, his eyes taking on a faraway gleam. "It was quite the place, in its heyday. When I was a little tyke, my parents used to pack up the Studebaker and the tent. It didn't matter that we were traveling less than a dozen miles away, that place was remarkable. We kids would make crafts, canoe on the lake, ride horses into the hills...and at night—oh! There was a band and dancing and campfire stories for the kids. It was a shame when the Campanella women decided to retire."

He seemed to ruminate for a moment, unaware of the way that his words swirled and bounced in Whit's head like tennis balls in a washing machine.

"Anyhow, over the years, Norm bought up much of the land adjoining the ranch and used it to graze cattle. The livestock are technically Clint's, but the property itself will be divided equally among the six of you. Once again, Norm has left only a few simple stipulations. First, he has asked—just as he did with the house—that no hasty decisions be made. Therefore, the title will not be officially turned over to the six of you until a minimum of three months have passed. An account has already been set up to take care of such expenses as utilities, basic repairs, and feed for the livestock. Second, someone must live on the property from the moment that notification has been made. In the past, Norm has had problems with squatters and trespassers, and he wants there to be a noticeable presence in the area to discourage any looting or vandalism."

They were about to inherit Come Back Ranch.

Good hell, Almighty.

"Last of all, any decisions about the final fate of the property and the transfer of the titles can only be made with all the beneficiaries physically present, except for Clint, naturally. The five of you must all come to a unanimous decision in regards to whether you will sell the holdings, or keep them and split things up. You'll be required to outline the details here in my office so I can draw up any other legal documents necessary. My services have already been prepaid, so please feel free to contact me anytime you have questions or when you're ready to move forward."

Finley seemed to have been turned to stone, but she finally jerked to her senses enough to gasp, "Why? Why would he do this?"

Grove's eyes held equal measures of tenderness and sadness. "I asked Norm that question. Do you know what he said?"

Finley shook her head.

"He said: 'These are my children.'"

At that, Finley burst into tears—and if there was one thing that Whit had never been able to tolerate, it was seeing Finley upset. He stood, hauling her against him, his eyes closing against his own emotions as she pressed her palms against his chest. Whit's arms wrapped around her waist, holding her so securely that he could feel every shuddering breath. Her warmth seeped into his body, spreading through his veins like molten honey, awakening parts of him that he'd long ago decided were dead.

Instantly, he knew he was toast. He'd told himself that he could come to town, pay his respects, then disappear again before his emotions could get the best of him. But in that moment, he realized he'd been kidding himself. Things between Finley and him had never been that simple. This woman could tie him in knots with a glance. To hold her in his arms was sheer torture and inexplicable bliss.

Even if she could never be his.

Grove cleared his throat, bringing them back to this room and the business that had brought them here.

"Whit, there is one more detail. A personal request from Norm. I can assure you this was important to him, but he in no way wanted to force you to do anything you wouldn't feel comfortable doing."

Here it came. The astonishing gift was about to be snatched away beneath a technicality.

You screwed up, physically and emotionally. So here you go, buddy. Everlasting purgatory."

"Norm tried to find you before his death to make the request in person, but...he's asked if you would serve as Clint's medical proxy."

Whit stared blankly at the man, sure that he'd heard wrong and that the words and their meanings had scrambled themselves in his brain.

"His...what?"

"Clint's medical proxy. You'll be given the legal authority to make decisions regarding Clint's care."

What the hell?

Whit was the person responsible for putting Clint in the hospital. In his mind, that was grounds enough for Norm to hate him for the rest of his life, not entrust him with Clint's well-being.

"I..."

"You don't have to tell me right away. I fully understand if you want to think things over or—"

"No! I'll do it! Of course, I'll do it."

In that moment, Whit knew he could never refuse. Clint had been his brother in everything but blood. And to have Norm extend the request meant...

He was forgiven.

The tremors began at the base of his feet and radiated through his body. He tried to steel himself against them.

Finley would think him weak.

But rather than stepping away, Finley rested her cheek against his chest. That fact alone helped him to breathe deep and regroup.

He could remain cool for her.

He could do anything for her.

Grove jumped to his feet. "Good. Good! I'll be getting in touch with the rest of your group as soon as possible, but I think we've made a good start today." He reached into his pocket and withdrew a set of keys. "I took the liberty of cutting keys for the lot of you. Finley, yours will open the Queen Anne, the garage, the storage shed, and the main house at Come Back Ranch. That smaller one will unlock the access gate leading to the property. Whit, you have a set for the ranch's gate and main house as well as the barn and the tack shed. Inside the residence at the ranch, you'll find a larger ring of keys hanging on the peg next to the back door. Those keys will get you into the motel's bungalows and all of the outbuildings. The house is already cleaned and ready for occupation, although things are Spartan. My dear wife filled the fridge with bottled water and a few essentials. She also put fresh sheets on the beds and towels in the bathroom. Congratulations."

As much as he wanted to stand that way forever, with Finley's arms around his waist, Whit knew that he had to get out of there. He needed fresh air…and…and…

Hell, he didn't know what he needed, but he couldn't stick around.

He held out his hand to Grove.

"Thank you."

"My pleasure. I'll be contacting you soon with details on how to access the account Norm set up. In the meantime, enjoy this rare gift."

Whit took Finley's hand—grabbed it might have been a better term—and pulled her outside.

Into the sunshine.

Into the fresh air.

But when he reached the door to the Bronco, he stopped, leaning his free hand against the roof. "Please tell me this isn't a sick dream."

It wasn't the inheritance Whit would mourn if it were. It would be Norm's faith in him.

"If it is, we're both going to have to wake up."

Finley stepped closer, resting a hand on his chest, and he couldn't keep himself from reacting—even though he knew it was the last thing he should do. In one movement, he leaned against the Bronco and drew her into the circle of his arms. But he kept the embrace loose. Almost…platonic.

Yeah, right.

"Did you have any idea he was going to do this?"

She shook her head. "I only knew he wanted me to help with the house. I envisioned myself packing up his belongings and getting the place ready to sell as soon as possible, not…this."

Bit by bit, the chill breeze seeped through Whit's clothing, assuring him that he wasn't imagining this scene— wasn't imagining this woman.

"Let's get out of here," he murmured, knowing that if he held her one more moment…

He would be completely undone.

He drove without conscious thought, heading out of town, pointing his vehicle toward the mountains in the distance. It wasn't until they'd been on the road for several minutes that he realized where he was headed.

"Do you…uh…want to go take a look at—"

"Yes."

Before he knew quite how it had happened, Finley had reached to take his free hand.

Dear sweet heaven above, he loved the way her smaller fingers fit between his own.

"It's been years since I've been to the ranch," she murmured. "Probably the summer after..."

"Graduation," Whit finished.

Going to the ranch had been their "grand hurrah." They'd loaded up with food and camping gear and headed into the hills above the main house. It would prove to be their final retreat before college and the rodeo circuit started interfering with their ability to get together as often as they'd like.

Within ten minutes, they reached the mouth of the canyon, and from there, Whit was forced to drive a little slower as the road wound up, up, growing narrower as jagged granite walls pressed in upon them from either side. Then, the canyon opened up to a glittering reservoir and the highway divided in two.

Whit automatically eased to the right, following the curves of the foothills for several miles, before slowing to make the turn to the access road which would lead to the Come Back Ranch.

"If you'll pull up to the gate, I'll jump out and unlock it," Finley said. She released his hand and reached for the buckle to her seatbelt.

"You're sure? I can—"

"It'll be quicker."

Whit realized that she was as eager as he was to see their old haunt.

He eased the Bronco to a stop in front of a pair of heavy iron gates. The truck hadn't completely rolled to a stop when

Finley opened the door and hopped to the ground. She wrestled for a moment with the chain and padlock, then the iron links dropped and she pushed the gate out of the way.

Whit rolled to a stop in front of her, then Finley closed the gate again before running back to the Bronco.

"I left the chain loose for now, but I thought I'd better close everything else in case there were any livestock on the property. Norm tried to keep the animals in the pastures by the barn, but who knows how secure the fencing is."

"Good thinking."

The road snaked up a small rise. On either side of them, thick stands of quaking aspen trembled in the breeze, the coin-shaped leaves shimmering in the sunlight. Beyond them were firs and pine trees, and the scrub oak and sumac which had turned crimson in the colder weather. Then, all at once, the trees opened up to reveal a sheltered valley.

Although it had been years since the Come Back Dude Ranch had been a guest property, evidence of its original purpose still remained. The paved access lane swung in a wide circle, leading first to the large cabin-like structure where Clint's aunts had lived and run the establishment. A weathered sign in front of the building still faintly bore the words CHECK-IN DESK.

Arranged in a U around the main office were thirty ground floor units for the guests. Each door and entrance had been given its own unique façade and adornments, and Whit knew from experience that a placard above each brass number announced the particular theme: Kodiak Room, Grizzly Room, Aspen Room, and at the far end, the Bridal Veil Falls Honeymoon Suite. In the center of the courtyard were the remains of a swimming pool and the smaller companion pools which had once been filled with steaming water from the hot springs. The old painted cement was chipped and peeling and the deep end was littered with silt and autumn leaves, but Whit could remember a time when that kidney shaped hole had been filled with crystal clear blue water and the antics of the Sinful Six.

Beyond the motel facilities, tucked away into stands of towering pines, Whit could see the other outbuildings: the low, window-lined arts and crafts bungalow with its fenced play area; the two-story gabled restaurant and game room; the stables where guests could arrange for horseback riding tours; and the barn, which was the gathering spot for hay rides and sleigh rides.

"It's all here," Whit breathed.

He didn't realize until that moment that he'd automatically applied the brakes so that he could take it in.

"Yeah."

Finley's single word response was equally reverent.

Granted, it wasn't in the best shape. Even from this distance, Whit could see that nature had begun to reclaim the parking lot. There were missing shingles and a few broken windows to the guest houses, and all that wood had begun to turn dark from the weather. But the kitschy fifties vibe hadn't been completely buried.

"It's pretty rough," Whit murmured.

"Rough" was an understatement. It would take a boat-load of cash to ever make it a habitable resort again—if such a thing would even be marketable. But the "bones" were there.

"I guess we should take a look at the main house first," Whit suggested. But when he looked to Finley for confirmation, he found her staring intently at the property, her brows furrowed.

"Is something wrong?"

She seemed to start, as if she hadn't been completely aware of him until he'd spoken.

"No, I—"

She was lying. He knew she was lying.

"Tell me."

Finley opened her mouth as if to offer him an automatic response, then sighed. "I didn't want any of this."

"None of us did. None of us could have dreamed that Norm—"

"No. That's not what I mean." She waved her hand in a gesture that encompassed the tree-filled valley. "This all...*complicates* things."

Whit could understand a bit of her concern. After all, the Sinful Six had gone from old friends who hadn't seen each other in years to property owners in what seemed like the blink of an eye. Without warning, they'd been saddled with responsibilities and options that they'd never had before—and there was still so much that needed to be ironed out.

"I know it's a big deal to inherit a property like—"

"No! You don't understand! I planned...I *need* to get out of this place—Larkspur, the county, the whole frickin' state of Wyoming, if necessary! I'm tired, Whit. I'm tired of the whispers and the gossip and the mistakes I made being dredged up every time I go into town."

Whit swallowed when he realized that *he* was one of those mistakes.

"I've paid my dues and done my penance and now that Norm has died, I should finally be free of it all. I nearly have enough money scraped together to make a move to another state and another life. There's nothing to keep me here anymore." She shook her head, offering a bitter laugh. "Sure,

I'll be named the Wicked Bitch of the West for abandoning Clint, but he's not going to get better. Ever. He'll never know if I go or if I stay."

Whit saw a sheen of moisture gather in her eyes.

"At least, that's what I thought. And now…now, I'm sucked right back into everything."

The words echoed in the confines of the Bronco. Whit's wonder died in his chest when he realized that what had seemed like a rare moment of forgiveness for him had become a burden to Finley.

"No one's saying we have to keep this place, Finley. We can sell the property and—"

"Three months. We've got to wait three months before we can even consider that option—and then, only after the Sinful Six can reunite and come to a unanimous decision. Who knows how long it will take to get everyone's schedules aligned enough to get us all together in the same room?"

The pain that radiated from her voice was so palpable that Whit couldn't help himself. He had to touch her.

He reached to slide his hand beneath the weight of her hair, absorbing the heat of her, his thumb reaching, sweeping, to caress her cheek.

"I'm so sorry. I didn't realize how bad things were for you here. I should have known."

He felt her trembling, saw her chest lift and fall with a series of quick, short breaths.

"You must think I'm horrible," she whispered.

"No."

He could never think that.

"Even though I'm about to run out on Clint?"

Judging by the man he'd seen in the convalescent center, he thought she was being rather harsh on herself.

"Norm wouldn't have wanted you to give up your own goals, Finley. You know that. Hell, you've been here for Norm and Clint all these years already."

Maybe that was why Norm hadn't named Finley as Clint's medical proxy. Maybe he'd known that Finley would always put the needs of others ahead of her own.

But Finley's situation suddenly reminded him that he also had a life outside of Larkspur. He had a fulfilling job—and while he might not have put down real roots in Reno, he felt grounded there. He'd impulsively agreed to take charge of Clint's care—and he didn't regret that decision. But could he do it long distance?

Shit.

This time, when he surveyed the layout of Come Back Ranch, a heaviness settled in his chest. For years now, he'd lived for himself. If he didn't like a job, he quit. If he got the itch to travel, he moved. But now...now, he was tied down with professional responsibilities in Reno and Clint's needs here in Wyoming.

Which meant that, eventually, decisions and sacrifices would have to be made beyond the fate of the Come Back Ranch. And even there, any choices he made would be rife with pitfalls. Especially where Finley was concerned.

As if she sensed that his thoughts had turned toward her, Finley looked at him then. For a moment, he was lost in the blue of her eyes and the vulnerability of her expression.

Knowing that he had to do something to allay her fears, he swept his thumb across her face, tracing the high arch of her cheek bone, first one way, then the other, coming to rest at the corner of her mouth.

"Look, no one's saying we're going to move in or anything," he murmured. "We're going to take a look around and see how the property has fared since we saw it last. Okay?"

She held his gaze. One second. Two. Then, she looked away. When she shifted, he let her go. Not because he wanted to, but because he knew he didn't have a right to do anything else.

He saw the way she straightened and squared her shoulders. Then, her gaze roamed over the buildings, the trees, and the slopes beyond.

"You're right. Let's go have a look."

In many ways, stepping from Whit's Bronco was like traveling back in time. How many summers had the Sinful Six spent in this place? If Finley closed her eyes, she could see the boys tumbling out of the Campanellas' van like rambunctious puppies, ready for the first adventure of the season. What to do first? Swim in the pool? Ride horses into the hills? Or hike up to the secret fort they'd made from a shallow cave in the granite cliffs up above.

But as soon as she opened her eyes, she was faced with the current reality and the changes that were irrefutable…chief among them, the man who stood before her.

Whit.

She'd always thought that when she saw him again, she would feel nothing but anger. After all, he'd been the one to escape Larkspur without offering her so much as a word of explanation. He'd left her to face the community's suspicions and the repercussions of their actions.

But now…

She found that she didn't really care about the past. All she could think about was...

The present.

Whit had walked ahead of her, moving to the wrap-around porch that led to the front entrance of the main office. He stood with his feet planted slightly apart, his coat swinging loose, his hat square to his brow as he dug the ring of keys out of the pocket of his jeans.

Western Male personified.

Lordy, lordy. If she'd known the man he would become, she might have paid more attention to him as a kid.

No. That wasn't fair. She'd always known the potential that lay within him. But he'd been so...*intense* that she'd forced herself to ignore him in favor of Clint's predictability.

Little had she known.

He must have found the right key because the door to the office swung wide and Whit glanced at her over his shoulder.

"You coming?"

She hurried to catch up, then brushed past him when he held the door open for her.

"It feels warm in here," she commented once he'd joined her.

"Mrs. Grove must have left the heat on for us. If we're lucky..." he reached for the switch on the wall and the lobby was immediately flooded with light.

Finley couldn't prevent the murmured "Oh!" that burst from her lips. Overhead, a huge chandelier made of antlers and faux candlesticks flooded the room with a mellow glow, illuminating the dark green carpet, fifties-era chrome and leather furniture, and the polished L-shaped counter that wrapped around half of the room.

Whit reached behind him, taking her hand.

Finley prayed he couldn't feel her reaction to his touch, the frisson of sensation that sizzled through her arm to radiate throughout her whole body.

If she'd thought that her reactions to Whit had been intense years ago, they were nothing compared to the storm of sensation that she felt now. She'd been a girl when she'd seen him last—and her emotions had been confused and chaotic. Now, she found herself reacting to him as a woman. A woman who was more than willing to embrace the chaos.

She blindly followed Whit as he led her around the counter. Here, a short passageway led to the private quarters which had once belonged to Maud and Geraldine Campanella. There was a small sitting room, and beyond it a corridor that led to a pocket-sized kitchen, a narrow bathroom, and two bedrooms.

Except for the kitchen and one of the bedrooms, the furniture had long since disappeared. Even some of the light fixtures were missing, leaving bare bulbs to dangle from the ceiling. But the spaces were clean and warm and seemed to be in fairly good repair.

"It looks a lot better than I thought it would judging by the outside," Whit said, still loosely holding her hand.

"It makes sense that the main house is in good repair. Maud and Geraldine lived here the longest. I doubt the guest quarters are this well-kept."

"Even so, I can see why Norm wanted someone to stay on the premises."

An awkward silence ensued, then they both spoke at once.

"I'll stay."

"I guess I could stay."

Whit's lips twitched at the corners.

"Unless you're really dead set on the idea, I'm more than willing to stay, Finley. Like Mr. Grove said, it's pretty Spartan. And I don't necessarily like the idea of your being up here all on your own."

She shivered slightly at the idea. It hadn't even occurred to her that by volunteering, she would be spending days and nights alone, in relative isolation, miles from the nearest neighbor.

"I...uh...thanks. But don't you have to get back to...Reno, wasn't it?"

He shrugged. "I've got time off due to me. It doesn't make a whole lot of sense to go right back. Not until Grove has had a chance to get ahold of the others." He shrugged. "Who knows? We might be able to iron out all the details within a week or ten days."

If only.

Then again, once all of the decisions were made, Whit would have no real excuse to stay.

"Besides, I'm sure I've still got papers to sign so I can take over as Clint's proxy."

Clint.

But this time, the mention of their friend's name didn't serve to be the damper that it usually did. Outside, it had already begun to grow dark and the dim wattage of the bulb overhead lent a mellow glow to the room. Like candlelight, the overall effect was intimate. Private.

"But you'll need to be in town."

"It's a twenty-minute drive. I can handle it."

Silence spooled between them, thick and sticky with everything left unsaid. Finley swallowed against the tight grip of her memories as she suddenly realized that she and Whit were alone, together, cocooned in a place that had once been a haven to them both. There was nothing to stop them from reaching out to one another.

Nothing but the emotions, past and present, that twined around them like clinging vines, warning them that once certain lines were crossed, there would be no going back.

EIGHT

*F*inley became acutely conscious of the way her fingers remained laced between Whit's, the slight roughness to his callused skin, the warmth of his body seeping into hers.

"Whit?"

His name was a bare puff of sound.

"Shh."

His free hand lifted, hovered in the air. Then he cupped her cheek in his palm—and she couldn't her instinctive reaction to lean into that caress.

"I…"

"Shh."

His green eyes seemed darker than ever, glowing from within. He took a half step closer. Then another. And another. Then he released the grip on her hand so that he could wrap an arm around her waist and pull her irresistibly closer.

Without thought, she moved her feet between his, allowed him to tug her even more tightly against him. Soon, they were pressed together, knees, thighs, hips, and the sensation was so astonishing, so welcoming, so overwhelming, that she clutched at his belt loops to anchor herself.

As she looked up, up, up, she became aware of his height and the impossible breadth of his shoulders. Then he was bending down, down, until his lips hovered above her own.

"I can't stop, Finley," he whispered. "I'm sorry, but I—"

"Don't stop."

Despite the urgency in his voice—an urgency that she felt to her very bones—his first touch was tentative, soft, hesitant. A mere brush of his lips, a mingling of breath.

She couldn't help herself. She eased forward into the embrace, pulling on his belt loops until he pressed more firmly against her. For such a tall man, it should have been awkward to kiss her at all, but by tipping his hips, bowing his shoulders, he knew how to make things easy, his nose brushing hers—not clumsily, but as a secondary caress. Then his lips closed over hers again, more firmly this time.

Sensation slammed through her, centering in the base of her belly, making her realize how long it had been since she'd felt this…this…utter hedonism and femininity, desire and possessiveness.

He framed her face with his palms as he deepened the embrace, parting her lips, touching her tongue with his. Then, as if an unseen boundary had been crossed, he plundered her mouth as his arms snapped around her waist, drawing her up, taking her weight.

Her own arms slid around his neck, her fingers plunging through his hair, reacquainting herself with the silky texture, the slight wave, the warmth of his scalp.

Somehow, in the embrace, his hat tumbled to the floor, but Whit didn't seem to notice—and she was beyond coherent enough thought to warn him. Instead, she closed her eyes, allowing herself to be swept away by the sheer pleasure of being in Whit's arms—not as a girl, but as a woman. A woman who was oh, so hungry for all of this.

When he broke away—more to allow them to breathe than for any other reason—he pressed his forehead to hers. His eyes remained closed as he seemed to savor the thunder of sensation that their embrace had inspired—and that reaction caused the warmth that had settled in her belly to seep upwards into her chest.

Finley supposed that the kiss should bring the past flooding back. After all, it was an embrace much like this one which had set a catastrophic chain of events into motion.

But she couldn't be sorry.

She refused to be sorry.

When Whit finally opened his eyes, she could all but read an apology being formed in his brain. But before he could speak, she lay a finger against his lips.

"Don't say it. Don't say anything."

The words emerged in a husky whisper that gave far too much away. Even she could hear the need and the echoes of passion that tinged her simple commands. But thankfully, Whit seemed to understand because he drew her close and wrapped his arms around her.

And for a time, he simply held her that way, her ear tuned to the ragged beating of his heart.

Whit waited until Finley had disappeared inside her house before backing his Bronco into the street and heading toward the main part of town.

He hadn't missed the twitch of the curtains at the large picture window, and he briefly wondered if Finley was getting the third degree from her mother or her sister.

Geez, it was like being in high school all over again.

Except they were both adults now. And as adults, the emotions between them seemed that much richer and more powerful.

He laughed softly to himself, shaking his head. Sure, he'd hoped he would run into Finley during his trip back to Larkspur, but this...

He'd never imagined actually holding her. Kissing her.

He was so busy thinking about the incredible turn of events, that he nearly didn't see the semi running a red light at the crossroads. At the last minute, Whit slammed on his brakes as a Peterbilt with a loaded cattle trailer barreled through the intersection, its airbrakes whining.

Damnation. If he'd been a few seconds earlier...

He swiped his palms over his thighs, his heart galloping wildly in his chest as he was flooded with the chaotic images of the after-effects of another accident, another highway. It took him several seconds to realize that the semi and trailer had similar markings to those in his notes.

Allowing a healthy distance between him and the vehicle, Whit turned the Bronco onto the main road and followed the semi until it turned into a service station. Hanging back near the convenience store, he pulled into one of the parking spots as the trailer came to a complete stop and the driver and passenger hopped out and began shouting at one another.

Clearly, they were upset about having run through the light. The driver circled the hood and gesticulated wildly at his tall, gangly companion. Then the two of them stalked to check the couplings to the trailer.

Since the gas station was well-lit, Whit dragged his phone from his pocket and took several photos of the rig and the two men.

He wasn't sure why he felt the need to document the vehicle and its occupants. Granted, the operators had run through a light, and it was clear that a mechanical problem may have led to the incident. The vehicle looked a lot like the livestock transport Thayne had described. Whit would have to check the tags, but the details didn't match exactly.

But even as Whit began to itemize all the reasons why he could head back toward the center of town, his instincts told him to stick around for a few minutes longer and remain alert.

The men seemed to find the source of their concern, then they turned to amble in Whit's direction. Keeping his phone low and against the dashboard, Whit continued to take pictures of the duo until they'd disappeared inside.

Starting his engine, Whit backed from his parking space and drove to the rear of the cattle trailer. Still snapping pictures, he recorded the tags and markings, then moved to the side opposite the convenience store. Temporarily out of sight of the huge wall of windows, he eased the Bronco into PARK and jumped out. Peering through the metal slats, he did his best to determine the size and type of cattle inside and snapped a few quick pics of the brands. Then he hopped back into the Bronco and finished documenting the Peterbilt.

Knowing he was already pressing his luck, he quickly left the parking lot and headed toward the center of town. He needed groceries. After that, he'd see if he could find a place in Larkspur that could provide him with some printed copies of the photos from his phone. Then he'd head back to the ranch and give Thayne a call. Once he'd sent him the files, they could compare their thoughts.

Whit had only gone a block before his phone pinged. Whit steered the Bronco to the shoulder. With his thoughts on work and Thayne, he expected to see the man's name on his caller ID. But when he checked the screen, he saw that Finley had sent him a text.

I LUV THE WAY I FEEL WHEN U KISS ME.

A bolt of sensation shot through his body, one that was a weaker version of the storm of arousal he'd felt holding Finley in his arms.

He'd never been much good at expressing his feelings— a fact which had led to much of the trouble ten years ago. This time, if he was going to make a difference, he had to at least try.

I FEEL THE SAME WAY.

He hesitated before adding.

I'M HAPPIEST WHEN I'M WITH U.

He waited, wondering if he'd said too much. Or too, too little.

But when he feared that he'd scared her away, his phone chimed again and a set of magic words appeared.

ME 2. AND I HAVEN'T BEEN HAPPY IN A LONG TIME.

He grinned. *WHEN CAN I SEE U AGAIN?*

TOMORROW AFTER MY SHIFT?

I'LL B THERE.

Finley pushed her cart down the bread aisle, knowing that she'd come to the grocery store for something...

But she couldn't remember what. She'd made a list on an app in her phone, but the battery had died and she'd left her car charger on the kitchen counter at home. Now...

Well, now, she didn't really care what staples she'd been asked to bring home. She kept remembering Whit's lips against hers, his arms wrapped around her waist.

Twice, she'd been kissed by Whit Patterson, and both times had been soul-shattering. It wasn't only his kisses, or the way his embrace made her feel inexplicably powerful and vulnerable, unsure and in control. There was so much more to it than that. So much more.

Which left her wondering if she were brave enough to play with fire.

Finley wasn't stupid enough to think that anything could ever come of a dalliance with Whit Patterson. He'd been gone for so long that she really didn't know anything about him. Except that he would leave.

But you're leaving too.

She shook her head to rid it of the thought. Yes, she might have plans to escape Larkspur, Wyoming, but she had her own goals to reach. And after everything that she'd gone through to make her way back to a place where those dreams were a possibility, she couldn't afford to waste them again by surrendering to the first man who'd...

Taken her breath away.

No. She had to be realistic. Besides, a kiss and a cuddle did not a relationship make. For all she knew, Whit was simply passing time with her, making his visit a little more enjoyable until the time came for him to return to Reno. Even with the responsibilities they'd inherited with the Come Back Ranch, he couldn't stay for long. He had a job and presumably a home. For all she knew, he had dear friends. Maybe even a relationship.

The moment that thought reared into her head, she shoved it away. Whit wouldn't be kissing her if he were dating anyone else. He wasn't that kind of guy.

Do you know that for sure?

Because he'd once kissed you knowing you were involved with Clint.

Finley shook that thought from her head, blindly reaching for a loaf of bread—any loaf of bread. She needed to get out of here and get home to her "real" life—and not stand woolgathering about a man who would probably be disappearing in a matter of days. If she couldn't remember what she'd come here to buy, she'd get the basics: bread, milk, fruit and vegetables. Anything else could wait until tomorrow.

Resolutely, she turned her cart toward the dairy section, only to come up short. There, not ten yards away, was Whit Patterson.

For a moment, she could only stare at him, taking in the long legs highlighted by a pair of well-fitting jeans—jeans that lovingly clung to the firm muscles of his thighs and the tight, rounded butt. Above that, he wore his Carhartt again, and she mourned the way that it obscured the upper half of his body. Then again, the bulky canvas did accent the width of his shoulders.

Stop it.

She must have telegraphed her lascivious thoughts because he glanced her way. She watched the slow montage of emotions—surprise, awareness, pleasure—before he turned to face her.

"Are you stalking me?"

Finley felt a rush of heat to her cheeks and immediately opened her mouth to disabuse him of that notion. But thankfully, she caught the gleam of humor in the forest green of his eyes. It was that hint of teasing that allowed her to be lighthearted in return.

"Mmm. So, it would seem." Even though her brain told her to stay away, her feet moved toward him. She glanced into his basket and laughed. "Stocking up on bachelor supplies, I see."

He only had a few items so far. A box of Pop Tarts, bread, cheese, lunch meat, a case of soda, and a half-dozen cans of soup.

"I'm easily pleased."

"I can see that." She couldn't help grinning up at him.

How could one man make her feel so happy just by being near?

"You might want to add something green or a fruit to the mix."

He pretended to shudder. "I wouldn't want to shock my delicate system."

That made her laugh.

"Seems to me, you could use a good home cooked meal, Whit."

"Are you offering?"

The words seemed to shimmer in the air around them, rich with promise.

"I could be persuaded."

"What would it take to persuade you?"

She hesitated, then said, "I'll have to decide my terms."

"Present your demands, your grocery list, and the night you want to do it, and it's a date."

Date.

Such a simple word—almost an archaic term in this day and age. But the nuances that lay behind it were enough to make a cascade of gooseflesh race down her spine.

"In the meantime, you'll make-do with Pop Tarts?"

His grin grew even wider. "I'll save those for breakfast."

"Ah. I was hoping you'd come to the diner again."

"Then…lunch?"

She couldn't help studying him from tip to toe, then back again.

"You don't look like you live on a steady diet of toaster pastries."

He bent close to whisper right next to her ear. "How would you know? You haven't seen all that much of me yet."

Yet.

Sheer awareness shot to the heart of her, burning like hot coals deep in her belly—and for a moment, she couldn't move, couldn't speak, couldn't react as she imagined herself sliding the coat from his shoulders, lifting his T-shirt from his head, then reaching for the snap at the waist of his jeans.

His low laughter skittered over her nerve endings as he grabbed a jug of milk and a small carton of cream from the dairy section, then moved away from her toward the check-out stands at the front of the store.

"See you tomorrow, Finley."

And Finley was left standing here, her body suffused in heat, her mind turning to pure mush.

A rush of cold air seemed to follow Whit into the convalescent center that night. But within a half-dozen strides, the chill dissipated beneath the warmth of the facility's central heating.

The nurse at the desk looked up, smiled. It was the same woman that he'd seen before. Sharla.

"I'm here to see Clint Campanella," Whit murmured, sure the woman wouldn't have remembered him.

Perhaps he'd been wrong in his assumption. Her smile brightened even more. "Of course, Mr. Patterson. Go on through."

Whit paused, holding up the sacks he carried. "I hope it's okay, but I didn't have time to eat before…"

She waved a dismissing hand. "Please, make yourself at home while you're here. We find that a relaxed atmosphere encourages more interaction with our long-term patients." Her eyes twinkled. "We also have a killer cafeteria, should you ever want to get a bite here. Our chef was trained in New York."

"Really?"

She leaned forward. "He's got a hot turkey sandwich that brings in a crowd every other Thursday. But get here early. It always sells out."

"I'll keep that in mind."

"Your lawyer brought some papers to our administrators earlier today. They asked me let them know if you visited again. I'll tell them you're here. I think they need your signature."

"Sounds good. I'll be staying for an hour or two."

He wouldn't have thought it possible, but the woman's smile grew even broader. "Wonderful!"

Whit made his way through the double doors, then down the corridor to Clint's room. This time, he found the door propped open.

The shock of seeing his friend lying so still had faded only slightly. Whit couldn't help pausing at the threshold, waiting for Clint's gaze to slice his way. But Clint's eyes remained barely open, staring into space while overhead, the television flashed with the bright colors of a kids' superhero program.

Whit relied on his instincts and stepped into the room with as much purpose and normality as he could scrape together.

"Hey, there, Clint. Looks like you've had a long day."

Long day, long week, long year.

"I grabbed some grub before I came."

Whit rolled the overbed table into position, then set the sack of food on top.

"I brought you a drink and fries, but then, maybe you've already eaten."

Whit continued as if his friend were alert and able to respond, even though he felt a bit like an insensitive jackass. But Finley had said to act as normally as possible, talk to him, stimulate his senses—whatever the hell that meant. All Whit knew was that Clint had always been addicted to a cold Dew and fries, and if the sight or scent of either of them could help, he was willing to try.

"There's a Broncos game on tonight, so I thought we could watch it together."

He set the sack and the drinks holder on the table, then dragged the recliner closer to the bed.

"I gotta tell you, the Broncos have been struggling since they lost that wide receiver, but I still have my hopes that they can get a win tonight."

Whit used the bed remote to change the channel and turn up the volume so that the room filled with the roar of the crowd and the deep tones of a former NFL player extolling the virtues of the Broncos' veteran quarterback. Then, he spread out a napkin and topped it with a paper boat heaped with a large order of fries from the Dairy Delight. He set the drink on the table as well, angling the straw toward Clint.

"Your Dew is cold and the fries are salty, just like you love 'em. I've got catsup if you need it. Let me know. Dig in any time," he offered casually.

He shrugged out of his jacket, throwing it onto the nearby couch before tossing his hat on top. Then he grabbed his own burger and took his seat.

The sound of the color commentary crew filled the silence for several minutes. But Whit couldn't seem to concentrate—on the television or his food. The few bites he took seemed to stick in his throat, refusing to go down, until he finally set his burger on the table next to Clint's food.

"Listen, Clint, we gotta talk. I know I screwed up all those years ago. We were friends. I should have told you how I felt about Finley from the very first. Maybe you would have understood." A humorless laugh pushed from his throat. "Or maybe you would have punched me in the face. I don't know." He shifted in his seat, leaning toward the bed, searching Clint's face for the slightest hint that his friend was even in there.

Just like Finley had said, there was no noticeable outward reaction. But Whit could *feel* his old buddy—whether it was memory or wishful thinking, he couldn't say.

"Once you staked your claim on her, I tried to keep things casual between Finley and me. Honest. And I don't want you to think that she did anything wrong, because she didn't. Hell, that year the two of us avoided each other like the plague—as if by ignoring our feelings, they'd wither up and die."

He linked his hands together between his knees, staring down at them, but really seeing a series of images from that last year that the Sinful Six had been together.

"If I'd known then, what I know now…" Whit began, then he shook his head, before muttering ruefully, "Hell, I probably would have done exactly the same thing. Bro Code and all." He sighed, not really sure where he was going with this one-sided confession, only knowing that by spelling it out to Clint, he was doing his best to explain it all to himself.

"The fact is, Clint, that my feelings for Finley haven't changed—even though I know they're as doomed as they ever were." He rubbed his thumbs restlessly together, then glanced up at Clint. "I kissed her today. And Lord help me, if it weren't for you, here, and everything that's taken place…I don't know if I could have stopped."

Once again, he searched Clint's features, but there was nothing but the steady rise and fall of his chest and the hiss of the ventilator.

"I suppose there are plenty of people around this town who will call me a bastard for moving in on a man's girl when he's down, but…she's been through a lot, Clint. All of it on her own. And today, after our kiss, I saw…I don't know, a spark of life in her eyes. So, I'm pretty sure she still has…feelings for me. That's why I'm being up front with you here. I don't know where any of this will go—if it will go anywhere at all. But I'm going to do it right. No sneaking around, no stolen kisses. I plan to, I don't know…*court* her. The way she deserves."

Whit waited, although for what, he didn't know. There was no sudden gasp, no blink, nothing. Nevertheless, Whit felt an inexplicable wave of peace wash over him. Maybe, as he'd supposed earlier, he'd needed to think things through and decide where he was headed with Finley to clear his mind.

And his conscience.

In any event, as the television blared and the players swarmed onto the field, Whit felt as if a huge weight had been lifted from his shoulders. His stomach growled in hunger and he reached for his food.

"I tell you, Clint. You don't know what you're missing if you don't at least taste your food. No one makes hand-cut fries like the Dairy Delight. I might have to eat them all myself if you don't shake a leg."

Then Whit leaned back in the recliner and took a bite of his hamburger.

"My money's on the Broncos to win the toss. What do you think?"

NINE

*W*hit shrugged into his jacket and slammed the door to the main house behind him. Surprisingly enough, he'd slept like a dead man his first night at the Come Back Ranch. Maybe it had been the absence of city noises, or the familiar ruffle of the aspen trees which had lulled him to sleep. In any event, as he strode toward the craft building, he was ready for work. Settling his hat more firmly over his brow to combat the wind, he tugged on a pair of leather gloves and surveyed the compound.

He hadn't come to Wyoming prepared for ranch work. He was going to have to stop in Larkspur and drum up a few basic supplies. He needed more practical boots—since he'd only brought his fancy Ariats with him—tools, and probably a ladder. And since he hadn't planned on staying for more than the weekend, he was either going to have to hit the laundromat every other night or augment his wardrobe.

Then, there was the list he'd already begun to compile. Towards dawn, he'd taken the ring of keys from the peg by the back door and he'd made a more thorough search of the property. He'd already known that the barn was in good repair. He'd been feeding a pair of horses and a half-dozen cows since taking up residence. But until that morning, he hadn't made a more detailed inventory of anything beyond the main house. The sun had barely topped the horizon when he'd begun inspecting the bungalows and he'd made detailed notes of repairs that needed to be made.

Surprisingly, the checklist he'd formed wasn't as long as he'd thought it would be. Granted, it wasn't that brief, but it was…"doable".

For some reason, the bungalows on the north side of the compound had suffered the worst damage—missing shingles, broken panes of glass, water damage, wood rot. Probably, those structures sustained the brunt of wind and weather. But the needs of the other lodgings seemed more in keeping with their age and having been shut up for a dozen or more years. Sure, they would need a good airing, new flooring, and some paint, but structurally, they seemed sound.

For the most part, the repairs were within Whit's skill set. He'd done enough ranch work to have basic carpentry and plumbing skills. If he could get to a hardware store, he could get a good chunk of the work done before he left.

Before he left.

In the past, he'd rarely taken a day off—whether it was as a cowboy or his job with the cattle cops. If he was honest, he'd avoided down time, knowing that solitude had a way of making him brood. On those rare occasions when he'd had time off, he'd been preoccupied with the cases he was investigating.

But since coming to Larkspur, it felt as if he'd stepped out of one life and into another one. He rarely thought about Reno or his job. Instead, he found himself becoming absorbed by what he'd found here—this place, plans for the future. And Finley. Always Finley.

If things were different, he would be tempted to fight to keep the property rather than sell it. Norm had amassed enough acreage for grazing to make the Come Back Ranch a successful enterprise. Granted, it would take a while to build it up to a full-fledged working ranch that could support a person. Maybe even a family. But Whit wasn't without marketable skills. He could get a "real" job to pay the bills and work at Come Back in his off hours.

As he let himself into the craft building and took a few cursory notes, Whit pushed aside the part of him that shrank away from the...*permanence* of his idle notions. Such plans were premature at best and preposterous at worst. The fate of the Come Back Ranch would be determined by the Sinful Six, not by him. And Finley...

Well, Finley had already made it clear that she had her own ideas for the future, and they didn't include staying here.

Whit finished his examination and carefully locked the door behind him. For a moment, he paused on the top step of the wrap-around porch. A gusting breeze rattled through the undergrowth and caused the last stubborn leaves on the aspens to shiver. As he absorbed the chill air with its hints of wood smoke, pine, and crushed foliage, he couldn't ignore the sense of...rightness. This was where he'd spent the happiest vacations of his life. It was hard to ignore the urge to see if he could recapture that magic.

Without Finley?

"Hell, you're losing your ever-lovin' mind," he muttered to himself.

Since he feared the restaurant would be beyond his abilities to assess, Whit ignored the two-story structure and strode toward the far side of the compound instead. He followed a familiar path—a part of him noting that all of the trails would have to be repaved or torn up altogether. Winding through bunches of sumac and scrub oak which had sprung up since he'd been here last, he followed the fenced pasture to a large, square structure which had once held equipment and vehicles for the Come Back Ranch.

As a kid, Whit remembered playing hide-and-seek in its shadowy confines. This was the place where the Campanella women had stored the old winter sleigh and the flat-bed wagons used for the hay rides. Opening the door, Whit stood for a moment in the dimness, waiting for his eyes to adjust.

He flicked on the lights overhead, but the bare bulbs hanging from the rafters were little help. It took a moment for him to pick out the hulking shape of Norm's vintage tractor. Beyond it was the squat outline of a baler and what looked like the spindly wheels of an alfalfa rake.

His boots echoed hollowly on the concrete floor as he moved further inside. There was the sleigh, looking dusty and a little bedraggled, and a riding mower. After that, beneath a pair of multi-paned windows, he found Norm's workbench— still cluttered with the remains of the wooden toys he made and donated to the charity drive each Christmas. Norm had always been careful with his tools. They were lined up on a peg board, each one carefully labeled.

Scratch tools off your list of things to buy.

Against the wall, there were several shapes covered with old cotton sheets. Pulling them off, one by one, Whit discovered that Norm had a belt sander, band saw, and drill press.

We're cooking with gas now.

Whit draped the sheets over the machines again, and updated his notes. Having access to tools—especially the power tools—would save him a lot of time.

There you go again, making plans.

He turned to survey the last portion of the building—where the Campanella women had stored the larger vehicles which had always made the best hiding places. The hay wagons were gone, but something large and bulky had been moved into the space in front of the massive sliding doors. A series of tarps had been layered on top and fastened down with baling twine.

Whit reached for the knife strapped to his belt. Cutting a few of the cords, he lifted up the corner of the tarp, then sprang back, dropping the covering again as if it had hidden a coiled rattlesnake.

"Shit!"

His pulse banged at his temples and seemed to pound in the base of his teeth. He stood hunched, gasping for breath, before he finally dared to draw the tarpaulin out of the way again.

There was no disguising the twisted metal, the shattered headlights, the flat tire that seemed bent at an impossible angle.

His car.

It was the old beat-up sedan he'd been using as his everyday wheels while he finished restoring the Bronco. He'd barely been able to fold his legs into the driver's seat.

Whit told himself to back away, to lock the doors to the equipment shed, and ignore what he'd found. But his body seemed to have other ideas. Without being entirely aware of his actions, he cut the bindings, then pulling the crackling plastic away from the wreck.

Someone must have tried to clean it up—or maybe it had been left outside for a time. Though his eyes scoured every inch, Whit couldn't see any tell-tale signs of blood on the glass. Rust had begun blossoming at the cracks and valleys caused by the crumpled metal—and even after being covered, there was a fine layer of dust coating the interior and exterior alike.

Whit felt a trembling grip his muscles—so much so, that he was forced to sink and rest on his heels. Looking at the crushed heap of metal and glass, he wondered how either he or Clint had survived.

Holy, holy hell.

Whit had been on duty during several serious automobile accidents—one or two of them destructive enough to enlist the aid of the fire department to cut passengers free from their automobiles.

But he'd never seen anything like this.

He rubbed his hand over his mouth, swearing again when he saw his fingers were shaking.

Shit, shit, shit.

Pushing himself to his feet, he strode toward the door.

He'd heard the stories—been told a hundred times what had happened. But because of the head injuries he'd sustained, he had a huge gap in his memories. Everything after the kiss with Finley was a blank up to that moment when first responders had begun loading him onto a backboard.

Why couldn't he remember?

The facts had been fed to him. If asked, he could recite all the details—they'd been seared into his brain by well-meaning friends, Elvis, the cops, the lawyers. But something about the events had always seemed like the retelling of a fantastical work of fiction—or events that had happened to a stranger. He remembered kissing Finley—that mind-blowing, life-altering kiss. And he remembered the unsettling thought that they weren't alone.

To this day, he couldn't have said what made him turn. Clint had been only a yard or two away, watching them. The shock, the disbelief, the absolute betrayal that had radiated from his features had forced Whit to back away from Finley. Then his friend had turned and begun running—and Whit had followed, full-tilt, arms pumping, feet pounding, knowing he needed to diffuse the situation.

Then…nothing.

He'd been told that he'd chased Clint to a local bar. That the two of them had been seen drinking and arguing. That they'd taken their argument back to the stadium parking lot where punches had been thrown. And when Whit stormed toward his car, this time it was Clint who'd been chasing *him*.

But for Whit, it was all a blank. There'd been Finley, that kiss, Clint running. The next thing he remembered was the blue and red strobe lights of police cars and pain, so much pain.

Damnit all to hell. The car was a mess. For that amount of damage, there had to be more to the accident than what he'd been told.

You were probably driving too fast.

Maybe you hit a patch of black ice.

Or you swerved to avoid another car.

You couldn't have known that the accident would occur on the other side of a blind curve. Nor could you blame yourself for the other cars which had slammed into one another in a freak chain reaction—including the one carrying Finley and Javi and P.J..

Only the cops had been blunt enough to tell Whit the truth.

Your blood-alcohol levels were pretty close to the limit.

What they hadn't said was that the blood sample had been taken hours after the accident. Which meant that maybe, just maybe, Whit had been driving while impaired.

He might have been young, but he'd never been stupid enough to drive drunk. Ever.

Until that night, apparently.

An old familiar guilt roiled in her stomach, but this time it was tempered by a healthy measure of confusion. Norm had known all of this. He'd even had evidence from the accident towed from the scene and stored in his shed. He had to have studied the wreckage inch by inch.

But he'd still named Whit in his will.

And appointed him as Clint's medical proxy.

Why?

What had Norm discovered in that hunk of twisted metal which had allowed him to trust Whit, even though his son was still locked into the consequences of that night?

As he carefully locked the door behind him and strode toward the house, Whit felt his guilt easing beneath a rabid curiosity. And something more.

Hope.

"Finley, there's a guy here to see you."

Finley slammed her locker shut and glanced up as she looped the strap to her purse over her shoulder.

"Who is it?" With her shift ending, the last thing she wanted was a customer showing up wanting to dig through the Lost and Found box.

Megan grinned. "It's that tall man you were with the other day."

"Whit?"

Megan shrugged. "He said he'd meet you out by your car."

"Thanks."

Finley hurried toward the back entrance before anyone else could find a reason to stop her. With the weekend approaching, the breakfast shift had been busier than usual—probably with campers deciding to take one last outing to Yellowstone before winter arrived in earnest.

True to form here in the West, mere days after a sleet storm had driven people indoors, the weather now hovered in the high sixties and the sun hung high in a cloudless sky. Unfortunately, that meant the diner's parking lot was filled to capacity, so Finley had to wind between a series of motor homes and jacked-up pickups before she managed to see her own economy car tucked into one of the rear stalls.

There, leaning against the hood, was Whit Patterson.

Finley couldn't account for the rush of joy she felt—then a slow burn of pleasure—and all from the simple sight of him. He had his head down as he scrolled through something on his phone. The brim of his hat obscured part of his face, but still left his sharp cheekbones and square jaw to her view—and the hint of a cleft in his chin. She'd always loved that faint divot. There had been times her fingers had twitched to touch it.

"Hey, there," she called out softly.

He looked up, automatically sliding his phone back into the pocket of his jeans. The simple shift of his hips was enough to make the pounding of her pulse ease lower.

"Hey."

He eased to his feet in a single graceful motion that belied his height, then reached behind him to grab a cellophane wrapped parcel. As he met her halfway, he held it out to her.

Flowers. He'd brought her flowers.

She took them automatically, her fingers parting the wrapping to expose a bouquet of sweet peas, daisies, baby's breath, and lobelia.

"They're beautiful," she whispered.

He'd remembered.

"Wildflowers—or as close as I could get." One side of his mouth tipped into a crooked smile, revealing the slightest hint of a dimple in his cheek. "If I remember right, you always said that carnations were funeral flowers, and roses were too, too predictable."

She couldn't help laughing. He'd remembered her philosophy on flowers word for word.

"They're beautiful. Thank you."

There was a beat of silence—long enough to cause her to look up.

Only to find that he was watching her. And for once, his emotions weren't hidden.

He wanted her.

He.

Wanted.

Her.

Before she could react, he murmured, "Not as beautiful as you." Then used a finger to tip her chin toward him. He kissed her, long and slow, his lips urging hers to part so that he could deepen the embrace.

She tried to step forward, needing to be even closer to the heat of his body, but he backed away.

"Uh-uh. Not yet."

Not yet?

"Have you eaten at all?"

"No, I…"

He sighed. "Finley, it's mid-afternoon. You can't work a busy shift without anything to eat."

"But—"

"Do you have any plans today?"

Beyond laundry, scrubbing the kitchen floor, and buying the groceries she'd forgotten the night before?

"No. Not really."

Billie and her mother would simply have to fend for themselves.

"I've got to go into Redmond to get supplies for the repairs. Wanna come? We could get something to eat on our way, or wait until we get there and go to one of those little places on Wilderness Drive."

"Let's wait."

This time, she got a whole smile. One slow, unfettered, Whit Patterson smile.

"Good answer." He tipped his head to the side. "I'm parked over there." He took her hand, easing his own ground-eating strides to a slow amble. "How was your shift?"

"Busy."

"That's good, isn't it?"

She nodded. "It's hectic, but it makes the time fly."

"And adds to your tips, I'm sure—which will add to your college fund."

He paused at the Bronco, opening the door.

"Yeah." She couldn't help smiling again. Evidently, her preference in flowers wasn't the only thing he'd remembered. "Every little bit helps."

This time, as she climbed into the high seat, he kept a hand at her elbow, providing her with support until she could slide inside and reach for her seatbelt. Then he circled to take his own place.

"I had the florist put those tube thingies on your flowers so they should be fine until we get back."

Tube thingies?

She pulled the cellophane aside from the stems to reveal that her bouquet had a source of water—and that little detail touched her almost as much as the flowers themselves.

"Thanks, Whit."

She bent to breathe deeply, inhaling the fresh summery scents, absorbing the tickle of baby's breath against her nose.

"You can set them in the back, if you want."

What she really wanted, was to bury her face in the blooms again and absorb the chaotic emotions ricocheting through her body. But she supposed that such behavior would only bruise the delicate blossoms, so she twisted to set them on the bench seat.

Tonight. Tonight, when she was alone and had all the time in the world, she would sift through her feelings. But not right now.

As she faced forward again, Whit took her hand. In the past, his grip had been loose, companionable, gentle, even. But this time, as he lifted her fist and pressed a kiss to her knuckles, there was a stamp of possession to his actions.

"I've been thinking things over since last night."

Since their encounter at the grocery store?

Or since their kiss?

Should she confess to him that she hadn't slept much at all? That she'd relived their embrace over and over again, dissected it, analyzed it, all in an attempt to understand why she was willing to step whole-heartedly into the same mistakes that she'd already made once before. She'd told herself that nothing good could ever come of a relationship with Whit—if he was even willing to offer anything that even approximated a *relationship*. She'd outlined all the reasons why it wouldn't work: they lived so far apart; she would be leaving soon; the past would never truly let the go.

But here, *now,* with his lips pressed to her skin, none of that seemed to matter.

"I want to court you, Finley. Would that be all right with you?"

Court her. Trust Whit to find an entirely old-fashioned way of announcing his intentions. But then, did men even "announce their intentions" anymore?

When she didn't speak right away, he seemed to take that as a signal to explain himself more in-depth.

"I want to do this right, okay? Hell, we probably already know each other better than most couples who date."

That might have been true of the old Finley and Whit. But to Finley, the man who sat beside her seemed like a stranger in many ways.

"I think we should take things slow. Date. Spend time together."

"B-but won't you be leaving soon?"

Whit shook his head. "I have a couple of weeks of vacation days saved up, and I called in a favor." He met her gaze before shifting his attention back to the road. "I'll be here awhile. Long enough for us to sort through things and decide...decide where this might be heading."

This.

This attraction.

This need.

This emotional vortex.

"I...uh, also paid a visit to Clint last night. Told him that I planned to keep seeing you."

The admission was made grudgingly—as if Whit feared that she would think him a fool. But the confession merely tightened this man's hold on her heart.

"So?" Whit asked, his eyes dark and green like a summer forest. "What do you say?"

Her breath left her lungs in a ragged whoosh—as if she'd been holding it for a very long time. And she realized that, ever since Whit Patterson had returned, she'd fought to avoid her response to him—the same response she'd had since his voice had dropped an octave and the colt-like gangliness of adolescence had faded beneath the greyhound leanness of an adult.

"Yes."

"Yes?"

"Yes, I'd like that."

And then, he laughed. Whit Patterson laughed.

"Well, all right, then."

TEN

*W*hen they arrived in Redmond, Whit headed for Wilderness Drive, parking on one of the side streets. Then, he helped Finley from the car. "Lifted" probably would have been a better term. Or maybe "controlled drop", because once she was free from the vehicle, he held her just enough so that she slid down the length of his body until her feet were firmly on the ground. Then, with his hands gripping the Bronco on either side, he bent for a soft kiss.

It took every ounce of self-control to keep the caress light, brief—and he didn't miss the way that Finley leaned into him as if wanting more. But he couldn't give in. Not now. Not yet. Not when so much was riding on the fact that he needed to do this right—even though he wasn't really sure what "right" meant.

He forced himself to lift his head. And when he caught Finley's slightly dazed look, he decided that his restraint was worth it.

"Let's find a bite to eat. Then we'll worry about the rest."

"Okay." Although uttered as a statement, there was a slight lilt at the end of the word—as if she wasn't really sure that she wanted to leave the shelter of the car.

That had to be a good sign, didn't it?

This time, as they made their way around the corner and onto the historical Wilderness Drive, Whit hooked Finley around the waist, drawing her tightly to his side. She looped her own arm around him. She must have felt the bulge at his back, because she looked up at him, her eyes quizzical.

"Are you carrying?"

His lips twitched. "I'm always carrying. Don't worry. I have a permit."

She opened her mouth—obviously ready to demand more of an explanation. But the last thing that Whit wanted was to get embroiled in talking about his work, so he diverted her by asking, "What are you in the mood for? Pancakes and eggs?"

When she looked up at him, slightly aghast, he laughed. He didn't have to be a genius to figure out that, after a morning of slinging bacon and hash, diner food would be the last thing she would want.

Her eyes cleared, becoming a bright, crystal blue. "You had me going there for a minute."

He drew to a halt, his gaze scanning the narrow street. At one time, Redmond had been a frontier town and a spoke of the Union Pacific. The buildings on either side were original to its heyday, and had fallen into disrepair, until a business-savvy developer hit on the idea of attracting the tourist trade with gentrified boutiques, summer condos, and up-scale eateries. Now gas street lamps and quaint signage framed such establishments as Outlaw Outfitters, and The Cobbler's

Bench, while restaurants and bakeries filled the air with their delicious scents.

"What are you in the mood to eat? Italian, Mexican? Sandwiches, hamburgers, steak?"

"I could hurt someone for Mexican right about now."

"Mexican it is."

He led the way to The Purple Iguana, signaling to the hostess that they had a party of two.

"Table or booth."

He and Finley answered at the same time.

"Booth."

"Booth."

The woman led them to a spot toward the rear of the restaurant, where she waited until Finley and Whit had taken their seats before handing them menus.

"Your waitress is Trish. She'll be right with you."

"Thanks."

Whit reached across the table to take Finley's hand, satisfying his need to touch her by tracing her fingers one by one.

"So why the trip to Redmond?" Finley asked softly.

His brain was barely able to make sense of the words. He was too busy absorbing this remarkable moment.

He was here.

With Finley.

Alone.

But a part of him finally recognized that an answer was required.

"I got to thinking that, once everyone else in the Sinful Six has been notified, they're going to need a place to stay."

She nodded.

"Most of their folks have moved on."

"Or were never much help to begin with," Finley murmured with a grimace.

He dipped his head to acknowledge that his father would probably be at the head of that list.

"Anyway, I took a closer look at the guest houses. Some of them are in horrible shape, but…" he shrugged. "Well, half of them aren't too bad. I think with a few repairs, a good cleaning and new flooring, we could come up with enough places for everyone to stay."

"Oh. Wow." Her eyes sparkled in the dim light of the restaurant and the single flickering candle placed in the center of her table. "The Sinful Six. Together at last."

"I thought we could stop by the building supply place. I need dry wall, shingles, and one or two sheets of plywood." He hesitated before adding. "Working on the ranch will help me keep my mind off you when you're at the Busy B."

A pink bloom began at the base of her neck and spread up into her cheeks.

How long had it been since he'd made her blush?

At one time, it had been a favorite pastime of his.

"Are you sure you should go to all that expense? If we all decide to sell…"

"It will bring a higher price."

"Then you should let me pay half."

Whit shook his head. "I dropped by Grove's office and he showed me how to use the account Norm set up for maintenance of the property." In truth, Come Back Ranch would need a lot more cash than the monthly allotments, but there was no way that Whit was going to mention that to Finley. He had some savings put aside, and he wasn't about to let Finley dip into her precious college fund for any other reason than tuition.

"If you're sure."

He squeezed her hand. "Positive."

The waitress approached, setting a bowl of fresh salsa and a basket of chips between them.

"Have you decided what you'd like to order?"

Whit was about to tell the woman that they'd need more time, when he happened to look up and see a wizened, bow-legged figure crossing the street outside their window. For a moment, Whit paused, his eyes narrowing, his mind churning to come up with a reason why he looked so familiar...

Hell. It was Martin Griggs.

Whit slid from the seat. "I've got to make a quick call. I'll have the beef fajitas, with... whatever you usually serve. And a Pepsi."

For a moment, his gaze locked with Finley's and he saw her confusion—and worse, a flash of an emotion that looked very much like disappointment. As if she expected him to walk out the door and keep on going.

Damn. Why hadn't he returned to Larkspur to be with her before now?

Sidestepping the waitress, Whit bent to place a quick kiss on her lips. "I'll be right back. It's for work. It'll only take a minute."

But as he strode toward the door, he still couldn't shake the feeling that she didn't trust him to keep his promise.

Finley couldn't help thinking that something was wrong as she watched Whit dig his phone out of his pocket and head for the door. Then, to her utter astonishment, he dodged between a pair of parked cars and headed west down Wilderness Drive.

"Miss?"

At the waitress's prompting, she glanced at her menu, scrambling for a choice that sounded coherent.

"I'll have the enchiladas."

"Shrimp, chicken, shredded beef, or ground beef?"

"Ground beef."

"Rice and beans?"

"Sure."

"And what to drink?"

"A…a diet soda."

By the time the waitress had gathered up the menus and Finley could return her attention to the windows again, Whit had disappeared.

What on earth?

She told herself that he'd show up any minute—the man had ordered his lunch, for heaven's sake. It wasn't likely that he'd leave her here, in this restaurant, a dozen miles away from Larkspur without her own means of transportation.

But there was a part of her, that mean little petty part, that wondered if he'd left her all alone. Again.

Stop it!

She took a chip and dipped it into the salsa, making idle circles in the scarlet sauce. But she finally sighed and dropped it onto her plate, acknowledging that she'd lost her appetite the moment that Whit had jumped to his feet. He'd said that he'd needed to make a call—and she'd seen him take out his phone. But why on earth would he leave the building? And he hadn't merely left the building, he'd left the vicinity.

Had she done something wrong? Said something wrong?

Finley tried to beat down the doubts that crashed into her head like breaking waves. There was probably a logical explanation...

But it was hard to push aside nearly ten years of history. Ten years with Whit missing from her life. Nearly a decade of feeling like a part of her had shriveled up and died. At first, she'd been able to tell herself that her feelings were simply due to the accident and the way she was processing her emotions over Clint's condition.

Those lies had been enough, for a time.

Until Whit Patterson had shown up after years and years of silence. And in that moment, it had been as if every emotion she'd jammed deep into her soul had been unleashed. Guilt at the way they'd parted. Shame for betraying Clint. Anger at the way Whit had never contacted her.

And want.

She *wanted* this man. Not just physically, but mentally, spiritually. When he'd announced he'd planned to court her, she'd felt a part of her opening up, much like the flowers he'd given her.

But that need, that passion, that return to sentience, wasn't without its misgivings. She might have known the adolescent Whit as well as she knew herself, but that didn't mean that she knew the man who'd brought her here today.

Brought her and abandoned her.

Stop it! She didn't want to be one of those women, those clingy desperate women who couldn't trust a man outside of her sight.

Then again, it wasn't Whit that she didn't trust.

It was herself.

She'd never been the type of person that men gave a second glance. Sure, she'd managed to hook Clint for a time. But, deep down, she knew that if the accident hadn't occurred, he would have changed his mind about marrying her. With Clint, everything in life was a competition, and she'd often wondered if he'd asked her to marry him simply because he wanted to beat Whit to the punch. Not that Whit would have ever asked her to marry him. Except for that kiss, he'd spent most of his time avoiding her those last couple of years. It had hurt her feelings at the time. But now...

Now, she realized that he'd been trying to preserve a friendship—with her and with Clint. Maybe he'd known, deep down, that if he waited long enough, her relationship with Clint was bound to run its course, progressing quick and hot like a brush fire, before it petered away from a lack of fuel. Other than their friendship, they had no real shared interests, no common ground. Eventually, Clint would become restless and move on.

And Whit? Was he any different? She'd never seen him date anyone more than one or two times, so she didn't have any history for comparison. And even if she did, they weren't the same people they'd been all those years ago. Too much had happened.

Sighing, she reached for the water glass and took a quick gulp. But as soon as she set the goblet back on the table, she glanced out the window.

And there he was, striding toward her, still talking on his phone, his head down and shielded slightly by his hat. In that instant, relief surged through her veins, then awareness, then panic.

What was she doing playing with fire this way? The most she could hope for was a few stolen days...

But as she watched him end the call, put the phone back into his pocket, and reach for the door, she tamped her misgivings deep into her heart.

For too many years, she'd allowed events to dictate her actions. It was time to follow her heart. Sure, she was bound to get hurt. Eventually. But she was tired of playing it safe. And alone.

That, more than anything, was worth risking burnt fingers.

As Whit slid into the bench seat opposite Finley and tossed his hat onto the empty space, he knew he had some explaining to do. So far, he'd veered away from talking about his personal life. There'd been a part of him that hadn't wanted to remind her that he didn't belong in Larkspur anymore, and that he'd be leaving soon. Hell, if he hadn't received that call from Thayne, he probably would have been gone already.

But as he raked his fingers through his hair and met her gaze—one that was carefully schooled to be neutral and without censure—he knew that there was no sense pursuing a future with this woman if he weren't willing to share a portion of his past.

"Sorry about that," he hurriedly offered.

For a moment, her defenses fell and she looked at him with such guardedness that he realized, just as he'd feared, there was a part of her that had wondered if he'd meant to come back.

Unfortunately, the waitress chose that moment to arrive with their food. As she settled the steaming platters in front of them, then the cold drinks, Whit was powerless to allay Finley's worries. Instead, he watched as she pasted a smile on her lips. One that didn't reach her eyes.

"Be careful. These plates are really hot," their waitress offered as she arranged things. Then she straightened to ask, "Can you think of anything else you need?"

"No, thanks," Whit said hurriedly. Right now, satisfying the hunger he felt was nothing compared to his need to reassure Finley.

"Let me know if you change your mind," the woman said as she backed away.

Whit waited until the waitress had moved out of earshot. Then, he immediately reached for Finley's hand. His first clue that she'd been entirely rattled came when she dodged his touch and reached for the silverware wrapped in her napkin.

Not wanting to push her trust any farther than he'd earned it, Whit said, "Sorry about that. I only meant to go as far as the curb but…"

He waited until Finley finally looked up at him to say.

"I got a call from a coworker the other day about a semi-load of cattle taken from a ranch near Lake Tahoe."

That caused a faint line between her brows.

"I work for Nevada's Agricultural Enforcement Unit," he continued. "Some people call us the cattle cops."

"The cattle cops?" she repeated.

"Yeah, we're a small unit. There's only six of us in the whole state. We're tasked with tracking down agricultural crimes—stolen cattle or equipment—or helping with brand inspections, if necessary. Then, there are times when we stand in for law enforcement for drunk drivers or traffic accidents until the sheriff's department or other police officers can arrive. In any event, I was given information about a hundred head of stolen cattle that they think might have made its way into Wyoming for an auction coming up next week. I was asked to keep my eye out for the trailer."

Her eyes widened. "You're a cop?" she repeated with a healthy dose of disbelief.

"Agricultural Enforcement Officer."

"But you…what? Carry a gun and a badge?"

"Yeah." Her expression was so comical, he didn't know if he should be amused at her disbelief or a little insulted. "I've got a department vehicle with lights and sirens, but I've also got veterinary supplies should the need arise."

The tension eased from her body. She arranged her napkin on her lap, then grasped her utensils and began to eat. "So…you saw the trailer and stolen cows on the road out there?"

"No. But I happened to see a man called Martin Griggs. We've suspected he's been involved in several cattle rustling cases over the past year, but we haven't been able to prove it." Seeing that Finley now seemed more relaxed and at ease, he unrolled his own silverware and began loading his tortillas with meat. "I trailed him for a couple of blocks. He got into a pickup and headed out of town. I was able to get the tag numbers and call it in. Thayne will let the officials here in Wyoming know that Griggs is in the area."

"You couldn't…I don't know, tackle him?"

Whit grinned. "No. We might suspect him of illegal activities, but we don't have anything solid on him yet. Besides, Wyoming has its own agency that handles these kinds of crimes."

Finley stared at him for a moment, her mouth ajar. "So, cattle rustling is still a thing? I mean, I thought such crimes disappeared along with the Wild, Wild West."

"Hardly. These days, criminals use trucks and trailers instead of horses to round up the stolen cattle. A lot of herds are kept at seasonal pastures where there isn't much supervision, so it can be an easy matter to load a couple hundred head onto a semi trailer, then drive off before anyone is wiser."

"That's amazing." Her head tipped. "And you're the big, bad *hombre* who brings them to justice?"

Whit shook his head. "That's not the official job description, no."

"But it's the truth, isn't it?" She offered a quick laugh. "It's ironic, don't you think?"

Whit had taken a bite of his food, so he lifted his brows questioningly.

"The only member of the Sinful Six to run afoul of the law, and now you're a lawman. Imagine that."

By the time he'd chewed his food so that he could respond, Finley had turned her attention to her own meal, so he left the subject alone. Finley might joke that he'd once "run afoul of the law", but the euphemism hardly described the terror that Whit had felt when, days after the accident, he'd been accused of vehicular homicide and thrown in jail. Granted, the charges had later been dropped, but not until he'd spent several days behind bars. By that time, the court of opinion had found him guilty of the accident.

After that, Whit hadn't bothered to go back to Larkspur. He'd wanted to put the whole experience as far behind him as possible. He hadn't known then that he would never be rid of the deep-seated panic he would feel every time he saw a patrol car in his rearview mirror. But as he'd hopped from ranch job to ranch job—seeing firsthand how devastating agricultural crimes could be—he'd seen another side of law enforcement. Hell, if it weren't for his interactions with Thayne Ruff, he might still be running. But Thayne had taken him under his wing, let him go on a couple of ride alongs, and It hadn't taken long for Whit to be hooked.

"Do you like your job?" Finley asked, taking a sip of her soda.

"Yeah. I do. I spend a lot of time outdoors, and I work with a bunch of really great people. I love the investigatory work and the chance I have to care for animals. The job is different every day, so it never gets old."

For a moment, her gaze was tinged with envy, then a spark of regret. "I suppose you'll have to be getting back soon."

He knew what she was thinking. Why were they even considering a possible relationship if he'd have to head back to Nevada?

This time, when he reached across the table, she didn't dodge his hand.

"Right now, I'm where I need to be," he stated, hoping she would believe him.

She seemed to digest that comment, because she offered a sweeping caress with her thumb and offered, "I'm glad."

ELEVEN

inley was feeling marvelously sated as they left the restaurant. Once again, as soon as they reached the sidewalk, Whit looped his arm around her waist, and she did the same. This time, when she encountered the pistol at his back, she felt a little glow inside when she realized what the weapon meant.

Whit had done well for himself.

But hard on the heels of that thought came a niggling regret. He might have found his way in the world, but she'd stagnated. She was stuck in the same town, the same job, the same house. It was as if the accident had thrown her into a perpetual loop.

But what else could she have done? Her mother, Norm, Clint? They'd all needed her. Even Billie had required a steadying hand from time to time.

"Penny for your thoughts."

She realized, too late, that her worries must have transmitted themselves to Whit.

"They're not even worth a penny. I was thinking of how much you've accomplished since leaving Larkspur. But me...not much has changed."

She felt him looking at her, but refused to meet his eyes. Why couldn't she learn to keep her mouth shut? The last thing she needed was for Whit to think that she wanted his pity.

Instead of speaking, he pulled her off the sidewalk to a narrow strip of grass that grew between two of the shops. Then, he faced her, tipping her chin up.

"Is that what you think?"

She opened her mouth, but closed it again, not wanting to sound even more self-indulgent. She shrugged instead.

He crooked his finger, using it to tip her chin. "Then you don't see what I see."

His voice was smooth, deep, velvety.

"I see a woman who's grown immeasurably since I saw her last. The Finley I once knew was skittish and shy. Sure, you had a streak of adventure to you, otherwise you wouldn't have lasted a minute with the rest of the Sinful Six. If called upon, you could hold your own in an argument or a debate, but you'd rarely volunteer your opinions on your own. The Finley I see now..."

He slowly backed her toward the outer wall of the shop. Then, when she had nowhere else to go, he threaded her thighs with his and bent toward her. "This Finley is strong. Poised. Fiercely protective."

He spoke the words against the shell of her ear, causing gooseflesh to cascade down through her limbs in a domino fashion.

"This is a woman who knows what she wants and isn't afraid to go after it. But she's also loving, oh, so loving. She can't bear to see anyone in pain."

The words were uttered in a soft whisper, the warmth of them trailing from her ear, along the curve of her neck.

"This Finley has sacrificed her own desires to help those she loves."

He moved back up again and began tracing the line of her jaw, the brim of his hat shielding them in a false sense of privacy.

"But now...now it's time for her to pursue her own dreams. And you know what? She's strong enough to do anything she sets her mind to doing."

He hovered over her lips so that she could hear the words, feel them, taste them. "And she's going to set the world on fire. Just you wait and see."

She fought to drag air into her lungs—not only from the picture he painted, the way he *saw* her—but from the desire that rushed through her limbs.

Dear sweet heaven above, she wanted to believe him. She wanted to believe this was the way he saw her. Even more, she wanted to feel him against her, pressed so tightly to her flesh that she could absorb a portion of his own strength and determination.

As if he'd heard her, his lips finally closed over hers— not tender, sweet butterfly kisses. No, he devoured her, proving in that moment how much he wanted her.

She was glad of the support provided by the wall behind her as he planted his hands on either side of her head, then proceeded to ravish her mouth. Finley was far from a passive participant, returning thrust for thrust, foray for foray. When his hands slipped behind her to pull her hips tightly to his, she gasped at the evidence of his arousal, her own hands gripping at his waist, his back, before finally tunneling beneath his jacket and shirt to find bare, hot flesh. Like a blind woman, she explored the indentation of his spine, the flat planes of his shoulders, then moved to rub her thumbs across the well-defined obliques.

"You have no idea what you do to me," he whispered against her lips.

That comment caused her to smile and she ground a little tighter against his hips.

"I have an idea."

He moaned. "Don't do that."

"Why not?"

"Because I promised you that we'd take things a step at a time."

"We are taking things a step at a time."

He chuckled softly against her lips. "By whose definition?"

"Mine," she whispered, then drew him down for another kiss.

He allowed her to control the embrace for several long minutes before breaking away again.

"We've got to get out of here. This is too public, too—"

She blushed, realizing that she'd been reaching for the button to his jeans. Too late, she became aware of her surroundings and the fact that they were only a few feet away from a crowded sidewalk.

"Oh, crap."

Whit laughed, resting his forehead against hers. "Give me a second. Maybe a minute. Or two."

She took a deep breath to help control her own galloping heart. "We could be back at the ranch in twenty minutes."

"Don't tempt me. We're taking things slow, remember?"

"Are we?"

He groaned softly, closing his eyes. "This wasn't part of my plan to court you."

"Why not? I think it's working."

He cracked one eye open. "It is, huh?"

"Yeah."

His smile was pure vintage Whit.

"Then I may have to alter my plans."

"Oh, so you have actual plans?"

"It's always best to be prepared."

"Then what's next on your schedule?"

He pushed away from the wall and took her hand. But rather than heading back the way they'd come, he led her toward the rear parking areas and from there to his Bronco.

"First, we're going to go get the building supplies I need—before I totally forget them."

"And then?"

He lifted her hand to his lips. "Then, you'll have to wait and see."

Whit took her back to Larkspur for ice cream at the Dairy Dream. One cup, two scoops, two spoons. Then, he headed for the frontage road to the radio towers, drove up on the hill and parked the Bronco beneath a stand of aspens so that they could look down at the glittering lights.

"It looks pretty from up here, doesn't it?" Finley asked as he killed the engine.

The glance he cut her way was all-knowing and filled with empathy.

"You've had a hard time, haven't you?"

He reached to unlatch her seatbelt, then pulled her across the bench seat so that he could drape his arm around her shoulders.

She grimaced, handing him one of the spoons. "I shouldn't complain. Overall, everyone's been very kind and supportive."

"But…"

"But sometimes, I enter a room and everything goes silent, so I'm pretty sure they've been talking about me."

"And what on earth would they be saying? 'Oh, look. There's that super-awesome Finley Fitzpatrick who's spent nearly a decade helping a grieving father and a sick friend, all while supporting her alcoholic mother.'"

Finley opened her mouth to insist that Alice wasn't an alcoholic. But then, she realized, *this is Whit.* If anyone knew the blatant signs of alcoholism in a parent, it would be Whit.

"I doubt they were being that kind."

Whit set the bowl of ice cream on the dashboard, then drew her even closer. "You never know. I'd be the first to agree that living in a small town can be a blessing and a curse. There's something about a close-knit community that can make a person feel safe, but it's hard to keep anything a secret."

She grimaced, toying with the buttons of his shirt. "I'll say."

"But the people of Larkspur know you, Finley. If they're whispering, it's not in a judgmental way. It's…simple human curiosity. The people who love you know the truth, that you've been a comfort to those around you. As for anyone else…" His chest rumbled with a low laugh. "Let 'em talk. There's not much else to do in a town this small."

Finley gasped in mock affront, poking him in the side with her finger. But she'd forgotten that he could be ticklish and he jerked, laughing even harder and reaching for her own ticklish spots. By the time the two of them had called a truce and calmed down again, she found herself feeling curiously…lighter. Until now, she hadn't realized how touchy she'd become about wagging tongues. But Whit was right. The people she cared about knew that the mistakes of the past had begun from a moment of youthful ignorance. Neither she nor Whit had ever intended to hurt anyone. And there wasn't anything on earth they wouldn't have done if they could turn back the clock. Barring that, they simply had to make the best of the situation they found themselves in.

She tipped her head to look up at him.

"You're pretty smart, you know that?"

Even in the dark, she could see the tenderness radiating from his eyes. "Not as smart as you."

The words were like sweet, sweet honey being poured into her soul.

"Are you going to kiss me?" she whispered, her gaze dropping to his lips.

He shook his head from side to side. "No."

For a moment, she felt a brief pinch of hurt. Then, she realized that he was smiling.

"Why not?"

He bent to press his lips to her hair. "Because, if I start, I won't be able to stop."

She could hear the irregular tattoo of his heart beneath her ear.

"Would that be a bad thing?"

"Mmm. A very bad thing."

"Why?"

His hand splayed over her back, slid down, down to her waist, then moved up to her shoulders again, setting her skin ablaze with each stealthy pass.

"Because I promised you we'd take things one step at a time, remember?"

"What if I give you permission to break your promise?"

Again, she felt him press his lips to her hair, then, his hand lifted to tuck her even more firmly beneath his chin.

"Don't ask me to do that, Finley." The whisper was barely audible and fraught with his own brand of frustration and need. "I want to do things right—no, I *need* to do things the right. As a sort of…penance…for the ways I hurt you in the past."

Penance?

"And…*reverence.*"

Reverence?

Dear sweet heaven above, that single word had the ability to seep into every battered corner of her heart.

"It's my new beginning Finley. *You're* my new beginning."

And even though her body ached with her need for this man…

How could she argue with that?

"But that doesn't mean that I can't hold you tight."

His arms wrapped even more securely around her.

"Or that I can't feel your heart beating close to mine."

She shivered beneath the intensity of his voice. Idly, she wondered if his eyes were closed, because the low, rumbling tone seemed to reverberate with a deep concentration—as if he wanted to absorb each thought, each sensation, each moment.

And wasn't that a turn-on.

"When I hold you like this, I can feel each breath you take, the warmth of your skin. You're so slight and delicate in my arms, but oh, so right. I could hold you like this for a hundred years and never be satisfied."

His words licked through her system, and for the first time in her life, she felt...*beautiful*.

His head shifted, and she was sure that she could feel his lips against her.

"I want to burn this moment into my memory so that I can take it out again and relive it a thousand times. I want to remember the smell of your perfume—wildflowers and honeysuckle." He shifted to place one of his broad hands over hers. "And the delicate sweep of your hands." His voice grew lower, huskier. "And the way you get me so hot just saying my name."

She wanted to assure him that she felt the same rush of pleasure each time they were together, but she couldn't bring herself to speak. She didn't want to destroy this moment when Whit Patterson—a man who was normally guarded and stoic—made love to her with his words.

"I missed you so damned much, Finley." The confession was aching, hungry. "You'll never know how many times I thought of you."

"Then why didn't you come back?"

That was the million-dollar question. No matter what had happened between them or the far-reaching ramifications of the accident, she would never have turned him away.

She felt him sigh against her.

"Because I was a coward, plain and simple. After everything that had happened, I couldn't bear to see you look at me with...disgust or recrimination."

This time, she couldn't remain still. She drew back, framing his face with her hands.

"I would have never done that, Whit."

His lips twisted. "Maybe, maybe not. Back then, emotions were still raw and I was...an angry S.O.B.. I lashed out at those who were closest to me. I didn't want to *feel* anything. It took me a long time to get my head on straight."

Finley had to admit that she probably hadn't been much better, but unlike Whit, she'd chosen to bury herself in work and responsibility. If she were honest, she might not have been as receptive to Whit returning in those early years. She'd felt so...resentful. Abandoned.

"So, what changed? Why did you decide to come back now?"

Whit's eyes seemed to glow in the dim light.

"When Norm died, I suddenly realized that life didn't offer a whole lot of second chances. I should have returned to Larkspur at least once, to tell him how much he meant to me growing up. Hell, even if he'd slammed the door in my face, I wouldn't have been left with this gnawing regret that I hadn't ever told him that. And the more I got thinking about it, the more I realized that wouldn't be my only regret. I had to see you, one more time."

"Why?" The word was a mere puff of sound.

"For the last ten years, you've haunted me Finley. You're there when I'm tired or frustrated or lonely."

He rested his forehead against hers.

"You're there when I see the sun spill across the mountains or heat shimmer off the desert floor."

His lips were so close to hers now. So close.

"I finally realized that I couldn't live with myself if I didn't see you. One. More. Time."

Then he was kissing her, softly, reverently—as if he wanted to absorb the texture of her skin, the shape of her lips.

Finley shuddered beneath the gentle exploration, her body seeing to fill with warmth and light. No man had ever made her feel this way—adored, worshiped. Leaning into his embrace, she opened her lips to his tongue, wishing that she had his ability to put her emotions into words. He needed to know that his arrival had been a reawakening for her. Until seeing him again, she'd gone through the motions of being alive, but in reality, she'd locked her emotions away. Better to feel nothing than to feel pain, sorrow...

Joy.

Passion.

But in that moment when she'd answered the door and found Whit on the front stoop of the Campanella's home, all those defenses had crumbled away to dust, leaving her raw and exposed and...hungry.

For him.

For his touch.

For the poetry of his words.

Finley couldn't restrain herself any longer. Still kissing Whit, she wrapped her arms around his neck, shifted to her knees, then straddled him.

Whit gasped beneath her, and she felt his broad palms at her waist and knew he meant to draw back. But she didn't give him a chance. Instead, she deepened their kiss—her tongue tangling with his, nipping, caressing—until his resistance vanished and he tunneled his hands through her hair.

He drew back only briefly to rasp, "You're killing me, Finley."

She smiled. "But what a way to go."

Then, there was no need to think as she settled more firmly in his lap and pressed herself tightly to his chest. Her breasts ached, her nipples straining against the lace of her bra. Vaguely, she could feel the hard plane of Whit's body rubbing against her—and the friction of clothing merely added to her arousal. But there was too much fabric between them.

Moaning slightly, she pushed at the edges of his jacket. "Take this off."

Whit released her only long enough to struggle free—just as she wrestled out of her own coat. The night air offered a welcome chill to her heated flesh—and vaguely, she noted that the windows were already beginning to steam over.

Acting purely on instinct, she reached for the hem to her shirt and swept it over her head.

"Finley, my Finley," Whit rasped.

Too late, she realized that Clint's engagement ring hung on a chain around her neck. But Whit didn't seem to notice. His eyes were on the delicate lace covering her breasts.

For a moment, Finley felt a shiver of uncertainty. She could never be accused of being "well-endowed". If there was one thing about her body which a man could find disappointing, it would definitely be her chest.

But just as she'd begun to rethink her impulsive action, she caught sight of Whit's expression—and it was not one of disappointment. Instead, he reached to cover one of her breasts with his hand.

"You've been wearing *that* under your clothes all day?"

And in that instant, he allayed all her fears. His eyes were glued to the red brassiere she wore and the sheer sweep of lace that only seemed to emphasize the pink of her nipples.

"Do you like it?"

Where had that *comment come from?*

"Oh, yeah. I like it a lot."

She leaned forward to whisper in his ear, "And the panties match."

Whit groaned and dragged her back into his arms. When his mouth covered hers, there was nothing restrained or reverent about his kiss. This was a plundering, powerful exploration, while his hands...

One hand remained at her breast, a thumb raking deliciously across her nipple, while the other pulled her so tightly against him that she couldn't ignore the ridge of his erection.

She lifted herself slightly to arch against him, reveling in the storm of heat and sensation that centered into her core. If she could only—

The sudden whoop of a siren cut through the haze of their passion. Almost immediately, it was followed by a tinny command issued through a speaker system.

"Move along! This is private property."

The order was followed by the brief flash of red and blue lights.

"Shit," Whit muttered. "I believe we've been busted by the sheriff, just like a couple of teenagers."

Finley scrambled for her shirt, then hunkered low in the passenger side footwell where she awkwardly tried to get her arms through the sleeves. But where she was clearly freaked out, Whit seemed more at ease with the situation—probably because he had his own badge and gun to wave around.

He shifted to start the Bronco and flashed his lights—and as if that were some secret code, the sheriff's car pulled past them, made a wide U-turn, and headed back down the hill again.

As soon as the cruiser's taillights disappeared, Whit regarded Finley with amusement.

"You okay?"

She opened her mouth, couldn't think of a reply and exhaled instead. Finally, she muttered, "No."

"Are you going to stay on the floor?"

Finley hesitated, then offered truthfully, "Maybe."

Whit chuckled and reached to help her onto the seat.

"Relax, Finley. We've got the windows so steamy, he couldn't see anything."

She wasn't so sure about that. It was one thing to bare herself to Whit, but to anyone else…

"You have your shirt on backwards *and* inside out."

She offered a very unladylike curse and fumbled to correct the mistake. But the fact that Whit decided to help her—laughing the whole time—didn't help.

Finally, he dragged her back to his side, wrapping his arm around her. But Finley couldn't relax. She kept watching for a pair of headlights to return. Whit put the Bronco in gear and backed up. Before shifting again, he leaned down to kiss her on top of the head.

"At least the man had good timing."

Finley shot him a horrified glance. "How?"

"He caught us at second base." Whit leaned closer to whisper, "And I was just about to make a move to steal home."

TWELVE

*I*t was a little after nine that night when Finley let herself into her mother's house. True to form, Alice was passed out in the recliner. In her hand, she held a highball glass, and on the table beside her was a nearly-empty bottle of Jim Beam.

Finley grimaced. It was time to confront her mother about her drinking again. But tonight…

Tonight, she had no desire to tangle with Alice's protestations that she was a "social drinker, nothing more." Nor did Finley want to suffer through an escalation of accusations that would lead to hysterical sobbing, which would then circle back to self-pity and her insistence that neither of her daughters had ever loved her properly. If they had, she wouldn't have to drink to forget her sorrows.

Screw that.

Finley looped her jacket over the coat tree and toed out of her shoes. Then she padded into the kitchen where she found a Mason jar under the sink. Normally, she might mourn the fact that she didn't have a proper vase for the flowers that Whit had given her. But tonight, the vintage jar seemed the perfect foil for the delicate blossoms.

She flipped on the light over the sink, then rooted through the junk drawer until she found a pair of scissors so that could trim the stems to the proper size.

"You know what's being said about you around town, don't you?"

Finley jumped, nearly coming out of her skin.

Had Sheriff Tucker known it was she and Whit in the Bronco? Had the rumors already spread?

Whirling, she found Billie standing in the doorway, her arms akimbo, looking every inch the disapproving parent ready to scold a teenager who'd missed curfew. But this time, even her sister's disapproving tone couldn't dampen her mood.

"Hello to you too, Billie."

"Do you have any idea what time it is?"

"Six minutes past nine. I would have stayed out longer, but I have the morning shift at the diner again tomorrow."

Billie's eyes narrowed when Finley refused to act cowed.

"And you've been with *him* the whole time, I suppose."

"With Whit? Yes. We went to Redmond."

Finley didn't bother to say why. She hadn't yet told her family about her inheritance, and she didn't plan on telling them until absolutely necessary. For now, it was her secret. Hers and Whit's. All too soon, the rest of the Sinful Six would start their pilgrimage back to Larkspur and she would have to say something. But not yet.

Billie seemed to lose all of her ire at once. She exhaled, her body appearing to fold in upon itself. Idly, Finley wondered if her sister were feeling ill. She looked...small. And vulnerable.

Billie planted herself on one of the bar stools and leaned her elbows on the Formica. She hadn't changed for bed yet. Instead, she was dressed in her usual "after work uniform", a pair of yoga pants and a camisole. But rather than looking comfortable, her sister looked like she'd spent most of the day boxing a kangaroo.

"Rough night?" Finley asked.

"Rough day. That temp agency has it in for me, I swear. I spent eight hours with thirty-one five-year-olds in Mrs. Rodenberry's all-day kindergarten class."

"Thirty-one!"

"According to the principal, there's a population bubble, whatever the hell that means."

Billie gripped her temples and Finley felt a twinge of concern. Maybe her sister was coming down with a bug.

"Headache?"

"Of the *massive* variety."

Finley finished trimming the stems and reached overhead for a glass. She filled it with water, then retrieved a couple of aspirin from the medicine cupboard.

"Here."

"Thanks." Her sister threw the pills to the back of her throat, swallowed several gulps of water, then shuddered, muttering, "Those kindergarten teachers are fucking saints."

Finley stifled a giggle, but a hint of her amusement must have shown because Billie stabbed the air with a finger. "Yuck it up all you want, but I'm not kidding about all the talk going around town. I had at least three people stop me at that school to see if the rumors were true."

At that, Finley stiffened. "Rumors."

Please, please, don't say that everyone knew she and Whit had been making out on the hill.

"That you and Whit are dating." She speared Finley with a gaze that could have stripped paint from the walls. "It isn't true, is it? You wouldn't be that stupid. Again."

When Finley didn't answer, Billie closed her eyes again, her face twisting in disbelief. "Geez, Finley, don't you ever learn?"

Finley tucked the last of the blossoms into the make-shift vase before turning to face her sister. "I don't really see why my social life is anyone's business but my own."

"Have you slept with him?"

"No!"

"But you're thinking about it, aren't you?"

Finley's mouth worked for a moment as she tried to formulate a response.

"Finley! Have you lost your mind?"

"Like I said, my love life—or lack thereof—is my business. And you, and everyone else in Larkspur, can keep your noses out of it."

"Can you really be that naïve? Look what happened the last time you got involved with Whit Patterson."

Finley's hands slammed down on the counter, making her sister jump. "Damnit! I'm tired of people throwing that moment in my face over and over again. We kissed. We were a couple of dumb kids and we kissed!"

"And your fiancé caught you."

"He wasn't my fiancé!"

Billie's eyes narrowed. "How can you say that? It's been ten years and you still wear his blasted ring around your neck!"

Finley's hand shot to the chain tucked beneath her shirt. The heavy weight of the diamond and platinum ring lay nestled between her breasts.

"I wear it because I don't know what else to do with it," she said wearily. "If I left it around the house, Mom would pawn it for her next get-rich-quick scheme."

"You wear it because you were going to marry the man."

"No. I wasn't."

"How can you say such a thing?"

"Because it's true!" Finley's hands fisted in aggravation. "He asked me, okay? He talked me into wearing his ring. But I never said I'd marry him. I didn't even want to wear the diamond. I told Clint I needed time to think things over, and he agreed. But only if I promised...I promised to..."

"Walk around town with an engagement ring on your finger, giving everyone in town the impression that you'd be married by the end of the year."

"I can't be held responsible for what the town assumed."

"And Norm. Norm thought the same thing."

Finley huffed in frustration. "After the accident, Clint was so...badly hurt." Her throat tightened, nearly choking on the words. "Norm thought that if I could be there, in the ICU, that Clint would...respond somehow. But the trauma center wouldn't let anyone but family into his room. So, when Norm introduced me as Clint's fiancé..."

Billie shook her head in disbelief. "You didn't bother to correct him."

"What was I supposed to do? I might not have agreed to marry Clint, but I'd...I'd told him I would consider it and..."

"You, selfish bitch."

Finley reared back at the venom in her sister's tone. "I did it for Norm!"

"You did it for you! You were too much of a coward to tell Clint the truth when he asked you in the first place."

"What truth? I was confused...and...and..."

"And you didn't have the guts to tell Clint that you weren't head-over-heels ready to commit to him. You know Clint. The man was confidence personified. It wouldn't occur to him that you had any doubts. That kiss you shared with Whit blindsided him."

Finley's eyes flooded with tears and the anger rushed away, bringing with it the same familiar despair.

Billie was right. This whole...*mess* could have been prevented if she'd been honest. With Clint. And herself. Instead, she'd shied away from the intensity of her emotions toward Whit, telling herself that her secret...*obsession* wouldn't last. Couldn't last.

So where did that leave her now? Chasing this unlikely dream with Whit?

Or continuing to manage the responsibilities she'd been carrying for years?

As Whit passed through the reception area of the Greensprings Convalescent Home, Sharla looked up from her post with a familiar smile.

"Mr. Patterson, how nice to see you again."

"I know it's late, but—"

"No, no. Go on through." Her smile widened even more. "We've got good news to share. Clint has been taken off the respirator. He seems to be much more comfortable. You'll find him sitting up. And he has a visitor."

Whit felt himself stiffen. It couldn't be Finley, he'd barely dropped her off—and the last thing he wanted was to encounter anyone from town.

"Actually, it's a good thing you came in tonight. Mr. Beaumont in Administration discovered that one of the papers he gave you yesterday was incomplete and he needs one more signature. I'll bring it to you as soon as I've finished my charts."

Hell.

That meant he couldn't just turn on his heel and leave.

He managed to mutter, "Thanks, Sharla." Then, with a purposeful stride that he didn't feel, he took the familiar path to Clint's room.

This late at night, the halls were quiet, the lights dim. Occasionally, he passed open doors where he was offered peeks into other people's lives—a family visiting an elderly woman, an old man sleeping slack-jawed, a wizened figure bent over a puzzle. But Clint's door was shut.

For a moment, he hesitated. Coward that he was, if he hadn't known that Sharla could appear at any moment, he probably would have continued out the back door.

Shit.

Was this what Finley had endured all these years, the uncertainty of every encounter with a person from town? Whit could hold his own in his job. There wasn't much that could make him hesitate. But this…

Hell.

He tapped on the door with his knuckle before he could change his mind, then resolutely pushed it open.

As his gaze scanned the room, he felt a moment of confusion, a leap of joy, then dread, then incomprehension, as the figure on the bed turned to look at him.

Look. At. Him.

For a second, the thought that Clint had miraculously recovered jolted through his body. Then, he realized that the eyes, the face, the body, were wrong.

His gaze leapt to the recliner, to the familiar form, the dark hair, the blue eyes that were half-lidded and aimed in the general vicinity of the television and the bright green of a soccer field, then back to the person on the bed.

"Whit?"

The figure uncrossed his legs and sat up. His dark eyes narrowed in the same moment that recognition thundered through Whit's veins.

Javi.

Javier Bartolomé.

The oxygen suddenly seemed to suck out of the room and Whit remembered the last time he'd seen his old friend. Javier had been seriously injured in the accident—concussion, cracked ribs, crushed hip. When Whit had tried to visit him in the hospital, Javier had shouted for him to leave.

Javi stood, his hands loose at his sides. But the casualness of his posture was deceptive. Whit recognized the erect posture of a fellow law officer, the innate awareness of the room and everything in it.

This was what Whit had been dreading the most, reuniting with members of the Sinful Six. With Finley, he'd known, deep down, that she had a good heart. Despite everything the past might pit against them, he'd known that she wouldn't turn him away.

Javi was a different story.

Javi had always been impatient, fiery, fiercely loyal. He'd been quick to anger and quick to defend. For those reasons alone, Whit braced for what might come next.

But when Javi rushed toward him, it wasn't with fists raised. Instead, he slugged him lightly in the shoulder, universal bro-code for a fond hello.

"You ol' dog! I didn't think you'd stay in town!"

Then, miracle of miracles, he held his arms wide and Whit found himself crushed in a powerful hug with Javi's broad hands pounding him on the back.

The greeting nearly squeezed the air from Whit's lungs, but it didn't matter. In that moment, he knew that all was forgiven.

When he stepped back, Javi's gaze raked over Whit's form. "You're looking good! You need wardrobe tips, as usual, but you're doing all right."

That made Whit laugh. Javi, as usual, was dressed in latest GQ fashion, dark turtleneck, dark jacket, dark trousers, with shiny rat-stabber shoes. His hair had been combed away from the sharp angles of his face and lacquered in place with some kind of manly hair-care crap.

"And you're bordering on the edge of sissy."

Javier laughed at that—probably because he knew there was nothing sissy about him. The man was ripped and carried himself with the innate assurance of a man accustomed to taking down the worst that society had to offer.

"How's S.W.A.T?" Whit asked as he moved into the room. He shrugged out of his jacket and tossed it and his hat onto the couch.

"Can't complain." Javi settled onto the bed again, fiddling with the adjustable mattress controls until he'd found the sweet spot for comfort.

"Hey, Clint," Whit said, squatting down to be at eye level for Clint should he care to turn his head. "You're lookin' stylin' without all the extra tubing." Whit took his friend's wrist, lifted his arm, and offered him a high-five—or the closest thing the two of them could manage. Then he settled Clint's arm in his lap again and repositioned the quilt draped over his lap.

"You don't think he's cold, do you?"

One of Javi's brows rose at Whit's fussing, but a glint of approval entered his eyes.

"Does his face feel cold?"

Whit touched Clint's forehead with the back of his hand, then his cheek.

"I don't think so."

Clint's fingers seemed to twitch, beneath the blanket. Even though Whit knew the reaction was probably involuntary, he moved Clint's hands so they lay on top of the blanket.

"Then I think he's okay. We've been sitting here, enjoying pizza and the game."

Whit settled back onto the couch, his gaze darted to the television high on the wall.

"Shit, what are you doing making him watch soccer?"

"Hey, the place has cable. This is an International League."

"Yeah, but Clint hates soccer, man. You know that." Before Javier could react, Whit snatched the remote from the edge of the bed and began flipping through the channels until he found a college football game. "You're going to set back his recovery another ten years if you keep that up."

There was a brief awkward silence as Javier met his gaze. The man didn't have to speak for Whit to know that Javi was wondering if Whit really believed his own words.

Whit resolutely held his gaze—conveying wordlessly that he knew the reality of the situation. Even so, he couldn't help the flare of defiance that settled in his chest. Clint was his responsibility now. If there was even a shred of a possibility that he could hear them, Whit refused to discuss the grim nature of his prognosis in Clint's presence.

To his surprise, Javi's expression slid into something akin to approval. Then he gestured to a box on the overbed table.

"Help yourself to a slice of pizza and let's catch up on old times."

Whit had just become aware of the aroma permeating the room—garlic, sausage, onions.

"Is that from Tony's?"

"Hell, yeah. Best pizza on the planet. I can't go through town without picking up a couple and taking them home."

Whit reached for a slice, grimacing.

"Anchovies? Seriously?"

Javi grinned, his teeth flashing white against his skin. "A guy's gotta have his protein."

Whit took a napkin, good-naturedly picking them off. "Do you hear that, Clint? The man still knows how to ruin good food."

Javi reached for his own piece. "I didn't think I'd catch you in town. I thought you'd be in and out once the funeral was over."

Had it only been a few days? With everything that happened, it seemed like so much longer to Whit.

"I decided to cash in my vacation time."

Javi swallowed his food, his brow creasing. "It wouldn't have anything to do with a lawyer named Grove, would it?"

"Partly. I take it he finally got in touch with you."

"I'm supposed to meet with him in the morning."

Whit nodded. "Finley and I talked to him as well. He's slowly tracking down the rest of the Sinful Six."

"What the hell is going on? Anything serious?"

"Depends on how you take it, I suppose."

"Come on, bro. You've got to give me a hint of what I'm up against."

As the familiar cadence of Javi's voice washed over him, Whit found himself sinking into the couch. Muscles that he hadn't realized had been held tightly in check began to ease. "I can give you the highlights, if you want."

Javi had taken a bite of food, so he nodded and lifted a hand to beckon with his fingers in that "give-it-to-me-straight" kind of way he had.

"Norm gave all of us, the Sinful Six, the Come Back Ranch."

The shock that settled over Javi's face was priceless. He coughed, hurriedly chewed and swallowed his food, then rasped, "Come again."

"Norm gave us the ranch. I'll let Grove give you all the details and stipulations, but it's up to us to decide what to do with the place."

Javi threw his half-eaten slice of pizza onto a plate and wiped his hands with a napkin. For a moment, his eyes softened as he seemed to focus on his thoughts—or maybe his memories?

"Who else knows about this?"

Whit shrugged. "Last time I saw Grove, he mentioned that he'd been able to do a conference call with P.J., but still hasn't found Liam."

Javi grimaced. "Yeah, he's fallen off the grid. The cell number I have isn't working and the last I heard, he was backpacking in Alaska."

"Backpacking? Liam?" Liam had always been bookish. A self-proclaimed nerd. In the past, he'd grumbled whenever the Sinful Six spent time in the mountains.

Javi shook his head. "I flew out to see him while he was in the hospital after the incident at Berkley—geez, it was a little over a year and a half ago. He'd been shot three times, point blank. I stayed with him for a couple of days until his parents could get there. I doubt he even knew I was there."

Whit shook his head in disbelief.

Why hadn't he known about any of this?

But the moment the thought entered his head, Whit knew. He'd cut himself off from the Sinful Six. Much like Liam, he'd changed his phone number and moved to parts unknown. About the time the shooting had occurred, he would have been working on the Double T Ranch and taking a butt-load of credits at a local community college so that he could finish up his degree and pursue his interest in agricultural law enforcement. He hadn't been too aware of local events, let alone a mass shooting reported on the national news. And he certainly hadn't thought that the victims included a dear friend.

"Did he...uh..." Whit cleared his throat when it emerged rough and ragged. "Did he make a full recovery?"

"From what I've been able to gather. I know they removed his spleen, and he went through several surgeries to repair a shattered femur. Last I heard, he'd also lost an eye."

"Shit."

"That was due to infection. He was hit by bullet fragments. They tried their damnedest to save it."

No wonder the man had decided to take a vacation from life. With all the surgeries and rehab, he'd probably had his fill of being told what to do.

But backpacking?

That had to be a mistake.

Javier exhaled in a gust, scrubbing his eyes with the palms of his hands. "Hey, listen…I'd love to stay and got caught up with everything that you've been doing, but I've been on the road since early this morning and I've got my K-9 in the truck. I don't want him to get too cold. I'm going to go crash at my mom's house."

"You're welcome to come to the ranch."

Javier rolled to his feet. "I'd love to, man, but Ma would skin me alive if I didn't spend at least my first night at home. If you're free, I'll head up to the ranch as soon as I've finished my meeting with Grove. I'd love to see the place again."

"I'll look forward to it."

Whit's throat grew inexplicably tight as Javi shrugged into his jacket, then offered a carefree, "Good to see you, man!" before he headed out the door.

The room settled into companionable silence with only the distant sound of the football game as accompaniment. For a few moments, Whit grappled with the fact that what should have been an awkward reunion at best…hadn't been awkward at all.

"Imagine that," Whit murmured. "If you would have asked me yesterday, I would have told you that my first meeting with Javi would have involved punches being thrown—or at least one of his famous stony stares."

He automatically glanced at Clint, seeking his own reaction. But Clint's eyes were on the television. For all intents and purposes, he seemed to be studying the latest offensive play.

Whit grunted in satisfaction. "I did the right thing by telling him to turn off the damned soccer game, didn't I? Obviously, Javi forgot the way you used to grouse about having to watch soccer for two hours before any of the athletes could manage to score. While football..." Whit grinned, squeezing Clint's shoulder. "Well, that was as much a religion to you as a pastime."

Whit pushed his own unsettled emotions aside and reached to fix a corner of the quilt which had begun inching its way off Clint's lap. Tomorrow would be soon enough to sift through his own chaotic thoughts—about the remains of his old car, his reunion with Javier, and how Whit intended to handle his promise to see to Clint's needs. So far, nothing about coming to Larkspur had gone as anticipated.

He resolutely turned his attention to the college game and the man seated nearby. He still had time to kill and Clint had spent most of the day alone. He may as well stick around and watch the game. There wasn't a television at the ranch. Besides, Sharla would be bringing him yet another form.

"Looks like Wyoming is up seven points. The Cowboys have got new recruits on the defensive line, and that seems to be helping."

He glanced at Clint and could have sworn his friend's eyes were tracking the movement on the screen.

"Even better, Javi left the pizza." Whit reached for the box and began picking off anything that even *looked* like an anchovy. "You'd better speak up if you want some, buddy, 'cause I'm hungry and this is the best pizza I've tasted in years."

He held a slice under Clint's nose, waiting until he was sure that Clint had inhaled the aroma.

Nothing.

Whit refused to let that dampen his mood.

"Let me know if you change your mind. You know Tony's. Best in the West."

Then he leaned back, stretched out his legs, and began a long-running monologue of the action on the screen.

THIRTEEN

*E*arly morning sunlight had gilded the aspen trees as Finley topped the rise leading to Come Back Ranch. Slowing her car, she wondered if she'd been a little too brazen to come to the valley so early without a warning. The clock on her dashboard read 7:45, and for all she knew, Whit was a late sleeper. She probably should have waited an hour or two. Or called first. But when she'd had an unexpected change to her schedule at the diner, she'd decided to surprise Whit and come help him with the repairs.

Uh huh. Right.

If she were honest with herself, her visit had little to do with the state of the guest bungalows and everything to do with Whit himself. Try as she might, she couldn't seem to shake the memories of straddling him, kissing him. Her dreams throughout the night had alternated between purely carnal delights and sheer terror when shadowy policemen seemed to pursue them both. She'd awakened so rattled…and so infinitely aroused…that she'd known she would have to see Whit again—*soon*. So, when another waitress had needed to switch shifts, Finley had been more than willing to go along.

As she began winding down into the valley, she could see a tall figure striding from the barn to the house.

Whit.

A flurry of butterflies seemed to settle in her chest—and she inwardly chided herself for behaving like a silly school girl. But the moment that thought appeared, she pushed it aside.

Why not? Why not indulge herself in the breathless excitement of a new romance? Heaven only knew she hadn't had many such opportunities in her life. And this was Whit Patterson. One of her oldest friends and a man for whom she'd held a secret attraction for years.

Even though she'd chosen Clint.

No. She wouldn't think about that now. She wouldn't think about the way her sister had all but accused her of cheating—or worse, abandoning Clint when he couldn't put up a fight.

It couldn't be wrong, could it? To move on? Even if it was with Whit, Clint's best friend?

She'd tried hard to be supportive in the last ten years. She'd stayed by Clint's side, hoping, praying that he would recover. She'd done everything that the doctors had suggested—talking to him, reading to him, filling their time together with sound and color. But nothing had changed. Nothing *would* change. And if she didn't allow herself to move on, nothing would ever change for her either.

Refusing to let her own thoughts ruin this time with Whit, she resolutely pushed her misgivings aside, and concentrated on the man himself. He must have seen her car because he altered his course. She watched as a smile spread over his features—a full-fledged, down to the bone smile.

That grin transformed his features in a way that took her breath away. She'd grown so used to seeing Whit school his emotions. After the accident, he'd grown stoic, even grim. Careful.

But this…this was a display of pure emotion.

For her.

For *her.*

She quickly pulled up next to the main office and parked. By the time she'd cut the engine, Whit was opening her door.

"Hey."

It was a simple greeting—one word, and so Whit-like. But that single syllable held such a wealth of emotion— pleasure, surprise, and a silky note of awareness—that she felt girlish shivers race to her extremities.

He barely waited for her to unfasten her seatbelt before he was reaching for her, drawing her to him, his head dipping for a long, slow kiss.

Sensation slammed into her body, chasing away any girlish notions of romance beneath a tidal wave of womanly pleasure. She lifted on tiptoes to deepen the embrace, her arms wrapping around his neck, her mouth opening to the forays of his tongue.

She'd never known that she could feel like this—hot and cold, desperate and needy. Sure, Clint had known how to kiss. But Whit…

Whit had a way of making her forget herself and her surroundings so that she could drown in the sensation of his touch, his exploration, his utter devotion. She could only pray that she was offering him a small portion of those emotions in return.

He lifted his head, slowly, reluctantly.

"I thought you had work this morning."

"One of the other waitresses needed to switch shifts."

"You should have told me. I could have met you."

She shook her head. "I thought I'd come here and help with the repairs."

"Wouldn't you rather stay in town and—"

She lifted on tiptoe to interrupt him with a kiss. "I'd really like to help."

Then after she'd helped...maybe there could be more of this.

Her offer seemed to garner his approval, because he smiled again—a smile that made her toes curl and her pulse flutter.

"Okay, then. Let's get started."

He led her to the first of the bungalows—The Kodiak—showing her that he'd already pulled out the carpet and padding, and repaired one of the interior walls with new drywall.

"There was a leak in a pipe toward the ceiling and another one further on in the sink itself. I finished fixing the one inside the wall, but I'm still working on the one in the bathroom."

Finley took a good look at her surroundings—seeing why Whit had suggested fixing up the units rather than leaving them as they were. As he'd told her once before, the "bones" of the bungalow were in good shape. Other than the leaks, there wasn't much that a good scrubbing and a coat of paint couldn't fix.

"Do you have a broom? Or cleaning supplies?"

"In the kitchen. If you don't see what you need, add it to the list on the fridge."

"I'll be right back."

By the time she returned, Whit was at the far side of the room, lying on his back with his head beneath the vanity.

The sight shouldn't have been a turn-on, but it was. Whit had stretched out, making her aware of how long and lean he was. His arms bulged as he wrestled with a wrench, and the tails of a plaid, button-down shirt rode up high to reveal the firm contours of his abdomen and the faint trail of hair that led from his navel to the waistband of his jeans.

For several seconds, she allowed herself to drink in the sight, wishing that she had the courage to approach him, kneel beside him and—

"Did you find what you needed?"

"Y-Yes. Thanks."

Get your mind on the job at hand, Finley.

But even as she began attacking the room with a cloth and spray cleaner, she couldn't entirely beat down her awareness of the man mere yards away. She was conscious of the creak of his tools, the way he bent one leg to help him angle closer, the soft curse when the wrench slipped.

As she turned to clean the multi-paned window, Finley realized that she hadn't had much contact with men in general since the Sinful Six had scattered. Sure, she'd had Norm— and Clint. But she wasn't accustomed to having a virile male nearby, especially one immersed in such a manly-man activity as household renovations.

"Finley, can you try the tap for me?"

She started slightly, wondering if he'd caught her staring again, but Whit's attention seemed riveted to the pipes.

"Sure."

She twisted the tap, heard an odd hissing noise and another muttered curse.

"Off! Turn it off!"

She bent to peer under the counter, suppressing a grin when she realized that Whit's face and the upper part of his shirt were completely soaked.

"Do you want a towel?"

"Not yet. I think I've got it."

He made another adjustment, then said, "Try the tap again."

She twisted it more slowly this time. Other than the gurgle of the tap, there were no other noises.

Whit offered a grunt of satisfaction.

"Everything good?" she asked.

"Yeah."

He shimmied from beneath the vanity, then rolled to his feet in one smooth motion.

"Want that towel now?"

He nodded and she fetched a dishtowel from the pile of cleaning supplies.

Now that he was standing, she couldn't help giggling when she saw him shaking his head like a dog. His hair was plastered against his skull and his shirt clung to his shoulders and chest.

But rather than giving him the cloth, she wiped the broad plane of his forehead, moved down the blade of his nose, his cheekbones, his jaw.

For a moment, the air around them seemed to shimmer with an electric energy. Meeting his gaze—that deep green gaze—she stepped closer, allowing the dishcloth to trail down his throat, linger at his Adam's apple, then move down, down to his chest.

"You're going to get cold in that wet shirt."

"Not if you keep doing that." His voice was low, gravelly, thick as molasses.

"You probably should change."

But he didn't move, and neither did she. Instead, she took his hand and closed his fingers around the towel. Then she reached for the buttons of his shirt.

"You wouldn't want to catch your death."

He made a sound, half-grunt, half-agreement.

The button slid free and she moved to the next one, then the next, and the next.

With each inch of progress, a heat built in her own body, moving lower and lower, until everything about her that was human and feminine seemed to blossom and grow heavy with arousal.

When she reached the last button, Whit's fingers snapped around her wrist.

"Finley…" It was a half-hearted warning to stop.

"Please. I want to look at you."

She watched as a ruddiness seeped into his cheeks and she wondered if she'd managed to make the unflappable Whit Patterson blush. Surely, he must know how beautiful he was. There must have been women who flocked toward him, attracted to his height, his strength, his masculinity…

Finley released the last button and spread his shirt wide. For long moments, she drank in the sight of him—the near-delicate wings of his collar bones, the flat curves of his pectorals, the ridges of his abdomen. Idly, she wondered if he worked out, or if he merely worked hard. This wasn't the bulkiness of a body builder. This was the lean, whipcord frame of a greyhound.

Without conscious thought, her hands lifted to push the shirt from his shoulders, revealing rounded biceps and taut forearms with a ribbon of vein-work pushing against the skin.

She could see evidence of his job in the unevenness of his tan. Although he'd clearly spent time with his shirt off, there were sharper demarcation lines at his neck and his wrists.

He stood that way, bare before her. And even though she'd seen plenty of men stripped to the waist, this time, it was different. There was an intimacy to the way he allowed her to look her fill, a shimmering heat that radiated from his body to hers and back again. There was no doubt between them that this exercise had begun due to her own curiosity. No. This was a prelude to something more—whatever that "more" might be. This was Finley stretching beyond herself, becoming comfortable with her attraction to Whit and testing her sensual wings.

She pressed her fingertips to his sternum—only her fingertips—concentrating on the warmth of his skin, the tensile strength of muscle, the faint bump of his heart. She explored the faint patch of hair that grew there, finding it soft, crisp. Buried beneath his faint tan, she found the evidence of scars—most likely from the accident. Finley trailed one of them to his side where she found a large mottled bruise that wrapped around his ribs.

"What happened?" she murmured.

"Loose bull. We wanted him to get in a trailer so he could be returned to his owner. The bull had different ideas. He pinned me against an iron gate."

Finley bent to press a soft kiss to the afflicted area. He flinched beneath her ministrations—not in pain, but in awareness, and she smiled against his skin. She'd never had anyone react so immediately to her touch. This close to him, she could see that his skin was pebbled in gooseflesh, providing a phantom trail of her exploration—which made her even more hungry to investigate.

Her fingers whispered down the length of his torso, circled his navel, before tracing the ridges of his abdomen. But when she reached the barrier of his jeans, something within Whit snapped and he hauled her into his arms, one palm tunneling through her hair, the other holding her tightly against his hips. Bending, he pressed his lips to the shell of her ear whispering, "Do you have any idea what you do to me?"

A soft laugh slipped from her throat and she rubbed more firmly against his hips and the ridge that pressed into her belly.

"I have an idea."

"You're driving me crazy."

"Bad crazy?"

This time, it was his turn to laugh, and the warmth of his breath against the sensitive skin of her neck caused a frisson of sensation to race through her extremities.

"No. Good crazy. Really good crazy."

Then his lips closed over hers and he began his own intimate foray, his tongue sweeping her mouth, testing the barrier of her teeth, slipping further inside to taste and tease. She willingly surrendered, then returned each gesture with one of her own, her veins filling with a wildfire that swept through her body before coalescing at that secret feminine part pressed so tightly against him.

Whit broke away to trail his lips down her neck again, ending at that oh, so delicious spot where it met her shoulder.

"I should have known I couldn't live without you," he murmured.

The words had the power to stoke her inner heat even higher.

"But you've done well."

He broke away, his eyes seeming to smolder.

"That wasn't living. It was existing." He cupped her face in his hands. "I've felt more alive and...*present* since coming to Larkspur than I have in years."

She stared at him, bemused, confused, not knowing how to respond. She felt the same. It was as if her world had suddenly taken on the colors of a children's cartoon. She wouldn't have been all that surprised if the forest animals suddenly burst into song. But even as she reveled in the headiness of this newfound joy, she couldn't entirely surrender herself to the situation. Not when they still had so many obstacles stacked up against them.

Whit's departure.

Her dreams to further her education.

Clint.

Clint might not be able to communicate, but his presence hung at the back of her consciousness. No, not his presence, his utter vulnerability. For the past ten years, she'd made him and his condition one of her priorities. Yet, now that she balanced on the precipice of transferring those responsibilities to another person, she found it difficult to let go.

Whit lifted his head, a frown appearing between his brows.

"What's wrong?"

She shook her head. "Nothing, I..."

But she couldn't continue, not when anything she said could be misconstrued by Whit. She didn't want him to think she wasn't fully committed to seeing where a relationship between them might lead.

She simply couldn't bring herself to believe that something permanent could ever become of it.

The moment the thought raced through her head, she mentally shrank away from her own cowardice. But the sentiment lingered in her heart like chips of ice. She trusted Whit, trusted in his feelings for her.

But she didn't trust that the circumstances surrounding them could be resolved.

And she certainly didn't trust the court of common opinion to approve of their relationship.

Could she find the courage to put her own needs above the reactions of her family and her community?

"Finley?"

"I don't know how all this is going to work out. I don't know how it *can* work out."

She feared that she was making a mess of explaining herself, but Whit seemed to understand because he drew her tightly against him, rocking her as if she were a child to be reassured.

With her cheek pressed against his chest, she could hear the faint thump of his heart, and the sound reminded her that this was real. *Whit* was real.

"We've got some challenges stacked up against us," he murmured. "I know that. And I know you've got even more on your plate than I do. You've got school to think about, your mom, Billie, even keeping tabs on Clint. And I know you'll get a lot more flack when people realize that we're seeing one another." He bent back so that he could meet her gaze. "I'm not saying that ironing all that out is going to be easy. But we're not under a time limit—"

"You'll be leaving in a week, ten days!"

He slid his palm up and down her spine in a soothing gesture.

"So, what? We've got phones. Cars. We'll come up with a way to be together as much as we can. We wouldn't be the first couple to have a long-distance relationship."

He would do that for her? Put his own life, his own wishes on hold?

Those green eyes told her the answer without its having been asked.

Yes.

"Just don't give up on us, okay? We've got a couple of weeks before we need to make any serious decisions. Let's enjoy *this*—" he waved a hand between them "—before we worry about all the hard stuff."

He was asking for a leap of faith—one that defied her own brain's insistence that she put logic over emotion. Judging by Whit's expression, he believed that they could find a way to forge a real bond.

And she wanted to believe him.

She nodded, swayed more by the determination that shone from his eyes than from her own conviction.

He grinned—that pure, unfiltered grin that never ceased to catch her by the heartstrings.

"Come on. We'll take a break for lunch."

"But it's only eleven."

"So? Are you on a schedule?"

"No, but—"

He bent to whisper in her ear. "Let go, Finley. The world won't fall apart if you loosen your grip."

She bristled, ready to point out that she was very far from being a control freak…but then, the truth seeped through the cracks.

Was he right?

Had she learned to cope by micro-managing? Was she so afraid of having events spin out of kilter that she clung to her lists and schedules and carefully planned activities?

"Let go," Whit whispered again.

She trembled from the mere thought of throwing caution to the wind and allowing her emotions to steer her actions rather than conscious will.

"I'll be there with you," Whit added. "I won't let you get hurt."

But Finley knew such things couldn't be promised. Life had a way of bucking the best of precautions—a fact she should have realized as she'd plotted and schemed and designed her life into something so…vanilla.

She'd never been all that fond of vanilla.

"Okay," she finally agreed. "Let's eat lunch—nothing predictable. I want Pop-Tarts and scrambled eggs and ice cream sandwiches."

Whit grinned. "I can give you two out of three."

"Then that will be enough."

Whit released her long enough to swipe his shirt off the floor. He took her hand and led her outside.

"Do you have to go to work later this afternoon?"

"Not until three."

He squeezed her hand. "Great. We can…"

His words trailed away and she looked up to see that he was focusing on a point in the distance. Following his line of sight, she saw an SUV topping the rise and winding its way into the valley.

"I locked the gate," she murmured, feeling a twinge of unease.

"I'm sure he already has his own key."

"Who?"

"Javi. He came back into town last night. I saw him when I went to visit Clint."

Just when Whit was sure that he'd managed to put Finley's fears to rest, he saw…no, he *felt* her take a huge emotional step back.

He immediately knew the cause for her withdrawal. It was one thing to feel their way through their relationship on their own, but this…this was a witness. Even worse, this was Javi, an old friend who had lived through the same chaotic events which had split the Sinful Six apart. Javi had supported Finley through the intervening years, so, in his mind, he probably still thought of Finley and Clint as a couple. There was no way to know how he would react once he realized that things had changed.

He felt Finley begin to tremble. "I can't do this. I know I'm being a coward, but I can't simply announce to him that I've abandoned Clint and—"

"You haven't abandoned him. You're still his friend."

"But—"

Whit released her to shrug into his shirt. But as Javi's Bronco took the last couple of turns, he touched Finley's shoulder, urging her to meet his eyes.

"We're not on a schedule, remember? If you're not comfortable letting Javi know that we're dating, then he doesn't need to know. We'll go on with our plans, have lunch, get a little more work done on the bungalows. I'll follow your lead. If you change your mind and want to say something to him, fine. If not, we wait."

She nodded, and Whit felt a jolt of pride. He knew how hard this was for her, walking into a situation without having a prepared battle plan at her fingertips.

But as he walked to intercept Javi's car, he was acutely aware of the emotional walls she'd automatically erected. Although she met Javi with a hug and exclamations of welcome, Whit sensed an air of reserve. And when she backed away, she carefully put space between her and Whit.

As the afternoon progressed, her tension didn't seem to ease. Instead, she insisted on making them all lunch—soup, sandwiches, and sodas—while Whit led Javi through the bungalows and outbuildings and reported on the repairs that would be needed in order to make the structures habitable.

Afterwards, while they ate their food and discussed possible uses for the property, Whit idly wondered what had happened to Finley's wish for Pop-Tarts, scrambled eggs, and ice cream sandwiches. With each minute that passed, his beautiful, mercurial Finley seemed to fade into the shell of the plotter and planner.

When she jumped to her feet and announced she needed to get back into town for work, Whit prayed that he would have a minute alone so that he could talk to her one last time. But Javi came along to accompany her to her car.

Damn.

She didn't quite meet Whit's eyes as she slid behind the wheel. Knowing he had to reassure her, he grabbed her door and said, "Fasten your seat belt. Lock your doors. And drive safely. It's hunting season and sometimes the deer in the area get spooked."

For an instant, she looked up and he saw a bit of her panic and a deep-seated disappointment in herself for avoiding a confrontation with Javi.

He touched her shoulder, briefly, softly, tacitly reassuring her that he wasn't angry. Whit might be more than ready to shout to the skies that he and Finley Fitzpatrick were together. But if he'd learned anything in the last ten years, it was that he couldn't force events to his own will. If she wasn't ready to take the next step, he would wait—he'd wait another lifetime if necessary. Because now that she was in his life, in his arms…

He wasn't about to screw that up.

FOURTEEN

*W*hit nailed another line of shingles onto the Grizzly bungalow, then lifted his ball cap, finger-combing his hair out of his eyes for the hundredth time that day.

He really needed a haircut. But he wasn't about to trust a barber he didn't know. Or to head into Larkspur for…pretty much anything.

The whispering had begun. Despite everything that they'd done to keep their relationship private, people in town were beginning to wonder.

Who knew how they'd found out? It wasn't Javi who'd been spreading tales. To his credit the man had spent the whole afternoon helping Whit with repairs—so much so, that Whit was far ahead of his original schedule. His friend had left for Jackson Hole the following morning, soon after phoning Whit and promising to come back to the ranch again in a couple of weekends—and he'd bring his tools.

There had been a hundred times when Whit could have mentioned their relationship to Javi. But Whit had promised Finley that he wouldn't, and he wasn't about to break that promise. So Javi hadn't been the source of the rumors.

Which meant that someone else knew—or people in Larkspur had seen them together enough to start putting two and two together.

He'd witnessed the increase in curiosity when he'd gone for groceries. Geez, he'd have to be completely oblivious not to notice the sidelong glances, the conversations that abruptly ended when he walked past.

He knew it shouldn't bug him—hell, hadn't he convinced Finley not to give the wagging tongues any heed? Besides, he didn't even know most of the people he saw in town, why should he care what they thought?

But he did care.

Not for his sake, but for Finley's.

Sighing, he dug into his pocket again. With the number of times he'd dragged his phone out, he would have completed more work if he'd nailed it to the roof in front of him. Once again, he found himself checking to see if he'd missed a call, or a text, or…

Nothing.

Damn it.

It had been three days since he and Finley had seen each other at the ranch. Three days. He hadn't called her that night. Javier had been too close to hand—and Whit had wanted to give her time to think things over, but maybe that had been a mistake. Since then, she hadn't answered her phone. He'd left messages, texted, but other than a couple of vague, one-word responses, he hadn't been able to pin her down for another of their "dates."

Shit. Had he screwed things up already? He'd wanted to do things right, take things slow. But maybe she'd decided such an approach was lukewarm at best.

Or maybe, the talk in town had become so obvious that she'd decided she didn't want to become the brunt of idle gossip again. Especially not in reference to him.

The distant sound of an engine and the crunch of gravel warned him that a vehicle was approaching. *Hell.* He'd grown tired of locking and unlocking the padlock, so he'd begun looping the chain around the gate. From a distance, it looked secure, but close up, it was an easy enough matter to get in. And with the deer hunt beginning that weekend, Whit had already grown jumpy from the sporadic gunfire in the distance. Had a happy band of weekend stalkers decided to make Come Back Ranch their base camp?

He shoved his phone back into his pocket, grabbed his hammer, and headed toward the ladder. He was only part way down when a car eased around the corner.

Finley.

The tension eased from his chest like sand rushing from punching bag. Where only moments earlier, the day had seemed bleak and cold, now he felt as if the sun had come from behind a cloud.

He shoved the tips of his work gloves into his back pocket and waited for her to come to a complete stop. Then, in two strides, he was there, opening her door.

"Hey, there."

She looked up at him and, just as quickly, the tension returned. He knew that shuttered look to her eyes. She had something on her mind, and it probably wouldn't bode well for him.

Damn it.

She knew.

She knew the whole town was speculating about them.

"Hi." Her gaze skittered from him to the bungalows. "You're making progress."

She wanted to make small talk first. He was okay with that. At least it wasn't an immediate crushing rejection.

"Yeah. I'm almost done replacing the missing shingles—at least, on the units that don't need major roof repairs." He pointed to the structures which had proven to be in the best shape. "I've concentrated on the ten buildings here. As of this afternoon, I've finished the drywall repairs and ripped out the carpets. The rooms will still need paint, new light fixtures and probably one or two more plumbing overhauls, but there's plenty of time for that. Even better, underneath all that hideous shag carpeting were beautiful hardwood floors that we can refinish."

"Aren't you taking on more than necessary? Even if all six of us stayed at the ranch, we'd have the extra bedroom in the main house and people could buddy up. You'd only have to fix a couple of the units."

"I know. I thought of that."

In truth, he hadn't originally planned to repair so many units. But when he hadn't been able to get ahold of Finley, he hadn't wanted to pressure her by searching for her in town. He'd made a daily sweep of the auction pens in Larkspur and even those in Redmond, and hadn't been able to uncover anything more for Thayne. That left him with most of the day free, and he would have gone stark, raving mad if he hadn't found a way to keep himself occupied.

"I didn't know if anyone might want to bring a guest or…a significant other."

Her gaze met his, then bounced away, so he satisfied himself with studying her features—her arched brows, translucent skin, the spattering of freckles, all of it framed by the soft gray fabric of her hoodie. But she seemed to take his answer at face value.

"Are you busy right now?"

"No, I was about to take a break."

Liar.

But once again, she didn't seem to find his overly-casual tone concerning.

"Could we talk?"

Whit's stomach tightened even more.

"Sure. I've got cold drinks in the house. Or coffee." Now that he wasn't working on the roof, he became innately aware of the chill to the breeze as it luffed against his T-shirt and kissed the sweat pooling between his shoulder blades.

Finley nodded, shoving her hands into the pockets of her jacket.

As they moved into the main house, Whit tried to study her expression. But she'd pulled the hood to her sweatshirt so low over her brow that he couldn't get a clear look.

Damn. What had he done?

As soon as they were inside, he set the hammer, his hat and work gloves on the counter and hurriedly scooped the morning's cereal bowl from the table, setting it in the sink.

"What would you like?"

"Coffee is fine."

He reached for a mug from the cupboard over the sink and filled it halfway with the black brew.

"Sugar's on the table. I've got cream if you want it."

"Thanks."

He crossed to the refrigerator, removing the pint-sized carton from the inner rack. He'd bought it for Finley, knowing that she liked her coffee more on the "tan" side, while he took it as black as tar.

Just as he'd anticipated, she added a huge splash. Sensing what she would need next, Whit pulled open a drawer, took out a spoon and handed it to her.

Her smile was rueful. "Thanks."

Needing to occupy his hands, he opened the refrigerator again and blindly took out a bottle of water. Twisting the cap, he drained half the contents before Finley finally looked up.

She took a tentative sip from her mug. Another. Then she grimaced.

"I suppose you figured out that I've been avoiding you the last couple of days."

His stomach seemed to suddenly freefall, but he tried to keep his tone casual. "Yeah, I…I figured you needed…space."

She sighed, set her mug on the counter, then—thank, God—she dragged the hood from her head. "I've enjoyed spending time with you."

She hesitated again, shoving her hands into the kangaroo pockets of her top.

"But…" Whit prompted when the silence seemed to throb with the sound of his own heartbeat.

"My sister has been hounding me."

"About what?"

She shrugged, biting her lip and seeming to look anywhere other than at him. "You. Me." She heaved a sigh. "Clint."

"Ah."

So, she didn't just have the town whispering behind her back. She had her own family to contend with.

"She's pretty much accused me of cheating on Clint."

Whit opened his mouth to argue that Finley had stood by Clint for years. How far did her loyalty need to extend? Clint wasn't going to get any better. Was she supposed to "stand by her man" until death? It wasn't as if the two of them had actually married.

But thankfully, none of that left his mouth.

"She hasn't said anything that I hadn't already been expecting. Not really. But to have her bring it up, again and again, has been...*horrible*."

Whit wanted to reach out to her so badly that the water bottle creaked in his hand and he realized that he'd been slowly squeezing it. He set it carefully on the counter, then leaned back, gripping the edge of the Formica.

Finley wrapped her arms around her waist. "I had to think things through, you know? I mean, it's one thing to subject myself to that kind of innuendo, but to let you take the fall for the way I've—"

"Whoa, whoa." Whit held up a hand. "You were worried about me? Your sister jumps all over you for what...going to lunch? Accepting flowers from a guy? Spending time at the ranch? And you're worried about *me?*"

"Whit, you don't understand. I've been through this, okay? And the talk has already started up in town again. I know you told me not to pay attention to it, but I can...*feel* people watching and whispering and..."

Whit plunged his fingers through his hair. Then he linked his knuckles together behind his head to keep from hauling her into his arms.

"Do you want to spend time with me, Finley? Do you want to...*be* with me?"

"Well, yes. But I've also come to the realization that I'm tired of hiding how I feel. I should have been honest with Javi—and the next time he visits, I will be. But I'm not waiting until then. I'm done being a coward. But you need to be prepared for the way this town is going to react to our dating."

Whit didn't wait for another word. He'd already heard the most important one.

Yes.

In two strides, he'd reached her and his hands wrapped around her waist, pulling her toward him. Then he was bending to kiss her, again and again, filling himself with the taste of her, the scent of her, knowing that if he lived to be a hundred, he would never be able to sate himself of his hunger for this woman.

For a moment, she seemed stunned and oh, so still. Then her hands clutched at his back, his waist, his shoulders, and she was giving back as much as she got.

"Y-you're not mad at..."

"At you? Hell, no."

"But the talk..."

"Damn the talk."

"But..."

He drew back, framing her face with his palms. "I don't care, Finley. Hell, if I'd known what had been worrying you, I would have put these fears to rest days ago."

"But they're saying—"

"I don't give a damn. Don't you see? I've been the brunt of gossip my whole life. It was inevitable with Elvis for a father. I stopped being concerned about the wagging tongues long ago." He bent to rest his forehead against hers. "It's you I'm worried about. I'll understand if you don't want that kind of hassle in your life, or if you decide that we've taken things as far as you're willing to go." He traced her lower lip with his thumb. "Just don't shut me out. If there's something wrong, something you aren't comfortable with...*talk* to me."

She blinked up at him, her eyes suspiciously bright, but then she smiled, slowly, tentatively.

"You really don't care, do you?"

"I care about *you*, Finley."

"Even though my sister isn't entirely wrong? I am cheating on Clint in a way."

And there it was. If anything could sink this relationship before it could ever begin, it was Clint.

"You aren't the only one struggling with the concept," he whispered. "He was my friend too."

He replaced his thumb with his lips, softly, without heat, wanting to reassure her in the only way he knew how. Then he drew back, trying to gauge the montage of emotions that flashed across her features.

Tenderness.

Hopefulness.

Regret.

No. There could be no regrets. He had to convince her that she wasn't doing anything wrong.

"I told him about us, you know," he murmured.

"Who?"

"Clint."

"What?"

Whit looped his arms behind her back, pulling her to him.

"I've been visiting him at night. We eat together...or rather, I eat and he...smells. Maybe."

Her expression eased from regret to incredulity.

"What?"

"You said to stimulate his senses, so for the last couple of nights, I've taken him a Dew or a beer—"

"You haven't!"

"Shh, don't tell the nurses." He couldn't help grinning at the way Finley's eyes widened. "Anyway, I tell him stuff. Like my progress here at the ranch. Or the way the Broncos are plagued with injuries." He paused before admitting, "Or that I intended to woo you."

"Woo me?"

Whit laughed offering a soft, "Woo-woo," in a sing-song voice. "Is it working?"

"You actually said that."

"Not in those exact words, but…yeah."

The incredulity faded beneath an emotion that looked very much like…wonder.

"You are an amazing man, Whit Patterson."

"You think so? Because I've been trying to impress you. Obviously, I haven't been doing that great of a job."

Her hands rested on his chest for a moment, lingering over the irregular *ba-thump* of his heart, then they slid up, up, to link behind his neck.

"I'd say you've done a great job."

"Yeah?"

"Yeah."

"Does that mean you'll let me take you to dinner?"

She pressed a kiss to his throat. His jaw. "I've got a better idea. Let's eat here, have a quiet evening, maybe see if the fireplace in the sitting room still works."

"Mmm. Sounds risky."

"I'm game if you are."

"There's not a lot to choose from meal-wise. Cereal. Sandwich meat. Pop Tarts. A couple of cans of soup."

"Delicious. I'm sure we could come up with a great menu from those ingredients. Besides, you've already promised me an unconventional meal."

"Pop Tarts, scrambled eggs, and ice cream sandwiches. I made sure I stocked the freezer."

"Really?"

"Yeah."

She eased closer—as if such a thing were possible.

So, what should he do now? Kiss her? Or start cooking? Truth be told, he wanted nothing more than to haul her into the bedroom, but he wasn't going to do that.

Much as his body begged him to surrender to his instincts.

At a loss, he blurted, "Have I told you anytime lately that I plan to take things slow with you?"

The moment the words left his mouth, he could have kicked himself. Not only was he beginning to sound like a broken record, but the words were no longer true. He didn't want to take his time anymore. He wanted Finley—today, yesterday, tomorrow. He wanted to haul her into his arms and into his bed. If she weren't so skittish, he'd open up the discussion of where she planned to enroll so he could start making plans on the best way for them to be together as much as possible.

But it was Finley who spoke first. Her lips twitched and she offered dryly, "We haven't seen each other in nearly three days. That's about as slow as it gets."

"I don't think that counts."

"Oh, it counts," she murmured against his lips. "It definitely counts. And I don't know about you, but I think it's time to pick up the pace."

In the end, they made grilled ham and cheese sandwiches cut into triangles and tomato soup, then sat at the table like a couple of kids after school, dipping the corners of their bread into their bowls.

Whit couldn't remember the last time he'd smiled so much—and laughed. As Finley regaled him with Billie's latest escapades as a substitute teacher for the local elementary school, he couldn't seem to help himself. He was so damned…happy.

If someone had told him that his outlook on life could change so completely in a matter of days, he would have scoffed at the idea. He was used to long hours on the road, nights spent poring over paperwork. If he spent much time at home at all, it was only to catch a Broncos game or a few hours of sleep.

But as the evening shadows lengthened and the sun dipped behind the horizon, he found himself building a fire in the sitting room while Finley dragged a quilt from the bedroom and arranged it on the floor along with a couple of throw pillows.

"Eventually, we're going to have to spring for furniture for this place," she murmured as she sat cross-legged, watching him feed sticks into the licking flames.

Whit didn't bother to point out that, only days before, she'd insisted that they sell the ranch as soon as possible.

She wasn't the only one who'd lapsed into thinking of the Come Back Ranch as a more permanent situation. Often, while he was seeing to repairs, Whit found himself organizing a long list of things to do—as if he planned to set up camp on the property for an extended amount of time.

Once he'd managed to build a large enough blaze to add a couple of stout logs, he turned to find Finley watching him. She had such a curious expression on her face—one that seemed at once somber yet intrigued, happy and melancholy.

"What?" he asked.

She offered a slight shrug. "I'm enjoying the view."

It took him a moment to realize that she wasn't looking at the fire. She was studying him.

A soft laugh pushed from his throat.

"I'm sure you can find something better to look at."

She seemed to consider the idea, then shook her head. "I don't think so. I like looking at you."

He became incredibly conscious of the path of her gaze as it slipped from his face, to his chest, then lower and lower. Each inch she studied seemed to warm beneath her regard.

"I was always afraid to look at you before."

The words had the power to steal the very breath from his lungs.

"Yeah?"

"Yeah. I guess I was too young to understand what I was feeling."

The silence spooled between them, broken only by the luff and snap of the logs being consumed in the fireplace.

"And what was that?"

Normally, he would have rued the way his voice emerged, husky, raw with need. But Finley was being so open about her emotions, he couldn't bring himself to hide his own.

She stood and the firelight limned her body and seemed to set her hair aglow.

"Need. Want."

There was more than a yard between them, but Whit felt every breath she took.

"It scared me."

"Why? I would never harm you."

"Sometimes…it hurt to be in the same room with you. I desperately wanted you to…like me."

He knew that it would be dangerous to move toward her. If he took a single step, he'd take another and another, then sweep her into his arms. But it became important that they say these things to one another. The past needed to be cleared away to make way for…

For what?

A future?

Yes. Please, God, yes. Let there be a future between them.

"There wasn't a day that I didn't like you, Finley."

But the word tasted tepid on his tongue. *Like* didn't even come close to the emotions he'd felt anytime she'd been near. Even now, the word seemed immature and inadequate.

"I loved you, Finley."

She grimaced. "As a friend, even a little sister."

A rueful laugh pushed from his chest. "Trust me. I never thought of you as a little sister."

"Are you sure?"

She took a step toward him and a light entered her eyes—one that he could scarcely credit being directed at him. He'd never had any woman look at him that way—with a mixture of hunger and promise, wonder and want.

"I swear, Whit, I only had to enter the room and you seemed to…mentally back away from me."

As the distance faded between them, his need increased until he felt as if he would be consumed and left a pile of ash. His fingers twitched with the need to touch her, to haul her into his arms, to kiss her again and again. But he remained where he was, old fears from the past still managing to twine around him.

What if he couldn't be enough for her?

"You scared the shit out of me," he finally admitted, his voice barely audible.

That admission caused her to pause in her relentless prowl toward him.

"Why?"

"Because I wanted you. Even then. But I couldn't have you."

"Why, Whit? Because of Clint?"

"There was that, but…"

She'd begun moving again and his throat became so dry, he doubted that he would be able to force the words free.

"But what?"

"God, Finley, you were so perfect. You still are. Even now, I worry that you'll come to the conclusion that I'm the last person on earth you should trust with your heart."

FIFTEEN

*H*e feared he'd gone too far when a shadow of doubt darkened her eyes. But there was no retrieving the words. Especially when she came to a stop in front of him, so near that the warmth of her body competed with the heat from the blaze behind him.

"Why on earth would you think that?"

"Look at who I am, Finley, who I was. No matter what I do, how hard I work, I'll always be that rough kid from the wrong side of the tracks. And you deserved—"

"Clint. That's why you pushed me toward him."

"I never—"

"You did! On those rare times that I had you alone to myself, you were always telling me how great he was, how stable, how reliable."

"I didn't—"

"Yes, you did!"

Whit forced himself to look back, to scrape together the memories of those months before the accident when he'd seemed to walk around with a permanent hard-on for Finley. Things had been especially rough for him at home. Elvis had been in trouble with the law for peddling drugs and he'd taken a lot of his frustration out on Whit. There were nights when Whit had slept in his car to avoid going home. His only real salvation had been Norm Campanella, the rodeo circuit, and his friends. But Clint...

Clint had a dad who loved him, a brick-and-mortar home, and a full-ride college scholarship. He was going to major in engineering while Whit...

Well, Whit hoped to scrounge up enough money to get an Ag degree.

"He was good for you," Whit whispered, finally admitting to himself that Finley was right. He *had* pushed her toward Clint.

"Yeah. As a protector, as a friend. But we never should have dated."

She reached out a hand, laying it flat against his stomach. Whit's muscles tightened in reflex.

Good hell, Almighty. She only had to touch him to crash through all thought and reason and awaken emotions that he'd never thought possible.

"Why were we so afraid, Whit? Why couldn't we see that by denying the truth, we were heading down a dangerous path?"

He shook his head, laying his hand over hers.

"This...*this* feels dangerous too, Finley."

Her head tipped to the side. "Maybe. But I'm tired of thinking, Whit. I'm tired of applying logic to a situation that isn't logical." She offered a soft, self-deprecating laugh. "I'm tired of being predictable."

She leaned toward him even more. Her free hand grasped his wrist, guiding him so that his palm rested in the lee of her waist.

"After all, you're the one who said that we should be more spontaneous and see where all...*this* can take us."

"But I also promised you that we'd take things one step at a time."

She released his wrist and slid her hands beneath the hem of his T-shirt. "Oh, I plan to take things one step at a time. And I intend to savor every damned step."

Her voice dropped to the barest of whispers. And even though he knew exactly where she was headed, he found himself flinching when she reached the bare skin of his abdomen.

"See," she murmured, her voice barely audible. "I'm not rushing anything."

"Fin-ley..."

Her name was a broken sigh. In one last burst of conscience, Whit supposed he should stop her and make sure that she really, really wanted to do this. But he found himself powerless. This was a Finley that he didn't know—one who was daring and in control.

"Come on, Whit. Give in. Just a little."

And he couldn't resist her. Even though he knew this could end up being a bad idea, a very bad idea, he couldn't say no.

Her hands continued to burrow beneath his shirt, moving up, up, until her fingertips brushed against his nipples and he gasped. That touch, that single hesitant caress caused more sensation to storm through his body than anything that he'd ever experienced before.

Because it was Finley.

Finley.

Grown up Finley who knew what she wanted—and damnit all to hell. She wanted him. *Him.*

He reached behind his neck to grab a fistful of his shirt, yanking it over his head and throwing it to the ground.

Whit had never really thought too much about his body. His job kept him fit, and hours on a saddle or slinging bales of hay took care of the rest. But when he saw the way Finley's eyes flared, he was glad that he pleased her.

With his shirt gone, she continued her foray, seeming to read each swell and plane like a blind woman. Her fingers skimmed over his pecs, danced around his nipples, then slid down, to explore his abs.

The rapt expression on her face would be more in keeping with an art critic at a museum. He couldn't seem to reconcile the fact that he could inspire such utter concentration. It had to be one of the most arousing encounters that he'd ever experienced. She seemed to memorize every curve and plane of his body, her fingertips moving whisper-light across his skin—barely making any contact at all. But as she explored and examined the hollow of his elbow, the vein work in his arm, the bones of his wrist, she blazed a path of fire and sensation in her wake.

When he would have reached to pull her close, she dodged away, circling him, her investigation continuing as she spread her palms over his shoulders, the muscles at the base of his neck, the wings of his shoulder blades. Then, with the tip of her nail, she traced the indent of his spine and the stacked ridges of his vertebrae.

Only after she seemed to satisfy herself with looking her fill did she continue her circuit and face him again. Whit had to clench his jaw to maintain a tight leash on his control.

Otherwise, he'd be yanking her toward him. Much as he wanted to, he couldn't do that. He couldn't scare her away. Not when she had found the courage to brush aside her usual reticence. He wanted her to feel safe in expressing herself, in being able to voice her own wants and needs. Hell, he'd give her the world, if she asked for it, even if it meant spending the rest of his life trying.

As she lavished her attention down his other arm, Whit realized that *this* was true intimacy—something he'd never shared with anyone else. *This* was a melting of mind and heart, an expression of true honesty and devotion. *This* was what it felt like to be truly accepted, despite all your faults and foibles.

He wondered if she'd guessed a portion of his thoughts, because she began to trace the scars that wrapped around his forearm. At some point when being thrown from the car during the accident, Whit must have raised his arm to protect his face. Deep gouges had faded into ropy ridges that never quite blended with his tan. She then moved to his ribs, where more scars streaked across his abdomen before tapering away near the waistband of his jeans.

"I'm so glad you survived," she murmured, so softly, he nearly didn't hear the words. "When we came upon the accident, I was so sure that you were dead. The wreckage…" she shuddered. "It's a miracle that you're standing here in front of me."

He'd never regarded his survival as a miracle. If anything, the weight of his guilt had often made him wish he hadn't walked away from the accident. But looking down at her—at the firelight gilding her hair and her features soft and intent and enthralled, he was grateful that he'd lived to see this.

She took another step toward him—so close, that he detected the haunting floral scent of her perfume. He could feel the warmth of her body, sense the...energy of her spirit.

"I never would have dreamed of doing this ten years ago. If I had..."

"If you had?" He barely recognized the strangled rasp of his own voice.

"I probably would have been the first documented case of spontaneous combustion."

He laughed at the picture she presented.

"I doubt that."

This time, when he reached for her waist, she allowed herself to be pulled tightly against him.

Her head moved infinitesimally from side to side.

"I don't. Even now, Whit..."

"What?"

"Even now, I feel like I could burst into flames."

That was all he needed to crash his lips over hers, firmly, forcefully—and she immediately opened up to him, kissing him with the same desperate need that surged through her own body. This was no gentle meeting of the minds, it was desire and frustration and hunger unleashed.

Her arms locked around his neck and he lifted her up, easily taking her weight, nearly coming unglued when she wrapped her legs around his waist, locking them at the ankles.

It would have been an easy enough matter to slam her against the wall and fumble with their clothes enough to drive into her. But he couldn't do that—wouldn't do that. He didn't want their first time making love to be quick and feverish and over too quickly. Like Finley, he wanted to enjoy...*every...damned...step.*

So, he wrapped his arms around her, holding her so tightly that the tight buds of her nipples drilled into his chest. He groaned, wondering if she were wearing the scarlet bra he'd seen once before. If so, had she donned the matching panties?

Finley wrenched away from their kiss, breathing hard.

"Still want to take things slow?"

He could only moan.

Her lips were trailing down his jaw, his neck. Then she added the tip of her tongue to the caress, sending a jolt of sensation to his groin. Hell, he couldn't ever remember being this aroused. And if he didn't find a better way to get at her—with his hands, his tongue, his teeth—*he* might be the one to spontaneously combust.

Whit managed to stumble toward the quilt on the floor. Half-leaning, half-falling, he managed to sink onto his back, drawing her down with him so that she lay on top of him, her legs tangling with his, her hair falling around them.

Finley's mouth—that sweet, sweet mouth—continued its exploration to the hollow between his collar bones, then traced the faint scars left over from the surgery which had pinned the broken bones back into place.

He took a shuddering gulp of air, his hands wrapping around her waist, his fingers spreading wide so that he could absorb as much sensation as he possibly could. He knew she would never admit it, but she was such a delicate thing—small boned, slim. But she was strong to the core, not just physically, but emotionally. There were those who might think her natural shyness hid a timid creature, but they would be wrong. Once she had an objective, very little could dissuade her. And currently, her objective seemed to be driving him to the brink.

Whit's hands tunneled beneath her sweatshirt, absorbing the silken texture of his skin. She trembled beneath him, from excitement rather than fear. And her mouth…

Good hell, Almighty.

She bent to place her lips over his nipple, licking, sucking, nipping.

At his gasp, she suddenly reared back, pushing herself up so that she sat astride him—and he groaned when her movements seated her more firmly against the bulge straining against his zipper.

Finley seemed to become aware of the fact at about that same moment, because an expression crossed her face, one that was satisfaction and arousal all rolled into one.

"At least you can't pretend that I leave you cold."

He framed her face with his palms. "You never left me cold, Finley. That was never the problem."

Whit prayed that she could see that he was telling her the truth. "Hell, I couldn't get enough of you, first as a kid. Then a teenager." A bark of rueful laughter pushed from his throat. "You only had to enter the room—shit, I only had to *think* of you—and my hormones started raging. Hell, I didn't know that I could *feel* that way. Hot and cold, nervous and aggressive—every conflicting emotion that you could think of, all rolled into one. I didn't dare approach you for fear I'd self-destruct or say or do something that would scare you off for good. But as painful and chaotic and confusing as it all was, I wanted you even then."

"Then why didn't you say something?"

He hesitated, wondering how he could put those chaotic years in words.

"It didn't seem…right. *I* wasn't right for you."

"Bull. You can't tell me that you held back all those years ago because of where you came from. Damnit, Whit, what did I have to offer? I was the product of an A-1 dysfunctional home as well. My mother could have drunk your father under the table—then there's her compulsive shopping and the get-rich-quick schemes. And Billie…she was out of control—she's still out of control. What did you think would happen if we got together?"

He fought through the fog of arousal and desire to put his thoughts into words. And it was then that he became aware of the chain which had come loose from her shirt. At the end was a pendant.

No, not a pendant.

A ring.

Clint's engagement ring.

He reached up, fingering the delicate solitaire, admitting softly, "I wanted more for you."

"Like what? What could Clint give me that I couldn't find with you?"

"Stability. Security."

"And what makes you think that Clint could have guaranteed any of that? Good grief, Whit, the man was obsessed with winning—and not only in regards to sports. Everything was a competition." Her lip trembled and her eyes grew dark. "Don't you see? I was his trophy."

Whit frowned. "No, you were—"

"Don't lie to yourself or to me. Clint only wanted me because, deep down, it meant that he'd won. He'd won in some stupid little contest the two of you had over me."

"No, Finley."

"Yes!" She pounded her fist against his chest. "Damn it, I could see it in his eyes every time we all shared the same room. The minute you were there, he would throw his arm around my shoulders as if to say 'Look what I've got!'" She took a deep, shuddering breath. "But it wasn't real, Whit." Her voice trembled and he watched as tears flooded her eyes. "It wasn't real!"

She suddenly sagged against him, and Whit wrapped his arms around her body, absorbing her sobs. And in that shimmering instant as the mood in the room shifted from passion to despair, he found himself grasping to understand what had happened. Finley had been alive in his arms, filled with a desire that he never would have thought possible. But now...

Finley sobbed as if her heart was broken, her tears falling onto his chest.

It wasn't real.

He grappled with the last coherent thing she'd uttered.

It wasn't real.

He scrambled to remember the months leading up to the accident. Finley and Clint had seemed so happy. So *right.*

But, yeah. Whit had been so wrapped up in his own self-doubt, he supposed that he had tried to push them together. On those rare occasions when he'd had Finley alone, he'd been self-conscious and tongue-tied and awkward. He'd relied on topics of conversation that he knew would be safe. School, sports...

And Clint.

Shit. Had he really been that stupid? Had he been so intent on avoiding his own feelings that he'd denied himself the one thing that could have made him happy? Even worse, had his friend picked up on his conflicting emotions?

It would be like Clint to see the situation as a twisted sort of race. Who could get the girl first? And it wasn't that Clint was being cold-blooded or calculated about the situation. Deep-down, Whit knew that Clint had cared about Finley. Hell, they'd all had a crush on her at one time or another.

But Clint…could he have stuck it out with her? Sure, he'd been willing to put a ring on her finger.

But had he loved her? Really loved her? Or had she been a prize to win? And once having tasted the prize, would he have been attracted to the next unattainable woman, the next competition?

Geez, he shouldn't even think about his friend that way.

Finley. Dear, sweet Finley.

That was why she was crying. Because she'd suspected the truth all along, that Clint had never really committed to her, not in the way that counted, not to the depth that she'd deserved. And through a string of unlucky events, she'd become trapped in that moment of doubt, not wanting to betray a man whom she cared for…

But hadn't cared enough.

And Finley, being Finley, hadn't wanted to speak ill of a man who couldn't defend or explain himself. So, she'd stayed by his side all these years, tied to the memory of a man who may or may not have married her, may or may not have given her the happiness she deserved.

Whit tipped his head so that he could press his lips against her hair.

"I get it, Finley. Geez, I get it."

Her sobs stilled and she tipped her chin to look at him through tear-soaked lashes.

Whit smoothed the hair away from her face, tucking it behind her ear.

"Since the accident, you've been trapped in the past, stuck in that instant when we both looked up and saw him watching our first kiss."

That embrace had been hot, uncontrollable, burning through them both with the strength and intensity of a wildfire. Yet something had warned them that they were being watched. And when they'd broken apart...

Whit still remembered the expressions that had raced over Clint's face. Shock. Anger. Betrayal. And then a stark, heart-breaking emptiness.

In that second, Whit had known the depth of his mistake.

Yeah, maybe Clint had unconsciously pursued Finley for all the wrong reasons. Maybe what they'd experienced together wouldn't have lasted. But Whit had seen how much Clint *needed* Finley. She was his anchor. His touchstone. And she'd been ripped away from him at a time when Clint had already been made vulnerable by injuries and a losing season on the circuit. He must have felt as if he'd been stripped of everything that had mattered to him.

By the same man who'd just stolen his rodeo title.

His best friend.

His brother.

Damn.

Whit remembered the way the color had drained from Clint's face. Then he'd backed away, turned, ran. And Whit had followed him...

But hitting the doors and dodging into the parking lot was the last thing that Whit remembered before the aftermath of the accident.

"He cared for you, Finley," Whit whispered. "He *did* care for you. You can't say it wasn't real."

Her chin seemed to crumple. "But it wasn't…*enough*. Not for me."

And therein lay the tragedy. Because she'd spent the last ten years in a limbo, unable to untangle herself from the past and move on.

"If it weren't for the accident—"

"But the accident happened, Whit. I can't wish it away."

He stroked her cheek, wiping the tears away with his thumb. "But you can't keep punishing yourself either. Because that's what you're doing. You're punishing yourself for the way you felt then and the way you feel now."

And that was the whole crux of the matter. Everything that he and Finley had been experiencing—the pleasure, the pain, the passion—could be destroyed if the two of them couldn't forgive themselves and move on.

Finley abruptly stood. "I've got to go."

"What? Finley, let's talk this through."

Whit sat up, reaching for her hand, but she dodged away. "Finley!"

By the time he'd pushed himself to his feet, she'd hurried out the back door to her car. Whit followed as quickly as he could, but she was already backing out.

"Finley!"

He pounded on the hood of her car as she drove past, but she didn't stop. And as he watched her taillights disappear into the darkness, Whit wondered if he'd ever see her again.

 #

Finley sat in the Greensprings parking lot, not really sure how she'd come to be here. She'd left Whit hours ago. For a time, her only goal had been to escape. She'd driven blindly, heading further into the canyon, so unaware of her actions that she hadn't realized how far she'd gone until the evening shadows had begun to lengthen. She might have continued going if she hadn't realized how futile her actions had become. Larkspur was miles away, but her thoughts and regrets still rode alongside her. Finally, in defeat, she'd turned the car around and headed back. Through it all, the same thoughts ricocheted through her head.

Why had she lost control like that?

Why had she said all those things—to Whit, of all people?

But now, as she leaned back against the headrest and closed her eyes, she realized that she couldn't have contained her emotions any longer. The things she'd told Whit…they'd been brewing for a long time. For years now, she'd tried to shy away from the truth, tamp down her fears and emotions, and convince herself that none of it mattered.

Tonight, she'd proven herself wrong. Her doubts, her insecurities, her inability to act had dragged at her like shackles, keeping her frozen in the past.

No more.

She might not have had the courage to act then—and she didn't know if she had the courage to act now.

But she had to try.

The evening wind was cool against her hot cheeks as she stepped from her car and crossed to the main double doors of the convalescent center. It was late, far later than she'd ever visited. She wasn't even sure if she'd be able to get in. For all she knew, the facility might be locked this time of night.

As luck would have it, one of the nurses appeared and exited the building. As she hurried toward the parking lot, Finley grabbed the door and slipped inside before it could close.

Since it was nearly midnight, there was no one in the waiting room, no one at the reception desk. The lights had been dimmed, leaving only the strip lights near the floor to illuminate the corridor. It didn't matter. Finley had been here so many times, she could have found her way in total darkness.

The fire doors had been closed for the night, but they weren't locked. Finley moved as quietly as she could, then hurried down the hall to Clint's room. By this time, the nurses had already come in to turn off the television and the lights and shift him onto his side. But his eyes were still open, seeming to stare straight at Finley as she approached the bed.

"Hi, Clint."

She bent to press a kiss on his forehead, then straightened. For the first time, she felt awkward, unsure of what to do next. Taking his hand, she absorbed the way his fingers closed briefly around hers. There had been a time when such a response had filled her with hope. Now she knew it was a reflex, nothing more.

In the past, visiting Clint seemed like visiting a sick child. She would fuss with the covers, offer a running monologue about the weather, then sit and read to him for a while. But tonight...

She wasn't sure. Maybe it was the fact that Whit had confessed about talking to him, *really* talking to him, that made her feel tongue-tied.

"I...uh, went to see Whit."

Such an innocuous way of describing an earthshattering evening.

She waited a moment, even though she knew he wouldn't respond.

"Actually, I've been spending quite a bit of time with him." She cleared her throat, searching for words. "He told me that he's been keeping you updated on the ranch and the...uh..."

Finley squeezed his hand again, and when his muscles responded in a way that made it seem that he clung to her, she felt at once like an idiot and a traitor. There was no sense continuing. It wouldn't do a bit of good to spill her guts to a man who probably couldn't hear her anyway.

But she couldn't seem to back away.

"Look, Clint, I'm going to go ahead and say this. I don't know if you can understand me...wherever you might be but..." She cleared her throat to ease it of the tightness. "I never answered you. When you asked me to marry you. And I should have. I knew the instant you pulled out that ring box that I needed...I needed to tell you 'no'."

The last word emerged as little more than a whisper. "Don't blame Whit. I'll be honest, I've always been attracted to him. Even before the accident, there was this intense...I don't know...*awareness* between us. At the time, I didn't have the experience or...or the courage to confront it. But that isn't important. What's important is that I should have been honest with you."

She lay her free hand on top of his, sandwiching his fingers in her grip.

"So, I'm telling you now what I should have said so long before. You deserved better then, and you deserve better now. You need a woman who loves you without reservation. And I'm not saying that because Whit and I...we're...we've met up again and we're...we're going to see if we can make a go of things together."

They were such weak words to describe the overwhelming emotions binding her to Whit, but courting and dating and yes, even "wooing" didn't seem to do them justice.

"I'm sorry for hurting you, Clint. I'm sorry for everything that led up to your being here. And even though I'll always be sorry for that, I can't keep living like…like a widow. I've spent ten years taking care of you and your dad—and I don't regret one single moment. But I have to move on. I can't keep hiding from…life."

In that instant, Finley realized how true the words were. Since the accident, she'd abandoned her own dreams for the future and immersed herself in caring for Clint and Norm, her mother and Billie. In the meantime, time had marched right past her and she'd been stuck in an endless loop of work, the convalescent home, and her mother's alcoholic binges. The years had marched steadily on, but she had stayed the same, ignoring the fact that, by now, she should have shown a measurable amount of *progress*. She should have grown or learned…something. Instead, she'd inured herself to anything but the most basic emotions.

Until Whit, like the proverbial knight-in-shining armor, had awakened her from her self-imposed sleep and brought a storm of emotions crashing down around her.

"I'll always love you, Clint. You know that. You've been my champion, my big brother, my protector. So, don't think you'll be getting rid of me any time soon. I'll still be your friend and you'll still be mine."

Not knowing what else to say, she reached into her shirt, removing the chain that she'd worn since the accident. Swinging from the end of it was the simple diamond solitaire Clint had insisted she wear.

Unclasping the latch, she tenderly looped the necklace around Clint's neck, then tucked the ring beneath his pajama top. Then she bent to kiss him on the top of the head.

"Sweet dreams, Clint."

SIXTEEN

*I*t was nearly one in the morning when Whit's phone chimed, signaling that he had a text. Normally, he wouldn't have bothered to look at it, even though he was wide awake. But after Finley's hasty departure, he was grasping at straws. Maybe, she was trying to get in touch.

Yeah, right.

He was so sure that it would be a memo from work or one of those annoying push notices from his apps that, for a moment, it didn't sink into his brain that Finley had sent him a text.

U UP?

He was in such a rush to respond that he had to erase his own garbled message three times before it made any sense.

YEAH. I'M HERE.

U SHOULD B ASLEEP.

THEN I WOULDN'T B ABLE TO ANSWER UR MESSAGE.

There was a pause as if she were digesting that remark, so he quickly typed,

CALL ME.

MOM AND BILLIE WILL HEAR.

SO?

Another pause.

I'M SORRY I LEFT THAT WAY.

Obviously, she wasn't willing to tell him what was on her mind, so Whit piled the pillows up behind him and snapped on the lamp.

U DON'T NEED 2 BE SORRY. U SHOULD NEVER BE SORRY WITH ME. WE'RE IN THIS TOGETHER, REMEMBER?

One second, two, three, then: *I KEEP FORGETTING.*

Whit smiled to himself.

THEN I'LL KEEP REMINDING U. I CARE FOR U. I WAS WORRIED I'D SAID SOMETHING 2 HURT U.

NO!

He waited, wondering if she'd offer him more, and to his relief, she did.

I NEEDED 2 MAKE THINGS RIGHT.

Right? What was she talking about?

I WENT 2 TALK 2 CLINT.

This time, it was Whit's turn to digest the information.

O?

I GAVE HIM HIS RING BACK.

A wave of relief hit Whit like a punch to the gut, then, just as quickly, a twinge of guilt. In his mind, he saw Clint lying in that hospital bed, completely defenseless. For the first time, he found himself hoping that Clint wasn't aware of his surroundings. If so, he would have another reason to hate Whit.

But there wasn't time to think about that. Right now, Whit needed to know how Finley was feeling about the turn of events.

R U OK?

The screen remained blank for several seconds, then a text box appeared.

YEAH. A LITTLE SAD 2 SEVER THAT LAST TIE 2 THE PAST, BUT I'M OK.

Whit could nearly hear the melancholy in her tone.

I COULD BE THERE IN 20 MIN IF YOU WANT.

Again, there was a pause, then, *NO. BUT THANKS. THAT MEANS MORE THAN U KNOW.*

He waited and soon enough, she continued.

I DON'T HAVE A SHIFT TOMORROW. R U FREE?

Was she kidding? He didn't have anything more important than her on his agenda.

ABSOLUTELY.

WILL MEET U AT THE RANCH.

WHEN?

SOON AS I CAN GET AWAY.

I'LL BE WAITING.

WHIT?

YEAH?

I ENJOY KISSING YOU.

The comment came out of the blue, shooting straight to his groin. Whit groaned softly, wishing he could instantly transport himself to be by her side.

O BABY, ME 2.

WILL U KISS ME AGAIN?

I'D DO IT NOW IF I COULD.

TEMPTING. VERY TEMPTING. BUT I'M BEAT. RAIN CHECK? I'LL MAKE IT WORTH UR WHILE.

Worth his while? Having her talk to him like this, teasingly, intimately, made him hard as a rock.

NO NEED FOR A RAINCHECK. IT'S A PROMISE.

Again, there was a moment's wait then,

I MAY NEED MORE THAN A KISS.

Geez. She was killing him.

I'LL GIVE U WHATEVER U WANT.

NIGHT, WHIT.

Damn. He could have continued for the rest of the night. But he knew she had to be exhausted, emotionally and physically.

DREAM OF ME, Whit offered.

O, I WILL. DON'T WORRY. SEE U TOMORROW.

Then she was gone, even though he continued to hold his phone for several minutes in case she had something else to say.

At long last, he set his cell on the nightstand where he could hear it easily—just in case. Then he reached to turn out the light. Settling back under the covers, he doubted that he'd be able to fall asleep—not when his body still thrummed with anticipation for the next day. But the moment his head touched the pillow...he slept.

Whit wasn't sure when his dreams changed—or when he became aware of the fact that they had changed. He only knew that he had drifted into a place where he wasn't alone...

And he'd been alone for so very long.

He dreamed of bright sunlight pressing against his eyes as he lay sprawled on his stomach. At first, there was a warmth, a presence. Then he felt a tentative hand against the small of his back. Small. Warm. Hesitant.

The warmth spread as the hand moved around his waist to burrow between his stomach and the bed, and a body pressed close to him from behind.

In his mind he imagined it was Finley…knew it was Finley…*needed* it to be Finley. The dream became so real, he could smell her perfume, feel her lips press against his spine.

Don't wake up.

Please, please don't wake up.

Her lips began to move down, down, pressing tiny butterfly kisses down the length of his back, setting his skin afire in their wake.

Don't stop. Don't stop.

He barely dared to breathe, afraid that the slightest movement could push the dream into his subconscious—because heaven only knew how many times he'd dreamed of Finley.

But not like this.

Never like this.

When her lips reached the spot where the sheet wrapped around his hips, she paused—and he was afraid that the phantom Finley would dissolve into nothingness. Instead, she shifted to lay her head on his shoulder, her fingertips making soft, swirling trails from his waist back up to his shoulders again, then reaching to skim across his arm, his wrist, his hand, before moving back to his shoulders.

And then, miraculously, those delicate fingers slid up to tangle in his hair—feeling so real, so warm, so tantalizing, that a frisson of gooseflesh seemed to spread over his scalp. At the same time, the weight at his back shifted and was sure that he felt the warmth of breath against his ear and the softly whispered words, "Wake up, sleepyhead."

Although a part of him begged Whit to ignore the words in case they might scatter this dream, he couldn't seem to help being pulled out of the last vestiges of sleep. His eyes flickered, absorbing the fact that he *was* facing the window and the light *was* warm against his skin and…

And the weight at his back hadn't shifted. Those fingers continued to trace up and down his spine.

He couldn't help himself. As much as he didn't want to interrupt the sensations, he had to know if he was finally cracking up.

Twisting, he turned onto his back, then blinked at the face hovering over his own.

Finley smiled at him, her eyes warm, her smile secretive.

"Good morning," she murmured.

Even when she spoke, he wasn't sure he should believe what he was seeing, or if it was a dream within a dream. Especially when he couldn't reconcile *what* he was seeing. She knelt above him, and if his eyes were to be believed, she was dressed in little more than his shirt.

His T-shirt.

"I was beginning to wonder if you'd ever wake up," she murmured.

"What…" his voice emerged too thick, too garbled. He cleared his throat and started again. "What are you doing here?"

One corner of her mouth tipped impishly. "I told you I was coming."

"W-what time is it?" He didn't want to give her the impression that he wasn't glad to see her—hell, he was ecstatic. But he still couldn't seem to wrap his mind around it.

"About six-thirty?"

"In the morning?"

She laughed. "Yes. I'm used to getting up at four."

"Why?"

"Work."

Duh.

"How'd you…how'd you get in?"

"I have a key, remember?"

A key.

But that still didn't explain why she was wearing his shirt—not that he planned on complaining. Especially when she knelt with her knees wide apart. The hem of the T-shirt rode high on her thighs and dipped low over that most feminine part of her in such a way that he was left wondering if she was *only* wearing his shirt.

As if she had become privy to his thoughts, she tipped her head to the side and asked, "Are you wearing anything under that sheet."

What the hell?

"Joggers."

She reached for the covers, lifting them briefly to reveal the soft cotton knit pants he wore most nights to bed. Dropping it again, she murmured, "Shame."

Geez, Finley.

"What's going on?" He managed to push the words free from his throat.

"I'm trying to wake you up. Am I succeeding?"

Was she kidding? He was more than awake. Every cell in his body seemed super-charged and she'd managed to give him a raging hard-on beyond anything he normally experienced in the morning.

"Uh, yeah."

She leaned toward him. "Then kiss me."

He couldn't have refused her if he'd tried. His hand snapped around her head, his fingers tangling in that glorious autumn-gold hair. Then he was pulling her toward him.

The moment their lips touched, there was no possibility of control. She'd shattered what little restraint he might have been able to scrape together. It was an immediate tangling of lips and tongues and breath as they strained to get closer to one another.

He felt her move against him, pressing against him. But when she shifted to straddle his stomach...

Dear, sweet heaven above.

He reared up into a sitting position, his arms wrapping around her waist, her back, pulling her tighter, tighter against him, knowing that he should stop things now...

But for the life of him, he couldn't think of a reason why.

When he finally managed to pull back—more to give them a chance to breathe than anything else—Finley's eyes opened. And the emotions that he saw there—passion, tenderness, *joy*—were nearly his undoing.

"What are you up to, Finley?"

She draped her arms over his shoulders. "I would think that's obvious. I'm trying to seduce you."

"Seduce me?"

"Mmm. Is it working?"

It was his turn to smile. "Oh, yeah."

He kissed her again, and again, and again—could he ever get enough of her? If he lived to be a hundred and woke to her like this every morning, he didn't think he would ever sate himself of the need he felt now.

Finley was the one to draw back the next time.

"I want you," she whispered. Then she squirmed slightly against him, making him acutely conscious of the fact that he seemed to be the only one of them wearing anything below the waist.

"Shit, where are your clothes?"

"On the floor."

"Why?"

"I told you, I planned on seducing you."

"I thought we agreed to take things slow?"

"No. You agreed to take things slow." She leaned forward, framing his face with her hands, her lips grazing his. "I've been waiting ten years, Whit. Don't you think that's long enough?"

Yes. Hell, yes.

But he had to put up a token protest. Just to make sure that she truly knew what she was asking. "Finley…"

"Ten years, Whit. And I don't intend to wait another minute."

Shit.

But then she was kissing him, wrapping her arms around his neck, crushing her breasts to his chest—and he couldn't have summoned a coherent thought to save his own life. There was only sensation and passion and…

Finley.

He reached to haul her even closer to him, bringing her down against him so that their hips ground together, moist to hot, hard to soft. Of their own volition, his hands grabbed the hem to the shirt she wore, dragging it over her head and throwing it behind them. Then his eyes slipped to her breasts, those small, perfectly formed, pink tipped breasts.

"You're killing me, Finley," he rasped, even as he bent to take one berry-like nipple into his mouth, sucking, pulling, until she bucked against him, making him so hard for her that he knew he had to gain control or he'd be exploding there and then.

But when that last shred of coherent thought convinced him to draw back, she arched into him, driving her breast more deeply into his mouth. She moaned, the sound so low, so filled with passion and wonder that he could only lick her, suck her, nip her with his teeth, before abruptly moving to the opposite breast to offer the same devotion.

Finley was rocking against him, her fingers plunging through his hair so that she could help control his movements. He was so far gone, that he nearly didn't feel the way she became suddenly still, rigid. Then her breath suddenly escaped in a shuddering breath that went on and on and...

Was she coming? Simply from having her breasts suckled?

He drew back enough to watch her, to see color bloom in her cheeks. Her lashes were down, her eyes closed, and her expression became rapt—as if she were looking within herself to absorb the sensations even more. Then, she suddenly sagged against Whit, panting softly.

"Finley, did you..."

She laughed softly. "Yeah. Oh, yeah."

Geez. He'd never had a woman so responsive, so...hot. They'd only been at it for a few minutes.

But then, if her blood was pounding nearly as hard as his, he supposed that it wasn't that remarkable. Hell, if she continued to rock against him, the way she was doing now...

Knowing he had to get control, just a little bit of control, Whit twisted to press her back against the bed. Bracketing her face with his hands, he rested there for a moment, only a moment, before pushing himself to his feet.

"Whit?" It was a complaint, a soft pant of worry.

"Shh."

In one movement, he shucked the pants from his body, then knelt back on the bed.

Her eyes trailed down his body to his erection, then widened slightly.

"Oh, boy," she murmured.

Whit couldn't remember the last time he'd wondered what a woman thought about his package. In the past, he hadn't had a lot of relationships. No one had ever compared to Finley, try as hard as he might to move on.

But with Finley, he wanted to please her.

"Do you want to stop?" he asked as he settled back on the bed next to her.

She rolled her head against the pillow. "No."

"You're sure?"

"Uh huh."

He leaned past her to reach for the jeans he'd left draped over the chair beside the bed. As quickly as he could, he took his wallet from his back pocket, opened it to retrieve a condom from one of the inner pockets, then threw his billfold and pants onto the floor. He tore at the package with his teeth, but when he would have removed the condom, she lay a hand over his.

"Not yet. I want to feel...*you* first."

"Finley," he tried to object.

"With my hands, Whit. I want a chance to...explore."

And how could he refuse? Especially when the request caused his blood to pump even hotter.

He tucked the foil packet beneath his pillow so that it wouldn't accidently fall out of reach, then he propped himself on his elbow above her.

"Explore away," he murmured, dipping to kiss her once, twice.

But when she reached for him, it was to lay a hand to his shoulder. Then, she slid down, down, to circle his nipple.

"Whit?"

"Mmm hmm?"

"I've never done this before."

"Never done what?"

There was a pause, then, *"This."*

He looked at her then, really looked at her, noting the flush to her cheeks, the way that she didn't quite meet his eyes. And then he knew.

Finley was a virgin.

He tipped her chin up, encouraging her to look at him. "Never?"

"No. Never."

He traced a finger over her brow, then down the curve of her cheek.

"Not even…"

"With Clint? He never even got to second base."

The thought surprised him—then pleased him more than it ever should. Especially when her cheeks bloomed with color and he remembered their own trip to "second base" and being run off lover's lane by the sheriff.

"Is that…all right?" she asked hesitantly.

His brows lifted. "Why wouldn't it be?"

One of her shoulders lifted in a shrug. "I'm over thirty, Whit. I should—"

He stopped her with a finger on her lips.

"Finley, there's no right or wrong age for any of this. It's the people involved. The intimacy."

That seemed to relieve her.

"Are you sure you—"

"Stop asking me, Whit. I want to make love with you. Right now."

He couldn't account for the relief that surged through him. He would never want to pressure her into anything. But if he were honest, he wanted her, plain and simple.

"What about you, Whit? Do you want to make love to me?"

He leaned down to whisper against her lips. "For more than a dozen years."

That seemed to surprise her. "A dozen, huh?"

"More than a dozen."

Her brows rose. "*More* than a dozen?"

"What can I say? I've been lusting after you since…forever."

Then, he couldn't wait anymore. He had to kiss her. Softly, tenderly, letting her know with every soft nuance of the caress that he was telling her the truth.

She must have believed his tacit reassurance, because he felt her relax into the embrace, then respond in kind. This time, he was careful to keep the pace slow and lingering. Now, more than ever, it was important to him that she feel comfortable with him. Trusting. He'd heard enough locker room talk to know that for some women, the first time making love could be fairly easy, or incredibly painful. And the thought that he would be the first to initiate Finley to the physical pleasures or pains was enough for him to keep his own passion in check.

For now.

Since her breasts had been so responsive, he ran the backs of his knuckles across one of her nipples. Immediately, it beaded up, becoming a hard point.

"You like that?"

Her eyes were nearly closed. Once again, she seemed to be concentrating on the sensations storming through her body.

"Uh huh."

"A lot?"

She offered a breathy laugh. "Yeah."

He bent to whisper against her ear. "I'm going to be watching you. Learning what you like, what turns you on."

"I should—"

He stopped her by brushing his lips across hers. "Shh. This time, we're exploring *your* body's reactions."

"But next time," she breathed against him "we do you."

"If that's what you want."

"Mmm…yes."

She kissed him then, completely, passionately, and even after the promise she'd been given, her hands skimmed down his back to cup the muscles of his butt. For a moment, he lost his concentration as her fingers dug into his flesh, pulling him against her so that his penis ground into her hip. He was about to chide her for jumping the gun and concentrating on his needs, when he realized that her actions were simply a means for her body to tell him what she wanted.

Lifting his head, he watched her face as his hand slipped down, down, cupping her intimately.

She gasped, her hips lifting to press him even more firmly against her.

Gently, he rubbed a single finger against her, feeling her wetness, delving between the folds of her body to her moist inner core.

"Is it okay if I touch you there?"

She nodded, her eyes still closed, her breathing becoming labored. Tenderly, he delved into her the length of his finger.

"Still okay?"

She offered him a smile.

Slowly at first, he withdrew, then slid back into her heat, miming with his finger what he hoped to soon do with their bodies. Finley seemed tight at first. Nervous. But as she grew more accustomed to his touch, he felt her sink into the bed and the muscles within her become more relaxed.

She was wet. So wet.

He bent to whisper next to her ear. "How about two fingers?"

She groaned, her legs shifting to give him better access—and an even better view.

As he stroked and teased, caressed and tested, he was amazed with how trusting she was with him. How open—and not simply in the view that she provided for him. As a virgin, he'd thought that she would be hesitant about showing herself to him. Finley had always been a little shy. And she'd never been the kind of woman to reveal a lot of skin.

But she lay before him, her legs slightly bent, her head flung back, her hands fisting into the sheets. She seemed completely at ease with allowing him to look his fill, to touch, to explore. Even more, she was so damned responsive, thrusting in upon his hand, shifting her body, or shaking her head if he tried something that she didn't find as arousing.

He could feel her body beginning to tense again and her hands gripped the sheets even more tightly. Her breathing hitched, and this time, he knew what he was seeing.

Finley, his sweet, responsive Finley, was going to come again.

"Ride it, Finley," he murmured, leaning forward to murmur the words against her breasts, even as his thumb grazed that bud at the heart of her.

She jumped, grabbing for his hand—and for a moment, he thought he'd done too much, scared her, hurt her. But then she was holding her palm tightly against him, guiding him, showing him how to give her the most sensation.

He lifted his head to watch her, wanting to see her expression again.

"Come for me, Finley."

She shook her head, even as she continued to guide his thumb.

"No, I want you to...to be inside me."

"Come for me first."

As if she needed nothing but his permission, she suddenly exploded around him, her heat convulsing around his fingers, a cry shuddering from her throat, her hands snapping around him to clutch at his buttocks so that he ground against her hip. She rocked against him, riding the sensations, her face filled with such naked joy and lust and arousal that he nearly came himself. Then, bit by bit, she rode through the waves of ecstasy until she lay panting, her muscles growing limp.

Before she could argue with him, he reached for the condom and covered himself, then maneuvered so that he lay between her legs.

She made a slight moue of regret. "But I haven't explored yet."

"Later," he whispered, kissing her on each breast. "I want you relaxed. Are you relaxed?"

Her soft laughter danced down his spine in a rush of sensation. "Oh, yeah."

"Tell me if…"

She lay a finger over his lips.

"I want you, Whit. All of you."

"Bend your knees. You can wrap them around me if you want."

He rested his weight on one arm, his body pounding so hard for release, he didn't know if he'd even be able to hold on long enough to do this.

With his free hand, he guided himself, hesitating at her entrance.

"I want you, Whit," Finley whispered, as if sensing his hesitation.

He eased forward, his own eyes closing as he concentrated on her slick heat and the way that she was tight, so tight. Even with as wet as she was, she seemed to sheath his head as if she'd been made for his pleasure alone.

He hadn't pushed very far before he felt the resistance.

"What do I do, Finley?" he whispered, the words barely audible.

Then she was there, her hands on his butt, wordlessly guiding him when to push, when to ease up. It soon became clear that the barrier wasn't going to simply give way—and he nearly pulled back, not wanting to hurt her. But then she wrapped her legs around his waist and shifted, tipping her hips ever so slightly. Before he knew what she meant to do, she reared against him, tearing the membrane that separated them.

Whit heard her cry out against him, even as he slid completely home. Then, he felt her teeth sink into his shoulder, felt her struggle to catch her breath.

"You okay?" The words were little more than a garbled exhalation of breath as he lay on her, still supporting himself with his arm, trying not to move.

There was no response at first. He felt her trembling against him, felt her body grow tight with...what? Pain? Fear? Regret?

Then she eased her head back to the pillow and looked at him from beneath her lashes.

"Are you hurting?" he asked quickly, the words nearly ripping from his throat.

She seemed to take a mental inventory before murmuring. "A little. But I feel good too."

She was going to be the death of him.

He'd never had anyone be so honest. Not just in bed, but about anything.

"I want you to move, Whit."

He wasn't sure that was a great idea, but he slowly pressed into her, then eased up, trying to offer her pleasure without a lot of friction—and it must have worked, because her eyes fluttered closed again and he could see that she was absorbing the sensations, testing the strange fullness that he provided.

"I love the way you fill me, Whit. It's better than I'd ever dreamed it would be."

She'd thought of them...*dreamed* of them? Like this? Together? Their bodies joined?

He could feel the heat pounding through his body, centering on that point of connection. His balls had drawn so tight that he wasn't sure how much more he could take.

"I...I don't think I can hold on much longer, Finley."

She offered a soft laugh—the laugh of a lover.

"Then don't wait any longer. I've already had my pleasure. Twice. And…I think I'm a little too sore to come again. But I want you to feel you lose control."

Her permission was all he needed. Although he told himself to be gentle, he couldn't seem to control his own reaction. He plunged into her, once, twice.

Then a world of sensation exploded around him and he gave himself up to the pleasure of loving Finley, mind, body and soul.

SEVENTEEN

*F*inley found herself drifting away, eyes closed. Her body thrummed with pleasure—and a little pain. But for the most part, she felt surrounded in a cocoon of happiness and a strange sense of...power. Never in her life had she been so aware of her own femininity and her emotions toward another human being.

She felt Whit roll off the bed and vaguely heard him move out of the room. She had the most incredible urge to sleep—maybe even sleep the day away. She was so certain that her dreams would be wonderful.

But when Whit returned, he pulled the sheet from her body.

"Come on, sleepyhead."

She groaned in dismay, then gasped, startled awake again when Whit scooped her up.

"What are you doing?"

Instead of answering, he carried her into the bathroom where she discovered he'd filled the claw foot tub with water. He set her on her feet.

"You're going to be sore, most likely, but a warm bath should help with that."

Finley turned to wrap her arms around his waist. "Why are you so good to me?"

At that, he tipped up her head and bent toward her—and his eyes were dark and warm and rich like a secret, untouched forest. "You know why."

And she did. She saw the emotions shining from those green depths. Tenderness, awareness...love.

This is what she'd been missing with Clint all those years ago—and deep down, she'd known it. With Whit, she'd always been comfortable at being herself. With him, she felt strong. Beautiful.

"You first," she murmured, indicating the tub with a tip of her head.

He laughed softly. "I can wait."

"I don't plan on wallowing in that tub on my own."

His brows rose infinitesimally. "I don't think we'll both fit."

"There's only one way to find out."

He released her and carefully folded himself inside. Finley hid a smile at the sight of him, so long, so tall, so lean, legs bent so that he could relax within the confines of the tub.

"Your turn," he said, holding out an arm.

For a moment, she was transfixed by the taut curves of his biceps, the hollow of his elbow, the veins that traced the length of his forearm before ending at those broad hands with their long, slender fingers.

Real. This was real.

Taking his hand, she allowed him to help her into the high tub and settle between his legs, her back resting against the broad plains of his chest.

The warmth of the water immediately seeped into her body—easing the strain of muscles she hadn't even known she possessed. Bit by bit, she felt the tension seep from her body—and with it came the realization that she'd been holding herself stiff and guarded for so long. But now...

Now, she felt...free.

She leaned her head back on Whit's chest, closing her eyes, enjoying the closeness. He'd wrapped one arm around her waist and used the other to dip a washcloth in the water, then use it to dribble warm water over her breasts and shoulders.

"Are you warm enough?"

"Mmm hmm."

"Feel good?"

She smiled. "Absolutely."

He leaned near her ear to murmur, "Happy?"

"Yes."

They lay there until the water began to grow cool. Then Whit soaped the washcloth and they helped to bathe one another. Once out of the tub, he dried her off, then carried her back to the bed and pulled up the covers.

When he would have left again, she snagged his wrist. "Why are you leaving?"

"I'm going to get us a bite to eat, then I'll be right back."

As he left the room, her lashes drifted closed. She would rest her eyes. Only for a minute. But when she heard Whit return, she found them much too heavy to open.

Seemingly from far away, she heard a soft clink, as if something were being set on the nightstand. Moments later, the bed dipped, and she felt herself being pulled close to Whit's side. He pressed a kiss to her head.

It took every ounce of will for her to say, "We should…eat."

He kissed her again. "There's plenty of time for that. Go ahead and sleep."

"Mmm."

She slid an arm around his waist, sighed in contentment, then did as she was told.

Whit couldn't remember the last time he'd awakened to the feeling that all was right with the world. He wasn't sure if he ever had. It sure as hell hadn't happened since leaving Larkspur. And he couldn't imagine a day under Elvis' roof when he'd experienced such a thing. If anything, it would have been the last time he'd spent time with his friends, right here at the Come Back Ranch.

But as he ran a finger up and down Finley's spine, felt the weight of her arm flung across his chest, and absorbed the warmth of her breath in the hollow of his shoulder, he couldn't remember ever feeling this…

Happy.

Which didn't mean that there weren't doubts lingering on the fringes of his consciousness. There were still so many unanswered details that needed to be worked out. Whit had no intention of letting Finley go. But he wasn't sure how he and Finley were going to make things work in the next few months. Finley wanted to go back to school—and he would be the last person to stand in her way. She deserved a chance to make her dreams a reality. But Whit…

Inexplicably, he felt himself pulled into two directions. Either he would return to Reno and the life and job that awaited him. Or he would stay here, tend to the ranch and be on hand to help Clint.

But how could either option blend in with Finley's goals?

His thoughts must have transmitted themselves to the rest of his body because Finley's fingers swept soothingly across his chest.

"What's the matter?" she murmured against his skin.

He would have to remember how sensitive she could be. She'd always seemed to know what he was feeling, even when he'd managed to hide it from the others.

"I'm thinking about my job," he murmured, not willing to voice his concerns. Not yet.

But Finley, being Finley, wouldn't be so easily put off. She lifted her head to study him with those blue, blue eyes.

"When do you have to get back?"

Damn. There were times when he wondered if she were psychic. She always had the ability to sweep aside the bullshit and find the heart of him.

"A couple of weeks at most."

She nodded, resting her chin on her hand.

"When are you planning on going back to school?"

"The first of the year."

"You…uh…" He hesitated, then asked, "Do you have something lined up?"

Those eyes looked away, but he wasn't fooled. The future weighed as heavily on her as on him.

"I've been accepted at the University of Utah and Boise State. I won't be able to get into the nursing programs right away, but hopefully, I can enter whichever one I choose by fall semester."

Damn. Both schools were hours and hours away from either Reno or Larkspur.

"It…uh…sounds like you've got everything all figured out."

Her gaze became troubled, a tiny line appearing between her brows.

"I thought I had. But now…"

So, she felt a measure of the same confusion he did. Granted, their relationship was new—at least in its current ideation.

"I suppose I could put things off until next fall."

He wrapped his hand around her nape, pulling her toward him for a searing kiss.

"No. This is important to you. We'll find a way—"

"Whit—"

"We'll find a way, Finley. I'm not about to put a crimp in your plans." He offered her a crooked smile, even though an ache had already begun to settle into his chest. "But I also don't intend to let you go."

That comment caused the shadows to lift from her eyes and she leaned in for another kiss. "Then I'll trust your word."

Trust.

In that moment, he realized that having Finley believe in him was as valuable as her devotion. And that thought alone was enough to spur him into finding a solution to their quandary. If it took a long-distance relationship or hours in a car to see her on weekends, he'd make it work.

He kissed her again, long and slow and sweet, absorbing everything about her that made her the woman he'd cared about for so long. Then he drew back, knowing that he needed to pump on the brakes. As much as he'd love to spend the day in bed, he also knew that Finley was sore. He could read it in the way she gingerly sat on the side of the bed before standing, or padded into the kitchen when she thought he was asleep, the rattling of a pill bottle letting him know clearly enough that she'd sought pain medication. As much as he might want to indulge in a little foreplay, he wasn't about to do anything that might cause her discomfort.

"Come on. Get dressed," he said softly. "We need to feed and water the livestock. I'm sure they're already wondering why we're late."

A flash of disappointment crossed her features, and he knew her thoughts without their having been expressed.

Plunging his hands through the tousled waves of her hair, he murmured against her lips. "I want you, Finley. More than you'll ever know. But you're sore and I won't be able to keep my hands off you if we stay in bed. So, let's feed the animals and get something to eat besides Pop Tarts." He kissed her again, this time with a little more intent. "Then maybe…this evening…we can get a little creative."

A spark seemed to light a fire in her eyes—nearly blowing his plans out of the water then and there.

Did she have any idea what she did to him with that look alone?

Knowing he would be completely undone if she continued to watch him that way, he nudged her toward the edge.

"Let's get going."

Within minutes, they'd managed to dress and found their way to the barn.

Finley hadn't investigated the property much beyond the main building, so she was pleased to see that the barn was in good repair. Here, Norm had a pair of Quarter Horses sheltered in the stalls and a healthy supply of baled alfalfa stacked up in the center aisle and the loft to see them through the winter. While Whit broke open a small bale of hay and forked it into the overhead feeders, Finley scooped oats into the mangers and checked on their water supplies.

For a moment, Finley paused to pet each of the animals, scratching their ears and stroking their necks.

There had been a time when the stalls had been filled with horses—and more had been kept in the pastures beyond. Trail rides had been offered through the foothills and sleigh rides during the winter. But that had been a long time ago.

"I'll see to the cattle," Whit murmured.

She watched as he grabbed another bale by its strings and hauled it outside to the fenced pasture.

Finley trailed after him, watching as he handled the heavy block of hay as if it weighed little more than a few pounds. Once at the fence line, he dug a small knife from a sheath at his belt and used it to cut the twine, then threw sections of the alfalfa into an old concrete feeding trough on the other side of the barbed wire.

"How many cows does Norm have?" she asked as she followed him.

"Only a half dozen."

He offered a short, high-pitched whistle and the animals that had been at the far-flung corners of the field began ambling back.

She shook her head. "I remember when Norm used to keep a couple of hundred head on the property."

Whit nodded, standing back to watch the cows jostle for position. "I suppose once his health began to fail, he kept things simple."

He paused, his hands on his hips, staring out at the pasture, and beyond that, the glittering lake where the Sinful Six had once spent so many afternoons swimming and canoeing.

"Norm had quite a piece of property here. These days, the land itself is probably worth more than anything you could ever run on it. But, with one or two new fences and a fresh infusion of livestock, this could become a real working ranch."

"A ranch-slash-motel."

He grinned. "The motel part would probably take a little more work."

She turned a slow circle. Come Back Ranch had a peace to it that she'd nearly forgotten. Here, a person could believe that they were miles away from civilization. The scents were richer—pine, hay, and the loamy earthiness of crushed autumn leaves. Aspen rustled overhead, their unique shivering leaves glittering in the sun like golden coins. Then there were the sounds: the wind soughing through the evergreens; the patter of squirrels rushing across the paths; the distant echoing rhythm of a woodpecker.

It really could be a lovely place to live.

If only.

If only she didn't have other plans. Plans which she'd already put off for too long.

Whit turned, and for a moment, sunlight spilled over the planes of his cheeks and jaw—and the sight of him looking so…content…nearly stole the breath from her body. She would give anything to see him like that every day of her life.

But a part of her—that secret doubtful part which had grown, oh, so suspicious of happiness—warned her that it couldn't last. This was a holiday romance, nothing more. All too soon, she and Whit would go their separate ways. It had to happen. Emotions this hot and sweet and powerful couldn't be sustained for long.

As if sensing a portion of her thoughts, Whit frowned.

"What's wrong?"

She shook her head and offered a light laugh—but the sound seemed false, even to her own ears.

He stepped toward her, tucking his gloves into his back pocket. Then he slid his hands around her waist, pulling her to him, hip to hip.

"What's wrong, Finley?"

Why did this man have to be so astute? With anyone else, she could have bluffed her way through the moment. But with him…

She had to be honest.

"It's beautiful here. At any other time, I might have been tempted to stay."

A warmth entered his gaze, conveying to her that he'd entertained much the same thoughts.

"But I've waited so long to get out of here, Whit. I want…no, I *need* to go back to school. I don't want to be a waitress all my life. I want to do something more…challenging. Meaningful. I've seen the medical professionals who have been so instrumental in Clint's care, and that's what I want to do."

He tucked a stray strand of hair behind her ear. "No one is asking you to give that up."

"But I can't do both, don't you see?"

He opened his mouth—probably to offer a blithe platitude. But then he seemed to reconsider.

"No. You're right. You can't do both."

"But this place…*you*…demand that I stay here."

He shook his head, leaning down so that they were eye level beneath the brim of his hat, his expression growing fierce. "No. I'm not asking you to do that." He framed her face with his palms. "I would never ask you to do that. Sure, the Come Back Ranch has made everything a little more difficult to sort out. But it won't be that way forever. Eventually, we'll get the whole gang back together and we can decide who wants to keep the property, who wants to sell. But that doesn't mean that you have to remain in Larkspur to do it."

She clutched at his wrists. "But don't you see? It does. According to the will, one of us has to live on the ranch at all times. You'll be leaving soon—"

"Javi—"

"Javier's life is in Jackson."

"Then P.J. or Liam."

"P.J. lives on a military base when he's in country and who knows where Liam might be."

"Then we'll hire a caretaker or lease out the house. We can give them free rent in exchange for watching the property and taking care of the animals."

For a moment, a brief spark of hope settled into her chest.

Whit must have sensed it because he pushed his point home. "We're going to sort through this—all of this. But first, I'm going to take you into town and we're going to eat. Nothing this important should be settled on an empty stomach. After we're done, we'll pick up more groceries and stop by your mother's house so that you can gather your things."

"My things?"

His arms looped around her back, pulling her close again, even as he bent his head for a kiss.

"I was hoping you'd…stay over tonight." His lips touched hers, once, twice. "I want to sleep with you in my arms, then wake up with your head next to mine on the pillow."

She couldn't resist sliding her own arms around his waist, splaying her hands over the indent of his spine.

"And is that all you want?"

"What else did you have in mind?"

She lifted on tiptoe to whisper, "Perhaps another bath?"

"Mmm. That could be arranged."

She trailed her lips along the line of his jaw, ending at the indentation of his jaw. Then, feeling bold, she nipped him softly. "And maybe…more of your expert attention in bed."

She felt him smile.

"Expert, huh?"

"Definitely."

"I could probably be persuaded."

She could feel the ridge of him against her and she lowered her hands to cup his buttocks, bringing him even closer.

He groaned softly against her, then bent to place a kiss against her neck, beneath her ear.

"I do believe that you are trying to distract me, Miss Fitzpatrick."

"Is it working?"

His laugh was low and rumbling, sending a skittering of gooseflesh down her spine.

"Oh, yeah."

Then he kissed her, long and slow and deep. One of those soul-wrenching kisses that had the ability to rock Finley to her very foundations and convince her that nothing mattered as much as this man. This moment.

But just when she would have chucked every goal she'd ever had for this moment to continue for an eternity, he drew back.

"I thought we'd decided to take things easy."

She laid a finger in the crease of his chin—that maddening, wonderful dent which had always fascinated her.

"And I thought that we'd already decided that ten years was long enough."

He shook his head, his grin becoming more pronounced. "I meant *today*." He put a scant amount of distance between them, then touched her cheek. "You've got to be in pain," he murmured.

Finley felt a heat seep into her cheeks. But then, when she met his gaze—and the tenderness and concern she found there—she pushed her embarrassment aside. This was Whit. *Whit.*

"Okay. Dinner. Supplies. Clothes. Then, I'm holding you to your promise to get…how did you put it? Creative?"

He laughed, looped one hand around her waist, and began leading her toward the Bronco.

"It's a deal."

EIGHTEEN

On their ride back to Larkspur, Whit pulled Finley into the center of the bench seat, then helped her fasten her seatbelt and arrange her legs around the gear shift before heading away from the ranch and merging onto the main road. Once he'd passed the first few hairpin turns, he draped his arm around Finley's shoulders and drew her close.

"Do you have to take the later shift at the diner?"

"No. I've got the whole day off."

Hallelujah!

Finley must have felt the same way, because she grinned at him, her eyes sparkling in the sunlight. "And I have three days off next week."

Three whole days.

Whit leaned to press a kiss against the top of her head.

"Best news I've heard yet. We'll have to plan something special."

One of her hands rested high on his thigh and she squeezed it slightly. "I'd rather spend time with you at the ranch. That would be better than any organized activity."

So true.

"I like that idea. Although we might need some furniture."

She glanced up at him, and he melted beneath her secret smile. "I'm pretty sure we'll have all the furniture we need."

In a single statement, she'd managed to send a raging hunger for her thundering through his veins. He tried his best to tamp it down.

Later. They had all the time in the world. Stay present in the moment.

He smiled, hoping that she could see how much he'd grown to care for her. He'd always been half in love with Finley. But this was different. As a twenty-something kid, he hadn't been smart enough to know what was right in front of him. He'd been attracted to her looks, her body, but he hadn't gone much deeper than that. He hadn't realized that Finley's generous heart and strength of character would prove even more binding in the end. This woman glowed from the inside out because she loved others just as fiercely as she defended them. And to be the object of that affection was powerful.

And humbling.

Glancing at her in the rearview mirror, he realized how much she had done for him—in only a few days. She'd given him acceptance, support, and forgiveness. But most of all, her gentle nature had soothed a savageness inside of him that he hadn't even known was there. She'd healed wounds that he'd thought had scarred over, but which had, in reality, festered beneath the surface. And her belief in him had given him the courage to confront people and situations that had once sent him running.

"Why do you keep staring at me?" Finley asked, her eyes meeting his in the mirror.

"Because you're the most beautiful woman I've ever known."

He watched a hint of pink touch her cheeks, and she looked away.

"Flattery will not get you out of helping me pack," she muttered.

"It's not flattery. It's a statement of fact. And if you don't believe me, I'll say it over and over again until you see what I see. You bring me to my knees."

Her mouth parted ever so slightly in astonishment at his words, the blush of color intensifying.

"You've made me so damned happy," he whispered, almost afraid to say the words aloud in case they tempted Fate.

She leaned into him, her head resting against his shoulder. "You've made me happy too. So much so, that I worry it can't last."

He ran his palm up and down her arm. "It will last. It has to last."

Because he didn't want to think of the man he would become if she left him.

Pushing that thought away, he attempted to steer things in a lighter direction. They were approaching the reservoir and the fork in the highway, so he slowed the Bronco. The precaution proved to be fortuitous when an SUV suddenly swerved in front of him. As he eased up on the gas, the other vehicle veered to take an exit to a scenic overlook where tourists could examine the man-made lake and take pictures.

Already, the parking lot was nearly full of RVs and camping trailers and—

"Shit!"

At the last moment, Whit swerved to take the exit as well, then tapped his brakes until the Bronco had slowed and he could ease into an empty parking place between a half-dozen Harley-Davidson motorcycles and a truck pulling a fishing boat.

"What's wrong?" Finley asked.

"Nothing, I…" He pointed to the glove compartment. "Reach in there and grab my notebook, will you?"

He fished out his phone, adjusting it to camera mode while Finley unfastened her seatbelt and fumbled with the flotsam in his jockey box.

Ahead of them an animal trailer had been pulled onto the verge. Whit began taking pictures of the trailer, then shifted his attention to the front. Two men leaned up against the hood of the truck talking, but they both wore cowboy hats, so it was impossible to see their features.

"I wish I had a telephoto lens—or I could get close enough to the trailer to get a look inside."

"Are these the rustlers you were looking for the other day?"

"I think so. Go to the last page in the notebook and read off the USDOT numbers I wrote down."

He heard her riffle through the pages, then she rattled off the letters and numbers.

"That's it."

"What do you need to see inside the trailers? The animals? Or something else?"

"Ideally, I'd like a shot of the brand on one of the animals to see if this is the load my partner, Thayne, has been trying to locate. But if I get too close—and that's Martin Griggs or one of the other suspects on Thayne's list—they might recognize me."

"Wait here."

Before he knew what she meant to do, Finley slid across the seat and stepped outside. He would have called her back, but one of the men straightened and turned slightly, giving Whit a glimpse of his profile.

Martin Griggs. If Whit could get a good look at the other guy...

In the moment he'd been distracted, Finley had begun to move. Whit swore when he watched her fluff up her hair in a way that begged a man to tunnel his fingers through the thick strands. Even worse, she'd tied her button-down shirt in a knot in her navel and walked with an exaggerated sway to her hips.

What the hell was she doing?

His hand moved to unsnap the pistol at his back as she walked straight up to Martin Griggs and began talking.

No, Finley, no! Griggs wasn't prone to violence, but he'd been known to fight back if he thought he was cornered.

Whit cracked his window, hoping to hear what she was saying, but with the gusting wind, he only caught snatches.

...boyfriend and I...New York...driving through...first real cowboys...seen...selfie...

Whit's hand closed around the door handle to his truck, even as he used his thumb to scroll through his contacts list until he found the Wyoming Livestock Board Investigators' phone number.

To his amazement, the two men laughed and posed behind Finley as she lifted her phone high.

"Say 'cheese'!"

She took a photo, then gestured to Griggs' straw hat. The older man grinned, causing his weathered features to quiver like a startled Bassett Hound. Then he muttered something and swept the hat from his head, handing it to Finley.

Finley donned the cowboy hat and took another picture, altered her pose.

Flash!

Then, she said something and the three of them huddled even closer. Whit nearly bolted from the truck when she made one of those pouty-kissy-selfie faces—which, considering the hair and the flash of navel, made her look like a sex kitten—and Martin Griggs wrapped his arm around her waist.

"Hello."

It took a moment for Whit to realize his call had been answered.

"This is Whit Patterson of the Nevada Agricultural Enforcement Agency. I need to talk to Brent Walker."

"This is Brent."

"Brent, I've been asked by one of my fellow officers, Thayne Ruff—"

"Thayne filled me in on everything," Brent inserted smoothly, obviously interpreting Whit's tension. "You got something for me?"

"I believe I have eyes on two suspects and the trailer in question. I have confirmation of the USDOT number, and I'm hoping to have confirmation within the next few minutes as to whether the trailer contains stolen livestock. Judging by what I can see from a distance, it's loaded. I've got no jurisdiction, so if you want to nail these guys, I need some of your men here ASAP."

"Where are you?"

"I'm currently parked on the Slick Rock Dam scenic overlook. I have Martin Griggs in sight and another unknown suspect."

"Hell, yeah. I've been wanting to nail that bastard to the wall for years. I'll alert the Wyoming Highway Patrol, then head to your location. Notify me if the suspects make a move, but keep your distance."

The line disconnected just as Finley pointed to the trailer.

"*...mind if I take a pic of the cows...never been this close...*"

She strolled toward the trailer and bent to peer through the slats—giving Griggs and his companion a great view of her behind. And they were looking, damn them. Whit had to clench his teeth and steel himself not to bolt from the Bronco.

Finley stuck her fingers through the slats, laughed, then said something to Griggs. He sidled up to her, but Finley was too quick, side-stepping him and peering through the louvers again as if searching for the right shot. Finally, she lifted her phone and Whit saw a flash, then another one.

Once again, Martin tried to ease up behind her—he even reached out, the bastard, as if to touch her backside. But Finley seemed to sense his movements because she straightened and seemed to half-skip, half-saunter to the end of the trailer where she took another set of pictures. Then, she turned and held up her phone.

"*...more pictures of...then I won't bug...*"

The two men glanced at each other, then reluctantly stood next to one another. Finley held up the camera, frowned, then motioned them to stand next to the semi and trailer while she circled to a spot in front of them.

"I'll be damned," Whit muttered to himself. "You little genius."

Judging by the angle of the phone, the photo would capture the two men—wide grins, hats tipped to a cocky angle—with the truck's logo and the trailer's identification number positioned behind them.

Just when Whit feared that she'd done too much and the two men were bound to catch on to her maneuverings, she offered them a quick wave, and shoved her phone into her rear pocket.

Whit slouched down in his seat and pulled his hat low over his brow. Swearing softly, he wondered if he should back out of sight. His Bronco was distinctive—and although Martin Griggs tended to work outside of Whit's stomping grounds near Reno, there was no telling if he would recognize it.

But once again, Finley seemed to instinctively know what to do. She began walking in the opposite direction—toward the railing that surrounded the outlook platform and the wooden placard that explained the historical and geological features of the dam. She snapped pictures of the water, the rocks—even the sign. Then she walked to the squat brown building that held the public restrooms.

From somewhere in the distance, Whit caught the plaintive whine of a siren and his eyes snapped to Griggs and his companion. Now that they'd stepped closer, he was fairly certain that the other man was the same one he'd seen running a red light on the outskirts of Larkspur.

The gusting wind luffed around the parked cars—and suddenly Whit couldn't hear the sirens at all.

Had he imagined the sound? Or had the Highway Patrol been intent on some other errand?

But then, the breeze shifted, and the sound became louder. There had to be at least one—no, *two*—cruisers heading toward them.

The men by the trailer seemed to realize the same thing because Griggs pointed to the semi and the two of them ran toward the cab.

Whit briefly considered his options. He'd been told not to interfere, but if Griggs took the vehicle onto the highway, then attempted to outrun the police…

At that moment, an RV began backing out of the parking space in front of the tractor trailer. Whit saw Griggs throw up his hands, his features moving in a way that left no doubt that he was shouting a string of obscenities. Then, he peered into his mirror.

Even from his poor vantage point, Whit could see the man's panic as the sirens were soon accompanied by flashing lights.

Unfortunately, Finley chose that moment to come out of the restroom.

Martin lunged from the semi and ran toward her, and there was no disguising the pistol held low to his side.

"Damnit!"

Whit darted from the Bronco, his hand already reaching for his own weapon. *Idiot.* If he pulled his gun, the Wyoming Highway Patrol would assume he was another perp to take down. But he had to get to Finley!

His boots skidded against the asphalt as he ran, hands pumping, legs scrabbling for purchase. But he wasn't going to make it.

He wasn't going to make it!

At the last minute, he launched himself into the air—and it was just enough to give him a burst of speed. For a few heart-pounding seconds, he was airborne. Then he hit Griggs square in the back, tackling him to the sidewalk. Immediately, Whit grappled to keep the man from raising his pistol. He threw all his might onto the man's arm and shoulder. Just when he feared Martin would still find a way to aim the pistol toward Finley, the gun clattered to the ground, and Finley, his sweet, sweet Finley, kicked it safely away into the grass.

Whit quickly twisted the man's arm to the center of his back, holding him there while his free hand fumbled for the flex cuffs he kept tucked in his holster. Within seconds, he'd wrapped the plastic bands around Griggs' wrists and pulled them tight.

Griggs began shouting epithets to anyone who would listen, but Whit ignored him, looking up at Finley.

"You, okay?"

She nodded. "I'm fine."

Whit rolled to his feet, then dragged Martin upright by his bound hands. By the time he'd tugged the man a safe distance from the gun that still lay in the grass, a pair of uniformed officers were running toward them.

Whit wasn't quite sure what would happen next—for all he knew, he could be slapped in handcuffs himself for "assault", but one of them jogged toward him calling out, "Are you Whit Patterson?"

"I am."

"We got a call to be on the lookout for a Livestock Board Investigator. You got ID?"

"In my truck."

"I'll need to see it, if you don't mind."

"No problem."

The second patrolman grabbed Griggs by the elbow. "We'll take him off your hands."

"There was another suspect—"

"A second unit rolled in behind us. The guy didn't even make it out of the semi."

As Griggs was hauled away, the patrolman moved to deal with the weapon, but Whit didn't give him a second glance. Instead, he reached for Finley, hauling her into his arms.

He wanted to kiss her and whisk her away to safety and scold her for taking too many chances. But all he could manage was tightening his grip to convince himself that she was all right.

Thankfully, her own hands clutched at his back.

"Is your job always like this?" she asked, a slight quaver to her voice.

A bark of laughter pushed from his throat. "It's almost never like this."

"Thank heavens."

A crowd had gathered around them and the patrolman threw Whit a steely gaze, clearly conveying that he hadn't been kidding about needing to see Whit's ID. Even so, Whit pressed a kiss into Finley's hair, then reluctantly drew back.

"I gotta—"

"I heard."

He gripped her hand, twining their fingers together. Even when he'd reached the Bronco and retrieved his badge and Nevada Agricultural Enforcement identification from his glove box, he refused to release her.

"You scared the hell out of me," he murmured for Finley's ears alone as the patrolman copied the information he needed into a pocket-sized notebook, then handed Whit's I.D. back to him and moved toward his car.

Finley squeezed his hand. "But I did a good job, right?"

Again, Whit offered a rueful laugh, his heart just beginning to settle into a normal rhythm. "You did an awesome job."

A tall, lanky figure dressed in jeans, a button-down shirt, a jacket, and a straw cowboy hat sauntered toward him.

"Whit Patterson?"

Whit automatically reached for his identification again, but the man waved it away.

"I'm Brent Walker." Brent Walker sported a huge mustache that had been waxed into spiraling curls. He held out a hand. "It's good to meet you, son."

Son? Walker couldn't have been much more than a dozen years older than Whit.

Whit reluctantly released Finley, but only long enough to shake Walker's hand.

"That's some fine work you did for us. I managed to get Thayne Ruff on the phone and the man's bustin' a few buttons over having trained you."

"This arrest was all his doing. I was just another pair of eyes."

The ends of Walker's mustache twitched as he grinned. "Well, I'd take a pair of eyes like yours any day. I'm short-handed, myself. Had a couple of officers move out of state this past month and I haven't been able to replace them, so I doubt we could have come to this happy ending without you. I don't have the manpower right now to chase down all the leads coming my way, so I appreciate everything you've done. If there's anything I can do to return the favor, you let me know."

"Thank you, sir."

"Call me Brent." He touched his fingers to his hat. "I hope we didn't interrupt you're plans, ma'am."

Finley smiled. "Not at all. I enjoyed seeing Whit at his job."

"I'll bet. You two have a nice day."

He backed away, returning to the knot of lawmen that were beginning to gather around the trailer.

"He seems nice," Finley said.

"Wait until he sees the evidence photos you took. He might offer you a job."

Finley laughed—and the sound hit Whit's bloodstream in a rush of pride and joy.

"He'd better not." Her nose wrinkled. "I think I've had my fill of cattle rustlers and livestock trailers for a while. Did you catch a whiff of that thing?" She stepped close, her voice dropping. A single finger reached out to slide down the placket of his shirt, then circle around the indent of his navel. The cotton fabric was no barrier to the intensity of her touch, and when she spoke, it was with a warmth—no, a *heat*—that was for his ears alone.

"Besides, seeing you on the job makes me realize that you can be a total badass when you need to be, Whit. And that…" Her laughter was low and rich and intimate. "That's a real turn-on."

Whit quickly glanced up to make sure they weren't being overheard, then said, "You think, huh?"

"I do. So, keep that in mind when we're getting…creative. We might have to play a round of lawman and the bad, bad cowgirl." Her head tipped. "Unfortunately, that may entail the use of your hat."

Her words sucked the very breath from his body and set his pulse pounding straight into groin. Despite the lawmen milling around them, he couldn't resist cupping his hand around her nape and bending to whisper next to her lips, "As soon as I get you back to the ranch…"

"It's a deal."

A few minutes later, Whit was asked to give his statement, so Finley returned to the Bronco and watched him work.

At first, it had been hard to reconcile the fact that her childhood friend had become a lawman. As a kid, he'd seemed to duck and cover whenever a patrol car approached—probably because his father was constantly being rounded up by the sheriff for one reason or another. And when they'd arrested him after the accident…

He'd tried to keep a stiff, neutral expression, but Finley had seen flashes of pure desperation and fear, then a weary acceptance—as if he believed he were beyond redemption.

But now?

Now, his posture and manner radiated confidence. He stood with his feet planted slightly apart, his shoulders erect, his hands moving in broad strokes as he gestured to the trailer and then to the pictures she'd taken on her phone. With his hat pulled low over his brow, his button-down shirt ruffling in the wind, and the championship belt buckle looped through his jeans, he could have been a cover model for *Western Horsemen.*

At one point, the other officers laughed—probably when they caught a glimpse of Martin Griggs posing in the "selfie" which clearly displayed the identification numbers on his truck and trailer. The officers glanced in her direction—one of the shooting her a thumbs-up gesture—and she waved. Then the group moved to the trailer to examine the cattle.

As they opened the loading door, Whit seemed to be doing most of the explaining. He slid her phone into his pocket, then retrieved the notebook that he'd collected along with the leather case which had held his ID.

Finley felt her heart melting beneath a wave of pride, but quick on its heels came a rush of panic. Clearly, Whit was good at his job—and it was just as obvious that he enjoyed it. But Reno was hundreds of miles from either of the colleges she'd chosen—and Larkspur was even farther away than that. How could they possibly keep their relationship going under those circumstances?

The instant the thought appeared, she pushed it away. She wouldn't think about that today. Right here, right now, he was hers and she would enjoy every minute to the fullest.

Whit began shaking hands with the other officers, then he turned, striding toward her. That image of him—tall, broad-shouldered, and every inch the cowboy—would be seared into her brain for the rest of her life. Especially when he only had to move in her direction for every womanly part of her body to clench in reaction.

The door squeaked as he climbed into the Bronco.

"Sorry about that."

"Don't be. I enjoyed watching you."

He shot her a look rife with disbelief, then shook his head, motioning for her to slide across the bench seat so that she sat next to him. As soon as they'd both fastened their seatbelts, he put the Bronco in gear, then backed out of the parking place.

"I think we've got what we need to put Griggs away. And since his accomplice is already singing like a sweaty tenor, we should be able to bring down his network as well. The guys in Nevada are over the moon."

"I'm glad. It's apparent you've all worked hard to make this happen."

He grinned at her—and she was struck with the fact that, a week ago, when he'd first arrived in Larkspur, she wouldn't have thought she would ever see such open joy radiating from his features.

"Most of it was fluke." He squeezed her shoulder. "If we hadn't left the ranch when we did, I doubt we would have caught up with them. You must be my lucky charm. I was with you when I saw Griggs in Redmond, and again today."

"Glad I could help."

"Are you hungry?"

"Starving."

"Then, let's get something to eat.

NINETEEN

Once in town, Finley directed Whit toward the center of town where a local family had begun selling street tacos from a converted school bus. After gathering up their food and drinks from the take-out window, they climbed back into the Bronco.

"You must be hungry," Finley teased. "That's an awful lot of food."

He pulled onto the main street, then reached for her hand. "It's not all for us."

For a moment, she felt a twinge of panic. Her time with Whit was so new—so precious—that she wasn't sure that she wanted to share him with anyone else.

Whit squeezed her hand. "Relax. I thought we could eat at Greensprings."

"Oh." The word was a bare puff of sound, revealing her surprise. But swiftly on the heels of that emotion came a twinge of guilt, then a flash of doubt.

In the past ten years, she'd visited Clint nearly every day. But lately, she'd only seen him a handful of times—as if Norm's death had made the visits more difficult.

No. Not difficult.

His death had signaled an ending of sorts. She'd visited Clint because he was her friend, true—and at one time, he'd been more than that. But over the years, it had grown harder and harder to see a lack of progress, so she'd begun to visit for Norm's sake. Now that Norm was gone, her trips to Greenspring didn't just remind her of Clint's condition, but of Norm's absence.

"I-I've only seen him a couple of times since Norm died. I'm not sure if I want…to visit him tonight."

She expected Whit to look at her with…what? Accusation? Disgust? But he merely regarded her with the same warmth he'd shown throughout the day.

He squeezed her hand. "You said you saw him last night."

She glanced away from Whit, not sure that she wanted to see his reaction to her confession. "Yes. That's when I gave him the ring back."

He lifted her hand to kiss her knuckles. "Then it's not so surprising that you're feeling a little hesitant. For years, you've been carrying around the weight of being Clint's fiancé."

"I was never really his fiancé. It was a mistake that I should have corrected years ago."

"Doesn't matter. You still supported Clint—and his father—as if you had accepted Clint's proposal. All these years, you've shouldered the burden of caring and supporting the two of them. I think it's only natural that you give yourself some time to shift from that role to that of being a friend."

Friend.

He rubbed her knuckles with his thumb. "Besides…it must be hard. Going to Greensprings and expecting to see Norm there. I bet he spent every free minute with Clint."

Finley felt a tightness grip her throat and tears sprung at the backs of her eyes—not from the reminder that Norm— her ally, her mentor, her stand-in father—was gone. But because Whit seemed to understand her chaotic emotions even better than she understood them herself.

"I miss Norm so much," she admitted. "I didn't realize how much I relied on his advice and his…company. I could talk to him about anything."

Whit nodded. "He was good for all of us."

She hesitated before admitting the rest of what weighed upon her. "But if we go to Greensprings together…"

She was such a coward. Such a coward.

But once again, Whit seemed to understand.

"You're afraid that people will talk."

"They're talking already."

He squeezed her hand until she looked up and met his gaze.

"Do you care?"

She didn't immediately respond. How could she? She'd never felt comfortable in the spotlight. In the past, she'd been quite content on the fringe, letting Clint and P.J. and Javi soak up the attention. They were the daredevils, the rabble-rousers, while Whit and Liam and she hung back.

But when the accident occurred, their roles had been reversed. Whit and she had become food for gossip and suddenly, everything they'd done had become part of the rumor mill.

Did she want to open herself up to that again? Did she want to feel eyes watching her as she crossed the street? Did she want to hear whispers die when she entered a room?

She was ready to back out of it all—lunch, a visit to Greensprings, even dating Whit. But then she met those eyes. Those forest green eyes, watched her with a mixture of warmth and determination, and yes, a portion of vulnerability. Unlike Clint, he'd never assumed that a relationship between them was a sure thing, or that she would wholeheartedly follow his lead. He was feeling his way through these tentative overtures with the same caution that echoed within her. And that, more than anything else, convinced her that she'd be a fool to turn him away.

"I'm not ashamed of you, Finley," he offered. "And I'm not ashamed of the fact that we're seeing each other. If there are those who can't accept that fact, that's their problem, not ours."

He paused long enough to let his assertions sink in, but Finley wondered if he had any inkling at the strength that seeped into her heart with each defiant word.

"As for Greensprings, Clint is our friend. We've both been as honest with him as the situation allows. Who knows? Maybe he's heard us and he's cheering us on."

"Or maybe he wants to leap out of bed and throttle us both."

"I'd love to see him try," Whit said with mock affront. But then, after checking the road ahead of him, he said more seriously. "I'd *really* love for him to try."

He glanced at Finley again.

"But even if he did, it wouldn't change my feelings for you, Finley. I've been half in love with you my whole life and it's time I did something about it."

I've been half in love with you my whole life...

The admission stole her breath.

Whit Patterson...in love with her?

Finley had never been under any illusions. She'd been a gawky kid, all knees and braces. Even Clint had regarded her as "one of the boys" until they'd graduated high school.

But Whit...he'd admitted to much more than that. Perhaps it was time that she borrowed a portion of his openness, especially in voicing her emotions.

Before she could summon the courage to tell him that she'd had a crush on him since the third grade, Whit said, "Greensprings?"

And in that instant, she couldn't have refused if he'd asked for dinner on the moon.

"Okay."

Whit walked into Clint's room to find his friend sitting in the recliner—and for once, it looked as if Clint's eyes were completely open and trained on the television bolted to the wall. Looking up, Whit winced when he saw a rerun of *Barney* with its purple dinosaur and its overly chirpy childhood actors.

"For hell's sake. Is that anything to do to a grown man?"

Whit set the sacks on the overbed table and started looking for the remote. Even so, he didn't miss Finley's disapproving frown.

"They're trying to stimulate him with the music and bright colors."

"That's not music. That's...torture." He finally located the remote tucked beneath Clint's covers. "Hell, Clint never watched anything like that when he was a kid. Why would he want to listen to it now?" He thumbed through the channels until he found a rerun of an all-star football game. "There. If they want to catch his attention, they should put on sports."

Finley squinted at the screen. "You really think that's going to stimulate his senses?"

"Sure. There's a marching band to provide music, the uniforms have bright colors, and..." he leaned low to murmur next to Clint's ear "...you'd rather be stimulated by a college cheerleader than a purple dinosaur any time of day, right?"

Finley giggled and began pulling the containers from the sacks. "How many orders of tacos did you get?"

"A lot." Whit nudged the table closer to Clint. "All right, my man, I couldn't remember if you liked chicken or beef, so I ordered half and half. There's also a couple of extra containers of hot sauce." He took the lid off and sniffed the contents, nearly clearing his sinus with the spicy aroma. "It smells like it can blow your head off, so it's gotta be good. There's also salsa if you want some."

He waved the hot sauce container below Clint's nose, being careful not to get it too close, then set it on the table next to the containers of tacos.

"I was going to get you a Dew, but you didn't drink the last one so—"

"Whit?"

He looked up to find Finley watching the pair of them, her expression suddenly intent.

"Do that again."

"What?"

"Let him smell the hot sauce."

Whit grabbed the container. "What's up?"

"I don't know, it could be nothing."

Whit waved the container in front of Clint's nose. "Look."

For a moment, Clint's eyes fluttered closed.

"You saw that, right?" Finley asked.

"Yeah."

But when he tried it again, there was no reaction.

Finley sighed. "It could simply be an unconscious movement, but I'll mention it to the nurses all the same."

"So, that's a different reaction?"

"I think so. He often has hand twitches, muscle spasms. He sometimes moans or makes unconscious noises." She sighed. "It's been so long that I know I shouldn't look for signs of something more, but…" she shrugged one of her shoulders. "I can't seem to help myself."

Whit wrapped his arm around her shoulders and pulled her close. "There's nothing wrong with having hope, Finley."

But even as he said the words, Whit couldn't help thinking that, at times, hope could be a dangerous thing. While there was nothing he would like more than to see Clint return to the land of the living…

If he did, Whit feared his relationship with Finley would be over before it ever began.

When they pulled up in front of Finley's house, there were no lights on.

"I guess nobody's home," Finley murmured. She hesitated only a moment before saying, "Do you want to come in?"

"Sure."

He killed the engine, then walked around the car to help her down. As they approached the front door, he kept his arm around her waist, matching his strides to hers.

"I don't think I've ever been inside," he murmured as she dug through her purse for her keys.

She offered a soft scoffing noise. "Sure, you have." But when she thought about it, she couldn't remember a single instance. When they were kids, she'd known her mother would be drunk or hungover—or at the very least, say something to offend her friends. So, Finley had done her best to keep them away. Only Clint—who'd been a golden boy in her mother's eyes—had been allowed free access.

After unlocking the door and stepping inside, Finley couldn't help glancing at the recliner. It would be her rotten luck if her mother had passed out in front of the television. But the room was empty.

"Come with me. This shouldn't take too long."

Whit followed her down the short hall to her bedroom. When Finley switched on the light, he whistled softly.

"So, this is the inner sanctum?" he murmured, his tone rife with amusement.

For a moment, Finley paused, taking in her surroundings with new eyes. When she'd been a teenager, her mother had gone through a "girly-girl" period—and she'd been determined her daughters would become the epitome of femininity and grace. Alice had immediately redecorated Finley's room with ruffled curtains, ruffled canopy bed, ruffled slipcovers on the furniture. Everything was pink, from light fixtures to wallpaper to carpeting.

"Wow," Whit murmured.

"Don't read anything into it. My mother is responsible. I've hated it from the very beginning. It looks like she hosed it down with Pepto-Bismol. But I was told if I changed it, I'd be thrown out in the street. After a while, it wasn't worth arguing with her."

"So…having lived inside a flamingo for more than a dozen years, how would you redecorate your ideal space?"

She'd already begun gathering clothes from her drawers, but at his words, she stopped to consider. "A pale, pale yellow, like the color of a summer sun when you're high in the mountains. And I'd get rid of all these frills and keep things simple and streamlined."

He seemed to consider that, his eyes narrowing as if he were trying to imagine the space with a different scheme. "Good choice."

Finley tugged on his wrist, pulling him further into the room so that she could grab the backpack hanging from a hook behind the door. Then she turned to face him, taking in the sight of Whit Patterson—a tall, lean, quintessential western man—awash in a sea of pink.

She laughed softly, then said, "There's one thing I'd keep as it is, though."

His brows rose and he surveyed the room again, an emotion akin to horror washing over his features. "What on earth would you keep?"

"You."

Finley leaned against the door until the latch hit home with a soft *snick*, then threw the backpack onto the floor near the foot of the bed. In two strides, she was in Whit's arms—

and he met her easily, lifting her up so that his lips could crash over hers.

With a twist of bodies and a tangle of legs, they fell onto the bed, Whit's weight pressing her into the mattress. Finley bent a knee to allow him to fit even more closely against her, then reached to tug off his jacket.

Whit shifted onto his knees long enough to wrestle out of his coat.

"And the shirt," she urged.

He reached behind him to tug his shirt over his head, fumbling to release his hands from the buttoned cuffs, then threw the garment onto the floor.

"You're sure you want to do this?" he murmured, his voice low and husky and smoky deep.

"Positive."

He pushed himself off the bed to shuck free of his boots and socks, then reached for his belt buckle. Finley, who'd been stripping off her own clothes, stopped to watch.

"What?" Whit asked, his hands hovering over his zipper.

"I'm enjoying the show."

He laughed softly and reached into his back pocket to remove his wallet. "Last one," he said as he threw her the condom packet.

"We'll need more."

His brows rose. "You think?"

His tone was silky and rich with his passion for her.

Her.

"We'll have to stop and buy some on the way home," she murmured.

Home.

When had the Come Back Ranch become home?

But as soon as that thought appeared, she knew. Whit had made the place home. With him, she'd felt a wealth of emotions that she hadn't experienced in a very long time. Happiness, excitement, passion. For the first time in years, she felt...

Complete.

She quickly removed the rest of her clothes, then welcomed Whit back onto the bed. This time, she gave herself over to the rush of passion and the sheer sensation of being skin to skin with Whit Patterson. Like a blind woman, she ran her hands over the breadth of his shoulders, the straining muscles of his arms, the long line of his spine. Then she gripped the rounded mounds of his buttocks.

Unlike last night, she knew what would come—what it would feel like to have him pressed close, moving against her, into her—and that knowledge alone set a wildfire burning through her veins. Before long, she felt the familiar tension deep within her, the encompassing *want.*

Wordlessly, she guided him to her.

"Not yet," he murmured against her throat.

"Yes, now. I want to come with you inside me."

He lifted his head, his eyes deepening to a smoldering green. Lifting slightly, he guided himself to her entrance, then began that long, slow slide into the heart of her.

Finley closed her eyes, concentrating on the sensations, the ache, the pleasure-pain which only seemed to intensify the sensations. With her hands, her knees, her hips, she conveyed what she wanted, and Whit offered her everything she requested—and more—kissing her breasts, her neck. Soon, her need knew no bounds, and he seemed to know that he should take the lead, increasing the rhythm of his lovemaking until she exploded with sensation, her arms gripping his shoulders, her mouth open against the side of his neck. Then, she felt his own release, and for a moment, she felt an answering tremor in his body before they both collapsed, breathing hard.

For a moment, she felt him shift and stand from the bed, her eyelashes flickering as she watched him remove the condom and throw it away.

"There's tissues and some wipes on the dresser."

"Thanks."

Moments later, he joined her again, lifting her from the bed long enough to throw back the covers. Then, the two of them settled into the impossibly small twin-sized mattress—Finley nearly laying on top of him, his feet dangling over the edge.

"You good?" he murmured.

"Mmm. Really good."

She smiled against his chest, her fingers tracing lazy circles. If she'd known that being with Whit Patterson would be so overwhelming, so completely soul-shattering, she never would have looked twice at another man.

Which left her...where?

Whit would have to leave eventually. They were fooling themselves to think that he wouldn't.

"I've been thinking," she murmured.

He chuckled softly. "That's good. Because when you're this close to me, I can't seem to rub two brain cells together."

He wrapped his arms around her in a quick hug, and she closed her eyes again, absorbing everything she could from this moment—the peace, the contentment, the way he made her feel as if she could accomplish anything in this world.

"I wondered if—"

The door suddenly whipped open, slamming against the opposite wall.

Finley gripped the sheets, twisting to see her mother looming in the threshold, her hands balling into fists.

"In my house? You dare to…be a little *slut* with this *asshole* in *my* house?"

"Mom!"

Whit sat up, automatically twisting so that he shielded Finley from Alice as she stalked toward them.

"Finley—"

"No, Whit!"

She knew he merely wanted to protect her, but as the anger bubbled up from a well of emotion that had been years in the making, Finley reached for his shirt and tugged it over her head, then scrambled from the bed.

Her mother stalked toward her, one hand lifted as if to slap her, but Finley barked, "That's enough!"

For a moment, Alice seemed frozen in place. Clearly, she hadn't expected Finley to fight back.

But Finley wasn't finished. "I'm not a teenager anymore. I'm over thirty and more than entitled to a little privacy in my own room."

"This is *my* house—"

"And *I'm* the one paying for the mortgage, the utilities, and most of the groceries! You haven't had a job in months, Alice."

"Don't you dare call me—"

"I'll call you whatever I want. If you want me to refer to you as my mother, then maybe you'd better start acting like one. I'm tired of being the only adult in our relationship."

"How dare you!"

"Oh, I dare. I'm sick to death of paying your bills and absorbing the debt from your hare-brained shopping sprees. I work hard, every single day, and it's about time I was able to spend those hard-earned funds on myself. So, I'm giving you notice right now. Come the end of the year, I'll be moving out. Once that happens, you're on your own."

Her mother seemed to shrink at the words, her cheeks going pale.

"You wouldn't. The house…my car!"

"You've got more than enough time to land yourself a job—although you'll be hard-pressed to find one in town considering the number of times you've been fired."

"But…Billie!"

"I can take care of myself, Mom."

The voice came from the hall and Billie stepped into the light.

Finley felt the heat rise in her cheeks—not from what she'd said to her mother, but from the way Billie was clearly getting an eyeful of Whit.

"I thought you were gone," Finley offered weakly.

"Obviously. I was asleep." She glared at Whit with a hint of the same venom that Alice had displayed. "At least I was until the headboard sonata began." She wrapped her arms tightly around her waist as if chilled, then offered yet another volley. "So, this is how you show your loyalty to Clint? Both of you should be ashamed of yourselves."

Finley's stomach seemed to plunge to the floor, leaving a rushing vacuum that felt so cold and hollow that coherent thought became impossible. Images rushed through her head—Clint bloody and broken after the accident. Clint in the I.C.U.. Clint at Greensprings. With each mental picture, she felt the same shift of emotions that had pummeled her at the time: guilt, fear, regret.

So much regret.

A phone began ringing in the background, and a tiny corner of Finley realized it was Whit's. But she couldn't move, couldn't speak, as her mother and sister continued to stare at her with such palpable disappointment and accusation that Finley felt as if she were crumbling into a million pieces.

She should have known.

She should have known that her time with Whit wouldn't last. This…romance that they'd shared was nothing more than a holiday fantasy which had been doomed from the very beginning. There was no way that such a relationship could last. Not with so much history weighing them down. A future was impossible against so much past.

"Get out," she finally managed to whisper. Then more forcefully, "Get out of my room. You won't have to worry about me or my behavior any longer. Obviously, there's no reason to wait for the first of the year. I'll be leaving Larkspur as soon as I can give my notice at the diner."

Alice raised her hands, "There's no need to—"

"Get out!"

Her mother stood for a second. Two. Then she and Billie stepped back.

They'd barely cleared the threshold when Finley slammed the door, then locked it for good measure.

The ensuing silence hung heavily on her shoulders, punctuated only by the incessant ring of the phone.

"Finley—"

"Answer your phone, Whit."

"No. We need to talk."

"Answer your phone." She turned to glance at him over her shoulder. Somehow, he'd already stepped into his jeans. "Just…answer the phone."

When he reached into his pocket, she turned away again, fumbling for her backpack. She began snatching clothes from her drawers and stuffing them inside—heedless of their condition or what she was grabbing. When she'd filled it as much as possible, she snatched a duffel from the bottom of her closet and began pulling things from the hangers overhead.

A part of her heard Whit in the background speaking on his phone—*Hello …yeah, this is Whit Patterson…*—but the rest of her was awhirl with disjointed thoughts and emotions. Embarrassment. Confusion. Anger, so much anger.

How had her life reached this point? Little more than a week ago, she'd been calm, controlled, knowing step by step how each day would progress and how close she was to her goals.

And now?

Now, she didn't know what to think or feel. She felt as if a tug of war was occurring between her past and the possibilities of the future, and no matter where she concentrated her energies, there was nothing but conflict and…

"Damnit all to hell!"

Her head reared up at Whit's sudden outburst. She supposed the time had finally come. He'd reached his limit with her. The scene with her mother and sister had been the last straw, no doubt, and he was about to offer her a not-so-fond *sayonara*.

But he wasn't even looking at her. He was grabbing his socks, tugging them on in fierce haste before jamming his feet into his boots.

"We have to get to Greensprings."

We.

The word snagged like a burr, allaying her fears and causing her heart to flip-flop in joy before the rest of his words could sink in.

Greensprings?

Whit glanced up, and for a moment, the lines and planes of his face seemed etched in granite. The incandescent lighting of the bulb overhead washed over his features, making them look gray and drawn.

"Clint has gone into cardiac arrest. They're trying to resuscitate him now."

TWENTY

*W*hit stood inside the doorway to Clint's room, his body still thrumming from adrenaline, his gaze darting from his friend to the medical personnel gathered around the bed.

"He's okay, Whit."

Glancing down at Finley, Whit realized that he was nearly crushing her fingers with his own. Immediately relaxing his grip, he lifted her hand to brush a kiss across her knuckles.

"Sorry."

She shook her head. "You don't need to apologize. I'm as scared as you are."

Unspoken between them lay the fact that Clint had been trapped in a vegetative state for nearly ten years and maybe, this could be the beginning of the end.

Whit vehemently shied away from that thought. He knew full well that this wasn't the way that Clint would want to live out the rest of his life, trapped inside a shell of a body he'd once had. He'd always been so active, bounding through life with an exuberant energy that was contagious.

But Whit wasn't ready to let him go. He'd spent so long running from the events of that night, that he hadn't realized how much he'd missed his family. Not Elvis. No. The Sinful Six were his family.

And Finley.

Finley was home.

The realization thundered through Whit, tightening his throat as he admitted to himself that the need, the joy, the absolute devotion he'd felt when he was with her hadn't sprung up since he'd returned to Larkspur. Those emotions had always been there—probably from the first time he'd laid eyes on her sitting cross-legged on the playmat in their kindergarten class.

Whit wasn't given much time to analyze the import of his thoughts because a middle-aged woman wearing scrubs and a lab coat separated herself from the other medical professionals and approached him.

"Mr. Patterson."

"Yes." He cleared his throat when the word emerged as little more than a croak.

"I'm Dr. Marion Furstenburg."

Whit released Finley only long enough to shake the woman's hand. Then he was reaching for Finley again.

"Mr. Campanella is stable again. His vital signs are about to be expected after being resuscitated, but he seems to be resting comfortably."

"What happened?"

"We're not really sure. Luckily, one of the nurses noticed that he seemed to be in distress when she took his scheduled vitals. I'd already been summoned by the time he went into cardiac arrest."

"Is he...uh...is he going to be okay?"

"It will require a full battery of tests before I can comfortably comment on his condition. I'd like to transfer him to the hospital in Redmond. They're more equipped to handle a cardiac emergency. With your permission, I'll arrange for his transport. In the meantime, he'll be closely monitored until we have a more definite diagnosis."

The answer was far from comforting. Essentially, they knew jack-squat and they weren't committing themselves to anything.

"Can we stay with him?"

"Absolutely." The woman hesitated before continuing. "In reviewing his charts, I noticed that you've only recently been appointed Clint's medical proxy."

"Yes, his father...passed away."

An expression of true regret tugged at her features. "I'm so sorry. Mr. Campanella was very devoted to his son."

"Yes. Yes, he was."

"In the next few days, you may be asked to reevaluate Clint's DNR orders. It's common procedure when there's a change in medical guardianship, so rest assured it isn't a reaction to Clint's current setback. Considering this evening's events, if you feel that any revisions need to be made, you might want to let one of the nurses know. They'll line you up with the proper staff to help you."

DNR orders? What the hell?

The weight of his role as medical proxy settled on his shoulders like a lead weight. Whit had known that he might have to make difficult decisions about Clint's care, but he'd thought he would have a chance to come up to speed with

Clint's condition and the needs associated with it. He hadn't even considered the possibility that he might have to determine whether…

He lived or died.

"Thank you, doctor."

The words came from Finley, along with another squeeze of his hand. Glancing down, Whit saw the concern in her features—not so much for Clint, but for *him*.

One by one, the other nurses slipped from the room, leaving Whit and Finley to stare at their friend and the monitors and cords that kept track of his condition.

"What…uh…" Whit had to clear his throat to even speak. "What are Clint's DNR orders right now?"

Finley took a deep breath. "Essentially, Norm didn't want Clint to die. He gave a time limit for life-saving procedures, but I'm not sure of the exact details. A few of the other guardians of long-term patients have opted not to have any intervention at all."

Whit stared at Clint. For the first time in all the visits he'd made, Clint's eyes were closed. His features were pale, a stark contrast to his dark hair, and his brows were furrowed as if in pain.

Again and again, the thought that Clint wouldn't have wanted this kind of existence hammered into Whit's brain. But to think that the vibrancy of his spirit could be snuffed out forever seemed…unthinkable.

"You don't have to decide anything right now, Whit," Finley offered gently.

She released his hand to slide her arms around his waist, and he held her, drawing comfort from her warmth, her gentleness, her essence.

"Has this ever happened before? His heart stopping."

"No. But he's had other scares and close calls."

"So, this...could be his body telling us that he's had enough?"

She shrugged against him. "Who knows? Maybe. Or maybe he's...I don't know...caught an infection."

"Do you think he's in pain? He looks like he's in pain."

He felt her studying the figure on the bed. "I don't know. They tell me that those in a vegetative state don't really feel anything. But sometimes I think I can sense an energy about him—and I swear I can tell if he's uncomfortable or out-of-sorts. But right now, he's so...still."

Not for the first time, Whit wished that Clint would open up his eyes, sit up, and proceed to offer one of his famous harangues on the best way to handle a situation. Damnit, even if he'd look at Whit, really look at him, maybe Whit could read his thoughts and know what to do. He didn't want his friend to suffer...

But he didn't want to give up on him either.

"Would you like a cup of coffee or a soda?" Finley asked. "It will take a while for them to arrange an ambulance, and it could be hours before we know anything for sure."

Her eyes were filled with such concern—not just for Clint, but for *him*. With everything that was happening, she worried about *him*.

In that moment, he was infinitely glad that Norm had possessed the insight to bypass Finley as Clint's medical proxy. She felt things so deeply—and she couldn't bear to see anyone else suffering. It was why she'd sacrificed so many of her own goals in the last ten years. To her, the well-being of her family and friends far out-weighed her own concerns—and it was the very best part of her. She was a natural-born nurturer.

"Have I told you what a wonderful human being you are, Finley Fitzpatrick?"

Her brows rose. "Because I offered to fetch you a cup of coffee?"

She laughed, and that soft feminine chuckle had the power to diffuse some of the tension that coiled around Whit like a snake.

"Well, that too. But there's oh, so much more to you. You have the power to make those around you feel loved."

A pink wash seeped into her cheeks.

"Martha Campanella would be proud," Whit murmured, realizing that Clint's mother—with her cookies and her folded clean clothes and her door that was always open—had been much the same way.

He wasn't sure, but he thought that Finley's eyes shimmered with a rush of tears. If they had, she quickly blinked them away.

"I'll be right back," she whispered, then backed from the room.

For a moment, Whit absorbed the silence of the room. Then his gaze returned to the bed and he was pummeled with all of the might-have-beens.

If a nurse hadn't caught things in time.

If they hadn't been able to revive him.

But even as the doubts and uncertainties swirled around him, a single overwhelming thought began to coalesce in his soul.

Moving closer, Whit grasped Clint's hand, holding it firmly as he bent close to Clint's ear.

"I don't know what you want me to do here, Clint, and there's no one else who can give me the right answers. So, here's the deal. Whatever you want, you're going to have to fight for it. I'm not going to make dying easy for you. If that's the outcome you're looking for, you're going to have to make that clear to everybody. But I'm hoping you fight even harder to live, buddy. I'll be here, every step of the way, and I'll do everything in my power to help you out. I'm not going anywhere, you hear me? So, fight to get back on track, damnit. Fight."

Finley had been partway down the hall when she'd realized that she'd forgotten her purse. She'd only taken a step into the room when she'd realized that Whit had moved to lean over Clint, speaking to him in low determined tones.

I'll be here, every step of the way…

…fight to get back on track, damnit. Fight.

Realizing that she'd caught a private moment, she snagged the strap of her purse, then stumbled into the hall again.

Although she'd shied away from the depth of her emotions for days, she couldn't avoid naming them any longer.

She loved that man.

Loved him.

How could she not? He was wise and sensitive and supportive. When he committed to something—or *someone*—it was with every molecule of his being. And he loved *her.*

But in those overheard words he'd spoken to Clint, she realized that, very soon, Whit Patterson would be moving back to Larkspur. He might not know it himself yet, but he wouldn't be satisfied with handling Clint's affairs long-distance.

Which meant that if Finley wanted to be with him, she would have to stay. Again. Put her life on hold. Again.

Her stomach twisted and she was filled with an old, familiar frustration.

She had to get out of Larkspur.

If she didn't alter the course of her life, *now*, while she had the chance, she never would. She would continue to stagnate, never learning or growing or challenging herself. And the thought of her future stretching out ahead of her—so barren of the opportunities she wanted from a job in medicine—filled her with panic.

But the alternative, leaving Whit after they'd finally managed to come together, was equally unthinkable.

What was she supposed to do?

Dawn was beginning to wash the sky with pink when Whit pulled into the driveway of Finley's childhood home.

"You're sure you'd like me to drop you off here?"

The last thing Whit wanted was for Finley to go back into that house and face the brunt of her mother's and sister's disapproval.

But Finley nodded. "I've got to get my stuff. I'll pack up my car and do my shift at the Busy B, then I'll meet you back at the hospital."

They'd finally received preliminary results on Clint's condition. Blood tests were showing evidence of a heart attack. Further tests and treatment would be done at the hospital in Redmond.

"You'll text me if you hear anything more."

"Absolutely."

When she reached for the door handle, Whit snagged her wrist, waiting until she looked at him.

"Are you sure you're okay? You've been through a lot tonight."

She tipped her head at a defiant angle, and when her mouth opened, he knew she was going to deny it. But then her chin trembled and she took a quick, gulping breath.

Whit reached to pull her across the bench seat and into his arms. Her hands snapped around his waist and she burrowed her head into his chest, but she didn't cry. Instead, she held herself stiffly, clearly fighting the emotion.

"What is it? Your mom? Your sister? Or Clint?"

She didn't immediately answer. But then, she exhaled, long and slow, and the tension in her body seemed to disappear with it, leaving her limp in his arms.

"The blowout with my family was inevitable—and it had nothing to do with you."

"I think that's debatable."

Her head lifted enough that he could see the sweep of her brows, the slender line of her nose. The rest of her features were still shadowy in the darkness.

"No, everything they said is merely a continuation of the same running argument we've been having for years. I never should have come back to this house when I left college. I should have found a little apartment and fended for myself."

Whit supposed the assertion had merit, but he also knew that when she'd moved back after the accident, it had been a chaotic time. Billie had still been in high school—as rebellious and out-of-control as any teenager could be—and her mother had been "recovering" from a divorce and back surgery by popping oxycodone like breath mints. Leaving her family to self-destruct would have been impossible for Finley to bear.

"You can't blame yourself for taking care of Billie and Alice."

"But I should have stood up for myself more. I should have settled the subject of my supposed engagement to Clint long ago."

Whit considered that point, then said, "You can't deny that handling the things the way you did gave Norm a great deal of comfort."

"I could have given him the same comfort as Clint's friend."

"Maybe. But..." Whit searched for a way to explain himself. "Clint was in I.C.U. for what? A month?"

"Six weeks."

"I know hospitals have relaxed things in the last few years, but back then, the trauma unit wouldn't let anyone into a patient's room but a direct relative. They stretched the rules to let you visit because you were his fiancé. I can't imagine Norm having to deal with all the treatments and successes and setbacks on his own. Having you with him in a semi-official capacity made the two of you a team." He bent to kiss her on top of the head. "You were always like a daughter to Norm, Finley. But going through all that together must have allowed Norm to feel like he could confide more of his struggles with you than he might have done with anyone else. I know having you here with me tonight helped me to sort through things with a level head, to look at them objectively and emotionally, and to feel comfortable with the decisions I made. Not to mention, you knew more about Clint's condition than any chart. I swear, you know more medical jargon than the doctors."

He felt her laugh softly, and the sound eased the iron bands that had clamped around his chest at the mere thought of her tears.

"But it was still a lie," she whispered against him.

"Was it?"

He tucked a finger beneath her chin and forced her to look up. "Finley, you cared for Clint. A lot. If it weren't for…our kiss and the accident…you might have married him."

She opened her mouth to argue and he placed a finger on her lips.

"Come on, Finley. If I'd moved away before the accident…can you honestly say that you wouldn't have considered it?"

Finley seemed to think about that.

"It would have been a mistake," she finally whispered.

"Maybe. Maybe not. None of us can ever say with certainty how our lives would have unfolded if we'd made different choices. There's a possibility that you and Clint would have married, bought a house with a picket fence, and had a dozen children."

"Hardly!"

"Okay, two dozen."

She poked him in the ribs, making him jolt.

"Ow!"

"And what about you, Whit? What would you have done?"

"Most likely, I'd be a bum."

"No, really."

He thought for a minute, then shrugged. "I don't know. I'd probably have a busted-up body from the rodeo circuit and a dead-end job. In many ways, the accident was the worst and the best thing that could have ever happened to me."

Finley's brows creased. "How so?"

"I was terrified when they charged me with vehicular manslaughter. Hell, I couldn't even remember the wreck, and they were telling me that I'd been involved in a six-car pileup and someone had died."

"But they couldn't prove you had anything to do with it."

"I didn't know that. All I knew was that I was locked up, had a public defender who seemed to dole out information with a teaspoon, and Elvis sure as hell wasn't going to pay any bail."

"We should have realized."

He slid his hand down her arm. "It was my fight. Anyhow, by the time I got out, I wasn't fit to be around. I was angry and alone—and I couldn't bring myself to come back to Larkspur where the court of public opinion had already convicted me. So, like a coward, I took up the itinerant lifestyle, moving from ranch to ranch, job to job. But those years taught me a lot. I learned to think for myself, solve my own problems, and work hard. I also figured out what I wanted to do with the rest of my life and how to get there. In the end, things worked out." He cupped her cheek in his palm. "Especially since all those struggles led me back here to you."

He bent and kissed her softly, gently, hoping that she could tell from the caress that, of all his accomplishments, meeting up with her again was the most important.

Her lips immediately parted, allowing him to deepen the embrace, to slip his tongue inside and taste her—a combination of sweetness and peppermint tea. As it had so many times before, the mere contact stampeded through his body with a rush of desire and tenderness and possession.

He'd been right in telling her that, if things had gone differently, she might have fallen in love with Clint and married him. But he was so damned grateful that she hadn't. With each day that passed, each kiss, each caress, his need for her intensified—and not only because of the physical pleasure she brought him. Heaven knew that she could get his body to respond with heat and desire and urgency like nothing he'd ever known. There were times that he wanted to shout from the rooftops that she was his, simply to keep her all to himself.

But it was more than that. She had the ability to soothe or encourage him with a glance. Hell, at Greensprings, he'd sworn there were times when she could read his mind. When the waiting would get to him, or he'd grow frustrated from the lack of answers, she simply had to touch him on the shoulder or shoot him a smile and he was pulled back to what was important.

Living in the moment.

With her.

Whit burrowed his hands beneath the hem of her shirt to feel the silken heat of her flesh beneath. He'd only just discovered her body—and he knew he'd never get enough—but it was her mind that fascinated her the most. He greedily wanted to discover all the nuances of her personality—her favorite song, what movies she liked, whether she relaxed with a thriller or chick lit. And he knew that he could spend the next hundred years with her and still not know everything.

He broke away to stare down at her.

"We seem to be crashing through my promise to court you, but I want you to know that I…I care for you, Finley. In fact…I'd say I'm falling in love with you. Again."

He watched as the emotions flitted over her features: wonder, joy, heat. But then her lashes fell and he felt her pulling away from him.

"What? Should I have kept my thoughts to myself?"

"No!"

She framed his face, kissing him on the lips in a way that left him in no doubt of her pleasure.

"I-I feel the same way, but…"

"But what?"

"You may not consciously realize it yet, but you've already made the decision to move back to Larkspur."

When he tried to object, she put her finger over his mouth.

"It's okay if you do, Whit. It makes sense. Clint's care is ongoing, and it will be so much easier if you're nearby. Then there's the ranch. Your being here would save us from hiring a caretaker. And you love it. You're so at peace when you're there. But…"

"But?"

"I can't stay, Whit. If I'm ever going to be something other than a waitress, I have to get out of here."

"I would never ask you to remain in Larkspur. My living here is no different than if I were in Reno. As soon as you know which university you plan to attend, we'll work things out. Promise."

It wasn't until the words were spoken that Whit admitted to himself as much as Finley that he'd be making a move—which left him open to a whole host of complications. He would need to sell his condo, pack up his stuff, quit his job…

But even as the list began to multiply in his head, he knew it was the right thing to do.

Nevertheless, he could feel the weight of Finley's doubts in the stiffness of her posture—and he doubted that there was anything he could say which would push away her fears. Too many times, her goals for the future had been pushed aside to make other people happy. Whit couldn't be one of those people.

Wrapping his arms around her, he cradled her head with his palm. "All these plans are short-term, Finley. We don't know yet where we'll be in a month, let alone a year. Clint's already shown us that he can toss one or two surprises our way, and the fate of the ranch is up in the air until we can get the Sinful Six back together. But you…you deserve to take the next step. We'll…swap places. I'll hold down the fort here in Larkspur—hell, I'll even do my best to keep Billie and your mother in line, if you want."

She made a sound that was half-laugh, half-sob.

"That's what you did for the last ten years, and I can take over. Go do whatever it is you want and need to do." He pressed his lips to her hair, willing her to trust him enough to continue loving her. "We've got phones. We've got cars," he reminded her.

She trembled slightly, revealing that he hadn't entirely convinced her.

But she was thinking about it.

TWENTY-ONE

*W*hit shifted on the hard, plastic hospital chair, trying to make himself more comfortable. He was too damned tall for the waiting room furniture—and the rows of chairs had been placed so closely together that he felt as if his knees were pressed up against his chest.

"Mr. Patterson."

"Yes!"

He jumped to his feet, shoving his phone back into his pocket, and wound his way through the mouse maze of legs and purses and book bags until he could approach the information desk of the emergency room.

The woman flashed him a professional smile that didn't quite reach her lips. "Sorry for the delay. They've finished Mr. Campanella's tests and he's being transferred to room 486. You'll go down that hall there, make a right. Go all the way to the end of the corridor, then take the elevators up to the fourth floor. Once there, you'll see signs leading you to the proper hallways."

"Thanks."

Less than five minutes later, Whit found the correct room and tapped lightly on the door before letting himself in.

Although he didn't think he'd ever get used to seeing Clint so still, there was a comfort in finding him stretched out on the bed, his dark hair pressed against the pillow. He seemed to be asleep, but as Whit stepped inside, his lashes flickered slightly.

A nurse in pale blue scrubs had been taking his temperature and she looked up as Whit entered.

"Hello. Are you family?"

Whit opened his mouth to clarify his role, but hesitated.

"Yeah. Yeah, we're family. I'm also his medical proxy."

"Ahh. You must be Mr. Patterson."

"Yes."

She stepped to the computer, her nails clattering on the keys. Then she said, "The cardiologist will drop by to see you as soon as possible, but he did want you to know that Mr. Campanella has had a mild heart attack. He's been given a blood thinner, so we'll be watching him closely, but his vital signs are good and Dr. Hildebrand is optimistic."

Thank god.

"My name is Jordan. I'll be in and out of the room, but if you need me, press the call button."

"Thanks."

She was nearly out the door when Whit stopped her with, "Jordan?"

"Yes?"

Whit had moved closer to the bed and he gestured to Clint. "Is he in pain? I just think he's…"

He paused, wondering what he should say. Frowning? Tense? Uncomfortable?

Maybe it was nothing, but even in the short time that he'd been in Larkspur, Whit had grown accustomed to the subtle expressions that flitted across Clint's face—whether they were involuntary or not. And Clint looked...

Different.

"I'll speak to the doctor."

"Thanks."

As the door bumped shut behind her, Whit pulled the standard hospital-issued glider closer to the bed. Then he took Clint's hand in his, mindful of the pulse oximeter clipped to his finger.

"You gave us a hell of a scare, Clint. But judging by the way the nurse seemed rather upbeat, I'm going to take that as a good sign." Whit squeezed his hand. "Nevertheless, this place can't hold a candle to Greensprings. It's pretty...beige. So, you're going to need to dig in your heels and get better so that you can get out of here. I'm pretty sure that smuggling pizza and sandwiches into the hospital will only get us into trouble—and where's Javi going to sit? Huh?"

Clint's lashes flickered again, and Whit hoped that meant they would open soon. Even if Clint didn't look him in the eye, Whit missed the illusion of his friend hanging on his every word.

"The repairs are coming along at the ranch. I can't wait to get you up there to see everything. I started asking about the possibility with Sharla, you know, the nice woman who says goodbye to you each night before she goes home. She had a word with your doctor, and buddy, they are giving a tentative green light to a field trip. You're going to have to get better first, and you'll have to sail through all your checkups, but this spring, when the weather is warm, we'll load you up in one of their vans and take you to the Come Back Ranch for the day. Granted, we'll have to have a caregiver tag along, but I think we can find a person who's cool and won't be too much of a wet blanket. You...you need to work on your strength first, okay? No more ventilators or pneumonia. And none of this heart nonsense. Geez, you're only thirty years old, man. No more fries for you."

Silence eased between them, washing into the corners of the room. But the quiet didn't bug Whit. He didn't know if it was the contact of his hand around Clint's or the sound of his voice—or sheer coincidence—but the furrow was disappearing from his friend's brow and his features seemed to relax infinitesimally. Even better, his eyes had opened and stared up at the ceiling.

"There you go," Whit murmured. "Don't let the change of scenery startle you. You're not at Greensprings, you're at the hospital—and they are giving you the royal treatment, let me tell you. I bet the nurses will be fighting over who gives you a sponge bath."

Nothing.

But the strain around Clint's mouth eased.

"I've already sent word to Javi. He's hot-footing it back to Larkspur. He should be here by tomorrow morning. I told him he might want to wait until we'd heard the results from your tests, but he wouldn't hear of it. Said he had get here in person so he could kick your butt for scaring us like that. He must have passed the word on to P.J., because P.J. called me as I was heading into the emergency room."

Whit laughed softly. He'd been worried about his first contact with P.J.—who tended to carry a grudge longer than anyone Whit had ever met. But after a quick "How the hell are you, Whit?" P.J. had immediately insisted on a "sitrep" concerning Clint's condition. Instantly, the intervening years—and the issues that had driven them apart—had dropped away.

"P.J. must be pretty good at his job, because he started rattling off all these medical terms. I swear, half of it was in code and the other half were these unpronounceable acronyms. I finally had to write down his most urgent questions. I'm to read them verbatim to your doctor and take notes on his answers. P.J. will call back tomorrow at about the same time. Until then, I'm supposed to text him with any updates. I think he would have hopped on a plane and made his way here if he could. He told me to tell you to stop being a pussy and get out of bed."

Clint's chest jerked and a sound that was half-cough, half-grunt burst from his throat. Whit glanced at him in concern, but Clint's eyes remained at half-mast and he stared into the white ocean of ceiling tiles.

Whit continued. He told Clint about his time with Finley—omitting most of the salacious parts. Even so, he found himself confessing, in a roundabout way, about being caught in Finley's bedroom by her mother and sister— another cough, another grunt—and how he was concerned that old fears might cause her to bolt.

"I'm worried about her, Clint. I'm in love with her— always have been. If I'd been less of a chicken-shit all those years ago, I would have fought you for the chance to date her." He glanced up at Clint.

Nothing.

"The thing is, I think the feelings are mutual. No. I *know* they're mutual. You should see the way she…lights up when I walk into the room. It's hot as hell…and a little scary. I don't want to let her down, but she doesn't seem to be able to trust that I'm here for the long haul. She doesn't seem to think that if I'm in Larkspur and she's at one of the universities…"

The words died as what he was saying finally sank into his brain.

He'd been expecting her to trust in him and his feelings—blind, stepping-into-the-unknown trust. But he'd forgotten that, for the past ten years, Finley had experienced a host of disappointments—quite a few of them at the hands of people who should have been supporting her. She'd given up her chance at college to take care of her mother. Rather than being grateful, Alice had continued with her self-destructive behavior, blaming Finley along the way. And Billie…

Well, Billie had always been a hellion. But even though Finley's influence had helped to pull her back onto the straight and narrow, Billie seemed to resent her sister for her help. If you added the way Finley had doted on a sick friend who had never fully recovered and a surrogate father who had died far too young…

"Geez, I'm an idiot, Clint. I've been expecting her to believe me when I promise that we'll work things out—but why should she? Hell, the minute things got tough after the accident, I took off. Deep down, she's gotta be wondering if that could happen again."

Whit released Clint's hand and dug into the pocket of his jeans for his phone. Within seconds, he had Javi on the other end of the line.

"Hey, how close are you to getting here?"

"I'm a half-hour out of Jackson."

"Can you do me a favor on your way through Larkspur?"

"Sure. Is Clint worse?"

"No, no. The doctor is supposed to come brief me, but it sounds like Clint had a heart attack. He's holding his own right now, but he looks a lot better."

There was a moment of silence as Javi digested the information.

"So, what do you need?"

"I'll send you a text with the address. I've got to call first and make all the arrangements. Once that's done, you can give the guy your name and pick up a package for me."

"Glad to do it. If you think of anything else you need, let me know."

As soon as he'd hung up with Javi, Whit began searching through the contacts of his phone. Time to quit one job and see if he could land himself another.

After spending the midnight hours at Greensprings, the morning at the hospital, and the evening working at the Busy B, Finley's head was pounding from exhaustion when she let herself into her mother's house.

But not Finley's.

Not anymore.

Her gaze automatically skipped to the recliner in the corner, but her mother wasn't there.

Hallelujah.

Unfortunately, just when she thought she'd managed to slip into the house unnoticed, Billie stepped into the doorway leading into the kitchen.

"How's Clint?"

Finley had expected to be grilled about her relationship with Whit, so the murmured query caught her off guard.

"He's doing better."

"Do they know what happened?"

"His heart started beating irregularly. Something they call…" Finley pressed a finger to her forehead in an effort to pull the medical terminology from her weary brain. "Uh…ventricular fibrillation. He's at the hospital in Redmond and they're doing a few more tests before they determine the cause and the best form of treatment. It's possible he was born with a heart defect that no one knew about or…or the accident caused some scarring…"

When she met Billie's gaze, it was clear that the medical jargon was making no more sense to her sister than it had to her.

"But he's…okay?"

"He's stable for now. I merely came to gather my things, then I'll head back to the hospital. Whit's still with him. I don't think Whit's left his side since the transfer."

Billie's lips thinned. "I don't know how he can even show his face there, let alone loiter next to his bed like a vulture."

"Damnit, Billie, what's your problem? Whit is Clint's medical proxy."

"Which is like putting the fox in charge of the hen house. Have you forgotten that it's Whit's fault that Clint is in this condition in the first place?"

"Billie! No one knows what happened that night or what caused that accident."

"He was drunk."

"If the police couldn't prove that, I don't know how you can. The accident was fully investigated and they dropped the charges within a few days. If they couldn't find the means to blame him, then why are you so determined to hold a grudge?"

"Because Clint deserved more out of life than to spend ten years in bed!"

The retort caused Finley to peer at her sister more closely. She'd never seen Billie like this before. Color flooded her sister's cheeks and she'd folded her arms tightly in front of her—barely disguising the fact that her hands had balled into fists.

Billie's chin tilted to a militant angle. "He also deserves more than a woman who professes to love him, then abandons him when times get tough."

The words struck Finley to the heart—not because Billie had uttered them, but because Finley had made the same argument to herself for the past ten years.

Before she could make a response, Billie marched to her bedroom and slammed the door—leaving Finley trapped, yet again, in a loop of indecision.

Was it wrong for her to want more out of life? She'd helped Norm watch over Clint for ten years. *Ten years.* Was she allowed to defer Clint's care to another person? Or was her decision to move forward with her own goals the epitome of selfishness? Heaven only knew that if Norm were still alive, she would continue on as she had, probably for another ten years. Why wouldn't her actions be interpreted as abandonment?

Or had the time really come to move into the next chapter of her life? Whit had proved himself more than able to care for Clint's needs—and he'd shown that he was more than willing to disrupt his life to assume the added responsibilities. If anything, Finley should feel free.

But saying she had goals and dreams and actually making the break to pursue them was becoming more difficult than she ever could have imagined.

Weariness seemed to grip her muscles like concrete as she moved toward her own bedroom. As she opened the door and flicked on the light to reveal a sea of pink, she realized that she no longer cared if anyone whispered about her behind her back. As Whit had once said, she'd probably grown so sensitive to the possibility of people gossiping about her that she'd begun to believe that every averted head, every murmured comment, was about her. Now, when she walked through the grocery store or served her neighbors at the diner, she realized that they had their own lives to consume their thoughts and attentions. If they asked her questions at all, it was merely to inquire about Clint's health or how Finley was doing. Sure, there'd been talk when she and Whit were seen together in town. But she realized that people would have been as curious if she'd been seen dating any of the locals.

It seemed the people of Larkspur had forgiven Whit for any involvement that he might have had in the accident.

So why hadn't Billie?

Sinking onto her bed, Finley realized that the source of the friction between her and her sister had arisen long before the accident. At one time, they'd been so close. Even when Billie had been in the midst of her most rebellious behavior, she'd confided in Finley, sought her out. But all that had stopped about the time that…

Finley had left for college?

No.

She straightened as the realization hit her. Billie's attitude toward her had changed about the same time that

Finley had begun dating Clint. Before then, Billie had always trotted along behind the Sinful Six in typical little sister fashion. She'd seemed enamored by the older boys.

Especially Clint.

"Oh, no. No, no, no," Finley murmured softly to herself.

Too late, she realized that Billie must have had a crush on Clint. When the events of that winter had tumbled one on top of the other—the supposed engagement, the accident, Whit's arrest—Billy must have taken them all to heart.

Finley jumped to her feet, about to rush to her sister's room, but she hesitated. What could she say without sounding insensitive or accusatory? Whatever her sister had felt all those years ago, she wasn't the same person any more than Finley was. She'd had her fair share of relationships.

But clearly, she still felt that she needed to watch over Clint—as if to ensure that his life remain as unchanged as possible.

Which left Finley right back where she'd started. She could either decide to maintain the status quo—and thereby placate her sister—or she could move on—which would bring its own host of problems.

Sighing, she curled up on the bed, hugging a pillow to her chest. Closing her eyes, she ignored the ache of her feet and the pull of muscles in her arms and shoulders. She'd forgotten how busy the evening shift could be. The groups who ate tended to be larger, which meant the trays she carried were heavier. With so many people, orders took longer to prepare, which meant tempers became frayed and small children became fractious.

She really, *really,* didn't want to spend the rest of her life as a waitress. Her job at the Busy B had been a godsend. She'd loved working with Herb Boyington and the rest of the crew—and the flexible hours had helped her to juggle all the demands of her crazy life. But after ten years...

She wanted a change. She wanted...

To grow.

The moment the thought slid into her consciousness, she realized that her decision had been made. She couldn't stay here—not without sacrificing the goals she'd set for herself. Now, more than ever, she wanted to pursue a career as a nurse. All the years with Clint being moved in and out of hospitals and convalescent centers had merely strengthened that idea. The doctors might stroll in and out of a patient's life, but the nurses formed bonds with the patients and their families that often made such difficult times more bearable.

She rolled onto her back and stared up at the ceiling, becoming more resolute with each minute that passed. If she didn't pursue her opportunities now, she may never have another chance. For once, all the loose details were falling into place. She'd been accepted by two possible universities, she had her tuition saved, and Whit would be here to see after Clint's needs.

The idea of having a partner to watch her back and assume a portion of her responsibilities was new and reassuring. But there was more to it than that. She trusted Whit to give Clint the same attention that she would have given him herself. And until now, she hadn't realized how hard it would be to walk away. Not without knowing that Clint had a person who would be as fiercely protective of his health as she and Norm had been.

Which left only one small facet of her plan left to decide. She'd grown to care for Whit, and she knew she was quickly falling in love with him.

No.

She'd *always* loved him.

But that love had evolved and grown into something more. So much more. There was no doubt in her mind that she wanted to be with him.

Nevertheless, there was a part of her that feared the timing was off. Whit insisted that they could make a long-distance relationship work. Finley wasn't so sure. She had no doubts about the strength of her emotions, but they hadn't really been tested. If there was anything that she'd learned in the past ten years, it was that life had a way of challenging even the strongest of bonds. In moving to Larkspur, Whit would already be uprooting himself from his job and home and way of life. Was it fair to ask him to sacrifice even more?

Even though being with him was everything she'd ever wanted.

But she couldn't think about that now. She needed to gather her things and get out of here. This house—this room—belonged to her past.

It didn't take long for her to fill a suitcase with the rest of her belongings. Other than her clothing, makeup, and toiletries, there wasn't a whole lot she wanted to take with her. She'd never cared for the furnishings, and she didn't want to hinder herself with too many possessions.

Once she'd hauled her bags out to the car, she returned one last time to fill a laundry hamper with bedding and towels, a half-dozen dishcloths, and her pillow. Then she eyed the room to see if there was anything she'd missed.

It wasn't until this moment that she realized she hadn't really collected a lot of "things." Perhaps, after her mother redecorated in an explosion of ruffles, she'd known that to add anything else would send Finley over the edge. Or perhaps, the space had never really felt like like a sanctuary to her. It had simply been a place to sleep. Her place…

Was with Whit.

She'd felt more alive, more comforted, more at ease with herself at the ranch and with him than she'd ever felt here.

Which left her with one last thing to do.

She moved to the closet, rifling through shoeboxes of heels and boots that she hadn't worn in years. There, at the very bottom, was a box with a pair of yellow high-top sneakers—the same shoes she'd been wearing when Whit had kissed her on that long-ago night.

She snagged the shoebox, tossing it on top of the laundry hamper. Then, unable to help herself, she opened the lid, pushed aside the tissue paper, and burrowed deep into the toe of the right sneaker.

Empty.

Finley dropped the sneaker and wriggled her hand into the other shoe.

Nothing.

For a moment, her brain couldn't seem to absorb the fact that she hadn't found the roll of cash she'd kept hidden there. She grabbed both shoes, shaking them—even though she knew they'd both been empty. Once again, she plunged her fingers down to the tips even as her stomach seemed to freefall. Blood rushed from her head to pulse in her extremities, making her lightheaded as she frantically pawed through the tissue paper in the box.

Gone.

Whimpering softly, she lunged toward the closet, frantically searching through each of the boxes, then tossing them aside until she reached the carpeted floor.

No, no, no!

The tuition money that she'd stashed away was missing. *Missing!*

She jumped to her feet, whirling in a circle as if the roll of bills had been left in plain sight. She'd added her tips to the stash only the day before. And she knew she'd been careful to put everything back in its hiding place. If she didn't, her mother had been known to...

Her mother.

The thought hammered into her head at the same time the front door slammed shut. Finley jumped to her feet and stormed into the living room.

TWENTY-TWO

"Where is it!"

Finley's voice felt as if it belonged to someone else, emerging high and shrill. But Alice didn't seem to notice. She unzipped her jacket and shot Finley a frosty glare.

"Your car is sitting in the middle of the driveway, Finley, so I can't get into the garage. You know I don't like leaving the sedan on the street. Anyone could come by and scratch the paint. Or those seeds fall from the trees and those sticky—"

"Where is it, mother!" Finley interjected, her voice a near shout.

Alice offered her a blank stare. "I honestly don't know what you're talking about."

"My money. It's gone."

"Money?"

Finley's hands balled into fists. More than anything, she wanted to launch herself across the room and shake Alice until her teeth rattled. Her mother might play the coy, southern ingénue, but Finley knew she was lying.

"My savings."

Alice opened her mouth—probably, to offer another vague rejoinder—but Finley stopped her before she could speak.

"Don't bother telling me you don't know what I'm talking about. It's obvious that you've taken it."

Alice bristled. "Are you accusing me of *stealing*?" Her mother huffed. "I'm not the only person who lives here, you know."

"So, you're going to blame Billie?"

"Blame me for what?" Billie stepped into the doorway, a mug of coffee cradled between her hands.

Finley shot a look over her shoulder. "I had nearly eight thousand dollars hidden in my room—money that I've been saving for years from my tips. I intended to use it for tuition so that I could go back to college and finish my degree. But it's disappeared."

The words snagged in her throat, in her chest. A wave of desperation added another layer to her anger.

There was no denying the patent look of surprise—then horror—that washed over her sister's face. Then Billie's eyes narrowed as she focused on her mother.

"And you were going to blame *me*?" Her tone rivaled Finley's as she speared Alice with a look of disgust.

Panicked, Finley tried to calm herself enough to sound civil, even if she didn't feel it.

"Just give it back—o-or tell me where it is. I won't say another word about this."

Her mother hugged her purse to her chest. "I haven't—"

"Don't lie to me! Not about this!"

For a moment, Alice maintained her defiant posture. Then her chin began to tremble and the façade crumbled. "You said you were going to leave," she mumbled, shifting from foot to foot like a guilty child.

"Mom," Billie warned. "Where's the money?"

"I-I used it to pay off half of my car loan."

The confession shuddered through Finley's veins like chunks of ice, locking her in place, freezing her brain in that one moment of disbelief.

Her *car?*

Vaguely, from outside her body, she heard Billie continuing to grill Alice.

"Good hell, Almighty, Mom, what were you thinking?"

"T-the money was lying around—"

"In her *room.*"

"She wasn't using it!"

"That doesn't matter, Alice. It was *her* room. *Her* money."

"Don't *you* start calling me Alice! I'm your mother and I deserve your respect!"

"For what? Being a lying, thieving alcoholic? I swear, Mom, you've done some horrible things in your life, but this…this has to be the worst. And I bet that money wasn't 'lying around' like you claim. I bet you went searching. Am I right, Finley?"

But Finley couldn't seem to latch onto Billie's question. Her thoughts stutter-stepped on one important fact.

"T-the payment. When did you make the payment?"

Maybe, she could call the bank and explain. Maybe, they'd be willing to refund the money.

Alice's mouth opened and closed for a moment, then she said, "Y-yesterday."

Too late.

The payment would have cleared. Since her mother had used cash, it would have been processed almost immediately.

"I think you should call the police, Finley," Billie said, touching her shoulder.

But Finley couldn't move.

Gone.

The future that she had dreamed about for so long was lost to her now. And she hadn't realized until then how the image of that roll of bills growing and growing in its hiding place had been the tangible evidence of her hope. When she'd been sad or tired or discouraged, the thought of that cash giving her a head start to a different life had pulled her through.

And now, she had nothing.

Her feet seemed to move of their own volition. She wasn't even aware of leaving the house and climbing into her car until she found herself pulling into a parking space at the hospital in Redmond.

She killed the engine, then sat with her fingers curled around the wheel. Of all the places she could have gone, why here? The last thing Clint needed was for her to bring negative energy into his room. He had a fight ahead of him, and she didn't think she had the strength to pretend that nothing was wrong.

So where did that leave her? She didn't have the money to get a hotel, and she was shaking so hard, she didn't think she could make it to the ranch. She simply wanted to go...

Home.

It was then, that she realized she'd instinctively gravitated toward the one place—the one *person* who represented safety, security, and a sense of...*belonging*. He was the shelter for her storm. And even though she was coming to him in defeat, she knew he would welcome her.

Grabbing her purse, she scrambled for her phone—only to realize that she must have left it at Alice's house.

That, more than anything else, seemed to be the tipping point in being able to control her emotions. As she hurried into the hospital, ignoring the cold wind that warned of an imminent winter, she lifted the collar to her jacket—more to hide her tears than to ward off the chill.

Keeping her head down, she strode to the elevator bank and punched the button praying that she could hold on a little longer. Tears might not be a strange sight in a hospital, but she knew that if she allowed herself to cry, she wouldn't be able to stop. And if she were going to lose control, she wanted to be in Whit's arms. He wouldn't be able to fix things. No one could do that. But he could offer his strength.

She hesitated at the closed door to Clint's room. For a moment, she pressed her ear to the wood, wondering if Javi had arrived yet. But she couldn't hear anything on the other side.

Hesitantly, she pushed the barrier aside enough so that she could peer inside.

Clint looked as if he were asleep. He lay peacefully on the bed—his body more at ease than she'd seen it in a long time. His ordeal must have dragged him into a deep sleep.

She stepped a little farther inside. There was no evidence of Javi. But there, on a chair at the far side of the bed, was Whit. He'd tossed his hat onto the sofa behind him and sat with his long legs stretched out in front of him. His head was down as he regarded his phone, but a noise must have alerted him to her presence, because he suddenly looked up.

Later, Finley couldn't have said who moved first. She remembered uttering a hiccoughing sob. Then the emotions inside her couldn't be held back any longer, and within seconds, she found herself being pulled into the room. Then, Whit was hauling her close, bending over her, into her, wrapping her tightly in his arms as if he warded off unseen blows.

Finley knew that she should insist they find a private spot—or at least go into the hall. But she suddenly crumpled, unable to stand beneath the burden of this latest, crippling defeat.

Whit instantly took her weight, lifting her and crossing to the sofa. As he sank into its depths, he held her even more securely in his lap, rocking her, holding her, absorbing her sobs with his body and the moisture of her tears with his shirt.

Finley couldn't have said how long she wept. The emotions roiled within her, escaping in a torrent of emotion—explosive at first, then easing, then becoming more sporadic with exhaustion.

Somehow, Whit knew that it was best for him to wait until the worst of the torrent had passed. He offered vague soothing noises, stroking her hair until she lay spent in his arms.

"What happened?" he finally whispered.

Finley thought that she'd already wrung every ounce of moisture from her body, but the tears welled up in her eyes again.

"I-it's gone. I-it's all gone."

"What's gone?"

"My m-money. M-my college money. My mother found my hiding place. She stole it and used it to pay for her car loan."

He grew still beneath her. In a very Whit-like fashion, he seemed to absorb the information, digest it, before saying, "I'm so sorry. I'm so, so sorry. Is there any way you can get it back?"

Finley bit her lip and shook her head. "I doubt it. Billie thinks I should call the police."

"There's time for that. When and if you're ready."

She loved the way that he didn't press her into a decision one way or the other. He seemed to know that, at the moment, it wasn't her mother's betrayal that hurt the most. She'd been disappointed by Alice often enough that, deep down, she wasn't surprised that her mother had taken the money. It was the ramifications that left her feeling weak and hollow.

"How much?"

Her chin trembled. "A little over eight-thousand."

Whit swore softly under his breath, then he gripped her even tighter. "You worked so hard. It must have taken years to save it all."

She nodded, not trusting herself to speak. Since her mother's employment history was limited at best, Finley had taken most of the responsibility for the house payment and utilities—which left very little once she'd been paid. After a time, she'd begun collecting a few of the bills that were given to her in tips—single dollars, sometimes a five, a ten—and tucking them away.

So much time and effort. Years of saving.

And it was gone. All gone.

The sobs came again, and Whit held her, offering her his strength and more. Without words, he conveyed his own emotions—regret, protectiveness, and a deep and overwhelming love.

He loved her. She knew he did.

"Do you want me to go beat the shit out of her?"

The remark came out of the blue—said only half in jest—and the absurdity of it caused her to choke, then laugh. When she gazed up at him, she could see that he hadn't meant the words. But there was a dark glint to the forest-green depths that conveyed that he wouldn't be opposed to confronting the woman.

"No," she whispered. Then she wrapped her arms around his chest and hugged him tightly. "At least not yet."

She felt him smile against her hair.

"We'll get through this."

"No. There's no way that I can—"

"*We.*" Whit said firmly. "*We* will find a way to fix this. You're going to college, one way or the other. We'll figure it out."

She opened her mouth to list all the reasons why it would never happen. But then, she realized this was Whit. *Whit.* He, more than anyone else, knew how much she'd longed to get her nursing degree. It wasn't simply a wish or a pipe dream. It was a *need* that she'd harbored for years.

Whit tipped her chin up, then wiped the tears away with his thumbs. "You believe me, don't you?"

The damned tears threatened to flow again when she met his fierce gaze. In the depths of those eyes, she saw his conviction and more.

"Yes."

"And can you believe everything else? That we can make this work? Me here, you at school?"

"Yes."

His eyes dropped to focus on her lips. "And will you believe me when I tell you that I love you, heart and soul, and that I'll never let you go?"

Again, she blinked against the sting of moisture. But this time, the source of her emotions was the blaze of heat in his regard, the fierce protectiveness, the glint of possession.

"Yes."

The word had barely escaped her lips when she was hauled close. Then his lips closed fiercely over hers. She willingly opened her mouth to the branding sweep of his tongue, even as her hands clutched at his shoulders, then wrapped around his neck to pull him even more tightly against her.

The pain was still there—the sting of dreams deferred. But the joy that swept through her held the warmth of the sun. In that moment, the last of her reservations melted away and she was once again filled with hope. Hope and love and the inescapable knowledge that with this man by her side, the future held limitless possibilities.

"Geez...get...room..."

Finley broke away, her head twisting toward the door, embarrassed that Javi had caught them in such an intimate embrace.

But the door remained firmly shut. There was no one there.

No.

There was still a third person in the room.

Her gaze dropped to the figure on the bed, to the half-open eyes that watched them.

Watched them.

"Clint?" she whispered, sure that she was mistaken. More than once, she'd been sure that Clint had been looking directly at her, only to realize that there was nothing purposeful behind his stare.

But this time, she saw one corner of his mouth twitch in a bare ghost of a smile. Then he looked slightly to the side, seeming to study Whit.

Finley felt Whit stiffen and knew that he was struggling to come to terms with what he was seeing…hearing. She watched his features shift, become blank, stoic. And in that instant, she knew that ten years of memories were racing through him like an avalanche, leaving one final emotion in its wake.

Guilt.

But Clint seemed oblivious to the brittleness that entered the room. He looked at Finley, the window, then Whit. Again, the corner of his lips twitched.

"Marry…herrr…" he whispered, the words slow, slurred, and barely distinguishable. Even so, their meaning slammed into the room with the impact of a gunshot.

Then his eyes flickered and closed again.

"Go get somebody," Finley urged. "A nurse, doctor—you saw that right? You heard him speak?"

"Yeah."

She scrambled to sit in the chair drawn up to the bedside. She clutched Clint's hand even as Whit lunged toward the door. But he'd barely pulled it open when Clint's lashes fluttered again.

"Wiiit…"

The sound wasn't really Whit's name, more a puff of air. But Whit turned to face the bed nonetheless.

Clint struggled to focus on his friend, his eyelids seeming too heavy to keep open.

"Myy…fault. I…wasss…drivvving…"

It was past midnight more than twenty-four hours later when Whit eased the Bronco to a stop in front of the main offices of the Come Back Ranch.

He couldn't remember ever feeling so tired…

And so fucking happy.

He glanced at the woman curled up on the seat beside him and couldn't help a soft smile, knowing that it was because of her. She loved him. Completely and unreservedly. True, it had taken personal tragedy for her to take a leap of faith, but that fact didn't bother him. He'd always known that change was hard for Finley. It was part of the reason why she'd stuck around Larkspur for so long. She didn't make a move unless she'd made her lists and plotted out a course of action.

But this time, she'd thrown herself into agreeing to a future with him without a second thought.

Which made Whit love her all the more.

Climbing from the Bronco, he reached for her, intending to carry her inside. He knew she was even more exhausted than he was—emotionally and physically. She'd endured a crushing blow once she'd discovered her savings were gone. After the confrontation with her mother and Clint's return to consciousness, he knew she was completely drained. But when he touched her, she jolted awake.

"What…?"

"Shh. We're home."

She pressed the palms of her hands to her eyes, then seemed to focus on their surroundings.

"Are you sure we should be here?"

Both she and Whit had been determined to stay by Clint's bedside. But after several rounds of doctors and dozens of tests, it had become apparent that no one could explain why

Clint had suddenly awakened from his vegetative state. Moreover, the simple return to awareness had exhausted him.

"Javi's with Clint, Remember? He'll keep an eye on him."

Since his slurred comments to Finley and Whit, Clint had fitfully slept. Over and over again, he would jerk awake and open his eyes. But after a sweeping search of the room—as if to assure himself that he wasn't merely dreaming—he would nod off again. Through it all, he hadn't tried to speak with them again.

In the end, it had been the nurses and Javi who had insisted that Whit and Finley go home, at least until morning. And it had been Clint's insistence—the barely perceptible shooing motion of two fingers—which had convinced Whit to surrender. He didn't want his friend sapping his precious energy by worrying about them.

"Besides, Clint kept fretting about you. You need rest."

"But—"

"We'll head back at first light. We can get a couple of hours sleep, shower, and change, then be back on the road to Redmond."

She opened her mouth as if to argue, then exhaled, silently conceding.

Whit would have carried her into the house, but she slid from the Bronco, smothering a yawn.

"I could sleep for a thousand years. But a few hours will have to do."

Crisp autumn leaves scuttled around them as they made their way to the back door. Finley had just reached for the knob when Whit said, "I'll meet you inside. I need to feed and water the livestock, then there's something I'd like to check."

"I'll help."

"Finley—"

"I'll help, Whit. I want to help." Her lips lifted in a ghost of a smile. "That way, I won't have to wait as long for you to come to bed."

He knew he should insist she get her rest, but he needed her nearby. After everything that had happened, he was finding it hard to believe that he hadn't tumbled into an alternate universe where things had a way of ending happily. If she were with him—his anchor, his rock—he could keep the turbulent emotions at bay.

In the end, the chores were finished quickly. The horses eyed them sleepily as Whit and Finley filled their feeders with oats and hay, and the cattle bellowed a disgruntled greeting. When Finley would have headed toward the house, Whit hesitated.

"You go ahead. I'll be with you in a minute."

Nevertheless, as he turned to cross the yard to the equipment shed on the opposite side of the compound, he heard her footsteps crunching on the gravel behind him.

"Where are we going?"

We.

He couldn't trust himself to speak. Not yet. He unlocked the door and flipped on the weak bulb that hung from the ceiling. A giant fist seemed to close around his chest, nearly cutting off his ability to breathe.

His boots rang hollowly on the concrete as he approached the hulking shape in the far corner. The light here was dim—too dim for his purposes. So, he dragged his phone from his pocket, hitting the flashlight app.

For a moment he hesitated. Who knew if Clint had been aware of half the things he'd said? He'd only uttered a half-dozen words. The effort of speaking to Whit and Finley had seemed to tax his abilities—to the point that anything else he'd tried to convey had emerged as little more than guttural noises. The doctors had warned Whit that it would take time to figure out what was going on in Clint's brain. He might have trouble absorbing the passage of time. He could have severe brain damage. And he would almost certainly have issues with his speech, mobility, and cognition. He could even slip back into unconsciousness.

But Whit knew what he'd heard.

He peeled back the tarpaulins, exposing the mangled car to the stark beam of light.

Behind him, he heard Finley gasp. "How long has this been here?"

"I don't know. Norm must have had it hauled to the ranch once the police closed the investigation."

As he reached for the door handle, his heart seemed to bang against the wall of his chest. Whit wasn't sure what he was looking for. He only knew that, for the first time in years, the guilt which had lingered deep in his soul like an unhealed wound urged him to look.

The hinges were bent and rusted, giving way with a god-awful squeal. Whit crouched on his heels, shining the light into the interior, taking in the collapsed dashboard, the twisted seats, and the spent airbag that hung from the driver's column like a macabre party balloon.

What personal belongings that might have once been here had been removed. The only remnants to Whit's earlier life were the coins in the cup holders and the parking decal hanging from the rearview mirror.

His gaze bounced from the shattered windshield, to the mottled stains on the upholstery—*blood? mud?*—to the fine layer of dust that coated the interior. Signs of violence were everywhere—and Whit had to swallow hard against the bile that threatened to climb up the back of his throat.

He and Clint were lucky to be alive.

Damned lucky.

He swept the beam over the back seat, the collapsed roof. According to the police report, the car had strayed over the center line and been struck head-on by another vehicle. The impact had launched them into the air. The police estimated that the vehicle had rolled at least three times, maybe more. In the midst of that ferocity, Clint and Whit had both been ejected.

Whit hesitantly leaned against the driver's seat, leaving a streak in the layer of dirt. The car probably hadn't been disturbed since it had been dragged here.

He tipped his phone to expose the floorboards—first on the passenger side, then on the driver's. But there was nothing to see. The right-hand seat had been pushed away from the dashboard as far as it would go, the back adjusted to a semi-reclining position, while the driver's side...

The driver's side...

"Hold this."

He handed the phone to Finley, absently noting that his hands were shaking.

As she shifted the light in front of him, Whit reached beneath the seat and tugged on the adjustment knob, then pushed on the backrest.

With a grinding clunk, the seat moved backwards several inches.

The strength seemed to escape from his body in a single *whoosh,* and Whit wavered, his legs giving way so he landed square on his butt. Then, he was dropping his head to his knees as he struggled to drag air into his starving lungs.

"Whit? Whit, what's wrong?"

He looked up at Finley, knowing that his eyes had flooded with tears—and he didn't care. This was Finley, the love of his life, his sweetheart, his lover.

"I wasn't driving," he whispered, the words nearly unintelligible.

In a rush, he remembered how he would grouse at Clint whenever the other man borrowed his wheels. Clint liked to sit with his knees bunched up, while Whit stretched his out as far as he could. Invariably, Clint pulled the seat closer to the steering column, then forget to return it to its original setting—which left Whit swearing and shoehorning himself behind the wheel until he could reach for the knob and release the catch.

Again, his gaze skipped to the passenger seat. It had been pushed all the way back.

"I was over there."

He watched Finley take in the scene with new eyes— watched her expression lift to one of wonder.

"You weren't driving," she repeated.

"Clint must have known I was pretty close to the limit. He must have taken my keys."

Which meant that their argument had blown over—at least enough so that Clint had taken precautions against Whit's endangering himself or anyone else.

Marry...her...

At the time, Whit had thought that Clint's comment had come out of the blue—a reaction to the embrace he'd witnessed in the hospital. But could it be possible that Clint and Whit had come to an understanding that long-ago night?

Not for the first time, Whit wished that he could remember the hours that had been stolen from him because of a head injury. He couldn't even be sure that Clint would recall what had been said that night. But it didn't matter anymore. The crushing weight of guilt flowed from his body like an outgoing tide.

Whit would never go so far as to say that he hadn't contributed to the accident. He'd been the one to start the chain of events—and he'd been the one to storm from the bar. But he wasn't solely to blame.

Finley knelt beside him and wrapped her arms around his shoulders. And in that moment, his heart seemed to take control of his body because Whit blurted, "Marry me?"

To her credit, Finley didn't flinch. She didn't even bat an eye.

"Of course."

Of course?

He drew back enough to meet her gaze head-on.

"You mean it?"

And there was that smile—a smile that could melt the farthest reaches of his heart.

"Yes."

He tunneled into his pocket, removing a small box.

"What's this?" she asked, only mildly curious. She seemed to be more intent on stringing a line of kisses up the line of his jaw.

"I had Javi pick it up on his way to the hospital. I couldn't seem to convince you that I was serious about the whole long-distance thing and…I thought this would help. Open it."

She grinned. She'd always loved surprises and he could only hope that this would be a good one.

But as she lifted the lid, her eyes widened and she made no response.

Worried, Whit hurried to cover the silence. "It's on approval. I called Mr. Savitch's jewelry store from the hospital and explained what I was looking for. You always said you didn't want a diamond solitaire. You wanted something with color. I chose an aquamarine—because they remind me of your beautiful eyes. I thought we could get you a wedding band with a bunch of smaller diamonds to circle around it. If you don't like it, we can go down together when we get a chance and choose—"

He didn't have a chance to finish, Finley launched herself into his arms and began peppering him with kisses.

"It's beautiful…and sweet…and romantic…and…" she paused to draw breath. "And I love you, Whit Patterson."

The last of his concerns scattered into the shadows.

"Yeah?"

"Yeah."

"And I love you. More than you'll ever know."

He plucked the ring from its box and slid it onto her finger. It was loose, but it could be resized. In the meantime, it wasn't so large that she couldn't wear it.

"I've also been thinking about your education."

She opened her mouth—clearly hesitant to bring down the mood of the proposal, but he lay a finger against her lips, his other arm wrapping around her.

"You're going to go to school, Finley. Quitting isn't an option. I've got some savings we can use for this semester. Once you've decided which university you'll attend, we'll pay your tuition and find you a little apartment. In the meantime, I think I've got a line on a job here in Wyoming. I've already had a word with Brent Walker, and he's extended an offer for me to interview with Wyoming's Livestock Board Criminal Investigators. If I can land the position, I can live here at the ranch—at least until we can get the Sinful Six together—so I won't need to worry about a mortgage or rent. That means we can use that money for your room and board. That will give us time to come up with a practical solution to make up the shortfall. I'm thinking…by the time fall rolls around, I'll have sold my condo, and that money will see you through the first two or three years. After that, we're home free."

He saw the spark of hope in her eyes, but it was quickly tempered with caution. The list-making Finley had returned.

"I-I can't let you do that, Whit. Who knows when I'd ever be able to pay you back—"

He stopped her protest with a kiss, one that was hot and passionate and that he hoped conveyed the depth of his feelings for her. He only pulled back for a moment to offer, "It's not a loan, Finley. It's an investment in the future. *Our* future."

Her eyes flooded with tears—and that was all the cue he needed to haul her back into his embrace and remind her how much that future meant to them both.

EPILOGUE

Late May

As she topped the rise which led into the valley of Come Back Ranch, Finley's heart fluttered in her chest like an excited bird.

Almost home.

She couldn't remember ever being this happy. She'd finished a full semester at Boise State and would be starting their nursing program come fall. But even with all those successes tucked under her belt, meeting those goals was only partially responsible for her mood. What excited her the most was that she had an entire summer to spend at Come Back Ranch.

With her husband.

As she twisted the wheel to negotiate the winding trip down to the buildings below, sunlight winked off the aquamarine solitaire and its circlet of diamonds.

She and Whit had probably had one of the fastest courtships on record. Despite his earlier protestations that they should "take things slow", less than two weeks after Whit's proposal, they'd eloped to a quaint wedding chapel in Reno. The event hadn't been planned. They'd gone to Nevada to load his things into a moving van. After landing a job with Wyoming's Livestock Board Criminal Investigators, he'd had little more than a weekend to pack everything up so that a realtor could begin showing the place to prospective clients. Getting married should have been at the bottom of their list of things to do. But in the short time she'd spent with Whit, Finley had learned that, at times, a person had to be spontaneous.

She hadn't regretted their decision. Within weeks, she'd become a long-distance bride, and she'd clung to those moments spent with Whit like a miser. True to Whit's promises, they'd found ways to stay in contact—phone calls, video messaging, stolen weekends. But this summer, she would have him all to herself.

Or would she...

As she finished the last bend, she saw that Whit's Bronco wasn't the only one in the parking lot. A boxy van had pulled up next to the swimming pool.

Whit had told her that he and Javi had spent two weekends repairing the filters, scraping away the peeling paint, then edging it with tile. Either they'd called in a handyman to help finish things up, or...

As she pulled up next to the Bronco, she saw the ramp that extended from the far side of the van.

No.

But as she fumbled to release her seatbelt and launch herself from the car, she saw a familiar figure in a wheelchair sitting beneath the shade of a beach umbrella.

"Clint!"

His head tipped up at her call and a huge smile spread over his lips. He lifted an arm slightly in greeting—his fingers still curled in stiff fists, but with more mobility than he'd displayed the last time she'd seen him.

She dodged through the gate and threw her arms around him.

"You look fabulous!"

A tinge of color touched his cheeks.

"Yoou...t-too..."

As the doctors had predicted, Clint's speech had proven to be one of the many challenges left from his coma. When he was tired, the words simply wouldn't come. But at times like this, when he was relaxed and well-rested, he found a way to make his thoughts known. In the past few months, he'd managed to confirm Whit's theory of the events leading up to the accident. He and Whit had argued, fought—and through it all, Clint had realized that what he felt for Finley paled next to Whit's emotions. But that hadn't meant he planned to give her up.

Nevertheless, when Whit had stormed to his car, Clint had known his friend shouldn't be driving, so he'd snatched the keys away from Whit and climbed behind the wheel. Several miles down the road, a rabbit had bounded into the highway. Clint had fought to avoid it and overcorrected, sending the car across the center line.

Finley drew back and eyed him up and down. Mere months ago, she never would have dreamed she would see Clint like this again. His skin still bore a hint of pallor from being bed-bound. But he was dressed in an outrageous Hawaiian shirt and a baggy pair of shorts. Sunglasses had been propped on the top of his head and his nose was covered with an extra layer of white sunscreen.

He lifted his arm again, gesturing to a muscular man dressed in flip-flops, swimming trunks, and a tank top. The guy was emptying a net bag of what looked like water toys—balls, noodles, kickboards.

"Thissh…Brock…"

"Of course." She held out a hand. "Whit told me that Clint had a personal caregiver so that he could get out and about more. I'm Finley Fitz—Finley Patterson."

Brock—who looked like an athlete more than a medical assistant—shook her hand. The strength of his grip made her realize that he would have to be in tip-top condition for his job. Clint was still at a point where he had to be lifted in and out of bed or his wheelchair.

"Nice to meet you, Finley. Clint's been jabbering about you non-stop all morning."

Clint snorted at that. Then he tipped his head toward the pool.

Brock seamlessly interpreted the gesture. "Clint and I were about to head into the water for a round of physical therapy. You're welcome to join us."

"Will you be staying the whole afternoon?"

"Actually, we'll be here the entire weekend. Whit set us up in one of the bungalows."

"Honnny…moooon…shuite…"

Clint and Brock laughed as if sharing a secret joke.

Finley remembered that day, oh, so long ago, when Whit had talked about fixing up the units so that there would be places for the Sinful Six to stay if they should ever return to the ranch. She felt a little tug at her heart at the rightness of that first "guest" being Clint.

"I would love to join you. Maybe a little later?" She hitched a thumb in the direction of the house. "I'd better say 'hello' to Whit first."

Clint guffawed, and Finley felt a heat begin to climb into her cheeks when he offered her an all-knowing look. But he hitched his head toward the house, offering, "Laa...terrr..."

Laughing, she backed away from the pair of them, pausing only once on the stoop to cast the men a final glance. Brock was helping Clint out of his shirt—revealing that Clint was still thin and pale and fragile-looking.

He hadn't emerged from his vegetative state unscathed. During the first few weeks, he'd sometimes regressed into long periods of confusion and sleep—so much so, that Finley had feared he might relapse entirely. Then, as his consciousness seemed more secure, he struggled with physical and neurological deficits. His doctors had warned him that it could take years of physical therapy for him to live independent of a caregiver. But Finley had a suspicion that Clint might surprise them all.

Brock muttered a comment to Clint that Finley couldn't hear. Clint tipped back his head, then laughed deep in his gut. And for a moment, she couldn't tear her eyes away.

Clint still had a long recovery awaiting him. But the friend she'd known all those years ago was still there. He might struggle with his words or rage against the limitations of his body. But the man she'd known—her one-time boyfriend, her childhood mate, her protective honorary brother—was still evident in the way he interacted with her. He'd made a comeback.

A comeback.

Maybe they should rechristen this place The Comeback Ranch in his honor.

She heard whistling coming from inside the main building and carefully opened the door, hoping she could surprise her husband. But he must have been listening for her, because she'd only taken a few steps into the kitchen when he suddenly appeared in the short hall leading to the rest of the rooms.

"Hey! You're home."

He held out his arms and she ran toward him, leaping into his embrace, her elbows locking around his neck and her legs around his waist. Then the two of them were kissing—hungrily, passionately, desperately. As if it had been years since they'd seen each other instead of ten days.

He broke away only long enough to gasp, "How were finals?"

"Aced 'em."

"That's my girl!" Then he was pressing her back against the wall and grinding his hips against hers.

She squirmed when she felt the hot length of him pressing up against her.

"I guess you're glad to see me," she murmured.

"I'm always glad to see you."

"I want you," Finley whispered, nipping at his jaw.

"Clint—"

"Is being entertained by Brock. Physical Therapy. We've got at least twenty minutes." She moaned as Whit thrust against her. Even through the layers of their clothes, the pressure was nearly more than she could bear. "Make that an hour. Maybe two."

He laughed, low in his chest, causing the fire in her belly to burn even hotter.

"Come here. I've got something to show you."

Finley waggled her eyebrows. "I bet you do."

"Not that."

She pretended to frown in disappointment, but her frown turned to a gasp as Whit twisted her in his arms, lifting her high against his chest.

"Close your eyes."

Finley considered ignoring his request—she didn't think she would be able to stop looking at him any time soon. She'd dreamed of this moment for so long, it was hard to believe that she was finally here with her husband. Not for a weekend, but for months.

But when she saw the glint of eagerness in his green, green eyes, she couldn't refuse.

As soon as her lashes closed, they were moving again. Then she felt Whit stop and heard the telltale squeak of the bedroom door.

"Okay, open your eyes."

For a moment, she couldn't take in what she was seeing. The last time she'd been here, the space had been Spartan at best—a dresser, a narrow bed, a single chair. But now the room seemed to glow beneath pale yellow walls, crisp white curtains—and the bed! A king-sized black iron bed filled most of the space.

"Billie helped me pick out the furniture and the linens. I figured she'd know what you would like."

"Billie?" Finley breathed in disbelief.

"Yeah. She chose the dresser and the wardrobe and all the pillowy crap."

Pillowy crap?

The description was quintessentially male, but she could tell he was secretly pleased by the bolsters piled high against the headboard and the crisp white duvet.

"It's pretty comfortable," he offered when Finley didn't immediately speak. "You told me once that if you could choose the color for your bedroom, it would be yellow, like a summer sun."

Once again, in the simplest of ways, he'd demonstrated the way he listened, really listened, to the things she'd said.

For a fleeting instant, Whit looked worried. "Well? Do you like it?"

She buried her face into his neck and clung to him, wanting to remember everything about this moment—the warmth of the sunlight on her face, the strength of his arms, the faint scent of soap and leather and man.

"I love it." She drew back, framing his face with her hands. "Nearly as much as I love you."

At that he grinned, lifting a foot to kick the door shut with a resounding bang.

"Wanna take it for a test drive?"

"Absolutely."

Read on for an excerpt from Lisa Bingham's

The Protector
In An Instant Series, Book 2

M aybe, things could have gone differently.
Maybe.

If he'd been carrying his weapon. If he hadn't had his head in his phone, hadn't been so concerned with shaving a few minutes off his "shit-to-do" list, hadn't been so intent on the latest batch of stupid cat footage sent to him by John-Not-The-Poet-Donne, he might have noticed the armed gunman braced on the other side of the double doors leading into the bank.

As it was, he nearly plowed into the back of the security guard.

"Sorry, man, I—"

"Get down on the ground! Down! Down!"

Too late, he looked up.

Even then, it took several precious seconds for him to take in the guard's pinched expression, his hands held up and out, a damp spot beginning to spread from his crotch to his knee.

"I said: Down on the ground! Down!"

Time seemed to grind to a halt as he registered his surroundings in shuddering, freeze-frame images.

A pregnant woman struggling to lower herself to her knees.

An old man staggering, his cane clattering to the marble floor.

Mr. GQ in the corner dropping a sheaf of bills that floated lazily toward his rat-stabber shoes.

And beyond them all, a woman with a swoop of dark hair, her eyes all wide and doe-like…

He'd never seen such unguarded terror.

"You too, asshole! Down!"

Just as abruptly, time leapt into a gallop as he became acutely aware of William Jefferson Clinton pointing an assault rifle in his direction.

"I'm not going to tell you again! Get on the floor or I'll drop you."

Before he could even bend his knees, the back of his head seemed to explode and the floor rushed up to meet him.

ONE

Kirk Webber felt the phone vibrate in his pocket. But as he snagged his bag from the TSA conveyor belt, he ignored the insistent buzzing.

Not now.

Not yet.

It was probably another message from Luca or Benny or Ian wondering if he'd made it to the airport, if he'd checked in, if he'd boarded.

Nag, nag, nag.

They couldn't possibly know that he couldn't afford to take his eyes off his surroundings. Not even for the scant few seconds it would take to read and answer a text.

Looping his rucksack over his shoulder, he jammed his feet into the flip-flops he'd donned for the flight and began the long slog down the terminal. Sure enough, he was destined for the last corridor, the last gate. And even though he'd booked the earliest flight of the day, the crowds were already a bitch to negotiate.

Tourists.

He hated Washington in the summer--and he hated Raegan International even more. Too many damned people.

His eyes scanned the crowd ahead of him, the seemingly floating torsos on the moveable sidewalk to his left, the anxious tide of debarking passengers surging toward the baggage claim area.

Already, his skin prickled beneath the surface and he could feel the cold sweat begin to gather between his shoulder blades.

Breathe, Webber, breathe.

He fought to keep his stride from breaking.

This was a bad idea. A bad, bad idea.

Moving out of his stomping grounds, out of his usual routine, off his customary routes was making him even more skittish. Hell, he was beyond skittish. He was one step away from panic. He should have stayed home. What had he been thinking, agreeing to this flight, this trip, this hare-brained plan?

Then again, he hadn't really been given choice. Just last night, Luca Raisch—that stoic, unflappable, seemingly unexcitable Swiss—had leaned over Kirk's blotter, fixed him with a fire-and-brimstone glare, and had growled, "Get your ass to that treatment center or turn in your weapon, your company identification, and pack up the contents of your desk. Those are your only choices."

And Luca hadn't been kidding.

Until that point, Kirk had thought that he'd been able to con his friends into thinking he was getting better. It had taken the threat of losing his job—the only thing that forced him out of bed each morning and gave him a shred of relief from the memories—for Kirk to realize that he hadn't been fooling anyone but himself.

He couldn't—*wouldn't*—lose his job. Even if he had to jump through another set of hoops like a pet monkey. Even if he had to negotiate one of the busiest airports in the nation. Even if he had to be cooped up in a tin sausage with a hundred-plus passengers, most of whom would be seated behind him.

Behind.

Him.

Kirk flashed hot, then cold.

Shit, shit, shit. Why couldn't he get his shitty-shit together? It wasn't as if he hadn't had time to recover, reflect, and rebound. He'd done all the required physical therapy. He'd met with a boat-load of M.D.s, P.H.D.s, and even a few double-D's, but he still couldn't walk the length of a public hallway without breaking out into a cold sweat, every nerve in his body jangling, warning him of impending doom.

Damnit all to hell!

Kirk abruptly veered toward a kiosk selling frothy fifteen-dollar-a-cup designer coffees and smoothies that looked like pulverized lawn clippings. Yanking open the cooler, he snagged two bottles of water. Handing the clerk a five, he ripped off the cap to one of the containers and chugged the contents while he waited for his change. As he held out his hand for the few coins owed to him, a stabbing pain settled over one eye. Brain freeze. He welcomed the pain, concentrating on the drilling sensation centering over his eye in the hopes that it would derail the morbid loop of his thoughts away from his memories for a few seconds.

Get down on the ground! Down!

He lobbed the empty bottle into a nearby bin.

Stop it!

Don't think about it. Not here.

As he grabbed the second bottle of water and returned to the concourse, his eyes began their habitual—*relentless*—scan of his surroundings.

Tired toddlers and exhausted parents dressed in matching Mount Vernon T-shirts at two o'clock. *Check.*

Pair of suit-clad businessmen twelve o'clock. *Check.*

Powerfully built man with bulky jacket straight ahead. *He's dressed that way in June? Why?*

No real exits.

No real cover.

Damnit!

"Get out of your own head, Webber," he muttered under his breath—not softly enough, apparently, because a woman in impossibly high heels and a teeny-tiny mini-skirt glanced over her shoulder and veered suddenly into the book shop. And it was a clear sign that he was cracking up because, even though her skirt barely covered her ass, Kirk didn't bother to give her a second glance.

You're almost there.

With his end-goal in sight, he was already searching the empty chairs for somewhere to sit—hopefully, with his back to the wall and a clear view of the waiting area. He'd just found the perfect spot—near the jetway door—when something caught his eye.

Long dark hair.

The slender curve of a woman's neck leading into a delicately rounded shoulder.

It's her.

He stutter-stepped, then abruptly stopped.

"Hey, douche-bag, watch where you're going!"

Kirk started, his attention momentarily drawn to a scrawny boy-man with enough hardware in his nose and lower lip to set off TSA's alarm bells. The kid flipped him the bird. It took all of the "adult" Kirk possessed not to return the gesture. By the time he'd managed to look back to that same spot…

She was gone.

Worse yet, his perfect seat was taken.

You're cracking up, bucko.

Yeah. He was definitely cracking up. Not only was he seeing things that weren't there. But that little inner nag inside his head sounded suspiciously like his old mentor, Niall Killrain—and the man had been dead for some half-dozen years.

No wonder Luca had been so insistent that Kirk hit yet another treatment center and another round of shrinks. And Kirk would do it. If only to get his job back. He'd go there, do his time, then head back. Then he'd do a better job of pretending that he was fit and healthy and…normal.

Even though he wasn't sure that he knew what "normal" meant any more.

Mia Papadopoulos hunched over the bathroom sink, her lungs burning as she fought to control the panic rising inside of her like a fetid tide. With one hand, she tried to keep the automated stream running. Someone must have designed the mechanism with water conservation in mind, because she was given about five seconds of tepid liquid before the whole thing stopped and she had to trigger the sensor again.

"Nervous flier?"

Mia jumped. But the woman who'd stepped to the sink beside her seemed more intent on reapplying her makeup than offering Mia anything but a cursory glance.

Since a response seemed to be required, Mia gave a vague smile.

"Let me give you a piece of advice, honey," the woman offered, the words slightly slurred as she tried to talk and outline the edges of her lips at the same time. "Pay the extra for first class. Then, the minute your butt hits the chair, punch the call button and ask the flight attendant for a shot of bourbon, a hot fudge sundae, and a pillow." She stabbed the end of her lipstick in the direction of Mia's reflection. "You'll be dead asleep before the plane ever lifts off the end of the tarmac."

As the woman turned and wrestled her luggage through the door again, Mia trembled.

A hot fudge sundae?

If only her anxiety could be cured so easily.

A glance at her watch warned her that the first boarding call had probably been issued. If she didn't hurry…

She fumbled with her purse, removing her phone. With trembling fingers, she hit her contact list, then her sister's number. Biting her lip, she listened intently as the ringing began.

One.

Two.

Three.

Four.

"Hi, this is Liz. I must be up to my eyeballs with work or off on a thrilling adventure. Leave your name and number and I'll call back. Promise."

And even though she knew she wouldn't leave a message, Mia stayed on the line for a few more seconds, listening to the strident beep, then the silence, until finally, reluctantly, she ended the call and slid her phone back into her bag.

"Swear to me that you'll get on that plane, Mia."

Mia filled her lungs with air.

"Swear to me."

Forcing herself to move, she swung her bag over her shoulder and strode out of the bathroom with what she hoped appeared a purposeful stride.

Just as she'd feared, a queue had formed at the gate, and an airline employee with a plastic smile was scanning the bar codes on passengers' boarding passes as fast as she could.

Knowing that if she allowed herself one last moment to reconsider she would turn tail and run, Mia forced herself to join the line.

Only for you, Liz.

Only for you.

Author Note

*T*hank you for reading *Wayward Son!* I had such fun bringing Whit and Finley's story to life and creating the jumping-off point for the new and exciting In An Instant Series. The next installment to the series, *The Protector,* is soon to follow.

I love hearing from my readers, so if you'd like to contact me or keep in touch with new and upcoming releases, I can be reached at my website, www.lisabinghamauthor.com, or on Facebook, www.Facebook.com/lisabinghamauthor.

Dear Readers

*Y*ou are so important to me and to my work. If you enjoyed Whit and Finley's story, please pass on your recommendations to friends, family, and other readers by leaving a free an honest review through the site where you purchased the novel, or through other social media and review platform sites. Your time and efforts are greatly appreciated.

About the Author

*L*isa Bingham is the bestselling author of more than thirty-five historical and contemporary romantic fiction novels. In addition to writing, she teaches English and U.S. History to exuberant teenagers. She is considered an expert in historical clothing and has served as a costume designer for theatrical and historical reenactment enthusiasts. Lisa has been lucky enough to live and study in such exotic locales as Brazil, Mexico, Europe, and the United Kingdom. Currently, she lives in rural northern Utah near her husband's fourth-generation family farm. She is married to her sweetheart of twenty-plus years and has three beautiful children.

Connect with Lisa Online

www.lisabinghamauthor.com

www.Facebook.com/lisabinghamauthor